Susan Sallis is one of the most popular writers of women's fiction today. Her Rising family sequence of novels has now become an established classic saga, and *Summer Visitors*, *By Sun and Candlelight*, *An Ordinary Woman*, *Daughter of the Moon*, *Sweeter Than Wine*, *Water Under the Bridge* and *Touched by Angels* are well-loved bestsellers.

All the Rising family accepted that May was Mama's favourite. May had her mother's own fragile, patrician beauty, and was as sweet-tempered as March was sharp. It was May who carried in the tea tray to Mama's bedroom. It was beautifully laid with the best china, and Florence sat up in bed and took May in her arms with a cry of gladness. 'I do love you, my darling May,' she smiled.

March was in the corner of the bedroom, looking after the new baby and staring at the pile of laundry, trying not to think how much soaking and boiling and blue-bagging it would need. Her sleeves were rolled up, her nine-year-old hands were red with washing. Florence suddenly realised March was in the room and she added quickly, 'I do love you all . . . so much . . . all of you.'

Later, when March was in the wash house, leaning over the sink, Alfred was almost certain he could hear her crying . . .

A SCATTERING OF
DAISIES

A SCATTERING OF DAISIES

Susan Sallis

This first hardcover edition published in Great Britain 1999 by
SEVERN HOUSE PUBLISHERS LTD of
9–15 High Street, Sutton, Surrey SM1 1DF.
Previously published in paperback format only
in Great Britain in 1984 by Transworld Publishers Ltd.
This title first published in the U.S.A. 1999 by
SEVERN HOUSE PUBLISHERS INC of
595 Madison Avenue, New York, N.Y. 10022.

British Library Cataloguing in Publication Data
Sallis, Susan
    A scattering of daisies
    1.   Domestic fiction
    I.   Title
    823.9'14 [F]

    ISBN 0 7278 5500 X

Printed and bound in Great Britain by
MPG Books Ltd, Bodmin, Cornwall.

1

April Rising was born in 1902, well into the twentieth century, the first of Florence's children to be born into the new era. Yet Florence still dated her letters 18 ... and then deleted the digits and started again. She wondered whether she herself should have been born sooner. There was something about writing a one and a nine at the top of her correspondence that frightened her.

The room in which April first saw the evening light, was newly oilclothed for the occasion. The wash-stand and giant clothes closet both leaned slightly outward with the sagging ceiling joists; the heavy Nottingham lace curtains, donated by Florence's Aunt Lizzie, smelled of must in spite of Florence's efforts; the ceiling flaked gently — one large whitewash petal floated in the ready chamber-pot, another in the china ewer of water on the floor beneath the matching basin above.

The rest of the house echoed the same paradox; a mixture of 'nice things' in a gently decaying setting. Number thirty-three, Chichester Street, Gloucester, amounted to a home that was just a bit more comfortable than its neighbours. All the houses in Chichester Street were rented by people who could ill afford new decorations. If their fortunes improved they would be likely to move into another house where the paint and paper might be newer. Or, just as probably, older.

Chichester Street was typical of Gloucester of that

time. The Romans had taken the city over and bridged the narrow Severn to push into Wales and their work could still be seen everywhere. The first William had recognised its strategic position and had taken the decaying monastery in hand, compiled his Domesday Book in its chapter house and set the pattern for the inland port for the next thousand years. Roman fortifications and Elizabethan dwellings crumbled together. The Parliamentary headquarters of the Civil War was hemmed in by a warehouse, and where Bishop Hooper had burned and burned and refused to die, slums festered into gypsy encampments, and every spring the Severn floods cleared the rubbish anew with its brown waters.

Chichester Street was an offshoot of one of the four roads sprouting from the Cross, the Northgate. It had been the drive and grounds of Chichester House, but that too was now owned by one of the rich merchants and let out to an impoverished cleric. The old carriageway was lined with two rows of pseudo-Regency houses, erected when the city had tried to be a spa to keep up with nearby Cheltenham. The Gloucester Coal and Coke Company had a slice of land there too, and dominated the houses with their gas container. At the top of the street, Goodrich's Dairy and the Lamb and Flag eyed each other with their bright windows. Mr. Goodrich kept bees in his garden and apple trees spread their branches over his wall. Otherwise there was little greenery. Two steps led up to each front door, flanked by a boot-scraper and a metal lid covering the entry to the coal chute and cellar. Window boxes were considered foreign. Some houses kept the privacy of their front room with a withered pot plant. The Risings used their front room for their work: Will Rising was a tailor.

The local midwife, nicknamed by Albert and March as Snotty Lottie because her year-long cold was never attended to during a lying-in, rolled April in a threadbare towel and laid her in the prepared drawer.

8

Satisfied with her strugglings and puny cries, she returned to Florence, holding a large meat dish, and sat on the bed to await the afterbirth.

Florence lay back exhausted, the relief from the pain and the pushing and the lump inside her making her feel so light she might have been floating above the bed. She remembered Lottie telling her it was a girl, and for that she was glad too. Her first-born had been a boy and for the first two or three years there had been certain indelicacies to be seen to. In the end he had been circumcised and Florence had wondered why it couldn't have been done immediately. She was prudish to a degree and the whole business of childbirth was a mental as well as a physical agony for her.

When she had her daily all-over wash, she dressed each part of her body before commencing on the next. Once she had caught sight of herself in the dark kitchen window, rigidly stayed from an eighteen-inch waist up, but minus drawers, petticoats and stockings as she prepared the wash cloth to deal with her lower parts. The sight had appalled her; this was surely how scarlet women must appear. She had made certain that in future she donned a petticoat and lifted it chastely on each side to wash from the hips down. To make assurance doubly sure, she got Will to fix one of the new-fangled blinds to the kitchen window though it looked out on to the high blank wall guarding the gas company's cylinder. She could not risk another reflection, which might well reveal the moment when, lower half petticoated, she scrubbed vigorously from the waist up.

She had undergone this physical and mental torture of childbirth four times now, and as she studied the ceiling, seeing in its patchiness a map of the Scandinavian peninsula, she felt not only relief at expelling the kicking lump that was April, but more relief still that surely she had done her duty and no-one would expect more of her. Four children: Albert, March and May within three short and terrible years; now April after an interval of eight years. This last birth would prove she was still a dutiful wife; there would be no need for further evidence.

She felt a flutter inside her and shrank against an inexplicable return of pain. Lottie said, 'Just another little push Mrs. Rising, just one more . . .' and dragged the sleeve of her black dress across her nose before thrusting the meat dish hard beneath Florence's buttocks.

'Good. Good. Everything there?' She poked searchingly and her nose dripped. 'Think so. Couldn't be better.'

Florence sighed. 'No need of a doctor then?'

Lottie fetched paper and rolled up the contents of the meat dish.

'Five bob!' she commented scornfully. 'Five bob to stand around and do nowt. And all the hot water — he's for ever washing!'

Florence adjusted the sheet. 'Our March will see to that, Mrs. Jenner. There's a good fire down below. I told her to keep it stoked up and the two kettles on the hob.'

'Right. Righty-oh.' Lottie spoke with the same familiarity which labour and childbirth made just permissible. But that time was over. Florence tucked the sheet firmly around her waist and tightened her mouth. Lottie went to the door and bawled for March.

'And bring up the hot water now my maid!' she ordered. 'You'mgot another sister and she en't even washed yet!'

There were no sounds of jubilation. Nine-year-old March disapproved of the whole situation as much as Florence did herself, and Albert had wanted — demanded — another boy. Will had wanted a son too, but he wouldn't mind over-much because girls were helpful in the workroom. He was busy there now and hadn't even opened the door to enquire of the children what was happening. Florence sighed; she did not blame him, indeed did not want him. A local landowner had recently died and Will had to alter the funeral suits of half a dozen tenant farmers. They all wanted letting out so farming couldn't be that bad. Will himself had come from Kempley just outside the city — that was how he had got the work — and had said, 'Never a farthing in their pockets, but plenty in their bellies. That's our farmers!' Florence had ignored the coarseness of this comment and asked, 'Is the work worth doing then? Shall we get paid?' And he had twinkled at her in the way that had won her heart so long ago: 'Our bellies will all be as full as yours is now my dear,' he had said. And then as she turned her head down to the button-hole she was sewing, he had pecked at her forehead remorsefully. 'Ah, Flo, you should be used to my country talk by now. And let me add, there will be plenty of goose-grease next winter for May's chest. That will please you, I'll be bound!'

They all accepted that May was her favourite. None of them minded — or so Florence thought. May, as fair as Florence was dark, but with Florence's own fragile, delicate, yet patrician beauty. May, sweet-tempered as March was sharp; as loving as Albert but without his demanding ways; with her father's easy-going nature combined with her mother's fastidiousness. May was a flaxen angel, and like an angel could disappear into another world at any time. May went into flannel drawers and petticoats in mid-September and did not come out of them until the first of June. May was rubbed with goose-grease every winter and dosed with glycerine and lemon at the first husky whisper of a cough. Where March would have protested furiously, she accepted it all with her sunny smile. Florence had overheard March once — at six years old mind you — inciting May to rebellion. 'Why don't you go upstairs — quietly — and change into your cotton cover-up? It's in the summer chest in the bandy room. I've been wearing mine since my birthday!'

'No you haven't,' May replied peaceably, skipping the issue as always.

11

Everyone would always know when March, May and April had been born, so March said angrily, 'Well, *your* birthday then! Go on cowardy custard. Do something for once.'

May obviously thought about it, then said, surprised, 'They only makes me wear my winter things cos they loves me.'

'I know *that*! But if it makes you hot and stuffy, it's a pity they do love you isn't it?'

Florence waited for May's reply; she knew it would be something special as it always was. When it came she crept away and felt for her handkerchief.

'But . . .' May's voice had been ultra reasonable. 'But March . . . I loves *them*!'

Now, as Florence let Lottie wash and bind her, she took her mind away from her present circumstances, by imagining May downstairs. May would be pleased it was a girl. May would become, on the instant, the little mother. April would have a sympathetic ear always from May. In fact Florence would have to guard against the child doing too much for her new sister. Of course, March, strong and capable March, would do her share too. She could push the baby carriage which might well strain May's chest; she could also fetch the bath water and change the napkins when she was home.

The thought brought Florence back to her surroundings.

'You need not bother with the baby Mrs. Jenner,' she said, fastening her nightgown firmly over the calico breast-binding. 'March is quite capable. I've been sending her down to young Mrs. Goodrich this past month for her to help out with the new baby.'

'So I did hear. An' guessed why.' Hard work now over, Lottie fished for her handkerchief and dealt with a drip. She never actually blew into a handkerchief, merely sniffed and wiped. 'Well, you can do with all the help you can get now Mrs. Rising. Some years since you had to see to a baby and you're getting on yourself too. I did begin to wonder . . . Mrs. Luker started same time as you and what was young Gladys? The eighth or ninth?'

Florence flushed. 'I haven't been in good health since May's birth.'

'No.' Lottie picked up her bag of tricks and prepared to leave, knowing she would get no confidences out of Mrs. Rising. But perhaps it was worth a last try. 'Of course Mr. Rising is a considerate man, en't he? I well remember when he arrived from the country to be prenticed to old Mr. Daker down the Barton — he was only a young shaver of thirteen then, but I allus said . . . I said, That young Will, I said, That young Will Rising — he's consid'rate.' She liked the word. It had a ring to it. 'Consid'rate,' she repeated.

'Thank you Mrs. Jenner. Mr. Rising will pay you on the way down, if you will just knock at the workroom door —'

'Not one to pester a woman, I'd say. And not one for the public either. Mind you —' she was in full spate so used her sleeve this time. 'Mind you, I'm not saying he don't like a glass with his neighbours. Many's the time he's bought me . . .' she snuffled a laugh and sniffed vigorously, 'a cup of tea!' She winked and her head jerked sideways as if pulled by the eyelid. 'But what I mean is, he en't one to come home roaring drunk and want —'

Florence said firmly, 'Tell March to come up straightaway with more hot water for the baby, will you Mrs. Jenner?' She was longing with all her soul for a drink of tea, but if she mentioned it she would have to offer one to Lottie too. 'And again thank you. You have been so kind.'

Lottie went to the door, disappointed. She thoroughly enjoyed discussing her patients' husbands, and immediately after a lying-in was the accepted time for many intimacies.

She said, 'Well, it were a sight easier this time than last. I thought young May 'ud never come. An' if that doctor had had his way she'd have been scarred for life.'

Lottie never failed to remind Florence, and May herself, that it was her expertise that had ensured May's

13

beauty. The doctor had actually taken the forceps from his bag when Lottie, dripping freely, had got her clawing fingers beneath May's armpit and started the spiral action of removal for which she was locally famous.

She closed the door behind her, leaving Florence shuddering at the memory. The next instant, March's clatter could be heard on the stairs. There was a metallic thump as she put the enamel pail on the step above her, doubtless splashing it over her pinafore, Florence thought with a sigh. Then the scuff of her boots as she caught it up. The stair drugget, again donated by Aunt Lizzie, was as unresilient as the old oilcloth had been and never absorbed any sound louder than the tread of the mice. And there were plenty of those. Florence sighed again; they'd have to get another cat. When the last one had died horribly from the poison put down by the Lukers, she had sworn they would never have another. But the mice were on the increase and they carried germs which might well infect delicate May. Or, of course, the new baby.

It seemed March, or some other member of the family, had forestalled her.

'Mother —' The door flew open and the bucket swung after it, followed — as if pulled by its handle — by the lanky figure of March. She plonked the bucket between her spread feet. 'Mother, guess what. We've got a kitten. She's black — all black, not a bit of white anywhere — and she's got the greenest, glassiest eyes you ever saw!'

Florence felt, for the fourth time, complete surprise that the life of the little household in Chichester Street had gone on normally, even excitingly it seemed, while she had been fighting a battle up here with only Lottie Jenner for company. Just for a second she forgot Lottie's undoubted commonness and felt a genuine closeness to her.

She said to March, 'And the kitten is far more interesting than your new baby sister I suppose?'

March glanced sideways at the drawer. There were a

great many nasty-looking cloths and sheets in the corner which she quickly did not look at.

'It's going to be called April I suppose?'

'She is going to be called April don't you mean?'

'Well. Is she?'

'Yes. Don't you like it?'

'It's the prettiest of all. March is just silly, nobody is called March.'

It was a perennial complaint. Florence smiled amiably, not realising how infuriatingly like May she looked.

'Then it's unusual, which is good. Distinguished. You will be the distinguished member of the family.' She put her head back, exhausted with the effort of talking. 'Now go and look at the baby, then you can wash her and bind her.' The baby must come first; she would ask for some tea afterwards.

March stared down at her sister. April was quiet now, disliking the rough towel but recognising that she had been handled and wrapped by someone who knew her business.

March said slowly, 'She isn't a bit pretty. And her hair's ginger. Like Albert's. What would you have done if she'd been born in October?'

'Called her October,' Florence said weakly but seriously. It was her whim that all her girls should be called after their birth months. It seemed to make them special, regal.

March prepared the wash-stand efficiently and lifted the baby on to it. She wished it had been called October. Then, what between its ginger hair and its ugliness, she could have loved it whole-heartedly. As it was, the musical name April must come between them.

There was a tap at the door and in came May bearing a tray beautifully laid with Mother's best china tea-cup, milk jug and teapot. Florence sat up with a cry of sheer gladness, made room for the tray, took May in her arms and wept. Dark hair mingled with gold. May said, 'Don't

15

cry, my beautiful little mamma . . . don't cry . . .' and
Florence sobbed. 'I'm crying with happiness darling. Oh
I do love you.' She looked up and saw March through her
tears, sleeves rolled up, nine-year-old hands red with
washing, auburn-brown eyes watchful. She added, 'I do
love you all — so much.'

March turned back to the baby, slid a penny into the
little lint pocket she had sewn ages ago, and bound it
carefully over the hideous, protruding navel. May would
be the beautiful one. March would be clever; distinguished and very clever. And this one, April, what would
she be? March glanced again at the pile of laundry in the
corner and tried not to think how much soaking and
boiling and bleaching and blue-bagging it would need.
She compressed her lips. April could be the worker.
April could help Father do the button-holes in the workroom, help Mother in the steamy wash-house and over
the hot cooking range. April would be . . . *useful*.

Downstairs, Will Rising finished sewing the last braces
button on to the last pair of expanded trousers and put
them on the pile. He flexed his shoulders, dropped his
neatly bearded chin on to his chest, then pointed it at the
newly-lit gas lamp. He clenched his hands then stretched
them, the fingers cracking and bending back slightly.
'Flexible fingers,' old Mr. Daker had said when he had
looked him over in the dark little shop down the Barton.
'Flexible fingers. Necessary for a pianist. Even more
necessary for a tailor!'

Will grinned at the memory, then stretched his grin
into a grimace and relaxed. Another of Mr. Daker's
maxims: take time to relax after a day's work. Old man
Daker had stitched by hand, sitting crosslegged in the
midst of his table like a tailor in a fairy story. Will had
never done that. Around his cutting table there were tall
stools and a comfortable chair before the treadle sewing
machine. He remembered once, creeping out from
beneath the Daker table where he slept, finding Mr.

Daker above him, standing on his head. 'Put yourself to extremes lad,' he had said on descending. 'Tension makes relaxing easier. To stand on the head ensures that the simplicity of standing on the feet is blissful. Sometimes even pain is worthwhile because its ending is so very good.' Will had thought of that very hard when he attended the barber's the following week to have a tooth pulled. It had worked. He wondered now whether poor Florence might have found comfort from such a simple philosophy if he'd passed it on to her. But Florence was stoical at all times. Will had quickly learned that — in a strange way — life itself meant suffering to Florence. Yet she bore it. Sometimes she almost seemed to enjoy the suffering.

He picked up the pile of trousers and carried them into the kitchen where March would help him press them tomorrow morning. By the ashy range sat Albert, clutching the new kitten. The unshaded gas mantel in the bracket above the mantelpiece spluttered. Flo would have changed that for a new one and ground the old one into silver cleaner by now. It had been a day and a half and no mistake.

Albert said, 'There's some milk left Dad. Shall we have bread and milk for supper? Or are you going to the public?'

'Might. Might not.' Will did not like committing himself. Daker had said that too. 'Don't give a customer a completion date. Not definite. Never. Never commit yourself lad.' He put the trousers on a corner of the table. 'If it's bread and milk, keep it away from these. I want to deliver them tomorrow.' He wouldn't mind popping along to the Lamb and Flag for an hour. It would be a nice change. And if Snotty Lottie was there she'd tell him more about the birth than Flo ever would. But Flo wouldn't like it. Flo didn't believe in the custom of wetting the baby's head.

'Will you be hiring a trap Dad?' Albert tried to encourage the kitten to settle around his neck like a

17

scarf. 'Can I come? I could help you take in the suits and hold the horse. And I don't mind not going to school.' He remembered a grievance. 'March didn't go today.'

'Because she had to help here. You know that. May went.'

'I could have helped here.'

'Button-holing?'

'Well . . .' he flinched as the kitten's claws dug in. Bright spots of blood appeared on his collar. 'Can I come Dad? The daffs will be out round Newent way. And the apple blossom.'

'We'll see. You'd better get that shirt off and soak it in cold water. The blood will stain.'

'March will do it,' Albert said carelessly as he nestled the kitten back into his elbow. 'She's got a load of stuff in the copper already.'

'Oh . . .' Will swallowed a curse. He had forgotten March would be fully occupied tomorrow morning with the maternity washing. 'All right,' he capitulated. 'You can come with me tomorrow. On condition you help me with the pressing first.' He cut short the boy's ecstasy. 'Can we go upstairs now? Since May came and told me it was another girl I haven't heard a thing.'

'Oh you have!' Albert looked for a twinkle in his father's blue eyes. 'Snotty Lottie came into your work-room, I heard her. She was talking for ages.'

'She wanted her florin, that was all.' Will looked disapproving. 'And what has your mother told you about using that name?' He really wouldn't mind popping in to the Lamb and Flag before closing time. From a sense of loyalty he had cut Lottie short once she'd assured him that Flo was all right and the new baby perfect; if he bought her a gin there would be no stopping her.

Albert was grinning, they both knew it was Will who had originally coined Lottie's name. 'Lottie's gottie an awful lottie snottie,' he said experimentally. The twinkle came at last. It transformed Will from a round-faced, straw-haired nonentity, into a replica of the King as seen

18

on their Coronation tea caddy. Albert laughed raucously just as March clattered down the stairs almost hidden by the pile of linen she was carrying.

'You can go up now,' she said tersely, bundling past them on her way to the wash-house. The copper was already full of the week's normal laundry soaking in soda and ammonia before having the fire lit beneath it tomorrow morning. What she could do with this lot, she did not know. Wearily she began spreading each layer in the shallow sink, letting the cold water run through the stains. Her mother had taught her long ago the main tenet of wash day: hot water for grease, cold water for blood. She turned the mottled brass tap on full so that the water splashed her pinafore. She didn't care. If only she had thought of taking up a tray of tea . . . if only Florence had wept into her mouse-brown hair . . . if only April had been born in October.

The scene that met Will's eyes as he went into the front bedroom delighted him. For the whole of his lifetime the institution of the family had been revered, the old Queen had made certain of that. In any case Will was a natural family man; the sight of his wife, flushed, beautiful, and still, after everything she had been through, refined, was enough to stir his heart. But when she was flanked, on one side by their exquisite daughter May, and on the other by the bundle of new life, and when the whole was lit by the soft yellow glow of gas, like a scene in the Theatre Royal, then it made Will stop in the doorway, it made tears start to his eyes, it made him eventually stumble forward and kneel down by the bed to take Florence's hand and press it to his lips.

'My darling. My beautiful darling,' he mumbled, keeping his head down.

Albert said, 'I thought you said it would be a boy? It's not very pretty is it?'

May said tremulously, 'Mamma . . . Daddy's crying. He's crying!'

'Like me. Because he is so happy.' Florence leaned over Will's head, kissing the silky hair and pressing the sheet to his eyes with her free hand.

'I suppose you'll want to call it April?' Albert queried, embarrassed and irritable with this show of emotion. He hated tears. It was the reason he could never feel close to May; she was for ever in tears about something. Now March . . . March never cried. She had a fiery temper, but she never cried.

'Her name will be April. Yes my darling.' Florence lifted her head slightly and smiled into her son's eyes. Strange that none of her children took after her. Albert was ginger, his eyes pale blue; March a little darker with strange, transparent, tea-coloured eyes; May heavenly blonde; and now this new one, ginger again. It did not occur to her that they had all inherited her long thin frame and sharp, defined bone-structure. But she saw that in his way Albert was going to be beautiful.

Will mumbled, 'I worship you Florrie. I worship you.'

He was like another child; she could love him freely now, just like another child. There would be no more . . . indignities. He lifted his head to smile wetly at her, and, unthinkingly, she pressed him to her swollen bound bosom.

'Dear heart,' she murmured. 'Dearest heart.'

May moved around the bed and put an arm across Albert's shoulders. 'Are you crying, Albert?' she asked hopefully.

Albert shrugged, more irritable than ever. 'No. I was thinking that if this one had been before you, it would have been much more sensible.'

'Why?' she asked, surprised.

'You would have been in proper order then,' he explained. 'March, April and May.'

May thought about it and then giggled deliciously. Albert, irritability gone in the face of such appreciation, said, 'Mother should have twelve girls really, shouldn't she? January, February, March —'

20

'She's *got* March,' laughed May. 'And April, and May. So the next would be —'

'June,' he supplied. 'Then July —' they gabbled through the year laughing inordinately. Will said in a low voice, 'You're all right Flo? You're really all right?'

'Of course.'

'I'll have to check on that. With Snotty Lottie.'

'Oh *Will* —' but she could not resist a smile. Then the smile went. 'Does that mean you're going to the public this evening?'

'Well . . . I must make sure you're really all right before I slide in beside you tonight my darling.'

She withdrew slightly. 'I made up the other bed in Albert's room dear. For tonight.'

'It'll be all right Flo —'

'The baby will disturb you Will. And you're so busy with the suits.'

'I've finished them dearest. Albert and I will be hiring a trap from Luker tomorrow and taking the lot of them out to Newent.'

'Will — you can't keep Albert away from school —'

'Just for once Flo! Good grief, May is always away for one reason or another.'

'You know I want him to go to the King's next year. He deserves to be a chorister with his voice.'

'And go to the King's he shall. Don't worry sweetheart. Albert will be a credit to you, March will be clever, May beautiful. And I . . .' he pressed himself ardently against the calico binding. 'I will always worship you.'

'What about April?' Albert asked loudly and cockily. He had been listening to the exchange in between May's idiotic comments, and knew that he would be able to go to Newent tomorrow. 'What will April be good at?'

Florence leaned away from Will and over the sleeping baby.

'She does not need to be good at anything,' she said

21

fondly. 'She will be the youngest. The baby of the family.'

Will stood up. She was giving in about Albert so that she could win over having her bed to herself.

'I'm going to the Lamb and Flag then,' he announced. 'Take care of your mother, Albert. Some of the bread and milk might not come amiss.'

Luker was in the public bar as he had known he would be; Lottie in the snug. He fixed to hire a trap for tomorrow and answered Luker's not-very-interested enquiries for Florrie and the new baby.

'Lottie —' Luker jerked his head in the direction of the snug. 'Lottie said it was normal. I did wonder after so long. And your wife being a bit on the delicate side. Now my Hettie, you see, she's kept going Mr. Rising. She's into the swing of things as you might say.' He lowered his voice, 'Expecting again you know. December. Not everyone knows — told Lottie of course.'

Will wiped froth from his moustache. 'But the last one — Gladys wasn't it — she was only born last month surely?'

'Well, February. But, yes, this is the best yet. Ten months between them. Bit of a record, eh?'

'I should say,' Will propped his mug on the brass rail around the bar. ''Course, only eleven months between our March and May. Calls for a drink. You on stout?'

'How about a drop of whisky? For the two of them. Yours just been borned. Mine just been made.'

Will felt like a giant refreshed after the unaccustomed spirit. He borrowed Sidney Goodrich's last edition of the *Citizen* and scanned it knowledgeably. Since the end of the war in Africa there wasn't much news outside the county boundary that interested him. He saw that some treaty was being signed with Japan and wondered why. Presumably Mr. Balfour knew what he was doing. He turned to the Hatches, Matches and Despatches. He'd have to send Albert along to the

Citizen office in Saint John's Lane early tomorrow with
an announcement of April's birth. He could probably
make it an advertisement in part: 'Mr. William Rising,
well-known tailor, and his wife, are proud to
announce. . . .'

Lottie's voice spoke in his ear. 'Wetting the baby's
head then Will Rising? Reckon I should have some
share in the celebrations. Reckon I did my bit. Not as
well as you did your bit — I'll grant you that —' her
cackle broke above the general hum of conversation
and he ordered quickly and hustled her back to the
snug.

'I want to thank you Lottie. . . .' She put her mouth
one side of her gin glass and her nose the other, and
swigged. When she emerged the usual dewdrop had
disappeared. Will grinned. He must remember to tell
Albert that tomorrow.

'Nothing to it. Not with your wife. Not with Florence
Rising. She were a Davies afore she married you.' She
swigged again. 'Welsh stock. Strong as Welsh ponies.
Anyway, she wouldn't scream and fight like Hettie
Luker. Not if you put the thumb screws on her.'

'No. No, she wouldn't scream. But strong . . . is she
really strong?'

'Don't you believe me?' She was suddenly drink-
belligerent. She thrust her head at him and there was
another dewdrop. 'She could have a baby a year and
not notice it. She'll outlive you Will Rising!' She sucked
the dregs from the gin glass and wiped nose and mouth
together on her silvery sleeve. 'Just like you've outlived
poor old Daker. D'you see that? You was looking at the
paper just now wasn't you? D'you see poor ole Daker's
gone?'

'No!' He felt the news like a hammer blow on his
chest. Mr. Daker who had apprenticed him because of
his flexible fingers and thereby saved him from being a
ploughboy. Mr. Daker who had stood on his head on his
cutting table and told him to bear pain gladly because

its eventual absence was then doubly wonderful. Mr. Daker was part of Will's life. When Will had started up on his own, Mr. Daker had sent along many a customer besides letting Will have all his alterations.

He said weakly, 'Are you sure? He's not sixty yet surely?'

'Don't believe me again?' She slid cumbrously around the table then back, holding the *Citizen*. 'Here's proof. Doubting Thomas.'

He read the small black-framed notice. 'Dearly beloved father of Hester and David.' He saw his name was Emmanuel. He had never imagined Mr. Daker to have a forename.

'I must get home,' he said. 'Florrie will want to know about this. I must get home.'

'Now don't you go telling her no upsetting news now mind. Not until tomorrow at the earliest.' Lottie put a restraining hand on his arm but he shook it off and stood up. 'Now Will Rising —' she stood up too, oddly like a bedraggled Queen Victoria in her rusty black. 'Just you remember. As one comes into this world, so another goes out. It's the law of nature and there's nothing we can do about it.'

Her words rang in his ears as he made his way back to Chichester Street with the April breeze suddenly keen and chilling searching through his waistcoat buttons for his very soul. As his new child had fought her way into the world, so Daker had gone out. Somehow it made Daker's death his responsibility. He wished he had gone to see him since his brief call for work last month. But there had been Sir Henry's death and the funeral and all the alterations to do. He had worked till three am for the past two nights, and Florrie had sewn button-holes till her fingers were raw.

He found he was crying again. It was the whisky. He knew that. But Daker . . . maybe if he hadn't rolled over on to Florrie that night nine months ago, Daker would be alive now. He broke into a shambling trot. He must

24

tell Florrie, shock or no shock. He must get into bed beside her and weep on her shoulder and let her smooth his hair and kiss his wet eyes and. . . . He wanted Florrie.

Albert went downstairs and got the milk jug off the stone floor of the larder, fetched a saucepan and tipped it in. He used a taper for the gas, hating the way it popped at him, then went out to the wash-house. It was quite dark now but the stars made the sky pale. He sniffed ecstatically, smelling frost. No school tomorrow. Kempley instead, and the daffodils and the red stone of Kempley Church and the wide shallow River Leadon, crystal clear and as cold as iron. Dad might let him paddle.

'March!' He opened the wash-house door and saw her leaning on her elbows on the sink, water pouring on to a pile of sheets. She was soaked from the waist down. 'March, come on. Leave that now. We're going to have bread and milk with Mother and she'll tell us a story. Come on.' He hesitated. She had lit a candle in a saucer on the shelf above her head where Mother kept the bar soap. He was almost sure she was crying, except that March never cried. 'Are you coming?' he repeated tentatively.

She turned off the tap and blew out the candle in one movement. They went back to the house and she put four bowls on to a tray and began to break bread into them without enthusiasm. Albert hovered over the milk saucepan.

'Put plenty of sugar on mine,' he ordered. 'Shall we take the kitten up? What are we going to call her?'

She made no reply and he added carelessly, 'She dug her fingers into my neck and made my shirt collar bloody. You'll have to wash it for me March. But it's all right, I'm not going to school tomorrow 'cos Dad's taking me to Kempley with him and the next day is Saturday, so —'

March screamed.

He spun round from the steaming saucepan just in time to catch her open hand on his face. She came up with her other hand, then again with the first, screaming and spitting all the time worse than the kitten. He thrust her from him and she fell in a heap against the table leg and there she stayed, hanging on to it, sobbing wildly, banging her head deliberately every now and then, completely hysterical.

The milk boiled over and put out the gas, and immediately the kitchen was filled with its stink. Albert flicked at the tap and left the milk to crust hard on the stove top. He did not feel his usual irritability at the sight of female tears. This was something quite different. This was a thunderstorm. He was reminded of Fred Luker in the playground at school, bawling all the awful words he could think of at the top of his voice before the Headmistress caned him. When asked for explanations he'd said, 'You got to get it out your system. That's what me mam says. Get it out your system. She has a go now and then. But 'course she don't have to put up with a caning for it.'

Neither did March. He knelt by her and watched her bang her head. Maybe she was caning herself.

'What's the matter?' he asked as soon as she stopped.

She spurted snot and spit worse than Lottie. 'Everyone. Everyone is the matter. All that washing. And now you with your shirt. I haven't had time to look at the kitten — got to wash the baby instead. And now you . . . going to Kempley . . . you *swine*! You spoilt brat!' She choked and he passed her his handkerchief. She used it and threw it on the floor. 'Nobody thinks I've got any feelings do they?' She picked up the handkerchief and tried to tear it but the good linen resisted her. 'All that fuss over May because she takes up tea! *Tea*! When the baby's lying there covered in the most awful slimy muck you ever saw!'

'I should have thought Snotty Lottie would have seen to all that.'

'That would have cost money you fool! Don't you understand *anything*?' She gave up the handkerchief and banged her head furiously. 'And now you've messed up your shirt —'

'I'll wash my shirt March.'

'And you're going to Kempley. You're leaving me here all by myself —'

'Mother and the new baby are —'

'It's *you* I want.' She stared at him malevolently and crashed her head against the table leg. 'Nobody loves me. Nobody cares whether I'm happy or not. Nobody loves —'

'I love you March.'

'No you don't. You're going to Kempley —'

'You can go in my place March —' Albert had never felt so fine in his life. The pale stars and the frost and Kempley . . . he would sacrifice them for his sister. 'I'll do the washing, don't worry. I —'

'You can't. You don't know how to.' But she did not bang her head and there was no anger in her voice. Her sobs died down slowly. 'Do you really love me Albert?'

'Yes.'

'How much?'

'I don't know . . . I. . . .'

'More than May?'

'Oh yes. And more than the new baby of course. And more than the kitten and —'

'More than Mother?'

He hesitated. 'I think so. I can't tell Mother things can I? Or say some words. I can tell you anything. Anything in the world. Like I told you when I fell down in Mrs. Luker's yard and looked up her skirt and saw she didn't wear drawers. Like I told you about my sore John Thomas and you got some of Mother's vaseline —'

'I love you too Albert.' She weighed her words carefully. 'I would die for you Albert.'

He said happily, 'I would die for you too March.'

'I'm happy you're going to Kempley. I don't want you

27

to stay at home. I want you to have good times. Even if I can't have them too.' She stood up and began sprinkling sugar on the bowls. In the pale green bowl, which was Albert's, she sprinkled a double helping. He brought over the skinny milk and poured it carefully. They went upstairs. They both felt the holy joy of renunciation.

Will stumbled into the bedroom feeling slightly sick at the heavy smell of sweet, burned milk. The room was dim, the gas turned down to a bead. On the heaped pillows of the double bed were three heads. The brown one raised itself.

'Hush Daddy,' March put a finger to her lips. 'Mother and May are fast asleep and the baby has just dropped off.'

Will felt frustration boil deep inside him.

'What's all this?' He did not lower his voice and he was quite certain Florrie was awake.

'We had bread and milk and Mother told us a story, then she said to get our night clothes on. She needs me here to see to the baby and that meant May had to stay too!' March sounded patronising and smug. She whispered a giggle. 'We used all the milk and Mother says she can't do any feeding herself for a while, so we put some of Mrs. Goodrich's honey on to a dummy and April just *loved* it!'

Will stared at Florence as if the intensity of his gaze could wake her up. She did not stir. He turned and blundered out. 'There's other nights, my girl,' he muttered as he felt his way to Albert's room and began to undress in the dark. 'There's other nights. And you're as strong as a Welsh pony remember.' He flung back the ice-cold sheets and got into the spare bed. On the other side of the room, Albert grunted and muttered March's name. Will remembered old Daker. He whispered, 'You could have stayed awake to hear about him. That's all I wanted. Just to share that. After all, we're meant to comfort each other aren't we? That's what marriage is for isn't it?'

28

No-one answered his question. He turned his head into the pillow. 'More like a nun than a Welsh pony.' It came to him suddenly that Florence would have made a good nun. Living with suffering. No screaming.

He slept at last.

2

Will and Albert were late leaving for Kempley. The girls, all four of them in the big bedroom, slept late, exhausted after a disturbed night. April simply would not believe there was no milk to be had and woke again at eight-thirty to demand her rights. March could spare her no more time; May had to be bullied to school and there was all that washing and no sound at all from Albert's room. She banged on the door as she scurried down the landing, lifting her skirt high above her bare feet, terrified of mice. May followed sleepily and took her time about setting out five cups and saucers on the part of the table not already occupied by the funeral trousers. She then sat in a chair cuddling the kitten and making no attempt to dress or fetch newspaper and sticks for the fire. March washed in cold water in the scullery, dressed hurriedly, discovering her clothes still damp from last night's swilling in the wash-house, and took the jug down to Mrs. Goodrich for milk.

Snotty Lottie was coming out of her door.

'Bab all right?' she called wheezily.

March, like her mother, did not believe in encouraging Mrs. Jenner. She raised the milk jug by way of reply. A breeze, funnelled into a near gale by the tunnel that was Chichester Street, almost took it from her; and Lottie gave up dealing with her nose and clutched her shawl.

'That's no good,' she grumbled. 'Bab's too little for that. I'll go on down and —'

'We're managing thank you Mrs. Jenner,' March said politely, terrified of incurring another florin fee. 'And — and my father isn't about yet, so —'

Lottie laughed horribly. 'Won't be the first time I've seen a man in his nightshirt — or without it! Won't be the last let's hope!'

There was nothing March could do. She watched Lottie go down the street, head bent, just a bundle of old clothes flapping in the wind.

Young Mrs. Goodrich was freshly aproned and bustling around the dairy laying out butter pats and cheeses for the day's business.

'I've heard,' she beamed at March. 'So I've lost my little nurse-maid.'

March smiled back. Young Mrs. Goodrich made her feel grown up, yet a cherished child at the same time. She watched her put the half-pint dipper in the churn and pour the contents carefully into Mother's china jug.

'I'd like to come still, and see little Charlotte. When there's more time,' she said shyly.

The dipper went in again and again. And again. 'You know you're welcome March.' Mrs. Goodrich dipped a fifth time. 'And if Granny or me can help you like you've helped us, then we'd be very pleased to do so.'

March knew that her occasional ministrations to baby Charlotte had been by way of practice for April and, in fact, a privilege. So she did not mention the washing. Instead she said huskily and gratefully, 'Just the quart Mrs. Goodrich. The jug won't hold any more.'

Mrs. Goodrich smiled. 'I think it will. Just a little drop more. Enough for a new baby at any rate.' She put the lace fly cover, weighted with beads, carefully in place. 'And she will be called April I daresay?'

March took the brimming jug with great concentration and nodded.

'And Mrs. Rising is well? And the baby strong?'

'Mother is fine. But the baby is crying a lot.'

'You take her that milk then. And tell your mother I will visit just as soon as we close this evening.' She came from behind the counter and held the door open. 'Now is there something I can bring? A pound of butter perhaps? Or a wedge of cheese?'

May and Albert would finish the butter between them, and Daddy would eat the cheese. March lifted her eyes from the jug and said, 'Mother is very fond of your honey Mrs. Goodrich. And so is April.'

'Then honey it shall be.' Young Mrs. Goodrich suddenly rested her hand on March's brown head. 'What a good girl you are March. I hope Charlotte grows up like you. You're a proper little Martha.'

'Martha, Mrs. Goodrich?'

'Never mind dear. Now mind the step. And walk as quickly as you can. You shouldn't have come out without your coat you know. The weather is very deceptive.'

March wasn't absolutely certain about the word deceptive, but she had a feeling it was what she was. She remembered how she had screamed and wept last night. Would young Mrs. Goodrich think she was so good if she knew about last night? But then, March was certain she would never behave like that again. The declaration of love between Albert and herself was sufficient to buoy her above her fierce temper and perpetual simmering resentment. She loved Mother and April of course, and — to a much lesser degree — May and Daddy; but her love for Albert was different. It was completely absorbing.

Will came into the bedroom barefooted, nightshirted.

'Why the devil didn't March wake me? Where is she? Where's May? What's the matter with the dratted baby?'

Florence was unperturbed. She had won her night and the day stretched endlessly ahead, all hers, even if April cried incessantly. She observed Will with

32

detachment and felt amused affection; he looked so funny with his pale gingery hair on end and his rounded calves emerging from the shirt. Usually a compact, well-made man, mild and pleasant of face, he looked this morning like a small bull pawing the oilcloth.

'March has gone for milk I expect. May is downstairs getting breakfast. Make sure she wears her muffler to school Will, the wind looks cruel this morning.'

He softened immediately at the sound of her gentle voice. She had brushed out her long dark hair and it lay like a shawl around her shoulders. How beautiful she was and how completely inaccessible.

'How did you sleep my darling?' he asked, the endearment only a slight afterthought. 'Did the baby keep you awake?'

'No. March was very good.' She smiled. 'They're good children Will.' She held out a hand. 'Four now,' she added softly. 'A regular family.'

He remembered she had said last night that April would be the youngest.

He walked over to the drawer and looked down on the squalling child. He said jovially and loudly, 'My mother had seven. But how she put up with this seven times over I don't know!'

Before Florence had time to reply to this comment or statement or whatever it was Will intended, there was a very perfunctory tap on the bedroom door and Lottie surged in, suddenly capable in her role as midwife. Will moved hastily around to the other side of the bed, making a jocular remark that would nevertheless show Lottie that as William Rising, tailor, he was outraged at being discovered in his nightshirt. Florence sat up very straight and emanated the same outrage. April yelled.

Lottie ignored the two adults and swooped on the baby.

'Did they starve you my little precious?'

She was different when she handled the baby; Will was amazed. Expertly she cupped the sagging head, unwound the sheet, lifted the long robe and examined March's work with the penny. She grunted satisfaction then changed the soggy napkin. Will managed to drape himself modestly — as he thought — in one of Florence's many shawls, and edge to the door, but there he stopped in spite of Florence's urgent dismissive gestures, to watch, fascinated by Lottie's expertise. Who would have thought, observing the old girl with her gin glass last night, that she had such a shining place in the scheme of things? Will had long known about her reputation: most of the women in the district would prefer Lottie to the doctor, and would have done if their fees had been reversed, but he had imagined a dark and sordid mystery at which she merely presided. It wasn't like that. He backed onto the landing — where Albert, on his way downstairs to find March, was much affected by the sight of the shawl-swathed rear of his father — but kept the door ajar so that he could see without being seen.

In any case, Lottie was only interested in April. The child was still crying but now, it seemed, in answer to Lottie's enquiries.

'Did they give you a nasty sticky dummy then?' she said through a mouthful of pins. April grizzled acquiescence and Lottie sniffed vigorously just in time. 'Never mind my beauty. Lottie's here now. Lottie will see to it.' She laid the baby on the bottom of the bed and approached Florence.

Florence said firmly, 'March has gone for milk Mrs. Jenner. She'll be another two or three minutes —'

'I saw her. Cow's milk!' Lottie sniffed then used her sleeve. 'And you with enough for two or three babies —' she unbuttoned Florence's nightgown so efficiently that Florence's flapping protesting hands were brushed aside like butterflies. 'And no good telling me there's nothing there yet. Your milk might not be in until tomorrow but there's something there for your baby. Nature provides, my girl. Nature always provides.'

Will watched with all his eyes as the calico was deftly unpinned and a huge breast exposed. Florence was weeping. Incredibly, after fighting her way tearlessly through childbirth, she was weeping at the sight of her focund body.

'There's nothing Mrs. Jenner! And it hurts!'

'Then it must hurt!' Lottie was inexorable. 'I remember we had this with baby March. Not with May though!' She seized a handful of flesh and with a brutality that made Will gasp, squeezed until her ancient purple knuckles showed white. Florence turned her head, covering her eyes with her hands.

'Don't — oh don't —'

A bead of clear fluid collected on the distended nipple, and then another. Lottie gave another grunt of satisfaction and reached for the baby. Will watched until April was sucking hungrily, then withdrew. He was breathing quickly. He went back into Albert's room and began to dress. There were coppers in his pocket kept handily for the gas. He counted out six of them. It was an expensive start to the morning, but worth every penny. When he got the money for the funeral suits he'd treat Lottie to another gin.

The trap made a reassuring rattle as it turned right at the Cross and began the long clatter down Westgate Street. Albert relished the trip even more than he would have done normally, because it was a gift from March. He clutched the springboard and lifted himself to see over the crowding houses to the cathedral spire. He knew that his mother wanted him to sing there one day. It meant going to the King's School and wearing that uniform and playing rugby football on Westgate fields, and first of all passing a scholarship. He must do it somehow. He was the eldest; he had to set a good

35

example. He was the only boy too. He sat down suddenly, overwhelmed by the abrupt realisation of responsibility. They came to the Causeway and the water meadows stretched either side of them, still soggy from the winter floods. The breeze was keener and began at last to wash away the clinging smell of steamy cloth which had filled the whole kitchen as they had pressed the funeral suits an hour before.

Albert said, 'May will be late for school.'

Dad let the reins go loose on Luker's pony and he trotted along busily, obviously enjoying the empty road and the river smells and the strong breeze. 'She won't mind. Nothing worries May.'

Albert thought about this. May cried a lot certainly, but it was not because anything affected her personally. It was because something was sad, or beautiful, or sweet.

He pulled the peak of his cap over his forehead and said gloomily, 'The trouble with May is, she's always happy.'

Dad put his head back and laughed loudly at this in a way Mother would disapprove strongly. But no-one was about. 'What's the trouble with that then my son? And what's so unusual? You're happy too aren't you?'

'Yes.' Albert was surprised about it. 'Yes, I am.' He looked up at his father, amazed. 'I'm quite like May, aren't I Dad? I'm a boy and I'm older and more sensible — May is so *silly* sometimes — but we're quite similar.' He was pleased with the mature word that proved his seriousness. 'Yes. We're quite similar,' he repeated triumphantly.

Dad was in a good mood. He laughed again, his small pale beard pointing to the sky. Albert loved him like this. Loved having him alone and forming a male alliance with him. He bounced on the seat and the trap swayed and the pony's rhythm changed hastily as the shafts leapt at his sides.

'Steady on!' Dad flipped the reins gently to reassure

the pony and guide him into the middle of the road which had narrowed now. It was crowded with fresh hawthorn hedges springing over the ditches and threatening to take their caps at any minute. The pony slowed and they both ducked under an apple tree, blushing pink with blossom, and drove past an orchard. Dad laughed again. 'D'you know, I used to walk this road every Sunday morning to see your mother? Ten miles there and ten miles back.'

Albert found himself reacting as May would have done. It made him feel guilty; his likeness to May made him feel guilty altogether, as if he were being disloyal to March. He made himself remember March's temper last night, her pain, her resentment.

He said, 'That must have been hard work Dad.'

'It was. I was only fourteen. I was thankful to get my apprenticeship with Mr. Daker. It meant I could see your mother most days. It meant . . . a lot.'

Dad's happiness seemed suddenly to fade. Albert said quickly, 'Look over there Dad. The blossom is all full on those trees. But not the other side of the road.' He jabbed with his finger.

Dad nodded, pleased with such keen observation. 'South side,' he said briefly. 'Lambournes — good apple that. They'll be ready a month before the others. Catch the market when the prices are up. Good bit of farming that, Albert. Good bit of business too. Always remember, catch the market in your favour. Whether it's buying or selling. Mr. Daker used to say that.'

'Tell me about when Mr. Daker used to stand on his head Dad.'

Albert grasped obscurely that his father wanted to talk about the old days and thought to please him, but Will's buoyancy continued to evaporate.

'Put yourself to extremes. That's what he said. That's what Mr. Daker used to say.'

Albert couldn't make head nor tail of this. 'What did he mean Dad?'

'If you stand on your head for five minutes, life seems rosy when you get back on your feet. Even if it isn't.'

This made sense because of March and her head-banging last night. She had been quietly happy ever since. He had told her about Dad wearing Mother's shawl like a skirt and she had giggled delightfully, her tea-brown eyes holding depths of amusement into which he had felt drawn and warmed. May had only smiled and continued to cuddle the kitten and invent names for it.

Dad said abruptly, 'Mr. Daker died. Yesterday morning. I can hardly believe it.'

Albert was undismayed, though he now saw the reason for his father's sudden unhappiness. Death featured frequently in playground gossip, but more often than not as a release from the workhouse. *That* was the real bogey, the real terror. Many old people from the city ended up in the workhouse. There was a workhouse at Westbury-on-Severn, and Albert had surveyed its grim high walls once while on a picnic to Newnham with the Sunday School. 'Solid stone,' the Sunday School superintendent had remarked with pride and doom. Albert imagined the beds, tables, even plates and cups, carved from solid stone.

'He wasn't in the workhouse though Dad,' he offered now as consolation.

It worked. Dad laughed, though without throwing back his head.

'That would be the final extreme, I should think,' he said appreciatively. Then, relapsing into moroseness, added, 'Though maybe that is what life is all about. It's so awful generally. It makes death more acceptable.' He looked down at Albert and let go the reins with one hand to hit him companionably on the shoulder. 'Why did I say that? When it's spring and the blossom is out and we've just decided our natural state is happiness?'

Albert spoke up with innocent, yet logical, wisdom. 'Well Dad . . . I suppose . . . if you're miserable sometimes, then you *know* you're happy other times.'

Will didn't laugh but he looked ahead and smiled as he caught a first glimpse of the little River Leadon where he had fished as a boy. How Mr. Daker would enjoy hearing Albert say that. And how true it was. If Will himself didn't occasionally feel out of sorts with Florence, would he know with such certainty how much he loved her in between? He remembered with horror how he had watched this morning. Watched and gloated. Yes, he had so nearly gloated because Florence was being forced to accept the physical realities of Nature itself. When he had always known that she was above Nature. All sensitivity and delicate manufacture, like a piece of porcelain, that was his Florence. He had known it when he met her first; known it in his twelve-year-old bones. She had stayed with the vicar at Kempley, pale and ill and dying — so the village children had said. When she talked to him among the gravestones where he helped his father with the weeding, it seemed her grandparents had sent her out of Gloucester while smallpox raged. Because she was so precious. Her own parents were dead, and only through her would the blood, if not the name, of Rhys-Davies live on. She was the last frail pennant of a line that went back to King Arthur. Will had stared at the thin white face beneath the shovel bonnet, and worshipped.

Albert, worried by the long silence, said in a small voice, 'I suppose, if it hadn't been for Mr. Daker, you'd never have been a tailor Dad?'

Will smiled down at his son, his world right again, Florence back on her plinth.

'It goes back before that, son. If it hadn't been for your mother I wouldn't have been a tailor. I'd have been a ploughboy. And you wouldn't be going to the King's. You'd be a ploughboy too.' He remembered a lewd jibe the village schoolchildren had made to him years ago in the school privy, and used it in a different context. 'The Risings are rising, Albert me lad! The Risings are rising!'

They rounded a bend, and stretching before them was

39

a golden sea of daffodils. Facing south, sheltered, cupped, held by a crescent of elms, the small trumpets of blossom seemed to be lifted by the breeze to make a silent fanfare for their arrival. In a corner of the field three gypsy women picked rhythmically, their baskets, high up one arm, already full. In two hours they would be on Gloucester Cross crying their wares. Albert voiced the sentiments of many of the townspeople.

'Newent daffs . . .' he sounded awestruck. 'It's really spring.'

Will slapped the reins on the pony's fat back and the trap lurched forward with new impetus.

'And we've got a new baby. With a voice like a bugle and yellow hair.' He laughed again, loudly. 'Not unlike a daffodil, eh?'

Albert laughed too, delighted that the shadow on the festivity had been lifted. Will had given two of his children the gift for happiness; and the need for it too.

May and Sybil Luker talked about babies during the dinner hour. The weather was fine and the yard sheltered from the stiff breeze; the boys had been banned from playing on the coal heap, so the two girls settled themselves comfortably on upturned buckets and opened their dinner tins. May's had originally held chocolates from the model village at Bourneville near Birmingham; Sybil's had held tobacco.

Sybil said knowledgeably, 'What you got to do is, give 'em something to suck on. All the time. Stands to reason don't it? If they're sucking they can't be screaming.'

'That was all right at first,' May agreed. 'March stuck the dummy into some of Mrs. Goodrich's honey and April loved it. But then she spat it out and cried again.' She picked up a square of bread, liberally spread with beef dripping and salted. She held it carefully on the crust so that her fingers would not get greasy, then she nibbled at it with her front teeth, chewing quickly like a rabbit. Sybil's meal was exactly the same, yet when she picked up the bread and fitted it as far into her mouth as possible, it looked much less delicious.

'Didn't your mam give her some titty?' Sybil giggled at May's expression. 'You didn't know, did you May Rising? You didn't know babies had to have titties?'

May was incapable of being shocked for long; curiosity quickly overcame her distaste for the coarse word.

'What do you *mean* Sybil?'

Sybil chewed enjoyably and explained. May nibbled right down to her crusts and listened, intrigued at first, then, as usual, touched.

'How *sweet* . . . oh Sibbie, how sweet. When we went to collect our kitten he was feeding like that. No wonder he has such a job to drink his milk out of a saucer. Oh Sibbie, how *sweet!*'

For an instant, there flashed into eight-year-old Sybil's consciousness that she almost loved May Rising. She said ardently. 'I'm ever so glad, ever and ever so glad, you've had a baby too. Perhaps Gladys and April will be best friends like us.'

'Oh they will. Of course they will.' May was sunnily certain, although in fact March had nothing to do with the Lukers, and Albert and Fred met only over a football and had none of the easy companionship she shared with Sybil.

'And I hope your mam will fall for another pretty quick too,' went on Sybil. 'Then our next will have someone to play with.' She stared at the high walls of Chichester Street Elementary and sighed ecstatically. 'Our families will be bound together for all eternity,' she concluded grandly, using the dialogue from a play seen by her father at the Theatre Royal.

May was gloriously impressed. 'How lovely!' Her enormous blue eyes watered. 'Oh Sybil how lovely.' She was just going to beg Sybil to tell her yet again about the play, when something else struck her. 'But . . . what do you mean? Are you going to have another baby? *Again?*'

'Not for ages,' Sybil said carelessly. 'I'm not supposed

41

to know. But I heard them going on about it the other night.' Sides, when Mam's expecting, she lets Dad do it any time. An' I can hear them night after night bouncing about in their bed.'

'Do what?' asked May.

Sybil was suddenly baffled. 'I don't know. Just bounce in bed I suppose. It makes them happy though. They laugh a lot.'

'That's nice.' May thought about it. 'That's lovely Sibbie. Bouncing in bed and laughing. Mother won't let us bounce on our beds because of the springs. Oh Sibbie, isn't it lovely having babies?'

Sybil giggled. 'Because you can be late at school and Miss Pettinger will let you stand up and tell everyone about your new baby and why it's called April?' She peered into May's chocolate tin. 'Can I have your crusts if you don't want them? They might make my hair curl like yours.'

The washing took all of a very long morning and March couldn't turn the handle of the mangle on some of the big sheets, so they hung dripping sadly in the yard. But they were clean. Damp and happy she went into the kitchen to take some food up to her mother. The kitten was on the table and she picked him up and held him to her face.

'Not allowed,' she told him and put him down by his milk. He lapped inexpertly then staggered to his tray where he began to paw at the sand. March watched, entranced. It was all so sweet and funny. If only April would behave like that.

She spread dripping carefully on to two slices of jaggedly-cut bread, dipping deep into the basin to bring up the lovely brown bits and streaking them in diagonal patterns across the bread. Then she swilled out the teapot, still half-full of tea from this morning, and rinsed the cups to go with it. It all looked as nice as when May had done it yesterday. She made the tea and carried the tray carefully up the stairs, glad when the kitten scampered after her because where he was, surely no mouse would dare to be.

Florence was sleeping but she roused immediately the door opened.

'March. Darling. Oh what a treat! My dearest girl.'

March glowed. She poured the tea and she and her mother ate together.

'Has April been good like this all the time?' she asked, peering into the drawer at the sleeping baby.

'Yes. I've been sleeping since Mrs. Jenner left.'

'Oh yes. Mrs. Jenner.' March recalled Snotty Lottie's unstoppable interference this morning. 'Dad gave her sixpence when she came downstairs.'

'Did he? I wonder whether that was wise. It might encourage her to come again.' Florence nibbled at her bread like May. 'However . . . she is excellent with the baby, I have to admit.' She smiled warmly at March. 'After tomorrow I shall get up, March. Your father will bring home some meat from the country this evening I daresay. Put it on the stone in the larder dear, and I will get up on Sunday and cook it. Then on Monday you can go back to school.'

March hesitated, on the verge of protesting. She enjoyed the importance of staying at home and taking over the household. On the other hand, there would be washing every day from now on; she knew that because of young Mrs. Goodrich's Charlotte. Even in the Goodrichs' well-ordered household the smell of washing permeated through to the shop.

She said, 'Mrs. Goodrich was in bed for more than a week. And she's stronger than you, Mamma.'

Florence smiled again. 'She has Granny Goodrich to see to things. And I don't want my little March getting old and bent like Granny Goodrich, do I?'

Florence rarely teased her children and when she did it was in moments of great tenderness. March felt joy blossom inside her like an explosion, not the deep pleasure that had flowed after Albert's declaration of love, but a flowering that was pure and unalloyed. Nevertheless it called again for personal sacrifice.

'I don't mind! I don't mind being old and bent for you Mamma!'

And Florence actually laughed; another rare occurrence.

'I can't imagine your back bending. Ever.' She stared down into her teacup as if reading the leaves. 'You have my pride March. It will keep your back straight even when it is breaking.' She looked up, discovering something with pleasure. 'Yes, you have my pride dear child. How interesting.' She was suddenly solemn. 'It can help you a great deal March. With your temper. You can control your temper by using your pride.'

March, on the crest of the wave because of her kinship with her mother, was in the trough now. She said, subdued, 'Where does my temper come from Mamma? Have you got one too?'

'No dear. I think you inherit that from Grandpa Rising.' Florence sighed. 'Your father is mild enough. So are Albert and May.'

Comfortingly, there came a sound from the drawer; a rude and unapologetic sound. Then April grizzled and began to cry.

Florence smiled again. 'Perhaps April will share your temper, March. Fetch her for me, will you dear?'

March lifted the baby lovingly. Grandpa Rising was an ugly little man who spoke in grunts, never words. She wanted nothing from him, but if she was forced to accept his unwelcome legacy at least April might share it.

She said, 'Shall I fetch some milk Mother?'

'No dear. Just give me the baby then take the tray downstairs will you? Then change your pinafore in case anyone comes calling — oh March it is wet! What have you been doing?'

44

'The mangle was dripping and the sheets were dripping —'

'And you are dripping!' Florence turned misfortune into another opportunity for gentle teasing. Then spoiled everything. 'And you must wash china in hot water with a knob of soda dear. Polish it well with a clean cloth. Then there will be no more smears like this.' She indicated her teacup and March saw that she had drunk only half a cup of tea. She carried the tray back down with less care. The kitten waited for her halfway down, and suddenly, before she could stop herself or even remember her pride, she put out a toe and shoved it hard. It rolled bonelessly to the bottom, picked itself up and galloped into the kitchen ahead of her. She followed it, placed the tray on the table, put the back of her wrist to her mouth and bit hard.

The visit to Kempley was everything Albert had expected. The tiny tied cottage where Grandma Rising had raised her huge family was even more ramshackle than usual and seemed full of babies; all rolling on the stone floor 'happy as pigs in shit' as Gran so vividly put it. Gran herself was dealing with a large bucket of boiling sheep's heads on the range, while Aunty Vi and Aunty Sylv cleared the recent dinner table and washed up at a sort of trough in the corner, where Albert well remembered having a bath with March when they had stayed here while May arrived. It was his earliest memory and set the pattern for all his future visits to his grandmother's cottage.

Shouting; you always shouted when you went to Kempley. It was the only way to be heard for one thing, for another it expressed the life force in you. Laughing; you laughed a lot even when there was nothing much to laugh at. And you laughed without discrimination. When Aunty Vi had tripped over the latest baby and broken her leg, everyone had laughed till their sides ached. Through Vi's cursing and bawling, through the

45

arrival of the doctor and the subsequent splinting and Vi's attempts to get about on crutches — through it all — the laughter had rung loud and clear. Even now Aunty Vi walked with a nautical roll and Uncle Wallie still clapped her on the shoulder and shouted, 'Anyone 'ud think you'd broke y'r leg our Vi!' And the shrieks of mirth went up anew.

'Got to that fancy singing school yet 'ave you my 'andsome?' Gran asked as she stirred and prodded and skimmed indescribable mess from the top of the bucket. 'Wun't speak to your ole gran will you? Not when you gets to that fancy school?'

'Not yet Gran,' he shouted. 'September. If I pass the scholarship.' He had to shout because Aunty Sylv was singing.

'You'll pass. You'll pass.' Gran threw the skimmings on to the back of the fire where they hissed furiously. She put down the spoon and turned to him. 'You'll be the pride of the Risings. You see lad.'

Aunty Sylv repeated 'The pride of the Risings,' and laughed loudly, and Aunty Vi, clattering away in the trough, joined her.

Dad came in from pipe smoking with Grampa and straddled a stool and they had to start on the stew. Albert found if he didn't look too closely at his plate and stoppered his nose, it tasted all right.

'Look at our Albert!' shouted Aunty Vi. 'He's got his nose all a-twisted round — what you doing that for, our Albert?' And they swayed about laughing so that Albert laughed too and smelled the sheep's head like a tanner's yard and twisted his nose frantically and had to be thumped on the back by Dad. Everyone managed to listen while Dad told them about April, and they were momentarily sober to hear of Mr. Daker's death. Then Albert told them through his gravy that they'd got a new kitten to keep down the mice, and they burst forth again.

All too soon it was time to deliver the suits. Grandma

promised them strong tea and stronger cheese on their return. 'Jack and Austin will be in then. And you'll catch your pa again in between the cows and the new grave.' This joke was much appreciated, though Albert knew that it meant quite simply his grandfather was digging another grave after he'd done the evening's milking. He watched them until the little red church at Kempley blocked them from view, then straightened with a sigh of repletion. The long winter had come between him and his country memories; he had been stupid to think Dad could stay in an unhappy mood for long. Not when he was going to Kempley.

He said, 'I wish you had been a ploughboy Dad. And me a ploughboy too.'

Will was amazed. He said, 'You couldn't stand it boy. Not all the time. It's like living on rough cider! And what about Mother? You wouldn't have had her. Not down here.'

Albert considered this. 'I'd have had March.'

'How? You wouldn't have had March without Mother.' Will laughed down at him. 'I couldn't be a ploughboy Albert. I love 'em — don't make any mistake about that. But they — they —' he searched for words to explain their tough insensitivity.

Albert used Gran's phrase. 'They're as happy as pigs in shit.'

Will looked alarmed. 'Don't ever let Mother hear you say that Albert. Else it'll be the last time you come to Kempley Cottage!' But then he grinned. Then laughed uproariously, sounding exactly like Aunt Sylv.

Albert said nothing. He could not find the words to explain that pigs living that way did not have to go to the King's School nor be responsible for so many women. They just revelled all the time in that unthinking happiness.

After school May was permitted in to the Luker kitchen to view Gladys being breast-fed. Hettie blushed slightly

47

under the astonished blue gaze, but was reassuring when she heard the whole story.

'Don't you worry your pretty golden head about your new sister dearie.' Hettie joggled Gladys to get her going again; she was always falling asleep in the middle of her feeds, and Hettie had to get tea with her still in position. 'I'll be over to see your mam ·just as soon as I've got this little terror to bed. A nice bottle of milk stout, that's what she needs. Our Fred can pop to the jug and bottle and get one for me. I'll bring it over and we'll have a chat. Everything will be fine and dandy. But you sleep in your own bed tonight, remember.'

'I'll remember Mrs. Luker. Thank you Mrs. Luker.' May continued to gaze as she backed towards the door. 'Oh Mrs. Luker, I think it's lovely. It's like our new kitten. It's so *sweet!*' She left the house still jabbering to Sibbie. She did not notice the bare boards in the hall and the bits of paper that always scuffed about underfoot in the Luker house. It was one of her gifts; May did not see unpleasant things.

If it had been anyone else in the world, Florence might have been frigidly angry; with May she was sorrowful.

'Darling. You must never say that word again as long as you live,' she begged, two bright red spots on her face, her hands to her ears.

'What is it really called then Mamma?' May put a knee on the bed and her arms around her mother's shoulders. She could not bear to distress her.

Florence took her hands from her ears where they had flown in self-preservation, and cupped May's face.

'My dear innocent child . . . it is Nature's way of feeding, darling. Nature's way.'

'I see Mamma. That's a very beautiful way of saying it, isn't it? Nature's way. Darling Mamma, you're not angry with me are you?'

'How could I be angry with you May? I could wish

however that you were not so friendly with the little Luker girl.'

'Sibbie?' May was loyal too. 'Oh Mother, she's the best girl in the school. I love Sibbie.'

'I know dearest. I only ask . . . try not to pick up her . . . er — sayings. You would not dream of dressing like her. Or going about unwashed as she does, so —'

'Mamma. I truly and honestly did not know titty was a bad word.'

'May!'

'Oh I'm sorry — I'm sorry Mamma.' May tugged the hands down from the crimson ears. 'Let's talk of something else. Please. What have you been doing all day? And how is my dearest little sister? And has Albert gone with Daddy to Kempley? And has March christened the kitten?'

Florence succumbed and embraced May fondly. They talked. April was admired. May prepared to go and help March get the tea.

'Mother. Mrs. Luker might come over and see you and the baby after tea.' Florence flung up her hands, but teasingly this time. 'Please be kind to her, Mother. Please. She wants to help you. Really and truly.'

Florence looked at the enchanting face framed in the angel-gold hair. She smiled.

'Very well darling. I'll be polite.'

'You're always polite, Mother. Be friendly.'

Florence said nothing for a moment. She was not friendly with any of her neighbours and, in fact, could not recall having a friend in her life. She nodded slowly. 'Very well May. I'll try. I promise.'

It had been another very long day. Albert slept intermittently, pillowed on Aunty Sylv's spongy bosom, smelling the natural smells of her that combined now to remind him of a human haystack. The bread, cheese and a huge mound of watercress, fresh picked by Uncle Austin, still took up the centre of the table,

49

the perimeter was crowded with arms, bare or sleeved, hairy or smooth. The babies were in bed. The two chickens, donated by one of the owners of the funeral suits, were packed in the trap and the horse was fresh and ready for the ten-mile trot back to the city.

Grandma said, 'Don't leave it so long next time our Will. We shan't be here for ever you know.' There was laughter at this ridiculous statement and Jack's voice bellowed, 'You didn't speck him to run down every five minutes our mother did you? Not when Flo's childing. God, he wanted to make the most of that I reckon! Eh our Will? Eh?'

Dad's voice, maudlin with cider, said, 'Little do you know our Jack. B'God. Little do you know.' Everyone laughed again. Aunty Sylv said, 'Drink talking. Eh Vi? Better get the lad up to bed praps.'

Aunty Vi gasped through her giggles, 'He's asleep our Sylv.'Sides, he's too young to understand.'

Albert lifted his chin to tell them he was not asleep and Aunty Sylv laughed louder than anyone, then leaned down and kissed him on the nose, then on each of his eyes. He relapsed again and dreamt that they were on the road back to Gloucester and the outline of the cathedral was black against the pale night sky and Dad was singing under his breath, 'I don't want to leave you but I feel I ought to go,' and the smell of the Kempley daffs was in his nose.

It had been a longer day for March. She had opened the door to young Mrs. Goodrich wearing a clean starched pinafore and a welcoming smile. Young Mrs. Goodrich had held on to the stone jar of honey in her one hand but had given March the bunch of golden daffodils from her other.

'Now dear, put them in the kitchen for tonight. Flowers shouldn't be in a bedroom overnight you know, and the family can have the joy of them until tomorrow.

Then take them up on your mother's breakfast tray. The gypsies brought them round this morning, fresh from Kempley, and I thought of your mother straightaway.'

March was overcome. The fact that she and Mother did not wish to be reminded of Kempley did not matter at all. Young Mrs. Goodrich's generosity and gentility did. March arranged the flowers in the Welsh pottery jug and put them in the middle of the table on the dark red plush cloth. When she lit the gas the kitchen looked almost as it did when Mother was about. She fetched May from the back parlour to see it. May came, dangling the scissors and a string of paper dolls from one hand. 'Oooh. They're beautiful March. No wonder Albert wanted to go with Papa. They're beautiful.'

Sometimes May's reactions were intensely satisfying. March kissed the golden head peremptorily. 'Go up and get ready for bed now May. I'll join you as soon as I've let Mrs. Goodrich out.'

'In our own room March?'

March nodded. April seemed to have stopped crying incessantly and she hoped her mother would not need her again tonight. March did not remember ever feeling so tired before.

She was not pleased to see Mrs. Luker.

'I won't keep your dear mother longer than a minute,' said Hettie breathlessly. 'I meant to come earlier but Sibbie fell and cut her leg and Fred was shoeing a horse with his dad . . . now you get on to bed dearie and I'll let myself out. You've got to leave the door for your father haven't you? So that ull be all right . . . and in your own bed I hope.'

What had May been saying over in that dreadful house?

Mrs. Luker actually came in to say goodnight to them on her way out. 'And you're all tucked up neat and nice and cosy. Just as it should be. No need to worry over your mother any more my dears. What some pretty

51

dears ... eh ... eh. ...' March wondered whether Mrs. Luker had been to the Lamb and Flag. She was no better than Snotty Lottie. March smiled against closed lids. Albert had said something this morning about Lottie. 'Snotty Lottie gottie lottie snotty.' Something like that. Albert was clever. Albert was beautiful. Albert loved her.

Florence held out her arms to her husband.

'Oh Will. My dearest husband. Why didn't you tell me about poor Mr. Daker? Mrs. Luker has just brought me last night's *Citizen*. Oh my dear, I am so sorry.'

He gazed at her. After the uproar of Kempley, his terraced house in Chichester Street was a peaceful haven and his wife more beautiful and refined than he had ever remembered. He sank to his knees by the bed and took her in his arms, and she, mellowed by milk stout, bent her dark head and kissed him.

'I didn't want you to know. Not yet. Not after the birth,' he murmured.

She whispered, 'My dearest. We're here to comfort each other in a cruel world.'

He held her gently, drawing comfort from her, until she fell asleep in his arms. Then he laid her head on the pillow and undressed, standing above April and looking down at her fondly as he compared her with the babies at Kempley. He was a lucky man. He must never forget he was a lucky man.

He climbed into bed beside his wife and put his hand on her waist. He thought of Albert. And his mother and sisters and brothers and the family scattered all over the Kempley and Newent area. He thought of the big funeral that would take place on Monday and how his suits would be there. And he slept with a smile on his lips.

3

They called the kitten Rags, and he grew leggily into a wonderful mouser. He spent every night at the top of the cellar steps and some mornings he had as many as half-a-dozen tails to show for his night's vigil. March no longer held her skirts high as she went upstairs; mice were unknown at number thirty-three. Thirty-one and thirty-five borrowed Rags occasionally, but Florence would never let him out of the front door in case he wandered across the road to the Lukers' and swallowed some of their poison.

Albert took the scholarship for the King's School and did not do very well, but he was given a place because of his voice. Mr. Filbert, who trained the choristers, said he had never heard such a true voice. Florence bought some royal blue and golden yellow Melton cloth from the Co-op in Southgate Street, and Will cut his suit. On August the twenty-seventh he left home with trepidation, walked along Northgate Street, cut down Saint John's Lane and through the cathedral close and presented himself at the arched door in the wall. Mr. Filbert gathered the new boys around him and took them into the music room. Albert relaxed immediately; his clear soprano soared easily without accompaniment. Mr. Filbert said, 'Where did you learn to sight-read boy?' And Albert answered literally, 'In the bandy room sir.' That was where Mother's piano was, plus a banjo acquired by his father. Mr. Filbert smiled and did not pursue the subject.

At midday Albert sat with the other boys at a long trestle table and unpacked his bread and dripping. The boy next to him had banana sandwiches and seeing Albert's envious eyes, offered to do a swop. He was as retiring as Albert himself, but during that first week they managed to exchange basic information and begin a friendship. His name was Harry Hughes: he had been a choirboy at Longford church: his father worked on the railway and put him on a tram every morning and he got off at Worcester Street. Albert began to wait for him where Alvin Street spewed its tenements into the Westgate. They would walk down to the cathedral together arm-in-arm, feeling a pair of real lads. They read Dumas together and evolved a clarion cry of comradeship. 'We'll live together! We'll die together!' They would proclaim this with exaggerated gestures and then snuffle and grunt their special, repressed laugh. Albert said to March, 'As soon as Mother is better, I want to ask Harry to tea.' March, immediately jealous, blurted, 'You like him better than me, don't you?' Albert said, 'I *like* Harry Hughes. I love you. You're my sister.' He knew by now the right thing to say to March.

They could all see that Florence was not well and it did not occur to her that she was pregnant again. She was still breast-feeding April and after his long celibacy during that pregnancy, Will was now very demanding. She imagined she was over-tired, nothing more. It was Lottie Jenner who enlightened her.

The Goodriches and the Risings were the only families in the street who sported a baby carriage for their offspring: the other mothers sat in their open doorways and nursed their babies on fine days and kept them indoors otherwise until they could use their own legs. Florence had wheeled April down to Chichester Street school one golden day in September, simply to give March and May the pleasure of wheeling her back home. The two small girls, trailed by an

54

envious Sibbie Luker, walked sedately behind the wooden handle, and April, sitting up now, gurgled at them enchantingly. It was a picture to remember. Florence found it easy to smile at the appreciative Lottie as she lumbered out of the dairy with her morning milk. At four o'clock in the afternoon.

'Lovely girls. All three of them. And the babby looks well enough considerin' she was early weaned.'

Florence regretted the smile which had encouraged Lottie to behave like . . . Lottie. 'She is not weaned yet,' she said against her better judgement. Florence still did not enjoy breast-feeding but she was proud of April's progress.

Lottie drew in her lips disapprovingly. 'Should be. For your sake Mrs. Rising. How far on are you? Three months? Four? Surprised you got any milk, but then, you thin ones are always deceptive.'

Florence stared, her surprise obvious, then she recovered herself with difficulty. 'It — it's early days yet Mrs. Jenner,' she said meaninglessly. She quickened her step to catch up with the girls and leave Lottie behind. It couldn't be. It couldn't. Yet she knew it was.

Doctor Green was blunt.

'Either you rest — lie down for twenty-four hours a day — or you lose this child. It's up to you.'

Florence knew where her duty lay and told Will about it that night. Will did not say a word. Once a pregnancy was confirmed, Florence would not allow him near her; the new baby became her duty before her husband. Will sat on the edge of the bed and stared down at his bare legs and accepted the cold fact of several months' more celibacy without protest. He could have said 'Alf and Hettie Luker make the most of their pregnancies.' But he didn't. Florrie wasn't Hettie Luker. He straightened his shoulders; neither was he Alf Luker. He must remember that.

It was Will who decreed that the children — all of them, even April — must be sent away. He would take the trap again and drive down to Kempley and see if his mother would have them.

'They'll be all right down at Kempley till Christmas,' he said defensively as Florence's horrified face turned towards him. 'And there's no other way you will stay up here in bed, I know that for a fact.'

Florence imagined how it would be: Albert out with Austin and Jack all day, Wallie thinking it amusing to introduce the boy to rough cider: her beautiful May among those coarse voices: April grubbing on the floor with the other babies.

She said, 'I'll write to Aunt Lizzie first.' She glanced at the new curtains. 'She's always been generous. I'll write to her.'

Will looked doubtful. It was one thing to send birthday and Christmas presents, quite another to receive their objects into a quiet, childless home. Especially when one of the objects was only five months old. But Aunt Lizzie was one of the mystical Rhys-Davies clan; and she was married to Edwin Tomms who owned two ironmongeries in Bath and might even be a Freemason.

Aunt Lizzie was overjoyed with the idea of having her nephew and three nieces on a three-month visit. She was not strong and number thirty-three Chichester Street offered little comfort to a semi-invalid, so she had never stayed there. The last time she had come for the day had been when May was christened and as Florence had never been able to afford the journey to Bath, they were virtual strangers to each other.

The children were not told the reason for this unexpected holiday and decided that Aunt Lizzie had summoned them for an inspection. Albert, long ago primed on his aristocratic Welsh blood, commented gloomily, 'I expect she wants me to change my name to Rhys-Davies.' March exclaimed in sudden terror, 'Or adopt you!' May, infuriatingly sensible in spite of her

56

romanticism, said, 'Don't be silly, Mother wouldn't part with a hair of our heads.'

Their chief concern at leaving home was the kitten. But the fact that Mother spent so much time lying down was useful in that respect as Rags very much enjoyed joining her on the feather bed in the big front room. They all went in to kiss Mother and assure her they were going to be good. May had her underwear checked and was given some wintergreen ointment for her chest; March was given last-minute instructions for April; Albert was told to be a little man and look after his sisters. They all stroked Rags, laughing delightedly as he rolled on to his back displaying his knotty curls. Then they were off, March pushing the carriage with one case balanced on it, Dad carrying another, Albert a canvas holdall. 'Like a moonlight flit,' Dad joked as they turned into Northgate Street where the pavement was high above the road and railed off beneath the railway bridge. 'It isn't night time Dad.' 'What do you mean Papa?' asked the children. Will shook his head, already breathing heavily. 'Step it out,' he said instead.

Bristol was the most amazing station in the world. Instead of wooden bridges over the line, it had tunnels beneath, tiled white like the public lavatories and echoing to every murmur. They saw a cattle train trundle slowly through between the platforms: twenty-four open wagons of lowing, terrified cows, heads tossing above each other's flanks, eyes rolling, bodies jerking as the wagons clanked together. May wept, though she was used to seeing herds being driven through the traffic of the Northgate on market days.

Bristol was amazing, Bath just beautiful. They changed to the Great Western line and travelled through a lush, enclosed Somerset. Hills wrapped them gently and the river was next to them, willow-edged and full of reflections, not a bit like their own Severn.

May breathed, 'It's lovely. Just lovely.' And March, holding April to the window, had to agree.

They emerged from the train, almost in awe. In the heart of their own city nothing was visible because it was so flat. Here, standing on the platform surrounded by their luggage, they could see the whole of Bath. The abbey, then the bays of terraces rising to woods; the river below, spanned by arched bridges; the green of parks. And though it was two o'clock of a November afternoon, no trace of fog. There might be a river mist later, but the sooty fog that settled over Gloucester on winter days was not here. And the smell was different too. As the train went on its way to Chippenham and Westbury, the sulphur smell went with it and left dampness. Not the muddy dampness of the canal over-laid with the vinegar of the pickle factory and the pulped wood from the match works, but the dampness of grass and leaves and the smiling, meandering Avon and the deep warm springs that the Romans had found.

March was silent through May's exclamations and Albert's grinning guffaws, but it was only because she could hardly believe her eyes. March did not have May's ability to see beauty through ugliness. Her home town was spoilt for her because of the grime and grimness; the countryside meant the squalor of Kempley Cottage. Bath was quite different. She was to discover ugly parts later, but that first impression remained. Bath was beauty and luxury. She surrendered the pram to May and walked through the booking hall in a trance. Already she knew that quiet, grey days in November would remind her of Bath for the rest of her life.

Aunt Lizzie was a surprise too. March could see she was a Rhys-Davies. There was the dark hair, though very much threaded with greys that were inclined to escape from their bun and frizz up on their own. There were the straight aquiline features and the brown eyes and the tiny, neat feet and long thin hands, but the

58

whole added up differently. Aunt Lizzie had had a sister to share the narrow confines of the Davies household and they had both escaped early to marriage. When Alice had died in childbirth, the baby, Florence, had lived in the gaunt old house in Westgate Street with no company save for a stiff governess, until she was sent to Kempley to escape the smallpox. All the laughter and fun she had known had come from Will Rising and their subsequent children.

Aunt Lizzie loved to talk, and March, the elder girl and the darkest of the three children, became her confidante. Before Will had left them that afternoon to catch the two trains back to Florence, she had set the pattern for their three months with her.

'Now darlings —' she patted Will's arm reassuringly. The fact that he had obviously impregnated Florence five times made him very special — Florence had always reminded Lizzie of a nun — but seeing him separately with his children like this, she could sense his attractions. She recalled her mother telling her in despair how ardent he was, and how poor Florence would never be able to stand against him; how she had wanted to send the girl abroad but Will Rising had threatened to kill himself if she went away. . . . There had been so many things, so many romantic things.

'Now darlings, I've looked out all my old games. Snakes and ladders and ludo and backgammon and . . . oh, ever so many things. You will have to amuse yourselves because I'm far too old to do it for you!' She laughed, obviously expecting them to deny this, but when nobody spoke, she sped on, 'Letty will take you for a walk each afternoon when she has finished in the house. And when I drive into town — or make suitable calls — you may come with me. Otherwise —'

'They're quite used to seeing to themselves Mrs. Jephcott — er — aunt,' Will said, liking the old lady better than before. At first he had hated all the Rhys-Davies because they came between himself and his Flo,

but when the old pair died it became evident that Aunt
Lizzie had not entirely disapproved of him as a suitor.
She had sent them the stair carpet and the curtains for
the Chichester Street house, besides remembering all
the birthdays. He patted the back of the hand that was
patting his arm. She was amazingly like an older
Florence.

'Then that's fine,' she beamed at them. 'I was afraid
you might feel dull here but perhaps, after all. . . . And
this is the new baby? She's going to look like you Albert,
isn't she? And what could be nicer?' She left Will's arm
and put her hand on March's head. 'And you are the
little mother March? Will you mind permitting Letty to
see to April now? Because I am so looking forward to
talking to you and hearing about your dear mother.'

She made no comment on May's beauty, her smile was
entirely for March, and her words gave March place
and importance.

'Oh . . . oh so am I Aunt Lizzie,' March breathed
delightedly.

'Then we'll ring for Letty now — the bell is by the fireplace dear — and she can bring our tea in here by the
fire and then take April downstairs and give her some of
that porage stuff and pop her into bed. I've given her a
room near Letty dear, on the top floor, so that you can
sleep undisturbed.'

'Oh . . . Aunt Lizzie . . .' breathed March.

May suddenly said, 'Daddy, do you have to go back
tonight?'

'Of course he does.' Albert, usually masking his
fondness for May in front of March, was piqued by
March's unaccustomed success. He draped a protective arm across the blonde head. 'Dad has to look after
Mother, don't you remember?'

'Please stay for tea at least William.' Aunt Lizzie flut-
tered above his coat sleeve again. One would expect him
to be well turned out as he was a tailor, but not to be
quite so much like the dear King when he had been the

errant Prince of Wales. 'You cannot return all the way to Gloucester without any refreshment at all.'

March was surprised when her father mentioned nothing about the sandwiches she had so laboriously cut for the journey; even more surprised when he carried Aunt Lizzie's hand to his lips in exactly the same way as he did Mother's. It affected May too and she began to weep silently as always, huge tears threatening to drown her blue eyes.

Albert said fiercely, 'We'd better say cheerio then Dad hadn't we? Tempus fugits and all that.' Albert had been doing Latin for exactly six weeks.

The children were hugged by Will in turn. March knew it nearly made him weep too to leave them, but she felt no reciprocal sentiment. She and Aunt Lizzie were going to talk while May and Albert played silly games and April was looked after, washed, fed and cleaned by poor Letty. But then Letty would be paid for doing it.

On November the fifth there was an enormous bonfire in Green Park and a firework display. The children drove along the Royal Crescent in Uncle Edwin's carriage and watched with all their eyes. March sat in the curve of Aunt Lizzie's arm, May on Uncle Edwin's knee; Albert in a Norfolk jacket and breeches knelt on the seat, his elbows on the folded hood. He thought how much more fun it would be if Dad was there, laughing and pointing his beard to the sky. It was strange; at home Mother was always serious and quiet and Dad full of fun. Here it was quite the other way around. Aunt Lizzie laughed more each day, but Uncle Edwin was more than just serious. He looked solemn even when May smiled up at him and asked whether he was quite sure he was warm enough.

Aunt Lizzie said, 'Are you warm enough kitten? That's the important thing. Your dear mamma will never forgive me if you catch cold while you're staying in Bath.'

March snuggled hard against the inside of Aunt

Lizzie's elbow, not minding a bit that Aunt Lizzie was as concerned as everyone always seemed to be about May. Aunt Lizzie's concern had a kind of indulgence to it; she used the same voice that she used to April. She never used that voice to March. March and Aunt Lizzie were equals in her sight.

A huge spray of sparks glowed against the night sky and gradually changed colour until they became a vase of flowers. March twisted her head to see whether Aunt Lizzie was enjoying it and saw that the dark eyes were not watching the fireworks at all. They were watching her.

'You see March dear. . . .'

After the fireworks, there was cocoa and little sugar biscuits by the fire, and while Uncle Edwin was unwillingly coerced into a game of dominoes with May and Albert, Aunt Lizzie talked to March. It was eight o'clock, when they should have been abed, but November the fifth was special. March watched the sparks collecting on the fire back — black-leaded every morning by Letty's underdog — and thought how pleasant it all was.

'My father — your great-grandfather that was — lost his inheritance because of an entailment. No dear, I do not understand it myself, but sometimes a great estate is entailed to a distant relative so that it will not be left to a woman or perhaps to a son who was not quite — er — regular. Born on the wrong side of the sheets as it were. And though dear Papa was brought up in the house and recognised as my grandfather's son, I rather think . . . however dear, this is mere speculation. All I know is that he was forced to leave Llanfenon when he was sixteen and he never got over it. He was embittered. At that age! What a fate! Guard against bitterness March, it eats at the soul like rust at iron.'

March touched Aunt Lizzie's hand; it was like one of May's stories but it was real. She said in a low voice so

62

that the others could not hear, 'Lemons are bitter too Aunt Lizzie.'

Aunt Lizzie recollected for a moment that she was talking to a nine-year-old child and spoke in the voice reserved for May and April.

'But lemons are clean and fresh dearest. Are they not? Not a bit like rust.'

March was reassured. She might be only nine but she knew she was capable of bitterness. She hoped it was the lemon kind and not the rusty.

'But you're not — em — embittered Aunt Lizzie.'

'I'm a realist, child.' Aunt Lizzie's smile became roguish. 'To pin one's hope on litigation is a dream in this country March. Remember that. I daresay laws and rules can bludgeon people into doing what they want occasionally. I find *persuasion* works better.' She laughed delightfully. 'Did you not take note of the way I persuaded your uncle to play with Albert and May? I kissed him my dear, and told him I was tired and you would soothe my nerves and could he possibly amuse the other two for me!'

March pondered this. Some of it was unwelcome: May got her way with Mother by means of a kiss and a hug. On the other hand she was also a dreamer and Aunt Lizzie obviously had no time for dreamers.

She looked up at Aunt Lizzie and laughed too and Albert said disapprovingly, 'Why are you laughing March?' They'd been at Bath just under a week and though he was making the best of it and nearly enjoying it in spite of himself, he did not expect March to do so. She was the one who wanted to go to school and become clever; she was the one who depended on his attention for her happiness. Yet here she was missing her precious school and Aunt Lizzie seemed set on taking her away from Albert. And she could still laugh.

She said with simple truth, 'I'm laughing because Aunt Lizzie is laughing!'

He was frankly jealous. 'Watch out you don't wake

63

May,' he said sternly. 'She's exhausted after all the excitement of the fireworks.' He made it sound as though Aunt Lizzie had forced them down to the park.

It was the first time the two gossipers had noticed May's comatose state and Aunt Lizzie pulled the bell while March dusted the crumbs from her pinafore into the glowing fire, suitably subdued. Uncle Edwin protested unexpectedly, 'We haven't finished the game yet my boy. A game must always be finished properly — that's something you should learn as soon as possible.'

Letty arrived and took in the situation at a glance. She bawled over her shoulder, 'Come on Rosie — stir yourself!' and in five minutes a drowsy May was helped upstairs and into her thickest flannel nightgown already thoroughly impregnated with wintergreen. As March followed her into the warmed bed, she felt sorry that Albert could not share her ever-present delight in this new existence. But his reticence did not mar anything. It almost accentuated her pleasure. And she adored Aunt Lizzie. Whatever Aunt Lizzie was and did, March would be and would do.

Teddy was born six weeks early on Christmas Eve. In spite of staying in bed, things did not go well for Florence. Doctor Green attended and Lottie was ousted by a professional nurse in starched white uniform. Ether was used, and the dreaded forceps, and Will, waiting on the landing in an agony of fear, heard the word 'haemorrhaging' and associated it always with the sickly gas smell seeping beneath the bedroom door. Somehow Florence clung to life. Pale and anaemic she would always be now, but she was alive. Teddy, under five pounds but healthy enough, was removed to a foster home known to Doctor Green, where a strong young woman, just delivered of a son herself, had enough milk for two or more.

Teddy thrived quickly, though Florence obstinately refused to believe it and sat white-faced through all the ten days of Christmas, unable to reply to the children's letters or do more than shudder at her daily diet of raw liver. On January the fourth Doctor Green made a bargain with her.

'If I go and fetch your son now and let you hold him for half an hour, will you start eating your liver and drinking your stout?'

Florence shuddered again, but nodded faintly and without much hope.

It was a cold day, the rain falling as sleet on to the thick oily water of the docks. The doctor drove his brougham carefully through the tiny back streets behind Gloucester prison to the house where the wet nurse lived. She had been the doctor's own kitchen-maid, and, in spite of her mean quarters, knew how he liked things done. Teddy and her own baby lay side by side in an upstairs room, well heated by a small fire and well ventilated too. Doctor Green nodded approval and especially so when he examined the children.

'You're doing a good job Kitty. A very good job. My patient will be very grateful to you. As I am. Not much money I'm afraid, but good warm clothing for your young Sir Nib here. The husband's a tailor.'

'Thank you sir.' Kitty was an amiable girl and would have suckled Teddy for the sake of her old employers, but her husband would want to render an account.

The doctor received the swaddled Teddy and pulled the shawl well up around his face. 'Once the mother is on her feet she will visit you until you wean the child, Kitty. We can't have too many of these outings while the weather is so unkind.'

'Certainly not sir. You tell her she's welcome here any old time. And she's not to worry one mite. That baby ent no trouble to no-one down here. An' he's not doing too badly by the looks of things.' She indicated just above her waist line, unashamed, and the doctor patted her shoulder approvingly. How much easier his life would be if all his patients were like Kitty Hall. He recalled Florence Rising's taut embarrassment at each examination and sighed.

But her joy at the sight of Teddy compensated for all the good doctor's trouble. She held out her arms with a little cry and stared down into the tumbled shawl incredulously.

'He's beautiful!'

'What did I say? Now fetch that liver Mr. Rising and —'

'He's so strong! He's stronger than April and she was the strongest of the children!'

'I said that too.'

Will brought the revolting liver, chopped as fine as he could do it on the bread board, with a little parsley added to make it just palatable.

'Oh that does look delicious.' Doctor Green took the dish and spoon, determined that Florence should not welsh on her bargain. 'Now, if you let your husband hold his son for five minutes Mrs. Rising —'

She relinquished the baby unwillingly and began on her liver, hardly noticing it. Her brown eyes, feverishly bright, never left that dark head and her hands shook as if eager to begin living again. She and Will had decided before the baby's birth that if it was a girl it should be named Elizabeth and if a boy, Edwin, in gratitude to her aunt and uncle in Bath. She had been glad not to be forced to stray from her month-names; now for the first time, she called the baby Teddy.

'We'll call him Teddy, Will,' she said, chewing desperately, her eyes watering, her hand held ready for the glass of water offered by Doctor Green. She gulped and gasped. 'Teddy. It suits him, don't you think? He looks so sturdy! And yet — and yet —' she swallowed again, 'he's dark like me. He's the first of the children to look like me!'

Will grinned at the tiny bundle. 'Oh I don't know, Flo. March has your eyes.'

66

Florence took another spoonful of her mess and chewed again.

'But Teddy — Teddy is a Rhys-Davies!' she said.

Will looked up quickly, his grin fading. 'Teddy he shall be if you like, Flo. But Teddy Rising. And don't you forget it.'

The doctor glanced from one to the other as he scraped the liver dish. He had wanted to say something at the time of the birth, but it had seemed inappropriate. Now he felt the time had come.

'Mrs. Rising . . . well done . . . a short drink will help it down, I think. Now. I have to say — to tell you — an unpleasant — er — fact. No good beating about the bush.' He looked at Will. 'Let Mother hold the baby again Mr. Rising. I think . . . yes . . . it would be best if she held. . . .' The transfer was made and the doctor cleared his throat. 'He's a very good specimen Mrs. Rising — that is to say — he's a lovely baby. As you see of course. All your children . . . lovely. But this one — this one must be the last my dear. I'm sorry. But I cannot be responsible if there are any more pregnancies.' She looked remarkably calm. It doubtless had not penetrated as yet. She was obviously one of Nature's mothers so it would hit her hard. He turned to Will. 'You understand what I am saying Mr. Rising? If your wife has another baby she will — er — forfeit her — er —'

Florence's voice spoke calmly at his side.

'We understand, Doctor. Perfectly. Please don't be anxious. We have five beautiful children, as you so kindly said. We are perfectly satisfied.'

Doctor Green looked at her. She meant it, at least for the moment. Of course in a year or two it would doubtless be a different story, but for now . . . well, she was an amazing little woman. Beautiful in a classic sort of way, and with that black hair folded over her brow she had the look of a nun. He smiled to himself and stood up.

'Time for young Teddy to go back to his meal ticket,'

he said heartily. 'Don't worry too much about it all, Mrs. Rising. As soon as you've had some of that liver and got strength back into your limbs, you can visit him every day. And we'll wean him early. There's a school of thought around these days that says babies can go on to solids as early as eight weeks.' He boomed a laugh. Mrs. Rising did not echo it, indeed she looked hopeful. 'Just eat up that liver,' he concluded quickly. 'As much as you can possibly manage.' He swaddled the baby again, pulling the lapel of his Burberry over the tiny head as he went out into the awful weather. He was pleased with himself. This time, disaster had been averted.

Will sat late over some turn-ups that night. Bitterness was a taste in his mouth and even the snowy rain slurping stickily over the smoked glass of his workroom had the look of gall. For one thing, he was exhausted. Since Mr. Daker's death last April, he had acquired most of his business, on the understanding that he paid ten per cent of his takings to Mrs. Daker as commission. Women. Old Daker had been a Jew, no doubt of that, but he had never struck bargains in quite the same way as his wife. It had seemed fair enough at the time. Florence had been doubtful, but he'd reassured her in his easy-going way. 'She's frightened, Flo. Frightened of being alone and poor. But David is nearly fourteen. Soon old enough to support all three of them.'

He'd been glad of the work at first. Mrs. Daker had put him on to a glazier in Barton Street who had supplied the new smoked glass window with his name let into it: 'W. Rising. Tailor.' Florence said it was in excellent taste and so much better than advertising in the Citizen. It was the nearest she had come to criticising his announcement of April's birth. It seemed to bring more work than ever. Complete strangers, taking their daughters to the new school in Denmark Road through Chichester Street, knocked on his door and enquired whether he tailored ladies' coats — navy-blue cloth, melton, with a half belt, suitable for school wear. He showed them March's, pockets full of moth balls for the summer. They were impressed. If he had more orders for next September, he might write a discreet letter to the headmistress suggesting that he become the school's recommended tailor.

Then there had been the upset over the new baby. He had reconciled himself to a few months' celibacy and had boasted in the Lamb and Flag of his prowess. Florence was his small wiry Welsh pony and as soon as the new baby arrived, she would do her duty again and March would be that much older to help out, and Albert would be singing solo in the cathedral, and May more beautiful than ever . . . he was the luckiest man in the world. Or so he had thought until today.

Angrily he laid the finished trousers on the pressing table, and, not finding the iron holder, picked up the iron from the gas using his handkerchief. Florence would have done the turn-ups for him while he tacked the new smoking jacket for one of Mr. Daker's friends, but he couldn't bring himself to ask her. He couldn't bring himself to speak to her since Doctor Green's departure. Mrs. Goodrich had brought in some fresh lamb's liver and he should have chopped it and taken it in to her while she sat with Mrs. Luker in the back parlour. Hettie Luker came over most evenings with a bottle of stout and bits of laundry, rough-dried and not very clean. He couldn't wait for Florence to be back on her feet so that his collars were decently starched and he didn't have to make do with the same shirt all week. But then, if he wanted Flo on her feet again he should have chopped that liver and taken it in to her.

Angrier than ever, he banged the iron back on to the trivet and folded the trousers into their creases and over a chair. His handkerchief had a large brown scorch mark across it, which meant it couldn't go into his top pocket for callers. He rammed it into the pocket of his trousers and banged down the passage into the kitchen. There was no sign of the liver on the table but Rags sat by his dish washing his face smugly. Will looked at the table, looked at the cat, and some of the temper which his father had passed to March exploded inside him. He leaned down and whacked the soft furry body as hard as he could. Rags sailed into the air with a startled squawk and landed feet first by the gas stove. Panic-stricken, he skidded beneath it then poked his triangular mask apprehensively from beneath the oven door. He couldn't believe his senses. The tall skinny dark one, yes. But not this one.

Will stared back, horrified at his own behaviour. He had never struck an animal or child in anger before. Never bullied his wife. Perhaps it would have been better if he had. He turned and strode into the back parlour. It was in darkness, the guard around the fire, the curtains drawn back ready for the morning. He closed the door on it and took the stairs two at a time. Voices came from behind the front bedroom door. Inside Hettie sat by the bed, recounting a small incident which proved how much Sibbie missed May.

'I'm not one to lie Mrs. Rising,' she concluded. 'Specially about children. Our Sibbie thinks of your May as her sister. More than her sister. They're like that!' She held up her forefingers side by side. 'Peas in a pod. Peas in a pod.' She smiled at Will, a wide self-congratulatory smile. 'And all the liver gone Mr. Rising,' she went on without a pause. 'I did chop it like you does and put in a bit of parsley and down it went as sweet as a nut!'

Hettie stood up and smoothed down her filthy pinafore. She was proud of her figure since her last birth six weeks ago. She moved her smile towards Florence.

'I'd best be going. Christamighty it must be gone ten and Henry wanting his supper I'll be bound.' Henry was the new baby. 'Oh, it's nice we birthed so close Mrs. Rising. Just like Sibbie and May is such friends so will Glad and April be. And now Henry and your little Edwin.'

Will said, 'I didn't realise you'd done the liver Hettie. Thank you . . . I've been kept late over some trouser turn-ups.'

Florence was distressed. 'Oh Will, why didn't you bring them in to me? I've been sitting idly talking to Mrs. Luker.' Will knew she didn't approve of him using Hettie's first name. 'Now, lock up quickly dear and come to bed.'

Hettie giggled and went to the door still smoothing her pinafore. Will followed, wishing there was a reason for the giggle, noticing for the first time the voluptuousness of Hettie's still swelling abdomen.

He said, 'Wait a minute Hettie. You'd better take an umbrella. You shouldn't have come over without a coat or anything.'

She laughed more loudly at this and came after him down the passage and into the kitchen. Rags was still beneath the gas stove.

Will said, 'Oh Christ. I thought the cat had eaten the liver and I kicked him there. Look at the poor little devil.' His voice dropped automatically into a slovenly drawl and Hettie's laughter increased accordingly.

'Oh Will Rising, I didn't know you could be . . . oh Will, you *do* make me laugh. Honestly!'

Will turned and saw her open mouth and very white teeth gleaming in the gaslight. The sleet, probably snow by now, brushed sibilantly against the dark kitchen window where the gasometer kept a constant watch for any indiscretions. She reminded him of his sisters, dirty, uncaring, full of senseless laughter that sprang from life; generous to a fault. . . .

He put his hands either side of her waist, leaned forward and kissed the open mouth. Immediately he sprang backwards as if she'd bitten him.

'Hettie I — my God — Hettie, I'm sorry —'

She put a hand to her mouth as if to stop the laughter, but her eyes danced and bubbled with it. They were blue eyes like his own and they were full of knowledge.

71

'Don't you dare apologise Will Rising! It ud be an insult that would!' She took a deep breath through her fingers. 'I never thought you'd look at me! Don't be sorry for that . . . for doing what you wanted!' She dropped her hand and took a step towards him. 'I'm honoured Will. I'm real honoured. Honest. I wouldn't lie to you Will. Not about something like that.' She was moving closer to him as she spoke those oft-used words. He noticed her neck was dirty and again he was reminded of Sylv and Vi. Pigs in shit. As happy as pigs in shit. 'I've never dared look at you Will. Not *look* at you. You know. Like that. Not till now.' She put her hands behind her back and undid her pinafore then slipped it over her head. Her fingers went to her throat and began on her blouse buttons. 'I've always said you was a handsome man. Like the King. And we all know what he's like, don't we?' She laughed yet again and showed those animal-white teeth and he smelled the comforting smell of stout on her breath. And if it was all right for the King. . . .

He said, 'I durs(n't Het. . . .' He sounded like his brother Jack. 'I durstn't. Supposin' . . . supposin'. . . .'

Again she laughed. 'Chrisamighty Will . . . you don't think any harm can come do you? I'm a month gone again a'ready. Cursed Alf last week when I found out, but now . . . it's a blessing in disguise en't it? A real blessing. . . .' Her hands took his and slid them inside her camisole and her laughter seemed to go into his throat so that they shook together and happiness burst inside him again as it always did. He couldn't be unhappy for long. It wasn't in his nature. They lay on the mat before the dead range and Rags came and sniffed at them and was sent flying back to the gas stove for his trouble. Hettie was laughing so much she hardly had the strength to pull down her drawers.

He could not face Florrie. He slept in Albert's bed and wept into the pillow. He had never touched anyone but Florrie, not until tonight. Since he was twelve Florence Davies had been everything to him. He had loved her with his whole being and he knew she had loved him with a tenderness and a selflessness he would not find again. He slept somehow, waking frequently in the hope that the incident with Hettie Luker was a fevered dream, groaning with despair as each time he realised it was not. In the morning he crept downstairs, hardly noticing the snow banked greyly against the windows. He boiled some water and made tea; scraped out the range and lit it; did the same to the fireplace in the back parlour. He boiled an egg for Florence and laid a tray as beautifully as May would have done.

She said, 'Oh Will . . . how kind you are!' and he felt terrible.

Later as he sat in his workroom and heard her moving slowly about, washing and dressing and settling herself in the back parlour, he wondered how they would manage until the children returned. They had to be alone together so often. It would be unbearable. And when Hettie came over this evening with the stout, what could he say? If he went to the Lamb and Flag she would be waiting for him when he got back. What could he do? He felt trapped in his own house.

It was time for him to make some dinner and take it in to her when the bell rang. He peered through the advertisement on the window and could just make out the bulky, well-wrapped figure of a woman. Not Hettie. Snow or no snow, Hettie would have slipped over the road hatless. This one huddled on the top step, level with the boot-scraper, head down and shoulders hunched against the east wind; it was his sister, Sylvia.

'Sylv!' He flung open the door and dragged her in. She was almost hidden in shawls and beneath them she was holding a large bundle tied just as his mother had tied his bundle when he had come to Mr. Daker. Sylvia, with her clothes? 'This is marvellous Sylv! Never been to see us have you? And not for want of an invitation — come in girl, out of that snow — never mind the oilcloth —' She was salvation. He led her into the back parlour, still exclaiming, so that she couldn't begin on any explanations just yet. She could have been about to report a death; it did not matter just so long as she was there between himself and Florrie.

Florence had kept the fire in and it was warm and elegant with the round table covered in a dark plush cloth and Florence sitting with her crochet in her lap. He was proud all over again.

Sylv took off snow-sodden gloves and exposed red-raw hands. Her face was red and raw too as if she'd been crying. Florence tried to get up.

'My dear! Whatever brings you here a day like this? Sit down — yes, I insist. Will — fetch the brandy.'

He pushed Flo back and drew up the other chair for Sylv. Then he hastened to the chiffonier and put sugar in a glass, then a thimbleful of brandy. Florence made distressed noises and Sylv kept saying, 'No need to fuss, Ma's all right. And Pa. Everyone — everyone's quite all right.' Then as the brandy thawed her throat, she added anxiously, 'You, what about you Flo? We heard about the new boy o'course, but the message didn't say nothing about you being ill. Hardly anything of you my dear — hardly anything at all!'

'I'm recovering fast. With the help of your dear brother.' Suddenly and unexpectedly, Florence picked up Will's hand from the back of her chair and put it to her cheek. 'He is goodness itself Sylvia. I cannot begin to tell you —'

Will snatched his hand away, then covered the rebuff with a laugh.

'So kind I leave you alone hour after hour while I'm in the workroom!'

'The work has to be done dearest. And you won't allow me to help.'

He couldn't bear it. He drew up a footstool and squatted between the two women. 'You'll stay for a few nights Sylv?' Hettie could expect nothing this evening if his sister was here. 'You can see we could do with your help. Florence has anaemia and the baby is out to a wet nurse, the other children all at Bath —'

'Why didn't you send and ask for one of us to come, Will?' Sylvia was looking better by the minute. 'Keeping it all to yourself like this. What are families for?'

'Florence wouldn't let me tell you —'

'Then she should!' Sylvia spoke unusually vehemently. 'I coulda come up before Christmas and saved all this fuss and bother.'

'There has been no fuss and bother Sylvia.' Florence spoke quietly but her voice over-rode her sister-in-law's. 'We have managed very well indeed.'

'Fuss and bother for me I meant m'dear.' Sylvia looked directly and appealingly at Florence then back to her brandy glass. Very carefully she placed it on the mantelpiece. 'Father would have taken it far more kindly if I'd been here for a month or two helping you out. As it is. . . .'

Will stared at her. She was all right, but she wasn't laughing.

'Come on. What's happened Sylv?'

She said roughly, 'Silly old bugger's turned me out!' At last she mustered a laugh. 'He reckoned four babies between Vi and me and not one husband, weren't good enough. Turned me out when I told him about the next one. Nearly told me to take the boys with me, but Ma stepped in and put a stop to that.' She met their eyes, defiantly. 'I didn't know what to do. Baby's due come April and the weather being like this —'

Will said in a strangled voice, 'God Sylv — not another one! No wonder Father kicked up this time! Who's the man?'

'Someone who can't do much about it Will. Same as last time and the time before that.' She looked at her red hands. 'Flo . . . I'm sorry. Vi and me . . . we're too old to get married now. And we can't keep saying no all the time —'

'That's enough Sylv!' Will was afraid Florrie would faint. 'Don't try to excuse yourself please!'

75

Sylvia flushed sullenly. 'Well, it's done. An' it can't be undone. An' there's nowhere else I can go. You going to turn me out too?'

Florence pushed her crochet to the floor as she reached across to take the big hands in her long delicate ones.

'Of course we're not going to turn you out Sylvia! Didn't you hear Will say we could do with your help? My dear, you are Will's sister — your home is here for as long as you need it!'

Sylvia looked up, surprised. She had thought Florence's disapproval would have shown itself in icy withdrawal if not outright dismissal. For a long moment her pale blue eyes stared into liquid brown ones, then she slipped to her knees with completely uncharacteristic humility and put her head in her sister-in-law's lap.

Will stood up and picked up the brandy glass and looked down at the two women. His sister and his wife. He had torn himself from one to reach for the other and had always thought them aeons apart. Perhaps seeing them together, like this, perhaps then he could view the incident of Hettie in perspective.

Meanwhile it was enough that Sylvia was here. Between him and Florence. Between him and Hettie.

He touched her shoulder.

'You're welcome to stay here Sylv,' he said benevolently.

4

Sylvia Rising pulled her weight at the Chichester Street house. For the rest of the month the snow was piled in drifts to the ground floor window sills, and while Will worked and reluctantly let Florrie help him — so long as she did so by the fire in the back parlour — Sylvia dug a way out of the front door and cleared the yard to the wash-house; kept the fires going, fed the cat and prepared huge sloppy meals of wet cabbage and potatoes and tough meat. Incredibly, Florence thrived. She eked out her liver with bread and butter and honey and small pieces of the heavy fruit cake Sylv produced twice weekly; she drank cocoa made entirely with milk, and after a glass of Hettie's stout one night she even shared bread, cheese and onions with her sister-in-law.

The respect which Florence gave to everyone was appreciated by the feckless Sylv and foundations laid for a lifetime of protective devotion. Sylvia washed Florence's smalls in the kitchen and dried them by the range; hers and Will's went into the copper with the linen and froze rigidly on the outside lines. Will's combinations were never the same again, they came halfway up his legs and were yellow ochre in colour instead of pale cream. In other ways Sylv's efforts were more successful. When Mrs. Goodrich and baby Charlotte were taken to the fever hospital near Tewkesbury, she stood over Hettie Luker during her visits in case any word should be dropped to Florence.

Will was not sure whether he liked Sylvia's devotion or not. Just as Albert in Bath was made uncomfortable by an unexpected invasion into his private territory, so was Will back in the sanctuary of Chichester Street.

He came down one morning to find Sylv scraping some mess from Rags off the floor with unaccustomed zeal.

'Don't bother with that Sylv,' he said. 'I'll do it later.' His sister appeared to have doubled in size since her arrival just two weeks ago, and it was all too evident from her heavy breathing that to stoop to scrub the floor was difficult.

'Flo might be down in a minute,' she panted. 'She mustn't see this our Will. It 'ud turn her up.'

He didn't deny it. 'Why doesn't it turn you up then?' he asked as he stepped over her to warm himself at the range.

She laughed. He realised how rarely that laugh sounded now. 'Oh get on with you our Will! I'm used to it'n course.'

He turned his back to the fire and straddled his legs. The warmth seeped inside his trousers and helped to thaw the frozen remembrance of yet another night in Albert's room. He said resentfully, 'She should be used to it too. Five children. She should be used to it.'

'Get on with you!' she said again, standing up, scuffing her shoe over the wiped oilcloth. 'Flo in't like us. We're rough.'

Unaccountably Will recalled watching Snotty Lottie — less than a year ago — squeezing Florence's breast. He said angrily, 'She should be made to do it. You're spoiling her Sylv. Next time, leave it — she's had to do it in the past!'

Sylv looked up, surprised. ''Course she has! An' she'll do it again brother!' She laughed stoutly. 'Not while I'm here though. Flo en't going to clean up cat shit while I'm here!' She wiped her soiled hands on her skirt and took the teapot to the stove. 'And that puts me

78

in mind of what I want to say Will. I mun't stay much longer. Flo wants her babbies back with her. They can't see me like this.'

'Rubbish!' Will moved a step away from the range and rubbed his backside. 'And anyway, what if they do? I'm not having my sister in the workhouse Sylv. And that's that.' He wondered, even as he spoke, whether he would have been so vehement before Doctor Green's dictum three weeks before.

She brought the teapot to the table and left it to brew while she cut bread and butter for Florence.

'It won't come to that Will. Leas-ways, I dun't think so. I hoped — when the snow gives over — I hoped as you'd go and talk to Pa.' She slapped half-inch slices on to a plate next to the sticky honey pot. 'He'll listen to you. 'Specially if you tells him that your kids are coming back from Bath and you dun't want them to see . . . owt.'

'He doesn't know they're in Bath. So that won't cut much ice.'

'Dun't be daft Will. You can explain about Flo nearly dying and having to be fed —'

'I'm not turning my sister away and that is that!' Will seized the tray, slopping the tea over the edge of the cup and not regretting it, nor the doorstep wedges of bread and butter. 'We need you here Sylv, surely you can see that?'

'You wun't need me when the little 'uns get back. You're always on about 'em Will. And Flo is too. I know little May can tempt her mam to eat food like I can't. And March gets the washing that soft. And you miss young Albert . . .' she took a deep breath. 'Chris-amighty. Don't you think I know how you feels? I can't wait to see my babs again. Ma'll treat 'em good, 'course. But I want 'em Will. I *want* my kids!'

He dug the edge of the tray into his waistcoat buttons. He'd never seen Sylv cry.

'Hang on till this lot thaws then —' he jerked his head

at the looming white-coated monster outside. 'I'll go out to Kempley as soon as I can. But if they won't have you back Sylv — you're stopping with us.'

He thought he might have an ally in Florence. It was the first time he had taken up her tray since Sylv arrived, and he surprised her tying the strings of her camisole. The room smelled of the translucent soap sent by Aunt Lizzie for Christmas. She slid into her blouse before she took the tray from him.

'Oh Will, how good to see you! I thought I had not heard the sewing machine.' She put the tray on the bed and lifted her face to him. He kissed her chastely. 'Darling, darling Will. I am so happy.' She smelled sweet. 'Nearly the end of the month and Doctor Green said Teddy could come home in February.'

Her thinness, well disguised by thick flannel petticoats, looked neat and trim. Especially compared with Sylv.

'And I suppose once Teddy comes home, so can the others.' Yes, Sylv was right, he was missing his family badly. Perhaps when they were all in the house again he would forget that he must be impotent.

Florence picked up a wedge of bread, dabbed it with honey and nibbled its edge just as May did.

'Well . . .' she looked up at Will. 'It is a little awkward, dearest. I wondered whether Aunt Lizzie could be prevailed upon to keep them until Easter —'

'Easter! Good Lord Florrie, it was you who was so anxious about Albert's missed schooling!'

'And still am. But . . . they mustn't be here when Sylvia's baby is born, Will. Surely you agree with me that such a situation would be impossible. I would prefer Albert to miss a year's schooling rather than —'

'They're coming home as soon as Doctor Green says they can,' Will maintained stubbornly. He could have told her that Sylv wanted to go back to Kempley, but he did not. Not then. She would know soon enough, and meanwhile she must face up to . . . things. 'Albert has doubtless already realised that there are more babies at Kempley Cottage than fathers to go with them! And if not then this is as good a way as any of learning the facts of life!'

Florence was bright red. She busied herself pouring her slopped tea from saucer to cup. Will left the room, glad to be properly and overtly angry with her. Already he saw that Sylvia must not be at Chichester Street when the children returned, but he was determined that if his father took her back, Florence should think it was at her instigation.

For the first time in her life, March had a cold that kept her in bed. Letty consigned April to her underling, Rosie, and took May and Albert for walks and refused to let them throw snowballs. Aunt Lizzie sat with March for an hour in the morning, and an hour in the afternoon. They played Lexicon and read to each other and talked.

Aunt Lizzie said, 'I felt I deserted your poor little mamma. She must have been lonely in that house with her grandparents. But I was trying very hard to have a family . . . and I missed my dead sister . . . I'm afraid I was very selfish.'

'Oh no Aunt Lizzie!' March said passionately. 'Mother was very happy. She has told us she did not miss her own mother and father because she never knew them. And she met Papa when she was fourteen and though he was only twelve he used to walk into Gloucester to see her every Saturday.' March blew through her blocked nose. 'She said Great Grandmamma felt bound to receive him because he looked so tired!' She had mentioned this before and knew it would make Aunt Lizzie smile sentimentally, which indeed it did.

Aunt Lizzie said, 'Yes. Florence must be a realist also, though she is a dreamer. She knew it was hopeless to wait for a Prince Charming — how could she meet anyone in that old house?' She added hastily, 'Mind you March, your father is a very handsome man. It would be difficult to turn him down.'

March nodded, though she had never considered her parents' courtship seriously. They were the two poles of her planet and that was that.

Encouraged, Aunt Lizzie proceeded. 'My sister made a love match and look where it landed her. Your dear mamma and I, we married where we could. With great affection of course but . . .' she sighed. 'I was lucky because Edwin inherited the business and some money. Yet you see dear March, I did not need it. None of my children were born alive. And your mother, with five of you, married a man with very little money. How odd life is, child.'

March was breathless. This conversation was quite the most interesting she had ever had. So . . . May was wrong, it was possible to marry without falling in love. Obediently she sniffed at the eucalyptus bottle and considered the prospects opening up before her.

Before she was allowed out of her room, Uncle Edwin came to visit her. He was a gloomy man, but May's constant smiling attention had by now had a cheering effect on him. March felt only a small qualm when his head appeared around her door.

'A little present,' he mumbled, standing between the bed and the fire. 'Thought May would be here. A little present for the two of you.'

March smoothed the sheet over her waist with one of the many small mannerisms she had picked up from Aunt Lizzie. 'May was moved in with Albert when I first had my cold, Uncle,' she said primly. 'I can knock on the wall for her if you like.'

'No. No, indeed no. You can show her. . . .' He approached the bed and held out what appeared to be a pair of wooden shears. 'You close the ends . . . so . . . and the monkey leaps . . . so.' A wooden monkey on a string turned frantic somersaults. March smiled.

'He's sweet. Oh, May will like him!'

'He's for you as well. May prefers dolls I imagine.'

'Oh Uncle . . . thank you.'

'He'll turn more slowly. Look —' He sat on the end of the bed and demonstrated. March took the toy from him and began to work it. Her brown eyes shone.

'My goodness child, you are very like your aunt. When I met her first. Just like you.'

March flushed with pleasure. 'I always wanted to look like May,' she confessed suddenly. 'But if I remind you of Aunt Lizzie, I would rather look like myself.'

Uncle Edwin actually smiled, delighted with the result of his compliment. 'May is a sweet little girl. She takes after your father's side perhaps. She is not a Rhys-Davies. You are.'

'Am I?' March was fascinated. Perhaps that was why she did not approve of Lottie or the Lukers.

Uncle Edwin said briskly, 'The toy is for you. I will find May something else. Now give me a kiss for it, child, and say nothing.'

He levered himself up and leaned over her. She lifted her face, smelling his tobacco smell and the frost on his clothes. He parted his lips, put them over her puckered mouth and sucked hard for a long two seconds. March had never been kissed in such a way before and wasn't sure whether she liked it, but when she saw how happy he looked she did not mind too much.

He lifted his head and stared down at her. Then he said hoarsely, 'If you want anything child, ask me. Anything at all.'

'Thank you Uncle,' she murmured.

After he had gone she lay down and played with the monkey, making him turn somersaults at a dizzy rate. She felt very powerful.

Two days later the afternoon post brought a letter from Florence saying that Will would arrive on February the fourth to bring the children back home.

Albert and May were like mad creatures. They went outside and pelted the thawing snowman with hard pellets of ice until he disintegrated entirely. When Aunt Lizzie went downstairs to order the meals, they fell about in front of the fire, giggling and making up songs about going home. Albert said, 'No more dominoes with Awful Uncle Edwin!' May said, 'No more walks with Letty!' Albert said, 'Petty Letty!' May shrieked and threw herself back against March's knees. 'Oh — oh — we'll see darling Rags again!' Albert said with great satisfaction, 'And I'll see old Harry Hughes. Good old Harry!'

March, sitting sedately in Aunt Lizzie's own chair, suddenly kicked out with her legs and sent May flying. May shrieked again but not with laughter. Albert said, aggrieved, 'What did you do that for?'

March clenched her hands into fists. She said tightly, 'She was hurting my legs. I'm not strong enough yet to have people flopping against me like that.'

May rubbed her back. 'I'm sorry March. I didn't know.'

Albert said, 'You cow. You don't want to go back home, do you?'

May said, 'Albert! Don't speak like that to March!'

March said, 'No, I don't. I don't want to go back to cleaning grates and washing smelly sheets and sleeping in the same bed with May and being more of a skivvy than Letty!'

'Shut up!' Albert shouted. 'Shut up! You're not to speak like that — I'll kill you if you —'

March went on as if he hadn't interrupted. 'I want to stay here where I'm warm and looked after and loved properly —'

Albert threw himself at her and dragged her out of the chair. They rolled together on to the floor. May screamed.

'I'm going to fetch Aunt Lizzie! You're not to fight — oh!' They crashed against her and she jumped away and ran out of the door still screaming. Albert knelt on March's stomach.

'Say you're sorry,' he panted. 'Say you're sorry — quickly!'

She sobbed and spat at him. 'I'm not! I'm not!'

'Say you love us better than you love Aunt Lizzie and Uncle Edwin! You've got to say it March! You've got to!'

Aunt Lizzie's voice was outraged above them.

'Get off your sister this minute young man!' She was stronger than she looked and helped him up by the scruff of his neck. 'Now go to your room. Go on. I don't want to see you again this evening!'

She gathered the weeping March into her arms. 'All right my dearest . . . just a quarrel . . . nothing to fret about . . . let Aunt Lizzie take you upstairs —' She sent May for Letty and ordered the bedroom fire to be lit again. 'Come on darling. A nice supper by your very own fire. Don't cry.'

But March could not stop. When Uncle Edwin presented her with a brooch without even suggesting a kiss, she wept again.

'I wanted a hairslide. Like May's,' she sobbed.

'Then you shall have it,' he knelt by her, rubbing her hand ineffectually. 'Tomorrow I will bring you a hairslide.'

She quietened gradually and when Aunt Lizzie came to kiss her goodnight, she was tranquil again. She waited until she heard the downstairs clock chime a quarter past midnight, then she slipped out of bed and crept down the passage to Albert's room where Albert and May slept in another double feather bed. Slowly and carefully she pushed at Albert until he rolled closer to May, then she insinuated herself into his place. The three children slept peacefully together. When Letty came in with their washing water, she gazed at them sentimentally.

'Three little angels,' she breathed to herself. 'Just

three little angels.' Faintly from above came the sound of April's urgent demand for breakfast. Letty sighed. The rumpus last night had been explained to her as a relapse in Miss March's health, but she had no doubt about April's weeping. 'Temper,' she went on as she poured the water carefully into the basin. 'That little one's got a temper and no mistake!'

Will went to Kempley to talk to his father and as the snow had gone, Sylv agreed to lend an arm to her sister-in-law as far as Bearland.

'It's over three weeks since I saw him Sylvia. In fact I've only seen him once. Doctor Green would have brought him again but the weather was so inclement.'

'Better leave him where he is m'dear. He'll be home for good and all very soon now.'

'I know. I know. But it's been a long time.'

They went beneath the railway bridge where melting snow from the ballast above dripped through. Everything was wet and dismal and smelled of soot. Florence said suddenly, 'I'm so lucky Sylvia. The children. Teddy. Dear Will. I'm so very lucky.'

Sylvia laughed. 'Sound a bit more cheerful about it then Flo!'

Florence leaned a little more heavily on the stalwart arm beneath her own. 'I want you to know, when your baby is born, you are welcome to come back to Gloucester.'

They turned into Saint John's Lane past the second-hand book shops and the Citizen office.

'You're a good woman Flo,' Sylvia said. 'A real good woman.'

Florence felt guilty as never before. 'I am not a good woman Sylvia,' she replied humbly. 'If I was a good woman, you would be staying at Chichester Street to have your baby and the children would remain at Bath.'

Sylvia glanced sideways, surprised. ''Tis my own

choice to leave your house Flo. You need feel no responsibility for it.'

They crossed Westgate Street and plunged into one of the narrow passages that led to the docks. The whole area was forbidding, yet number sixteen Prison Lane sported a polished brass knocker and the step had been stoned to gleaming whiteness.

"Ten't too bad,' Sylvia said reassuringly. "Tis better than Kempley Cottage!' She laughed but got no answering smile. Florence was looking suddenly tense and stood aside while Sylvia knocked on the door. She was shaking slightly like a young girl meeting her lover. Sylvia squeezed her arm. "Tis all *right* our Flo,' she whispered. 'You knew where it was . . . certainly en't no slum.'

Florence summoned a smile. 'I don't care about the house.' She looked around her as if seeing the street for the first time. 'I'm looking forward so much to seeing Teddy. Oh Sylvia . . . I'm looking forward so very much!'

Sylvia smiled back. She had never seen her sister-in-law so excited before. Always a bit apart, that was Flo. Like a nun.

Kitty Hall made them tea and settled them by the fire in her tiny kitchen before she went upstairs to fetch Teddy. She placed him, round, sleeping and content, in Florence's arms and went back for her own son. Teddy did not open his eyes but his lashes were dark and his wispy hair as black as Florence's own.

'You're right Flo,' Sylvia said, looking down at him. 'He's a beautiful child. Not a Rising though.'

'No.' Florence's hand shook as she adjusted the shawl around Teddy's face. 'No, he's not a Rising.' She forced herself to look away from him as Kitty came back down the bare wooden stairs. 'I must thank you Mrs. Hall. He is looking so strong and well.'

'Not a bit of trouble Mrs. Rising.' Kitty sat back from the other two and kept her baby tucked well into her

87

elbow. 'I shouldn't have brought this one down,' she apologised. 'But he does cry so when little Edwin goes from him.'

Sylvia said in her broad Kempley voice, 'Aye, they'll miss each other when this 'un comes back home Flo. You'll have a job keeping Teddy quiet I reckon.'

Florence smiled down at the baby in her arms. 'He can cry all he wants to,' she said. 'So long as he's well, I shan't mind.'

Kitty, relaxed by Sylvia's country presence, poured more tea and remarked conversationally, 'A pity yours weren't to be borned a bit earlier. Then you could have done my job.'

Sylvia laughed easily. 'I might look big, but I barely have enough for my own generally. Yet Flo here — my goodness, she fed the other four and couldn't stop the milk this time. Could you Flo?'

It had occurred to Florence that Sylvia, doing the laundry, would know only too well the difficulty she had had to staunch her liberal flow of milk. She wished she had not found it necessary to mention it. Not that it mattered when she had Teddy in her arms. This one she would have fed so willingly. The thought of him at Kitty Hall's breast gave her her first pang of jealousy.

Sylvia misinterpreted her flushed cheeks and silence. 'I'm sorry Florence.' She turned back to Kitty. 'He looks a good weight on what you give him Mrs. Hall.'

'The doctor weighed him yesterday and he's nine pound. Considering he was five pound borned the doctor was very pleased.'

'I should think so!' Sylvia waited for Florence's reciprocal gratitude. 'That's very good Flo isn't it? Nine pound!' she prompted.

'Very good.' Florence forced herself to smile at Kitty. Then her joy in the baby excluded any other lesser feeling. He was hers, so completely hers. His conception, whenever it had been, had been a time of horror, when the only way she could stop from crying out, was to hold herself apart. So it seemed as if Will had had nothing to do with it. Certainly, physically, there was no trace of his father in him. Yes, he was hers. Hers. She held him closer, pressing him deliberately into the softness of her breast as if she could absorb him into her being. And as if her feeling echoed in him, he opened his eyes wide and brown and looked up at her. Then he smiled.

'My saints, he's young to be grinning away like that,' Sylvia said, looking over Florence's shoulder.

Kitty laughed. 'He can't see proper yet I don't reckon. 'Tis the wind.'

Florence said nothing. She smiled back at Teddy, then lowered her head and kissed him. His little fists came up and minute nails clawed at her chin. Florence laughed. And at that rare sound, Sylvia laughed too and all three women filled the tiny house with their merriment. Florence looked around her at the leaping firelight, the hard wooden chairs, the scrubbed flagged floor, the rag rug; she knew, surprised, that she had never been so happy before. Not like this. Not so happy that every small detail of the scene was printed on her mind. She thought: I'll never forget it; the smell of soot and baking and warmth and babies; the taste of Teddy overlying the raw liver; the sense of well-being; the three of us with our babies. I'll always remember this and know that I was happy.

Something happened as they were leaving that helped cement the occasion into Florence's very self. The babies were put back in their small cocoons upstairs, the fire banked and guarded, the window opened. Kitty assured them yet again that Teddy was bathed every day and powdered well afterwards, also that his midday feed now consisted of arrowroot spooned into him according to Doctor Green's instructions. He would be fully weaned in another month. They went outside, Kitty and Sylvia shawled, Florence neat in a tight-waisted coat made by Will ten years ago and newly trimmed with left-over braid. The little cottage, hemmed in by the high wall of the prison on this side, was almost in darkness. Suddenly the sound of marching feet echoed from side to side, bouncing up from the cobbles sharply and ominously. Sylvia took Florence's arm.

'What is it?' she asked, looking at Kitty.

'Some of the prisoners.' Kitty opened the door wider. 'Step inside until they pass. It is sad to see.'

They crammed behind Kitty in the passage. The tramping of feet drew nearer, accompanied by another dreadful sound: the clanking of chains. Florence shivered and Kitty said, "Tis only till they reach the new prison. They take them by barge down the river to Bristol. Then they're allowed to work in the fields — oh, all sorts. 'Tis just to transport them.' She turned her head as an order was rapped out and the feet stopped. 'Oh . . . 'tis my husband with a message for me. I'll be only a minute!' She flew outside and the two women left in the passage had a full view of a grim sight. Half a dozen men, shaven and dressed in drab grey uniforms, stood outside the little cottage, chained to each other by their wrists. But it was their attitude that distressed both Florence and Sylvia. It seemed as if all the spirit had left them and they drooped where they stood. Like ancient blinkered horses in the traces, they waited for the next order.

Kitty ignored them and went to the end of the line where a stocky man in smart blue began to talk to her earnestly. She listened then flew back. 'Needs some food,' she gasped. 'He has to go with them to Sharpness —' she disappeared down the passage and Florence and Sylvia, thoroughly uncomfortable now, confronted the man and his charges. He touched his cap, but could not come nearer to introduce himself. Florence murmured, 'Should we go and speak to him?' Sylvia tightened her grip on her sister-in-law's arm. 'No. Will would not like it.' She lowered her voice still further and added, 'Lice.'

As if the single word had penetrated at least one pair of ears, a man looked up. His chain clinked warningly and Kitty's husband growled in his throat like a dog. The man seemed not to notice. His eyes went to the two women and even through the murk of the January afternoon it was possible to see their blueness. He stared. Florence looked away immediately but Sylvia narrowed her own eyes and stared back with the honesty — some said brazenness — which she always gave to men. He focused on her completely. For a very long minute they looked at each other without faltering. Then Kitty rushed past them with a package which she gave to her Barty. An order was rapped out and the men marched clankingly on.

Both women were quiet on the way home. Florence thought how lucky she was. Teddy was so healthy. Will and the children. Sylvia. Teddy. . . .

She said suddenly, 'Did you know that man Sylvia? That convict outside Mrs. Hall's?'

'No.' Sylvia trudged solidly through the darkening afternoon, Flo's arm tucked firmly into hers. 'And then . . . yes.'

'How do you mean dear?'

'I've never clapped eyes on 'im before. But when I looked at 'im, I sort of recognised 'im.' Sylvia shook her head, baffled by her own feelings. 'No. That en't right.' She looked down at the slight figure beside her and said tactfully, 'You wouldn't understand Flo. What I mean is, I reckon if things were a bit different, we could 'a bin friends. 'Im and me.'

'Ah.' Florence thought she understood only too well. It was the side of Sylvia that she tried not to think about. 'Ah.' She turned her mind quickly away, just as she had when she had seen her own reflection in the kitchen window that time. She thought of Teddy again.

And Will and the children. But especially of Teddy.

Old man Rising agreed grudgingly to have Sylv home
for her lying-in. Jack and Austin drove in with some
crates of poultry the next market day and took her
back with them on the wagon. Will and Florence
had a week together before he fetched the children.
They were awkward together; she was afraid he
would not keep to the attic room and did not know
that the image of Hettie Luker was still between
them. It was a relief when the fourth of February
arrived.

'Have you had a lovely time?'

Florence looked at them all as the prisoner had
looked at Sylvia. April was fat, her hair a mass of
ginger curls. May had new stature; she it was who
carried April from the baby carriage and asked
Albert to fetch a clean napkin. Albert guffawed
constantly and looked uneasily at his sisters.

May said, 'Lovely. Lovely. And Daddy is such a
gentleman — you would be proud of him. He kisses
Aunt Lizzie's hand and bows — oh she thinks he is
marvellous. Doesn't she March? She says how handsome he is and —'

March said, 'Mother, Aunt Lizzie wants me to
visit by myself this summer. Could I? D'you think I
could?'

Albert said, 'Where's my brother? I thought I had
a brother instead of all these girls? Where is he?'
He laughed loudly and pushed March and Will
frowned.

'It's all right Father . . . Mother, may I visit Aunt
Lizzie —?'

Albert said, 'Well, *we* don't want to go if that's
what's worrying you March! You and Aunt Lizzie —
always talking! May and me having to go for walks
with that crazy Letty, and play dominoes with
boring old Uncle Edwin!'

'He's not boring!' March looked at Albert without annoyance. 'He's not a bit boring. I love him very much.' She spoke with great deliberation.

Albert flushed darkly and Florence intervened.

'Tea is laid in the kitchen. Boiled eggs and fruit cake. It'll be like Christmas having you all back. And Rags has missed you too. Come along — we've so much to talk about!'

April sat in the high chair for the first time and made them all laugh a great deal. Rags lay on his back in front of the range just as he'd done when they left. May talked about the fireworks and Christmas morning in the abbey. March asked some surprising questions about the Rhys-Davies' inheritance and though Florence answered them prosaically, May's eyes shone with the romance of it and March said, 'So one day, if it's all sorted out, we might be rich?' Florence laughed and shook her head. 'That is the way your poor great grandfather thought, March dearest. Put it out of your head.' Albert laughed shrilly. 'Be a reellist March! I heard Aunt Lizzie say that — be a reellist!' Will chuckled. 'Well, if your Aunt Lizzie is a realist, Flo, she's done very nicely out of it.' Florence shook her head, 'I've done better, Will. A good husband and five beautiful children. I've done very much better.'

Later, as she carried April up to her bed while the girls unpacked their treasures, he followed her into the bedroom.

'Flo. It will be all right now we're all together again, won't it?'

He was like a child asking for reassurance. Of course she knew it would be perfectly all right once Teddy was home. She looked at him, her face unusually bright. 'I hope you are as happy as I am, dear husband,' she said.

He took her in his arms suddenly and held on to her like another child. April lay on the bed and examined her toes. They clung together. Then Will cupped her face and kissed her quietly. At that moment he was quite certain that their love was grander than anything earthly and could transcend the physical.

They had never been so close.

5

The first thing April Rising could remember was watching her sister May in a concert at the Corn Exchange in Southgate Street. Until her family told her the actual facts, she was inclined to confuse it with the more auspicious occasion of Albert's solo at the cathedral when he sang Faure's Requiem in honour of a lamented dean. That took place when April was two years old and her memory consisted of huge columns climbing to heaven, a peculiar vibratory note on the organ which put her off organ music for ever, and Albert apparently screaming for help. This had led her to scream also and to be removed.

April's musical ear was much more suited to the sentimental songs with which that period abounded. She was quite certain — at three years old in fact — that May was not screaming when she tripped on to the stage in white crepe paper and told everyone she was a 'dainty, dancing fairy'. She loved both her sisters, but May was her favourite. May never lost her temper, shared all her treats, was beautiful and fun.

The concert was in aid of Blind Babies, and May had suggested to April that they tie scarves over their eyes and spend half an hour each day finding out what it was like to be blind. April hated it until May pushed up the blindfold so that she could see her feet. March scoffed at them both and told them they were 'ludicrous' which was even worse than being ridiculous. But April never forgot what it must be like to be blind and she clapped her tiny palms until they were sore when May curtsied, kissed her hand at her assembled family, and retired reluctantly into the wings.

That evening April announced that when she grew up she would be a misery. She spoke with such exaltation that May questioned her and finally discovered she wanted to be a misery like at Sunday School.

'A missionary!' May said, smiling lovingly. 'Why not indeed?' May had many of her mother's phrases.

Albert sniggered — the loud guffaws of three years ago had long been subdued into the accepted King's School snuffle.

'Let's see Ape . . .' Florence was out of the room otherwise this name would not be permitted. 'Old Livingstone was a bit of a misery wasn't he?'

April nodded vigorously, delighted when March and Albert laughed and May hugged her and Daddy slapped his knee. She was encouraged to expand. 'Praps I'll sing like May and give the money to the miseries. 'Cus I don't want to go all the way to foreign parts.'

At that, Will picked her up and sat her on his knee and kissed her ear lobe. Florence, entering with Teddy on her hip though he was a hefty two-year-old, had to know what it was all about. April listened in a dream of content. This was how it had been at the concert. She was Daddy's girl, he was always telling her so. Albert was specially his too. Mother claimed Teddy and May for her own. And March needed to belong to no-one. March was strong. When Gladys Luker pinched April as they sat on the front step once, March had smiled brilliantly, taken a piece of Glady's arm between pointed finger and thumb, lifted it slowly and started to twist. 'Do you enjoy it Gladys dear?' she had asked. Later, May, finding both children weeping copiously, had kissed April's red mark and shown both of them how to spit on their forefingers and massage their wounds. She had then sat between them and told them

96

a story about how little girls must be kind to each other and never pinch.

So April listened to the chatter of her family above her head and watched Teddy eating the bits of coal left in the bucket from last winter and was utterly content. Soon it would be bedtime and she would put on her own nightie and kneel with Teddy to say 'Gentle Jesus meek and mild. . . .' And she knew that to the end of her days she would remember May singing, 'I'm a dainty dancing fairy.' And the awful head-fluttering note of that organ and the hugeness of the place where Albert had screamed. . . .

Teddy too was happy enough; though never content. He had no caution, no decorum whatever. He had recently acquired the knack of holding his water and now performed publicly whenever necessary. If Albert had done this, Florence would have died of mortification. She screened Teddy as best she could with her long, fashionable hobble skirt, but she smiled at him all the same. Already he showed great ingenuity in getting in and out of scrapes. The coal bucket was always his goal, but he had also fallen out of his cot, thrown his wooden horse through the kitchen window and regularly coasted head-first down the druggeted stairs. March was the only one who got cross with him, so he saw no need to mend his ways. Even Hettie, on the few occasions he and April played in the Luker house, kissed him when he knocked Henry over. Henry was older than Teddy by a few weeks, but much smaller so it was hardly a contest. When Teddy discovered he could also send Gladys Luker flying, he felt more confident. Hettie laughed at this too and told him he was a bigger bully than his father. Gladys wiped her nose on the back of her hand like Lottie Jenner and took an early opportunity of pulling April's ginger curls as hard as she could. Again, May was the peacemaker.

*   *   *

When Teddy was three and the Christmas holiday finished, Florence reluctantly agreed to both her babies attending a private school in Midland Road. The Misses Midwinter were highly recommended by one of Will's clients. They took a dozen children aged three to seven for a shilling each per week, and taught them refined manners, the three R's, music and dancing. Will was delighted. It was all part of their climb up the social ladder. He and Florence hired Luker's trap and took the children down past Daker's in Barton Street and over the level crossing by Park to Midland Road. They were nervous and Will kept talking. 'It's called California Crossing,' he improvised, 'because a fellow called Clarence built it. They called him Cal for short, then California Cal and —'

Florence laughed to show April that it was a joke but as a train snorted past, reverberating the road like an organ note, the child said fearfully, 'Will we have to go over Cally . . . Cally . . . by ourselves?'

'Certainly not!' Florence forced a reassuring smile. 'March or I will meet you. And we will come through the subway. It's a tunnel and you will love it.'

Miss Midwinter was terrifying. She took them into the back parlour for their 'perticlers' which April thought might be her drawers but turned out to be the catechism. She did not smile when April announced her intention to be a 'misery'. And she asked with great significance whether Teddy could 'behave'. She had grey hair arranged in hundreds of small curls over her forehead like Queen Alexandra. When she finished writing she clipped a pair of pince-nez on to her nose and peered over them.

'When I wear these,' she announced, 'I am about to address a child. When I address a child, that child immediately stands.' She waited. Suddenly April understood and was no longer afraid. She took Teddy's hand in hers and pulled him from Florence's knee. Together they looked over the edge of Miss Midwinter's

98

big desk and received approving smiles. It was so easy. You watched for the glitter of the gold-rimmed glasses . . . you stood . . . you were approved.

A little girl of six appeared as if by magic. Miss Midwinter announced that her name was Bridget Williams and she was the granddaughter of Alderman Williams and she was to be a friend to April and Edwin Rising.

Florence smiled at the solemn pig-tailed child.

'When I was your age, your grandfather used to come to visit my grandfather,' she said encouragingly.

Miss Midwinter thawed on the instant. 'Ah . . . and your family Mrs. Rising? Old Gloucester stock, I knew the minute I set eyes. . . .'

'I was brought up by my grandparents. Next to Bishop Hooper's lodging.' Florence surreptitiously unfastened the buttons on Teddy's new sailor jacket. He was slow with buttons and she had made his trousers so that they would slip over his tiny hips.

Miss Midwinter was delighted. 'Mr. Rhys-Davies? Of course — the scholar! I can see him now, walking the cloisters . . . his white beard and his frock coat — and I can see the likeness. Of course! And especially in little Edwin. My sister and I are delighted — delighted, Mrs. Rising —'

April liked that bit very much indeed. And she liked Bridget Williams too. In fact within three days of starting school, she loved Bridget Williams. And on the strength of that long-ago connection, Mrs. Williams eventually invited April to tea at their house. They lived in the country at Barnwood and got there in a motor car. April could remember March telling her that quite soon she was going to buy a motor car. Now April understood why. When she got home from Barnwood she fetched the sovereign from the locket Aunt Lizzie had given her at Christmas and tried to give it to March.

'What's that for?' March asked ungraciously. She had had a talk with Miss Pettinger that morning and had been told that in that lady's opinion March's disposition was unsuited to the teaching profession.

'For your motor car,' April said. 'Mr. Williams' motor car has a folding-back roof for the summer. Could you get one like that March? And can I have a ride in it if I give you some more money?'

'May I have a ride in it,' March corrected.

'May I have a ride in it please March?'

'No,' said March. 'And if you think a single sovereign will help — it will take a hundred of those to buy a car!'

April said confidently, 'You'll get one March. And you'll have to let me have a ride in it if my sovereign was the first one you had!'

It hadn't occurred to March to save for the motor car bit by bit, she had imagined it would come in one fell swoop. She smiled unwillingly at her small sister then, uncharacteristically, gave her a hug.

'You're my favourite sister,' she said. 'And I'll get a cocoa tin from Mother and we'll save in it for a car. And your sovereign will be the very first!'

April felt guilty. She wished she could tell March that she loved her better than May also, but she could not. The tin was duly labelled and put on the mantelpiece in their bedroom. It grew heavy very quickly but when April peeped inside one rainy Sunday afternoon it seemed to contain nothing but her sovereign and a lot of farthings. Albert was paid three farthings for weddings; they must come from him.

Bridget had to be asked back to Chichester Street for a reciprocal tea. The invitation was given and accepted; March would meet them out of school and walk them home and Will would hire the trap to drive Bridget home in the evening. April was so excited she forgot to stand up when Miss Alicia spoke to her and forfeited her teacher's smile. Teddy made it worse by piping up with an unsolicited excuse.

'Bridget Williams is coming to tea Mishalisha!' It

was the best he could do with the sibilants of the name. 'April's all sited!'

Amazingly Miss Alicia then smiled. It was the first time that April realised Teddy was her favourite.

'Ah I see. So no work will be done properly today.'

The laughter brought in Miss Midwinter, and soon April was chanting with the other four-year-olds, 'Mrs. D., Mrs. I., Mrs. F.F.I., Mrs. C., Mrs. U., Mrs. L.T.Y.' She was top in spelling and tables and Teddy was bottom. But Teddy was still the favourite.

The three of them held hands, Teddy in the middle, and ran down into the subway, then stood directly under the railway line until a train went over their heads. March, walking sedately behind, put her fingers in her ears and went quickly up the other side. April would have preferred to do the same, but Bridget and Teddy thought it was thrilling to be underneath a moving train. Bridget ceased being the quiet girl she was at school and Barnwood, and screamed loudly to produce echoes. Teddy screamed too and March hurried back and grabbed his hand, making him walk with her. Bridget said contentodly, 'I like being friends with a huge family like Queen Victoria's. Papa says it will be good for me to rough and tumble for once.'

They had boiled eggs for tea in the back parlour. Mother had drawn faces on each egg, some smiling, some downcast. When they took their egg cosies off and saw the faces they laughed, and Bridget laughed loudest of all. There was a pot of Mrs. Goodrich's clear golden honey and piles of white bread and butter and a big fruit cake. After tea Bridget wanted to play outside. 'Like a street arab,' she said sunnily. So they joined the Luker children who were giving wheelbarrow rides to the Lamb and Flag and back. April bowled her hoop, Bridget jumped feverishly on to the wheelbarrow and Teddy looked for something else to do. Something which would impress Bridget Williams once and for all.

101

He staggered down Luker's side way with a heavy rope from the dray.

'Come on! We'll make a swing. Over that branch there!' He pointed to one of the Goodrich apple trees.

April was fearful. 'What about the bees? We mustn't, Teddy. Go and put that rope back and Henry will let you have a ride on —'

But Bridget was bored with the wheelbarrow and the hoop.

'Go on Teddy! I'll lift you up! Come and help me April — you with the dirty face — come on!'

Gladys, thus addressed, pinched April furiously and Bridget was left to lift Teddy as best she could. April couldn't help noticing through her tears of pain how much Bridget enjoyed holding her brother's plump little body aloft. Then the rope was over the branch and Teddy swung away from Bridget, whooping like an Indian. For three glorious seconds he swung in short arcs above the other children while they clamoured for their turn, then there was a hideous groan from the arthritic old apple tree, then a sharp crack, then he descended on to the unyielding pavement. April registered the ghastly sound of a human body, plump and resilient, hitting stone. The next instant Bridget began to scream.

Teddy had a broken arm and mild concussion. Hearing the news Bridget spluttered noisily, 'If God will make Teddy live, I will be his servant for the rest of his life!' And May, romantic realist that she was, said sensibly, 'Don't be silly Bridget, Teddy isn't dead by any means. And he certainly doesn't need a servant!'

Fred Luker drove Bridget back to Barnwood with March for company. Coming back it was almost dark and March was suddenly conscious that though Fred Luker was the same age as Albert, he was grown-up. His short, burly form squatted sideways opposite her, and his silence was patently embarrassed. To relieve that embarrassment she laughed lightly.

'It's good of you to look after us like this Freddy. After all Teddy isn't very popular with Henry and Gladys I understand!' She was glad to hear how cool and adult she sounded. But in the long pause which followed it was obvious Fred Luker was still at a loss. Then at last he cleared his throat, turned and spat over the side of the trap into the road. March tightened her lips.

'I — I . . .' more throat clearing. 'I dunno nothing about the little 'uns Miss . . . er . . . March.' He hawked and spat again. 'No-one called me Freddy for a long time.'

'We used to call you Freddy when we played.' She and Albert, Fred and George had 'played' no oftener than three times. 'And you used to call me Marchy.' She tugged her single brown plait to the front and brushed her chin with its frayed end. 'I hate my name. Marchy is better. But when I'm grown up I shall call myself Marcie.' March would not have dreamed of talking like this to anyone else; with Fred Luker it was rather like confiding in a dog. Or an ox.

He looked at her outline, chin raised against the darkening sky, silky hair brushing it gently. He blurted, 'Your April did tell our Glad that you be saving for a motor car. That right?'

'It is.'

'I got one.' Fred's voice was harsh with triumph.

'You *what*?'

'I got a motor car. In the yard.' He rested on one elbow and flapped the reins on the pony's back. 'Breakdown. Towed 'n back with Jenny and left 'n in our yard for a mechanic to call.' Jenny was the carthorse who pulled the goods dray which earned most of Alf Luker's money.

March was awed. 'What's it like? April says Bridget's has got a folding roof.'

'This one's got everything. An' . . . I got 'er started too.'

103

'You *what*?' repeated March.

'Got 'er started. Druv 'er down the side and back.'

They passed Barnwood House where all the rich loonies were locked up, clattered under the railway bridge and slowed for the Pitch.

March said, 'I'll never save enough to buy a car. Never.'

Fred spat again, judiciously. 'Reckon you could. You got brains. You could be a secerty. This bloke what's got the car . . . 'e's got a secerty. She's arranging for the mechanic to call . . . she arranges every bloody thing for 'im. You could do that.'

March swallowed at the vicious swear word, but decided to ignore it. 'D'you really think so . . . Freddy?'

''Course you could. . . . An' if you wants to come an' 'ave a drive now . . . tonight . . . you're welcome!'

'Freddy!' March jumped about on the seat like Teddy. 'Freddy! May I really? Oh Freddy!'

She waited in the blackness of the side way while Freddy unharnessed the pony and put away the trap. She felt guilty, knowing she should go straight home to comfort Mother and reassure April about the Williamses. The workroom light was on, so was the front bedroom's; Father working in spite of everything, Mother in bed. No-one would see her if they looked out. As for the Lukers hearing anything, nothing was more unlikely. Through the thickness of the wall she could hear the noise of the eleven children like bees in a hive. She pressed her back against the rough stone, taut with excitement. It crossed her mind that a week ago she had suffered agonies of jealousy when May was given a paintbox for her birthday. It was accepted that May was artistic and March was practical, yet March had wanted that paintbox so much it hurt her. Now . . . now she had something that May would want, yet be frightened to accept. Through the darkness came the astounding roar of an engine followed immediately by a terrible smell. March shrank against the wall and wondered whether her courage was trickling away.

The roar changed note slightly and started to hiccough as it came closer. March peered into the road again expecting a constable or the Goodriches — already alerted to sudden disaster that day — to appear. No-one stirred. Below, on the corner, the lighted door of the Lamb and Flag suddenly opened and someone fell into the gutter. Then the enormous bulk of a two-seater Delage loomed at her side and Fred's voice hissed urgently, 'Come round this side Marchy — come on now — make haste!'

She made haste and was hauled up by his side. The car bounced into the road, the leather seat was slippery, the door much too shallow, she held Fred's arm and her breath squealed in her throat.

'Not frightened Marchy? This en't nothing. She can do thirty or more. Look at that there shine on 'er!'

His words barely made sense but she could see that in the light from the gas lamps the car gleamed richly.

He turned slowly and inexpertly into Northgate Street and pulled out the throttle. They roared to the top of the Pitch in two minutes when it had taken ten to come down in the trap. March kept bouncing and squealing and Fred started to laugh and swung round in a huge circle at the top of the Pitch so that she was thrown about helplessly. They returned jerkily — 'Easier goin' up than down —' panted Fred as he grabbed and released the big brake lever on the running board. 'Yes,' said March, holding the door and the edge of her seat and her breath. Somehow they turned back into Chichester Street and edged up to the yard again.

'Oh Freddy. Oh . . . that was lovely.' March let her breath go ecstatically.

'You sound like your May. Everything is lovely for her.'

'Not for me. But this is.'

She got out and waited for him. The smell of the

exhaust fumes was no longer terrible and she sniffed them sharply like Mr. Goodrich sniffed his snuff. And she remembered Uncle Edwin.

They walked down the side way and into the road and she turned and put her arms around his neck and kissed him.

'Thank you Freddy. Dear Freddy.'

He was aghast. He stood there watching her dart across the road and up the steps of thirty-three. Then, inspired, he called softly, 'G'night Marcie. Sleep tight.'

When Teddy came out of hospital, even Florence's devotion was taxed to the limit. His arm was heavy with plaster and pulled at his tiny shoulder until the pain made him cry. For perhaps an hour each day he would rest it on the table and practise his letters, puzzled and amused at the unexpected difficulty of using his left hand. Then frustration would overtake him and he would demand a story in a petulant voice, or, if Florence was established in the chair with some sewing, he would want a drink of cocoa and a buttered nobby.

Will said, 'What that boy needs is a good thrashing.' He had never touched one of the children in anger and his words shocked Florence.

'Poor Teddy. He's never known a time when he hasn't had companions. When you go to Daker's next, Will, walk on down to Bearland and ask Mrs. Hall if she would like to bring little Tolly up for an afternoon.'

'Bearland is in the opposite direction from the Barton,' Will pointed out. Then seeing the pleading in her beautiful eyes, he inclined his head over his sewing with mock gallantry. 'I am yours to command, my lady Flo. As always.'

Florence was certain they had never been so happy. But there were times when she wished Will's sincere concern for that happiness did not seem . . . slightly ironic.

* * *

Kitty, big with her second child, was a port in a storm as usual. The weather was unexpectedly sultry and she did not feel up to the walk through the city to Chichester Street. However if Mr or Mrs Rising could bring little Teddy down to Bearland, she would be delighted to look after him each and every day until his arm healed. Young Bartholomew was looking forward to having his old playmate no end.

So it was that Teddy and Tolly were playing five stone on the scrubbed step of number sixteen Prison Lane, when a man, shabbily dressed, swarthy, with unexpectedly blue eyes, shambled from the docks towards them. Tolly, heeding his mother's instructions for such a situation, retreated down the passage beseeching Teddy to come with him, but Teddy was curious, and, as always, completely unafraid. 'I can smell the sea on him,' he declared. 'Let's ask him where he's been — Tolly — cowardy custard — Tolly —' but Tolly was in the kitchen looking for his mother.

The man took another few steps, his knees buckling under him. He reached out with one hand as if pointing at Teddy, then crashed to the cobbles and lay face down, head sideways on the outstretched arm, rear end pointing to the hot sky.

Teddy galloped towards him, pumping with his one good arm. He crouched by the man, put his plaster near his head and leaned on it. The man's eyes, open and strangely alert, surveyed him.

''Tis the heat boy. Don' be frit. Get me water.'

The words and accent reminded Teddy powerfully of *Treasure Island* which May was reading to him at bedtime. The man definitely smelled of boats and the sea. He scrambled back to his feet and shouted to Kitty and Tolly just emerging from the cottage. Kitty hesitated then turned back for water.

Teddy said confidently, 'Just coming. What's your name mister?'

The man replied automatically, 'Dick Turpin. Four, five, eight, nine.'

Teddy hugged his plaster to his midriff, annoyed. Albert sometimes bammed him along like that and it wasn't particularly funny. Dick Turpin indeed. 'I'm the one who didn't run away,' he reminded the man coldly.

The man closed his eyes. 'Thanks boy. Thanks,' he whispered.

Kitty arrived with her Barty's shaving mug full of water, determined not to contaminate her glasses or cups. Tolly stood back, obviously following further instructions, while she put the mug near the man. He saw it, grinned feebly at the two figures standing well back, felt for the handle and lifted the mug to his mouth. Half of it slurped on to the cobbles, the other half disappeared without the man seeming to swallow. He put down the mug and supported himself on one elbow, straightening his legs painfully.

'You're Mrs. Hall,' he said in a low voice. 'The wife of Bartholomew Hall, warder of Gloucester prison?'

Kitty took a pace backwards; confirmation enough.

'I ain't in no condition to harm you or the children, lady . . . wondered if you could help me in my search for a . . . long-lost relative.'

'Where does he live?' Teddy asked avidly.

''Tis a lady, boy. Friend o' Mrs. Hall's I b'lieve. Staying 'ere two or three year ago when I passed by. Could not claim kinship then Mrs. Hall . . . you knows why.' The man pushed up his sleeve and Teddy saw some marks there. They meant nothing to him, but Kitty drew back again. The man put up a pleading arm. 'I've paid for what I done — you of all people must know how I've paid!' He lay back and took some deep breaths, then spoke with his eyes closed. 'She's the only one 'ud 'elp me — I know that. Tell me where she lives . . . please.'

Kitty said nothing and Teddy asked, 'How can we? We don't know her name or what she looks like or anything.'

Kitty warned, 'Teddy —'

The man said, 'She was big. Wrapped in shawls — sleet and slush everywhere. Blue eyes, grey bonnet —'

Kitty gasped. 'If it was three years ago it was Mrs. Rising and her sister-in-law.!'

Teddy was full of importance. He took a step forward and stooped down, holding his plastered arm. 'That's my aunty. Aunty Sylv,' he announced. 'I'm Teddy Rising and Aunty Sylv is my father's sister.'

Kitty said, 'Teddy! You don't know . . . and get away dear — germs —'

The man growled, 'I'm not diseased Mrs. Hall. Just starved and done in. Thanks boy.' He opened his eyes and looked, then nodded. 'Yes. I remember the other woman now. She was your mother all right.'

Teddy said cockily, 'And I've got three sisters and a brother and he's a bishop's page now 'cos his voice is breaking and he can't sing for a bit and —'

'Where's she live?' interrupted the man.

Kitty put her hand on Teddy's shoulder. 'Come on dear. We've done what we can —'

'Kempley Cottage —'

'Teddy, you are *not* to speak to this man again!' Kitty propelled him back up Prison Lane. Tolly ran ahead and held the door ready to slam after his mother as if he expected a siege.

'Thank you boy!' called the man.

The door slammed. Teddy said, aggrieved, 'Why did we have to leave him Mrs. Hall? He was interesting!'

'He was a no-good down-and-out,' Kitty scolded. 'And you shouldn't have ought to have told him where your aunty lives! What if he goes there and makes a nuisance of himself?'

Teddy was amazed. 'Everyone's a nuisance at Kempley,' he told her. 'If they get too much of a nuisance, Gramps and Uncle Jack throw them out.'

Kitty was partially reassured. When Florence arrived to collect Teddy she made light of it.

'I think it was someone your sister-in-law knew from the country,' she said deviously. 'I doubt whether he will look her up after all. He is probably at the Salvation Army rescue home by now.'

Teddy was not able to jog his mother's memory by referring to Dick Turpin as an ex-prisoner, and after hearing his garbled account of the incident, Florence dismissed it from her mind. She certainly did not wish to question Prison Lane's suitability for Teddy; not at the moment. The new school in Denmark Road was well established now and Will had twenty-two navy-blue uniform coats to make before September; he needed all the help she could give.

She fully intended to tell him about the mysterious 'Dick Turpin' but that night he scattered all their wits with an announcement. They were to move house. They were sitting in the back parlour, almost afraid to move because of the flashing summer lightning.

'Frightened of a few fireworks in the sky!' he scoffed at the three oldest as they huddled over the Happy Family cards as if it were midwinter. 'And these are the travellers who saw the firework display at Bath if you please!'

April, turning the pages of Teddy's book for him in the empty hearth, glanced fearfully at the uncurtained window. 'Gladys Luker says her cousin was struck by lightning and burnt to a crisp. They only knew it was him 'cos there were just four teeth in the road. And that was all he had. Four teeth.'

Will said, 'Forget about the weather for a moment — you can wallow in your gory stories when I've told you mine. Which isn't a bit gory, but much more exciting.' He had their attention, they stared at him over their cards and books, even Florrie over her eternal button-holes.

Will grinned. 'How would you like to move? Yes, move, young Teddy! Not very far. But into a much bigger house where I can have a workroom that will hold two sewing machines and a pressing table as well as a cutting table. Where you can have a bedroom each if you want it.

110

Where the bandy room can be downstairs so that we can use it in the winter.' Florence leaned forward; she loathed carrying coals to the fireplace in the attic, which meant her piano was not used for six months of the year and grew damp. Will twinkled down at her. 'A house with a garden — plenty of trees and a lawn big enough for tennis. The wash-house on the side so that you don't have to go outside to do the laundry — room for indoor lines when it's wet —' Children jumped and leapt around him and Teddy's plaster caught him painfully on the shin. 'Tell us Dad! Where? When? How can we afford it?'

Will held up a restraining hand and answered the last question first; it was a matter of great pride to him. 'We can afford it because the Risings are rising!' He looked at Albert and they both remembered the old joke. 'We're doing well — your mother is working every minute she can spare to help me, and if I had more room I could afford to employ a sempstress part-time, which would mean —' The children leapt again like a bubbling cauldron. 'Where is the house, Father?' and Will laughed and relented. 'Further up the street. Chichester House, no less.'

The silence was awe-struck and completely satisfactory. A retired vicar lived in Chichester House and had done for the past twenty years. He was a recluse and used the back gate which led into Mews Lane.

May said in a low voice, 'Has the reverend died, Daddy?'

Will shook his head. 'When Mr. Amies came for the rent last week he told me the old man was going into a home for clerics and the house would become vacant, and was I interested? The rent is twenty-two and sixpence a week — twice what we are paying now — but with the increased business —'

'The house will keep us poor, Will,' Florence warned. 'All those rooms to heat. And the garden. . . .'

'The children will do the garden.' He played his trump

111

card. 'And they will never need to play in the street again Florence.' He looked sternly at Teddy. 'You will play in the old stables at the back and break your limbs in private my lad. D'you hear?'

April breathed, 'Bridget could come to tea again, couldn't she?'

'I think we might just put up with her once more, might we not Florrie?' enquired Will, twinkling again.

'And — and there will be room for my motor car!' March said amid much laughter.

Albert said, 'Can Harry stay a night now?'

'*May* Harry stay a night Albert.'

'Well, may he? There's never been room before but —'

'Yes, he may, my boy.' Will put an arm on Florence's shoulder. 'Perhaps you'd like to have your Aunt Lizzie down too Florrie?'

March forgot about Harry Hughes. 'Oh, I'll always love summer lightning after this! It will remind me of Aunt Lizzie!'

'Everything reminds you of Aunt Lizzie,' grumbled Albert. But for once he smiled as he said it.

6

Florence worked hard to make Chichester House into a home, but though number thirty-three had been too small for them, this new house was too big. They had been there three days when the staggering news of two deaths was brought by Sibbie Luker: Mrs. Goodrich and her daughter Charlotte had been killed by a tram in Worcester Street. Florence could hardly believe it.

'To escape the fever — do you remember they were ill when Teddy was born? And now to be struck down like this! It's too cruel.'

Sibbie said virtuously, 'Mam says all the trams should be taken off the roads. This could never have happened with a coach an' horses —'

'Of course it could,' snapped March, grief making her impatient. Mrs. Goodrich had been the only genteel person in the street and had always shown a preference for March. And Charlotte, little seen, tiny, delicate, had called March 'Aunt' and wanted to sit in her lap.

Florence sighed. 'It was meant to be, Sibbie. And, somehow, they were meant to go together.' She touched Teddy's shoulder unobtrusively. 'They could not manage without each other.'

'That's a lovely thought Mamma,' breathed May. 'Perfectly beautiful.'

Sibbie said, 'Mam says these things always go in threes and she wonders who will be the next.'

'Stuff and nonsense!' Will stood up, spilling French chalk on the newly-swept floor. 'Off you go to school you girls. Albert, you'll be late! April, Teddy, coats and hats and wait for me at the gate!' He spoke in a lower voice to Florence beneath the immediate hubbub. 'I'll see to the little ones. You go and sit with Granny Goodrich. Tell Sid I'll be along later.'

So it was that the three older Rising children went to their first funeral.

It was September the first and the apple and plum trees, neglected for years, were yielding their over-ripe fruit to the children and the wasps, and Florence was trying to make jam, sort out her linen and press finished school coats all at the same time. The weather was warm and golden, and after four weeks' grace school had started again and the big old house was quiet. Will wandered around it before he began the tricky task of cutting a ladies' riding habit; he had gone on a tour of inspection with Mr. Amies, the rent collector, otherwise there had been no time to explore his new domain. For the past month it had been dominated by children and it had been as much as he could do to gather his things around him in the new workroom and make a routine for himself. The bereavement in the Goodrich household had shaken him more than he cared to admit; he imagined it being Flo and April — Flo and any of them. He knew he could not manage alone. At the back of his mind he wondered about a third death. . . .

The house was big; Flo was right, it was too big. But he did not view it as a dwelling. It wes a symbol of his success. It had been here long before the twin rows of terraced houses and it still sat in the midst of its own grounds quite separate from them. In fact they belonged to it, tenantry. Yes, the rest of Chichester Street was tenantry to Chichester House. Which made him a bit of a squire. He grinned, well pleased with the image. It was how he felt. A bit of a squire.

He wandered through attics still cluttered with stuff left by the old vicar. Four big rooms with board ceilings smelling of sweet wood. Then down to the middle floor where five bedrooms were grouped around a square landing, and a bathroom led off from one of them. A proper bathroom with a closet and a gas geyser and two steps leading up to the bath. Woodworm in the closet seat; he must tell Flo to get some beeswax down those holes. There were views from all the windows, pleasant leafy views with no glimpse of the gasometer. From the bathroom he could see the four-square cathedral tower. He leaned out and watched Flo lugging in another basket of plums. Maybe it *would* be more expensive living here, but there would be plenty of jam next winter to sweeten the outlay!

He grinned as he went down the wider, shallower stairs into the tiled hall. It impressed clients, did this hall. And the house was double-fronted so that Flo could have her parlour looking out at callers, and he could still have a front room for his work. Mr. Daker had stressed the importance of a front workroom. 'Take them down a dark passage and you've lost them already my son,' he'd always said. But over the road at number thirty-three that had meant the parlour being in the middle room, dark with a view of the wash-house. Will said aloud, 'Yes. It might be pricey but it knocks spots off what we had before!' As if in reply to this remark, the outside bell jangled on its spring and the next minute Sylvia appeared in the garden, bundled up as if it were winter. Will rapped on the parlour window and hurried to the front door.

'Thought you'd come and see the palace, did you?' he welcomed her, grinning broadly. 'You're a one for turning up unexpected our Sylv — but welcome just the same!'

He expected her to remind him that she had visited him only once before, but she bundled into the hall

115

without a word and looked around her vaguely. It was enough to overwhelm anyone, of course.

'Come on,' he encouraged. 'Straight through to the kitchen same as before. Flo's jamming the plums.' He clapped her on the shoulder as if she were another man. She hadn't brought a bundle of clothes with her this time.

Flo looked up from the steaming preserving pan and gave a small cry of pleasure. Her wooden spoon went down, she wiped her hands on the towel nearby and held them out to her sister-in-law. And as before Sylvia lowered her head to them without her Kempley laughter, and it was obvious she was near tears.

Will fussed about behind her, drawing chairs to the plush-covered kitchen table, covering her emotion with enquiries for Jack and Austin and Wallie and his many sisters. 'Mam all right?' he asked sharply when she at last collapsed into a chair and he saw her face.

She nodded slowly. ''Tis Pa. He's gone my dears. Dropped dead in the field next to his shires. Master 'ad him put on a gate and brought 'ome. Ma laid 'im out nice. Austin's gone to Newent for the undertakers. Jack's telling the others. I wanted to come and tell you.'

'Thank you Sylvia.' Florence fetched the teapot automatically.

Will was stunned. 'The third death,' he muttered. 'The third one to go.'

Sylvia said, 'A good way too. In harness. He really were in harness. But Ma. . . .'

'Is she taking it badly?' Florence asked.

'She is that. Master will want the cottage see. Jack and Austin was casual workers and not entitled to the tenancy. It were tied to Pa. So we'll have to get out.'

Florence and Will were silent. They both knew that this was a worse catastrophe than the actual death. But inevitable.

Sylvia went on, 'Vi is taking the boys — mine as well — and going with Wallie.' Wallie had a smallholding

116

along the Dymock road and could always do with extra hands to weed, prick out the seedlings, pick flowers and fruit and sell them wherever they could be sold. 'Jack and Austin are off to Wales. To the mines.' She glanced sideways at Will. 'That leaves Ma, And me.'

Will said nothing. He was unwilling to take his mind away from the shock of losing his father. Surely he could be given a little time for grief before he had to start worrying about the others?

Florence looked at him as she reached again for Sylvia's rough hand. 'You will come here. Of course. You and Daisy. And the boys if you wish. You know that Sylvia.'

'The boys will be happier with Vi and Wallie. And me . . . I shall be all right. But thank you for Ma. Thank you Florrie.'

Will said brusquely to cover his silence: 'What do you mean you'll be all right? You'll come here with Ma. No more to be said.'

Sylvia withdrew her hand from Florence's and stared down at the flagstones. 'I — I shall be getting wed. I think. Quite soon.'

This news created much more of a furore than the previous items. Flo exclaimed with delight and Will opened his eyes wide with astonishment.

'Who?' he asked with uncomplimentary disbelief.

Sylvia kept her eyes to the ground and explained quickly in a low voice. 'I saw 'im first when I were with you before, Will.' She glanced at Flo and away again. 'Down at Kitty Hall's, d'you remember Florrie? He were a prisoner then —'

'A *convict*?'

'Not any more!' Sylvia lifted her head angrily. 'He's been punished and he's out now.' She smiled proudly. 'He came to me.'

Florence put two and two together. 'Dick . . . Turpin? Was it? Teddy told me he collapsed outside Kitty's cottage — back in the spring that was. Is it the same man?'

'Yes. Yes. Name you don't forget, eh?' Sylvia looked at her hands this time. 'He was near done when he got to Kempley an' Pa wouldn't 'ave 'im in the cottage, so I kep' 'im in Master's barn. No-one did know.'

There was a short silence. Florence looked uneasy. Will said, 'Where is he now then?'

Sylvia thinned her lips and took a breath. 'He don't know about Pa's dying. He left last month to find work. So we could get married.'

Will followed up remorselessly. 'He asked you to marry him?'

"Twas understood.'

Florence gestured to Will over Sylvia's head. 'Then you can come to us until the wedding day. You can be married from here. Nothing could be nicer.'

Sylvia shook her head. 'No. No Florrie. You don't see what I'm telling you. 'Tis the same now as before — when I was expecting our Daze. And the girls are older now. It would be worse. There's April and young Teddy. And Albert is just at an age when . . . no, I can't come 'ere.'

There was another silence. Florence's face was flaming red. Will said, 'You fool Sylv. Christamighty. Four kids and no husband. You damned *fool*!'

"Tis different this time. Dick will be back. 'E'll be back. You see.'

'And where d'you go meanwhile?'

'We'll go in the workhouse for a while. Me and Daze. Just till — just till —'

Will made an explosive sound of disgust and flung over to the boiling kettle where he made the tea angrily.

Florence said, 'When is the baby due my dear?'

'Roundabout March's birthday I reckon. Now don't you worry your head Flo, we'll be all right. And it's different this time. Dick an' me . . . we think a lot of each other. A lot.'

Florence took the teapot and poured tea, pushing a cup across the table to Sylvia. Then she went to the preserving pan and stirred thoughtfully. Will sat down and humped his shoulders. It was a mess. Bad enough poor old Pa dying, but they couldn't even bury him without trying to think of all these other things.

Florence said from the depths of the steam above the jam: 'You can't go to the workhouse. That's for sure. And Will was talking of taking on a sempstress anyway. And all this food . . . my goodness, we've got work and shelter and food . . . enough for an army.'

'I am not coming here Flo, not in my state. But I thank you —'

'And number thirty-three empty just across the street,' Florence continued, dabbing her wooden spoon on a saucer to see if the mixture jelled. 'Eleven shillings a week. That's all. If we can't find that it will be a poor look-out. Don't you think Will?' She emerged from the steam and gave one of her rare smiles. 'Your — Mr. Turpin — will be able to manage the rent when he comes back Sylvia. Meanwhile if you can help Will in the workroom, I'm sure we can arrange something.'

Will and Sylvia stared at her as if she were an angel. Steam clung to her hair like a nimbus and she did indeed look ethereal. As they applauded her joyously, she smiled again and shook her head. 'My tea will be cold. Will, fetch the bread from the crock, Sylv must be hungry.'

The funeral was as untidy as Walter Rising's whole life had been. The vicar had no-one to take his place as grave-digger, so his sons hurriedly dug a grave the night before, taking it turn and turn about while a big harvest moon saved the use of lanterns. Hubbard the undertaker presented his bill before he brought the coffin. It was twenty-two and sixpence, and each of the eleven children found two shillings towards it and ignored the odd sixpence. Mr. Hubbard, lips tight, wore his secondbest topper and walked ahead of the five brothers as if they were not carrying one of his coffins at all. Behind the brothers, Albert supported his grandmother. She and her six girls wore a motley collection of black shawls, muslin veils and bonnets. The other grandchildren ran about even during the service. The rest of the mourners had come straight from the fields and looked it. March, trying hard to think of Grampy Rising, understood why his temper had been so fierce. It was all so . . . messy!

There were no funeral meats. The gaffer wanted his cottage the next day and Will took as much as he could back with him in the trap. The weather seemed set fair, so much of the bedding was removed. Teddy and April sat on rolled-up feather beds in the well of the trap and May held Gran's precious brown teapot on her lap. It began to drizzle as they crossed the Causeway and Florence opened umbrellas and held them in strategic positions. April, thinking of Bridget and her grandfather who was Alderman Williams, suddenly started to cry. 'We haven't got a grandfather at *all*,' she wailed to the skies. 'He wasn't very nice but at least he was some sort of grandfather!' March shushed her quickly but put a sympathetic arm around her neat school coat. She agreed that Grampy Rising had not been very nice, but at least he was now gone and perhaps the whole sad business of Kempley Cottage could be forgotten.

She had not reckoned on the ability of the Risings to bring their environment with them. Wallie borrowed a flat wagon for the rest of their belongings and they arrived the next day like a pack of gypsies. The house, which had always been bare and shabby, was now like a barracks. Florence had left the drugget on the stairs because Chichester House had a polished staircase that needed no covering, but the thin carpet seemed to shred away almost overnight and the wood beneath became splintery in another day or two. The table and chair legs were kicked, there were no curtains — Kempley Cottage had never had any — the brass beds sagged to the floor, the mice came back to wallow in the dirt in spite of frequent visits by Rags. If Sylvia had not been in an unusual state over her new baby, the house might have looked better; after all she had kept it before. But Sylvia wanted this child as she had never wanted her others. So the brass was not polished and the step went unscrubbed, and soon number thirty-three looked a twin to the house opposite where the Lukers lived.

However, Gran, Sylvia and Daisy were well received in the street. Lottie Jenner called often to drink tea with Gran, and on several occasions Gran took on Lottie's layings-out when she was under the weather after a session at the Lamb and Flag. Hettie Luker would have loved them simply because they were Will Rising's relatives, but she liked them for their own sakes too. Their easy-going generosity, their laughter — which returned very soon after the funeral — their feckless-ness with Daisy, made them her sort of people. The more respectable residents of the street admired their ability to work even if this did not extend to keeping house. Gran and Sylvia worked all hours at finishing for Will and Gran went out scrubbing each morning before breakfast. Even little Daisy hawked round chestnuts that winter and shared her earnings with her cousin April.

It was not only Daisy who repaid the generosity from Chichester House. Gran and Sylvia were not too proud to do their week's shopping as late as possible on Saturday afternoons. They would scrimmage around Eastgate Market by the light of the naked gas lamps, taking the squashed vegetables from the the fruiterer's stall at a penny a sack, delving through the bloody shambles of the butcher's for one of Gran's favourite sheep heads, buying up stale bread and buns from Fearis'. Gran delighted to take a basin of home-made brawn with her when she carried Will's finished work back to him on a Sunday and Sylvia would take a pot of jam and

121

some goose-grease from Flo with one hand and return a basin of dripping with the other.

Florence was too wise to refuse these gifts although she frequently gave Rags the brawn and used the dripping for frying, saving her own carefully rendered pork and beef fat for toast and sandwiches. An intuitive relationship between the two houses flourished. Albert was the favourite as always; May and April were always welcome; Teddy was a continual surprise and they viewed him warily, as slow-moving cows might watch a playful puppy; March was a visitor treated with respect, Flo a visitor treated with love. Strangely enough, Will — completely at home during his evening calls — was odd man out when they were all together.

Will felt as ambivalent about his family's closeness as he had about Sylvia's visit four years before. Half of him wanted to cut right away from them and the dirt and chaos they brought with them. The other half found it relaxing: a relief. Also, by visiting number thirty-three each day, he felt he was driving a wedge between the alliance of Sylvia and Florence. An alliance which he saw would soon include his mother.

There was another reason for his daily visits. He usually found Hettie Luker there, gossiping in the kitchen. There had never been another touch exchanged between them, nevertheless he had not been unaware of her adoration over the years and it was flattering. Now, in the company of the Other Risings, Hettie would tell a joke, wink and give him a nudge. One filthy November night she followed him into the wind and rain, stumbled on the boot-scraper and was suddenly in his arms. Laughing hysterically she delivered him a smacking kiss. Then, shocking at first, but provocative and amusing as time went on, she grabbed at him, laughed wildly and shouted, 'It's still there then! Standing up for its rights too by the feel of things!' He had watched the darkness of her hurry over the road and knew he ought to think of her as a whore.

122

But Hettie Luker was no whore, any more than Sylv or Vi were. She made him feel a bit of a devil. Like the King again. He chuckled as he bent his head and fought his way up to Chichester House.

About this time, Fred Luker sold his father's one good horse and bought a car. Uncomplainingly he took Alf's punishment, then went out to clean it, sporting two black eyes and a bleeding mouth. March, coming home from school, was waylaid by Gladys, who led her furtively down the side way to the stables.

March gasped, 'Freddy! What's happened — your eyes —'

Fred said brusquely, 'Nemmind that. Small payment for this, eh?' He took her into the dark interior where she could just see the gleam of metal. 'Tidn't no Deelaje nor nothing,' he cautioned as she grabbed at his arm. "Tis one of they Austins. One of the first 'e made I reckon. Fifteen year old. One or two things I dun't unnerstand so I be going up to Brum to see 'im and ask a question.'

'Brum?' March hung on his arm as she had done last Whitsun when he'd taken her for that first spin.

'Birmingham. Just near there. Place called Northfield where 'e's got 'is factory.'

'But Freddy, you can't just go! I mean . . .' the enormity of his proposal overwhelmed March. For anyone to beard the lion of car manufacture in his own den was bad enough, but for Freddy to do so was incredible. His cap, always worn sideways, his filthy shirt and big misshapen boots . . . . 'Freddy Luker. You're wonderful,' she amended with conviction.

'Aye. I know that,' he wasn't joking. 'But not that wunnerful. I wants you to help me Marchy. If you'll help me I'll teach you how to drive — let you take the wheel.'

'I — I'm not fourteen till March —'

'Dun't you *want* to drive the bloody car? I only got it

123

— got *this* —' he jabbed a finger towards his eyes ' —
'cos I thought you'd be so bloody pleased!'

She was about to tell him just what to do with his car
and his beastly black eyes, then she paused. To take
Aunt Lizzie for a drive in her own car meant being able
to drive.

She said, 'Of course I want to drive. But would I be
allowed to?'

'No-one need know if you're so bloody bothered!' He
softened suddenly at the thought of himself and March
secretly in his beautiful Austin. 'Be better that way. No
bloody fuss.'

'All right Freddy. And thank you.'

He put his hand on hers to keep her by him. 'Dun't go
yet Marchy. You 'aven't 'eard 'ow you can 'elp me, 'ave
you?'

'Oh. I thought you meant . . . sort of encourage you.'
March was not unaware of how her sudden kiss had
affected the eldest Luker son, and she was not
displeased. She remembered how Uncle Edwin had got
so much pleasure out of his wet kisses when she was a
little girl.

'I wants that, too. En't going to get none of it from my
bloody family, that's for sure.' Freddy led her deeper
into the darkness of the stable and pressed her hospit-
ably down on to the running board of the Austin. He
said nervously, 'I've used Pa's money and me own to get
this, Marchy. Can you get 'old of five bob for me fare to
Brum?'

March found she was enjoying the darkness and
sense of intrigue. There was the car money in the cocoa
tin. Apart from April's sovereign which had started it
last Easter, there wasn't much. Would she be justified
in using that sovereign?

She said, 'I'll bring the money tomorrow. On my way
to school. Will you be here?'

'Thank you Marchy.' Relief made him collapse by her
side. Their legs were pressed tightly together. March

124

glanced sideways and could see the greasiness of his face shining in the half-light.

'What did you call me Freddy?' she asked softly.

'Marchy . . . I mean, Marcie.'

She leaned forward and put her lips to his. 'That's better,' she whispered. 'And Freddy?'

'Oh Christ. What?'

'I'd much rather you didn't swear any more.'

'Oh Christ . . . Oh Christ I'm sorry Marcie.'

She laughed. She felt light-headed. She kissed him again and felt him tremble all over and smelled his sweat. Then she turned and ran down the side way, past the waiting Gladys, up the street and through the door in the wall of Chichester House. Like her father she felt . . . marvellous.

At Christmas Florence insisted that her in-laws should come and share dinner. She tried to contact Vi, Jack and Austin, but it was hopeless: the short distance between Wallie's smallholding at Dymock and Gloucester defeated the Other Risings, and as for the boys they were as good as gone for ever. Neither Gran nor Sylvia seemed to mind. When Florence suggested to Sylvia that she might be missing Sam and George, Sylvia looked surprised. 'I know they're all right m'dear,' she said as if reassuring Florence. 'Every season comes in its turn. In winter you can't 'ave summer. 'Tis no good 'ankering for it.'

It sounded to Florence as if that could be interpreted as 'out of sight out of mind'. Gran's stoic acceptance of her loss and Sylv's of the absence of her sons and the father of her unborn child, must not be seen as heartless however. Florence was fast learning to accept them as they were.

So they ate their goose and sage stuffing around the big dining-room table, the ten of them, and Rags was allowed to sit on May's lap and lick each of the plates in turn, by which time the fire in the bandy room had taken hold and they retired there to sing carols and doze, drink tea and play dominoes and feel frankly bored.

Florence was playing 'Hark the Herald Angels . . .' when there came the faint tinkle of the garden door. Will stood up with alacrity.

'Probably one of the Lukers to wish us a merry Christmas and collect a mince pie or an orange.' It occurred to him they might well be accompanied by Hettie. No-one would mind if he bussed her beneath the mistletoe Teddy had suspended above the door. He hurried out.

Florence stood up and closed the vicar's heavy old velvet curtains. 'It's completely dark. How can Hettie let the children out at this hour?' she asked. No-one answered. Teddy, thoroughly irritable, knocked down the house April had made with the dominoes; March dragged him away and Albert turned to the bamboo table loaded with old *Citizens*. Not even his fondness for Gran could induce him to be sociable this year.

The door opened again and Sylvia manoeuvred her bulk out of the armchair and stood stock still, staring and clutching her bodice like a heroine in a play. Everyone turned to look. A man stood diffidently in the doorway, dwarfing Will who was just behind him.

Teddy, who had embroidered the incident in his mind many times over, announced, 'Crikey-dikey! It's the escaped convict!'

Florence said, 'Hush Teddy dear. No swearing please!'

Sylvia swallowed and spoke steadily. 'My dear. I knewed you'd come.' She walked forward, her abdomen carrying the rest of her with it. The man opened his arms wide and engulfed every last ounce of her. They stood rocking from side to side for so long it became embarrassing. The Rising girls fidgeted, Teddy and Albert exchanged glances, Daze suddenly let out a wail of jealousy, Gran rolled her eyes and made snicking noises of exasperation.

Will made his voice heard. 'This calls for a celebration I reckon — eh? Get by the fire our Sylv . . . warm your . . . er . . . this gentleman. Albert come down and help me with the cider. Newent cider our Mam. From Hayward's farm. Payment for an alteration I did for him.'

They put the poker in the fire and mulled their cider and made a terrible sparky mess roasting chestnuts to go with it. Through it all Dick and Sylvia did not speak. They smiled at each other. Sylv smiled at her family. Dick ducked his head at them. But apparently they had no words for each other or for anyone else.

Florence played more carols and May sang a solo, and in an effort to keep the ball rolling April said ecstatically that May should have proper singing lessons.

'No money for extras like that,' Will said with unusual sharpness, affronted by the arrival of this stranger laying claim to his sister. It was one thing to turn a blind eye to suitors he had never set eyes on, but this was bordering on the brazen. 'We have to earn our money the way we know how with so many mouths to feed.'

The silent Mr. Turpin looked up at that and suddenly smiled, his blue eyes crinkling 'irresistibly' as May told Sibbie later. Then he stuck his hand inside his waistcoat and brought it out clutching a wad of notes.

'I can look after some of 'em from now on,' he announced proudly. 'My own won't want again, and them she'd live with —'

Gran said, 'Where d'you get that money young man? Truth now. We don't want no constables a-knocking on our door! Shabby we might be but honest we definitely is!'

'I earned it old lady.' The face flushed and the eyes were angry. 'An' if I 'ears anyone making out different, they'll be sorry.'

A row sprang up immediately. 'No-one threatens me!' Gran squawked. 'Not even me own 'usband threatened me — 'e knew better! Will, you 'eard what 'e said!

No-one threatens your mam — tell 'im!'

'You called me a thief missis an' —'

'I think it behoves some of us to watch our tongues,' Will said ambiguously. Daisy yelled. And at last Sylvia spoke.

'Be quiet all of you!' she spoke sternly but not very loudly. Everyone was quiet. 'There's bound to be misunderstandings. We expect that, Dick and me. But he's my man and he's come back to look after me and the baby.' She turned to her daughter. 'Daze, you will sleep with Gran from now on and stop that silly blubbering. If you're a good girl Dick might let you call 'im Daddy.' She put her arm through his. 'Come on now my dear. You'm tired and so am I. Goodnight everyone. Good night Flo. I do thank you for a wonderful Christmas. 'Tis the 'appiest in my 'ole life.'

May watched them go out and her father follow them hastily. Then she turned to March and Albert and said breathlessly, 'That was the most romantic thing I've seen. Ever. When I marry, that is how it will be. He will find me out of every girl in the world. And I will cleave to him through thick and thin —'

'Oh shut up May!' Albert said.

'Albert! Mother doesn't like you to say shut up!' May reminded him amazed. March was also surprised.

'I don't care. Just shut up. All that love business . . . it's sickening!'

March said, 'Look, they're all going now. I'll see them out and bring up some bread and milk, shall I? Like before. And May and I can play our duet and April and Teddy can dance —'

'So can Mother and Dad,' said Albert. 'That leaves me. What plans have you got for me March . . . or should I call you Marchy?'

March glanced at him sharply and saw that he knew. She whispered, 'I'll tell you about it . . . it's nothing. Honestly.'

She told him while the others sped the visitors down

128

the street and she heated milk and broke bread into a basin. He did not seem very interested after all. He had seen her standing in the side way with Fred and heard him use that special name.

'It's just that . . . he's beneath you,' he said sulkily. 'All the Lukers are rubbish and you know it. Or you did know it.'

She said, 'Yes, but if they can help you to get what you want, Albert . . . don't you see? When I'm grown up I'm going to buy a car and drive straight down to Bath to take out Aunt Lizzie. You can come, too.'

'Oh . . . rubbish,' he repeated.

It was in the small hours that same night, when she woke to the heavy anti-climax of after-Christmas and heard someone on the landing. Carefully she edged away from May — they had chosen to share a room still — and padded barefoot to the open door. It was Albert mounting the stairs with a glass of water. In the light from the bead of gas, she saw that he was weeping.

'What is it?' She followed him into his room, fully lit, a pile of books tumbled over the bed.

'Nothing. Clear off.'

Stunned, she watched him drink then get into bed kicking the books to the floor. He looked up at her. 'Well? What are you staring at?'

'I thought you loved me.'

'I do. That's why I want you to go away. Go on March. I'm different now. Keep away from me.'

She made a stifled exclamation and went to him. He tried to push her off, but she knelt on the bed above him, her arms in a strangle-hold around his neck. Suddenly he crumpled and began to cry again, pushing his head into her shoulder. She slid to his side, kicked her legs beneath the clothes and, shivering, held him to her. The crying was awful. A blubbering boy's sound that she had never heard before.

His tears soaked through her nightdress and were immediately cold in the freezing night. She pulled him lower in the bed, stroked his strawberry blond hair and kissed his forehead.

'Tell me . . . tell me . . .' she whispered.

He began to talk, unable to hold back any more. His voice came in gasping sobs, husky with shame and disgust. She felt her own body go rigid against his and could not believe what he was saying.

'But the bishop . . . he couldn't . . . he's a man of God . . .'

'He does it to all the pages. Harry told me. He picks the pages for that very reason, March. So there must be something in me!'

'But why? Why does he do it?'

'I don't know. It's like Aunt Sylv tonight. That's how it is March. When he kissed me first I didn't understand . . . realise. And then — and then —' March listened again, believing this time, feeling sick. He told her the same story a dozen or more times. Once the flood-gates were open he could not stop. She went with him through every degrading experience, building from that first kiss which he had thought a blessing, to after last night's Midnight Mass when he had disrobed his master.

At last he whispered, exhausted, 'What can I do March? What can I do?'

'Leave school,' she said promptly. 'Now. Don't go back in January —'

'I thought of that. But what would Mother and Dad say? I'd get no end-of-school report —'

'D'you think they'd care about that? When you tell them what the bishop is really like, they'll — they'll —' March did not know what they would do exactly because a bishop was next to the King, but she knew they would do something.

'I couldn't tell them March . . . I couldn't. And anyway, there was a boy once who made a fuss. He was

130

expelled for lying and his father lost his position . . .
no-one believed him.'

March could understand that. Adults frequently
disbelieved children for no reason at all.

'Just tell him you *won't*! You won't let him do anything
any more.'

'He laughs. He says I will like it quite soon . . . oh
March, shall I? Do you think I shall start to like it? It's a
horrible dream . . .'

March dried his eyes on the corner of the pillow case.

'That's all it is. A dream. It won't happen again. I
promise you that my dearest brother. I'll think of something. You know I'm the clever one in the family, so I'll
think of something.' She kissed his hair. 'And even the
dream will go away because I'll be here. I'll be here all
the time Albert. All the time.' She put her mouth to his
eyes and he closed them obediently. Then she held him
close to her until he was asleep. She did not sleep for a
long time. It was very cold and she was high in the bed
supporting Albert. She did not mind. She wanted to
stay awake with a cold brain that could sift facts and
this new knowledge very carefully. She made plans and
cast them aside. If Albert was powerless to frighten the
bishop, so was she. She had to find someone important
who would side with her.

Uncle Edwin brought Aunt Lizzie for a New Year visit.
They arrived in an old-fashioned hansom from the station, Aunt Lizzie swathed in scarves but noticeably
thinner than when March had visited her last year.
Uncle Edwin, in spite of the familiarity of March's
annual holidays at Bath, was still a shadowy figure,
largely ignored by everyone. Except March. He looked
better for being older, his hair was now white beneath
his curly-brimmed bowler. As soon as she saw the way
he handed his coat so casually to May in the hall, she
knew he was the one to help.

They were both enchanted with Teddy, who

131

informed Aunt Lizzie she was a 'Christmas apple'. Uncle Edwin pronounced Albert 'a man'. Aunt Lizzie hugged May and patted April on the head. They both smiled at March, including her with themselves, adults for whom little compliments were unnecessary.

They celebrated that first day of 1908 traditionally. Pork and turnips at midday, a sedate walk down Henry Street to view the new high school for girls in Denmark Road, then back along Worcester Street and home for buttered pikelets and fruit cake and carols in the bandy room. There was ginger wine and the Christmas port and gentle reminiscing for the women while Will and Uncle Edwin discussed the cowardly way Campbell Bannerman had given in to the trade unions. As self-employed men they could agree on this one point until the cows came home. March yawned and wondered how she could get Uncle Edwin alone and whether she would be able to tell Albert's story when she did.

It happened the next morning. Her father and Albert were filling the dozen coal buckets for the day, Aunt Lizzie was lying in and Uncle Edwin was permitted the sitting-room in glorious isolation with the morning papers.

March crept in ostentatiously and raked at the glowing firebars. Neither of them spoke, not even to exchange a 'good morning', yet their silence heightened a mutual awareness to the tension of a violin string.

He gave way first.

'Well March?' He lowered his paper and looked at her as she fiddled with the irons in the grate. 'Have you come to talk to your old uncle?'

March smiled and quite deliberately patted her hair with one of Aunt Lizzie's mannerisms. She said quietly, 'I would like to talk, Uncle. To ask your advice. But if you would prefer to be quiet, then I am content just to be with you.'

He drew in an audible breath, let the paper fall to the rug, scrubbed at his eyes with the back of his thumbs. He looked at her again. 'My goodness, you look more like your aunt as each year goes by.'

She settled herself on a low stool; she felt odd; slightly sick and hot from the waist up.

'How are you Uncle Edwin? And how is the business?'

He leaned back, surprised. 'I am tolerably well. Yes, tolerably well I think. And as for the business — that is something ladies do not understand March. Remember that.'

She was deflated and slumped on the stool wondering how she could tell him and what he could do when . . . if . . . he knew.

He misunderstood her dejection. 'That is not to say ladies do not understand how to use the end results of business, March dear.' He leaned forward again and touched her shoulder. 'Do not imagine because Christmas is over, you cannot ask me for another present. Our presents have always been a special joy for me March. A special secret.'

She said in a low voice, not looking at him, 'You told me once, I could ask you . . . anything.'

'I have not forgotten, March.' He sounded hoarse and his grip on her shoulder tightened. She let herself be drawn towards him , . . on to her knees, her head on his lap.

'I do not know how to say it Uncle. First I have to tell you . . . something. Terrible.'

He ran his tongue around his lips. 'Tell me March,' he commanded.

She whispered, 'It's Albert . . .'

'A girl.' He was disappointed. 'He's got some girl into trouble.'

March had no idea what he meant. 'No. It's the bishop. Oh Uncle it's so horrible. What the bishop does to him . . . it's horrible . . .'

He knew what she meant but wanted to hear her say it. He gathered her to his shoulder and she felt his arms tremble. After all, he was an old man.

'Just tell me March dearest. Don't be afraid. I will deal with it for you, but I must know exactly what has passed between Albert and the bishop. Then I can act.'

She sobbed with relief. Her cold midnight vigils were over; it was her turn for reassurance and sympathy. She drew a breath and began to speak in short truncated sentences. When Uncle Edwin showed no sign of shock and continued to stroke her upper arm with his shaking old hand, it became easier. Each time she paused he said softly, 'Go on. Go on dearest.' And gradually the whole sordid story unfolded. March wept with the relief of it and felt quite literally that she had laid a heavy load on Uncle Edwin's lap.

'I've promised to help him and I don't know what to do. I don't know what to do.'

She could feel Uncle Edwin breathing into her hair and when he spoke his voice was muffled by it.

'Poor little March. Dear little March. Uncle Edwin will see to it. Don't worry any more.'

'How? What will you do?' She was frightened that he would do the wrong thing; implicate Albert; or Father.

'I will go to see the man.' He seemed to be kissing her scalp.

She said, 'But he'll think that Albert has told you! He'll blame Albert!'

'Give me another name, my dear. The name of one of the other boys.'

She said without thinking, 'Harry Hughes. Harry Hughes is in the same form as Albert.'

'Then I shall tell him Harry Hughes has confided in me. I shall not give my name. He will assume I am a relative or friend.' His voice became stronger as he lifted his head. 'I shall have to rely on my demeanour and bearing to frighten him. Do you think I can do it March?'

She looked up. Her face was streaked with tears; she was almost unbearably beautiful and vulnerable. She whispered adoringly, 'Oh yes Uncle. Oh yes.'

134

And then, because she knew it was the proper payment now, she reached up and kissed him.

That night she crept out before supper for a driving lesson with Fred. She was almost dizzy with happiness. Fred wound energetically and the engine jumped under the bonnet. 'Throttle!' he bawled and March throttled obediently. She drove them to the bottom of Westgate Street and on to the waste ground where February floods would come. She did not grind the gears and by the light of the moon and the flickering oil lamps on the car, she manoeuvred successfully around the ruins of old buildings that could have been there when the Romans came to Caer Glow or when the Parliamentary forces had billeted themselves in the city. Fred was cautious with his praise.

'Din't put 'er through it like you usually do,' he said running his hand lovingly over the upholstery. 'You'm getting better Marcie, I'll give you that.'

It was better than a paean coming from Fred. She relinquished the wheel for the run home. She needed no more practice. She could drive. Fred could keep his lessons and his car; Uncle Edwin would buy her a car in the summer. When she went to live with Aunt Lizzie for good.

She ran back down the side way without saying goodbye and he stared after her like a hungry dog. She knew he was there and she did not wave when she reached the street. She thought her brief eighteen-month friendship with Fred Luker was finished.

7

At the end of January 1908, Sylvia Rising was married
to Richard Turpin at Gloucester Registry Office in
Saint John's Lane. Florence, Will and old Mrs. Rising
were there, and afterwards they all went to the
Cadena for a cup of tea and a fancy cake. It was
snowing, big white wet flakes that stuck to eyelashes
and veils and piled beneath shoes and boots, but Sylvia
looked warm and enormous and very happy. Dick
called her 'Mrs. Turpin' and she pretended she did not
know who he meant. 'I din't know you'd brought your
mam along Dick —' and he said dramatically, 'I en't got
no mam any more my child, but I 'ave got me a bran'
new wife!' And they both laughed uproariously.

Florence went home with a headache and Will was
strangely irritable. That night when he went down the
road to see his mother, Sylv and Dick were in bed
already and Hettie and his mother were far gone on the
stout Dick had brought in from the Lamb and Flag. Will
took Hettie's hand and led her up the hall and into his
old workroom now full of junk. In the thick cold darkness, their usual kiss was not enough. Trembling, he
fought his way through her layers of clothing and
pushed her down on the bare boards. Afterwards he
had to dress her again she was so far gone, and even
the snow outside did not revive her. Sibbie Luker
answered his knock and smiled knowingly as she said,
'What you bin doing to 'er Mr. Rising?'

He didn't like that. Sibbie was the same age as his

136

May. His irritability was still there, so he went on down to the Lamb and Flag to conclude a wedding day as it should be concluded. And there Lottie made everything twice as bad by elbowing him for a drink and saying, 'Hettie not 'llowed out tonight Will?'

As he spat snow on his way back home, he did not feel guilty as he had done that first time; far from it. It was Flo's own fault now. She couldn't expect him to behave like a monk for the rest of his life. But he wished Hettie did not have such a long tongue. Dammit, if it got back to Alf Luker there might well be trouble.

Albert's duties with the bishop were minimal and absolutely straightforward during his remaining time at the King's School. Although he begged March to tell him what she had done, she was obdurate in her silence, and as the weeks passed he was tempted to believe she had done nothing at all and it had just happened. Even, at times, that he had imagined the whole thing.

He was happy again. Mr. Filbert was training Harry and himself with the men's choir, and had asked them both to attend practices after they left school. Harry was to be articled to the cathedral solicitors and Albert was not far away; it was ideal. They had similar natures, unadventurous and content with their lot. Harry's father was a railwayman and Harry would have liked to have joined the G.W.R., but there was no money in it and lawyers were always rich and respected.

On March the third there was a party at Chichester House: it was March's fourteenth birthday. Harry was invited, Sybil Luker, David Daker, Bridget Williams and Tolly Hall. Daze was there, invited or not.

It was the first time David had come to see the Risings. After Mr. Daker's death, Will had made several attempts to encourage a friendship but Mrs. Daker suddenly turned to the faith she and her husband had left before their marriage, and decided that David would not play with non-Jewish children. Frustrated, Will had still taken April and Teddy with him when he made one of his calls. April, usually so friendly, had stared at the sloe-black eyes of David Daker and hidden her face in her father's trouser leg. Teddy, following Albert's example, had said pertly, 'Hello David. Daker the Baker.' Will did not take them again.

Now David, a tall lean man of sixteen, leaned nonchalantly against the piano in the bandy room, letting it be seen by his faintly insolent glance that he had come for the sake of his business only. He was dressed in a suit he had made himself, with the new cut-away jacket and narrow lapels, showing a waistcoat and a drooping watch chain. March and Albert thought him unbearable, May still brimmed with sympathy for him though his father had been dead for five years; April was still vaguely frightened of him, and Teddy did not notice he was there.

They had supper in the dining-room, the table pushed level with the chiffonier to make a proper buffet. There were sandwiches of every kind with tiny labelled flags stuck into them, mince pies, plum trifle, apple turnovers, wedges of Christmas cake, ginger beer served in wine glasses and tea for the ladies.

The younger ones sat on the fender surrounded by plates and glasses and Bridget recounted the terrible tale of Teddy's Accident for the delectation of Daze and Tolly. 'It was all my fault and I said I'd be your servant for ever after, and I have, haven't I Teddy?'

Daze and Tolly, bored stiff by the old story, exchanged glances. Daze said rebelliously, 'How? How have you been Teddy's servant, Bridget Williams?'

Bridget glanced at them in return. 'I help him with his spellings. And I told Miss Midwinter it was my fault when he spilled the ink.'

April gasped. 'That's lying Bridget! And cheating!'

Teddy said swiftly, 'I don't need any help with spellings. And I wouldn't have cared about Miss Midwinter knowing I spilled the ink. Those things are nothing. If you really want to do something for me Bridie ...' he grinned provokingly. 'I want one of those new scooters like in Marshall's toy shop in Eastgate street. I wanted one for my birthday and I didn't get one. And I wanted one for Christmas and I didn't get one. You get me one Bridget. You get me a scooter.'

'She can't,' Daze said flatly.

Tolly commented, 'They're a lot of money. My Pa says it's wicked to charge all that money for two wheels and a bit of tin.'

'I want one all the same,' Teddy said blandly, looking at Bridget.

'She can't get you one,' repeated Daze.

'I can!' Bridget picked up her wine glass defiantly. 'I can Daisy Rising. So there.'

April said, 'You're not to, Bridget. You're not to ... and you're not to do Teddy's spellings any more. You'll lead him into bad ways!'

But Teddy was already smiling with anticipation. He squeezed April's arm painfully. 'We'll share it,' he whispered. 'We'll share the scooter all the time!'

David Daker said, 'Let me fetch you something sweet, Miss May. A mince pie perhaps?'

'That would be nice.' May's face dazzled at him like a flower. 'Sibbie, would you like a mince pie?'

' 'Drather some trifle — stay there May, I'll help David to fetch it.' They passed Bridget carrying a cake. 'Stuck-up little madam,' commented Sibbie, looking at David to see how he would take it.

David had already sensed that Bridget Williams was on a higher social rung than anyone else. He smiled suddenly, and his saturnine face lifted into good looks. Sibbie stood by him while he hovered uncertainly with a plate. Then she loaded it confidently. They both knew where they were.

Will said, 'Flo dearest, shall I go down the road and see how Sylv is getting along? Everyone looks well settled here.'

Florence glanced over her teacup, well satisfied. Granny Goodrich had come out of her shell to help her prepare all the food and she was now sitting back like Flo herself, enjoying its fast disappearance. Of course it must remind her agonisingly of the loss of her daughter-in-law and little Charlotte ... but perhaps it was not all pain.

Will pressed her hand. She was more beautiful than ever tonight in a severe shirt-waist with long tight sleeves fastened with a row of tiny buttons from elbow to wrist. Desire flamed in him. 'I'll go on over to my mother then, Flo. I won't be long.'

Florence looked doubtful. 'Be back for the dancing Will. You must lead off with March.'

'Of course. Don't fuss dear.'

'I'll come to the door with you.' They went into the tiled hall, ice-cold, piled with coats, hats, mufflers, the enormous Goodrich umbrella. Florence found Will's things, wrapping him into them with tender care. She opened the front door and took a deep breath of the frosty night. The sky was high and milky and made the gas lamps beyond the garden wall look sickly yellow. 'Oh Will ... oh Will, we have so much.' She was almost frightened and hung onto his arm. 'We have too much.'

He too was affected by the hugeness of the night and the thought of the warm crowded room behind them in the midst of an empty universe. He held her face and kissed her lips tenderly. He said in a low voice, 'Flo ... dearest Florrie ... you're forty years old, my darling.'

She smiled her slight smile. 'Don't remind me Will. I know it.'

140

'Surely it would be all right now. . . . No chance of another child.' He kissed her again, smelling her clean fragrance with half-closed eyes.

She drew back. 'Oh Will how can you think of such things now?' He knew she was blushing. After eighteen years of marriage. 'My dear, we're much too old for that sort of thing.'

He straightened and pulled his knitted gloves over already cold hands. He knew with sudden clarity that she would never sleep with him again. The knowledge was a knell in his heart. He shivered.

'Will, you're cold. Come back inside — they will send over when the baby is safely delivered.'

'No. No, I must go.' Hettie would smell of stout and sweat and the meal she had just cooked, but she would be warm and welcoming. He needed her as he had never needed her before. 'I must go. Now.' He was halfway down the path, last year's leaves crackling under foot with frost. Florence watched until the garden door closed after him. Then she too shivered. It really was very cold.

The adults cleared the food into the kitchen and sat around the big table drinking tea while water boiled for washing up. The children — though David Daker could hardly be called a child — played hide-and-seek all over the house. It was noisy, disorganised, and an opportunity for the younger ones to let off steam. Albert chased March with Harry tagging along obediently, then quite suddenly disappeared, leaving March alone with Harry in the bandy room.

March said, 'Pax! Pax now Harry! Where's Albert?' She got behind the upright piano, her rich brown hair already tumbling from its pins. Her flannel blouse was tight and beginning to smell under the arms. She clasped her hands primly on her waistband and repeated on a rising inflexion, 'Where is Albert?'

'Gone to help your mamma —' the King's School snigger bubbled nervously through Harry's nostrils.

141

'He says I am to collect my forfeit. And bring you down-stairs and —'

'Forfeit?' March wanted Albert very much indeed.

'When I catch you, you must pay a forfeit before I let you go.' Harry side-stepped to one side of the piano and she to the other. He struck a bass chord that set her nerves on edge.

She said, 'First you have to catch me!' then feinted towards the table and immediately doubled back. Harry played rugger and caught her quite easily. They struggled.

'Let me go!' March was furious. He must surely smell her blouse, flannel was notorious for holding a smell.

He was at a loss, but Albert had spoken of nothing but March and how she must be the belle of the ball. He gasped, 'A kiss! A kiss is all I demand fair maid!' And without giving himself time for second thoughts of what he guessed awaited him, he lowered his head.

The next moment he was sitting with his back clapped against the hot fender and every ounce of wind knocked from his body. March ran out of the bandy room, trying to push her hair back into its pins. As she lifted her arm, the sharp smell of sweat made her eyes water with fury. It was all Albert's fault for leaving her with that — that — lummock!

Every time David Daker looked for May, he found Sibbie, and as May ran off into the darkness, Sibbie stayed right where she was, next to him. The third time it happened, she hung on to his arm when he made to run after May.

'I've found you,' he reminded her. 'You have to go back to the parlour now. That's the game.'

Sibbie pouted. 'And you have to come with me.'

'I've still not caught May however.'

'Well, I'll be off again if you go now. You have to make sure I go back to the parlour, even if you have to drag me there.'

'I'm certainly not going to do that.'

'Don't you like me David? I like you.'

'You're making that obvious.' He lounged against the passage wall, his face a white blur, but his attitude one of boredom. Sibbie played her trump card.

'I'll let you see under my vest David.'

He said, 'Good God little girl. I've seen what you've got and more.'

She was completely enthralled. He had sworn so beautifully. And she guessed he must be telling the truth because he was so matter of fact about it.

'I'm thirteen you know,' she tempted. 'I'm six months older than May. She's a little girl. I'm not.'

He said cruelly, 'She's a lady. And you're not.'

She took a step back and came against the wall. An old nail, driven in for a long-ago picture, scagged at her best blouse, and tears sprang into her eyes. She wasn't a needlewoman like May and her cobbled darn would show dreadfully. David Daker was turning away from her, going after May again. She said sharply, 'She doesn't want you. And I do!'

He laughed carelessly as he disappeared into the darkness. 'What a shame,' he whispered back. 'What a great pity. For you.'

She stayed where she was and deliberately worked the nail head through to her shoulder blade. She hoped it would bleed. She hoped it was a rusty nail and she'd get blood poisoning and lie near death's door in the infirmary and David Daker would visit her and lean over her bed and murmur, 'How can you forgive me Sibyl? Please recover and I will spend my whole life making you happy.'

May was prosaically in the parlour, talking to a subdued Bridget who had fallen down the stairs.

'I thought I was supposed to catch you?' said David, all his mystery and panache gone in the full gaslight.

May laughed up at him. She was exquisite. He'd never seen anything like her. She made him forget the

143

drudgery of working for his mamma in the small shop in the Barton, counting every penny. May was refined in the true sense of the word. All the dross, all the superficiality was gone from her. She was like a candle flame, pure, dancing, coolly yet warmly alive.

'You *were* supposed to catch me,' she agreed. 'But I escaped. And here I am, back home!' She stood up and caught Bridget's hand in hers. 'Come on. Harry and March are helping Mamma in the kitchen. Let's go and see if they're ready to start the dancing.'

She was talking to Bridget — David realised this with a sinking heart. He followed her into the hall and as she turned towards the kitchen, he noticed a glimmer of white at the top of the stairs. He paused. If it was Sibbie still after him, he'd go up and twist her arm behind her back until she cried. It would be some compensation for May's indifference. He waited by the newel post and April came slowly down the stairs until she saw him, then waited herself. Her heart beat uncomfortably. She hadn't really enjoyed the game since Bridget fell down the stairs and she had left Teddy and Daze enjoying a strictly forbidden pillow fight. Now her way was blocked by the dark and terrifying David Daker.

She said in a small voice, 'Excuse me, have you seen May?'

He didn't answer her. The gas mantle popped suddenly and she jumped with it and that made him smile. But it wasn't a friendly smile.

She quavered, 'Teddy's burst one of the pillows I think. And he won't stop and . . .' her voice died away as his foot went on the bottom stair. He was still smiling, his teeth whiter than his pale face. But it was his eyes that were so terrifying. They did not move from her for an instant and they didn't blink. She blinked herself, rapidly, half a dozen times. Then she said, 'I don't think we're playing the game any more. I think I heard March say it was finished.'

144

He was still silent and his other foot was on the next step.

She retreated and he advanced.

She said, 'Oh dear . . . oh Mr. Daker, I'm frightened. Please don't . . . please . . .'

At last he spoke. In his deep, man's voice, he said, 'I'm coming to get you. April Rising. Youngest of the Rising girls. I'm coming to get you!'

April squeaked a scream like a mouse, turned and ran up the stairs. They seemed endless and very slippery. Mother did not like them clattering up the polished wood in shoes, so their outdoor shoes were kept in the hall flanked by a row of home-made slippers with felt soles. The soles skidded desperately as April pounded up one step at a time on her five-year-old legs. She could hear David Daker laughing quietly behind her as he took the stairs two at a time, and she knew if he caught her she would go mad on the instant. Her reaching arm gripped the landing banisters and she swung on them expertly, just avoiding his grasping fingers on her skirt. The bathroom door was open. She let the impetus of her swing take her through it, slammed the door, turned the key and sagged against the lock, trembling in all her limbs. There was no sound at all from outside.

'You can't get me,' she called tremulously. 'I've locked the door — it's no good trying to get me.'

Nobody replied. She stared in terror all around the tiny room. There was nowhere he could get in. The window opened only at the top and was of frosted glass. There was a ventilator above the pot-bellied gas geyser and another beneath the lavatory cistern. She looked through the geyser vents in case he was in there.

She said, 'You can't get in. No-one can get in.'

There was no reply and after another few moments she sat on the broad mahogany lid of the lavatory and stared at the door. Was he out there or had he gone

145

downstairs immediately she'd got inside? She was cold now, sweat drying on her bare arms and face and chilling her right through. She got up and stood in the bath to pull at the gas chain and light the room thoroughly. Daddy always said the gas light warmed the bathroom; she tried to believe it. She clambered back out of the bath and looked at the door again and thought how silly she was, it was only a game. And then with a slowness that was awful, the door knob began to turn.

She knew that she had turned the key, yet at the first movement of the knob she doubted it and flung herself against the door to block his entry. 'Go away!' she called, hysterical now. 'Go away — or I'll scream for Teddy!'

The door knob twisted back, there was a short silence, then the laughter again. His voice said, 'I'll be out here whenever you open that door April. Just waiting.'

'I won't come out then! I won't come out at all!'

She sat on the lavatory seat again and folded her arms. Teddy would come downstairs in a minute. Dear Teddy who would tackle anyone or anything on her behalf. He'd protect her from Devil Daker. Yes, that was a good name for him. She must tell that to Albert. Devil Daker. She went back to the door and put her mouth to the keyhole. 'Devil Daker!' she called.

Dick and Hettie sat close to the kitchen range. Will sidestepped through the usual mess on the floor.

'What's to do?' His accent slid sideways as it always did with Hettie. 'Nothing happened yet?'

Dick said nothing, just spat into the fire. Hettie lifted one shoulder. 'They'm up there. Lottie and y'r mam. Something en't quite right I shouldn't wonder.'

Will shot a warning glance at Dick. 'Sylv's as strong as a horse,' he said. He'd heard those words before and they had not proved true. 'Young Daisy is enjoying herself over there.' He jerked his head towards the door and looked at Dick.

Dick ignored him and hoisted himself out of his chair.

146

'If owt 'appens to Sylv, that'll be it. I shall be off like a shot. You wun't see me 'ere no more.'

'Nothing will happen to our Sylv! I told you she's —'

'I dun't care about the babby. That's all she do talk about, the bloody babby!' He lifted his head and stared at the ceiling. 'You can 'ave the babby!' He spoke loudly as if talking to Heaven. 'Take it an' welcome! But not Sylv. Anything . . . not Sylv.'

'Look Dick, sit down.' Dick was taller by a whole head than Will and seemed to fill the small kitchen. 'Sit down and I'll make us all a nice cup o' tea. Christamighty, I coulda brought over some food, there's enough back 'ome to sink a ship!'

'Goin' well, is it?' Hettie asked, smiling up at him, biting her lip, her light blue eyes full of anticipation. 'Good of you to leave it to come and enquire for your sister. Good of 'im, innit Dick?'

'What? Ah. . . .' Dick prowled to the door. 'I'm a-goin' to go up. I'll stop outside the door. Can't wait down 'ere no more.'

They did not try to dissuade him. As soon as his tread rasped on the bare stairs, Will was at the door securing it, Hettie busy with her buttons. Will turned down the gas as Florence had always insisted, then came back to her. Just for a split second he felt a surge of disgust that was almost nausea as he caught sight of her billowing folds, the abdomen stretched and permanently gross after too many babies and too much stout, the breasts pendulous and flaccid. Then her arms went round him and he buried his face in her neck. 'Christamighty Het . . . Christamighty. I want you tonight. It's been awful . . . awful my love.' He forgot the wide night and the frost and the stars and beautiful Florence. Or perhaps he did not forget them at all. Perhaps they were all sublimated in the coarse body of Hettie Luker.

*   *   *

David Daker bowed low over April's stockinged knees.

'Will you forgive me enough to dance with me, little lady?'

Bridget screamed with delight. 'Go on April . . . go on . . . a proper dance!'

April said, 'I don't know . . .' even as she stood up.

He had been waiting for her outside the bathroom door, just as he'd said. She'd heard Daze giggling and Teddy saying, 'Are you waiting to go in there Mr. Daker? I'll bang on the door shall I?' And she had screamed, 'Teddy! Teddy!' and unlocked the door and hurried out to find David Daker still laughing and telling Teddy that he had trapped April in there so that she couldn't get 'home'. Teddy had laughed as well, then Daze — though Daze did not know what it was all about, but like her mother she would laugh at anything. Then David had looked at her with his sloe eyes and said, 'You weren't a bit frightened were you April? I knew you weren't when you called me that wicked name.' Then he picked her up and carried her to the bandy room where the piano was striking out some commanding chords and Mr. Goodrich was leading March to the middle of the floor. Sibbie and May and Bridget and everyone had looked at them as they came in and David had said, 'Look what I've caught. One Rising. One female Rising. Very pretty. Very, very pretty indeed.' And everything was suddenly wonderful.

It went on being wonderful. He danced with her again and again. He danced with Sibbie too. And with May. But he came to April every time. She wasn't quite comfortable about it because he kept looking at her and laughing even when she didn't say anything very funny. But everyone else laughed too. Mother smiled from the piano and Albert's friend called her 'the belle of the ball'. Only March, in a clean white blouse, frowned disapprovingly.

Sylvia's screams were ringing through number thirty-three as Hettie and Will squirmed on the floor of the kitchen. Will lifted his head. 'Oh God. . . .' He tried to concentrate, but could not.

Hettie said, 'It dun't matter my love. It dun't matter. Another night. Plenty more nights.'

'Oh God. . . .' More screams, and more. Then silence. Will staggered to his feet. 'What shall we do? What shall we do Het?'

'En't nothin' we can do my love. Surely you knows that after your five.'

He shook his head. 'Florrie never screamed or cried out. Never. Not even when she was bleeding to death after Teddy.'

'Christamighty.' Hettie sat up slowly and began to button herself. Her drawers lay where she had kicked them, beneath the gas stove where Rags had crouched that first time. She listened; there were no more sounds. ''Tis all right now Will. Babby must be borned. Come on back.'

He shook his head again, shoulders hunched. 'Not tonight Het.' He shouldn't have remembered Florrie and her stoicism. He wanted to cry.

Then the door opened. Dick stood there looking at them in the half-light. Hettie sprang up but it was too late, he'd seen her bare legs and open blouse and anyway she spoiled it by diving for the gas stove and her drawers.

Will said, 'Dick — listen — we haven't — not tonight —'

Dick said, 'Babby's borned dead. Sylv's all right but the babby's borned dead.'

Hettie stopped her scrabbling and stared at him, hair round her face.

Will said, 'I'm sorry Dick. But so long as Sylv's all right. Eh?'

Dick said, 'Bloody fool. 'Tis all my fault en't it? I said, din't I? You 'eard me — the two o' you! I said to take the babby — and the babby's took!'

Will said, 'Pull yourself together Dick. She's going to

want you any minute now and she en't going to want to see you like this. She'll be quite bad enough herself. Come on, sit down. Any brandy in the house Hettie?'

Hettie went to the dresser, poured and returned. They sat Dick in the chair. By the time Granny came through the door, the whole scene looked normal. In the circumstances.

Will did not know how he went back to the party and danced with March and avoided Florence's reproachful look for being late. But he did. He danced with every one of the ladies present, even Daze. He held her with special tenderness because the small sister she might have had was dead. Then he helped find everyone's coats and wraps and he handed Bridget into the family Daimler as it arrived in Mews Lane, and told April to find Daze a nightie and let her sleep in with her for tonight. He drank the cocoa that March made and kissed his three girls goodnight, clapped Albert and Harry on their shoulders, hoisted Teddy into his arms. It had been a good party, he agreed with them all, a very good party. And there was no reason why May shouldn't have one; April too when she was a little older. No reason at all.

And then, just as had happened before, he found Florence asleep or feigning sleep, and he had to take his grief upstairs with him. Was she really frightened that he might try to climb into bed with her after all this time? He smiled wryly and then began to cry as he remembered Sylv's agony of body and spirit. Little did Florence know. Little did she know.

There was no party for May. The whole family were surprisingly stricken by the loss of Aunt Sylv's baby and May herself spent more time sitting with her grandmother and being a little mother to Daze.

March was relieved that there would be no more socialising in Chichester House for a while. She had tried to be polite to Harry Hughes for Albert's sake, and look where it had got her. And as for that insufferable David Daker making a fool of little April — she had no wish to repeat any of it. The summer would go on very pleasantly now until the annual visit to Bath. Certainly there was the boredom of the Whit-walk and the business of leaving school and receiving her attendance prize, but she was still warm with the knowledge of saving Albert. Moreover she could drive a motor car.

She brought her plait forward and tickled her chin with it, wondering whether she dared ask Uncle Edwin another favour quite soon. Although really, it was she doing him the favour. He probably needed a personal secretary without realising it. And if he bought a motor car she could drive him to the office besides doing his typing for him.

She flipped her plait over her shoulder again and smiled at the bright May sunshine. She had always wanted to live in Bath.

Gladys Luker suddenly popped out of their side way, dirty-faced as usual. March thought it was a pity April and Teddy would be going to Chichester Street school next autumn; Bridget might be dreadful but at least she wasn't common. Sibbie was the only Luker who was presentable and that was May's influence. March could have wished that she had had the same effect on Fred, but he continued to wear his flannelette shirt without a collar and had even taken to using a thick leather belt to anchor it inside his trousers rather than braces. He looked no more than a navvy. Luckily the driving lessons had all taken place during the dark evenings and only Albert knew of them.

Gladys hopped in front of her and walked backwards. 'Our Fred wants you,' she said.

'Is that so?' March replied coolly. She side-stepped Gladys and quickened her step, not only to avoid Fred but because she was passing thirty-three on the other side. Aunty Sylv might be sitting outside for a breath of air. Aunty Sylv did not like sitting indoors any more and she didn't like Granny's company much. She spent part of each day at Chichester House 'being quiet' as Florence explained it. March knew that since the baby had been born dead Aunty Sylv had gone a bit queer.

Gladys leapt in front of her.

'Our Fred says it's important. Real 'portant.' As March did not take any notice of this she added desperately, 'March, please come and see our Fred! 'E'll 'it me else!'

The thought of Gladys Luker being hit did not bother March; Fred had a right to hit his sister just as she hit Teddy when he was more than usually obstreperous. But if it was that important it might well be to her advantage to investigate further.

She said, 'All right. Five minutes.' She turned on her heel and went down the side way. Gladys kept watch.

Fred was shovelling horse's dung into a stiff sack. The ramshackle stables in the sunshine stank to high heaven, as did Fred himself. Nevertheless his grin was wide as he saw her.

'Hello Marcie. You en't stopped by since end of Febr'y.'

March stepped delicately on to the mounting block; there was actually steam coming from the sack. She breathed shallowly.

'No. You're working when I'm home.' It was true yet she felt slightly uncomfortable. She had almost cut Fred since the end of her driving lessons.

Fred shrugged, not offended. 'Well, I suppose the lessons were over when the light nights come along, eh?' he grinned again. 'Didn't want to be seen with Fred Luker, eh Marcie?'

She said defiantly, 'I told Albert about it. About the lessons.'

'An' about the kissing?' He guffawed at her expression. 'No, you never, did you my maid? Never tole 'im about that.'

Wishing she had not mentioned Albert's name, she said quickly, 'Boys are all the same! Always wanting . . . that.'

152

His grin died as he stared up at her. Standing there on the mounting block she looked like an angel aureoled in light.

'What d'you mean? Who bin kissing you Marcie?'

'You of course.'

"Oo else? You meant someone else — come on —'

She shrugged. 'Oh, just a boy at my party. Nothing.'

'That bloody David Daker — why din't you tell me — I'd bloody well kill 'im —'

'It wasn't David Daker you idiot. Never mind.' She jumped down. 'I must go Freddie. Mother will be waiting tea.'

"Alf a mo. I en't told you. I'm gonna start a cab service. What d'you think of that Marcie? A motor cab. All me own.' He followed her down the side way, taking off his cap and knocking it against the wall so that dust flew. 'I'm gonna make a fortune Marcie. See if I don't. Next thing you know I'll 'ave a char-a-banc.'

She reached the safety of the street and turned to look at him. How on earth she could have kissed him she'd never know.

She said deliberately, 'It was Harry Hughes. The one who kissed me. He's going to be a solicitor you know.'

He said nothing. He watched her all the way down the street and his face was without expression.

Albert was in the fruit enclosure picking gooseberries into his spread handkerchief, head down. She peered at him through the netting.

'Albert, I thought it was your practice night with Mr. Filbert.' She wished with all her heart he would look up and say he preferred to be with her.

'I'm missing it. Don't say anything to Mother.'

'Why? Why are you missing it? Are you ill?'

He turned his face down further. 'Harry's not going.' His head came up and she saw he had been crying. 'Harry's been sacked, March! Sacked from school! Some trumped-up charge about him pinching money from the lockers — you know Harry wouldn't do that!'

She couldn't take it in at first. Jealousy of Harry almost overwhelmed her.

Albert's distress turned to anger. 'You *know* Harry's not a thief March! And you know why he's been sacked — you're the only one who does know!'

She stared, then said through stiff lips, 'What do you mean?'

He left his handkerchief and the few token gooseberries and pushed his way blindly through the wire gate.

'That — that — *swine!* Harry won't say anything of course, but the bishop must have — must have — asked him.' He looked at her painfully. 'You know what.' He hung on to her shoulder and turned his face towards the clear blue sky and the fruit trees budding. 'Oh March, if only I'd said no. Like Harry must've done. I'd be proud to be sacked . . . now I feel a miserable coward. And there's nothing to be done about it. Harry. Or me.'

March let out her breath tremblingly, terrified that Albert would sense through his contact with her shoulder that she was the cause of Harry's expulsion. She clenched her fists. It couldn't be that. And even if it was, it was nothing to do with her. Uncle Edwin had taken the matter into his hands.

Albert said, 'I think I'll go up to the attics for a while. Don't say anything to Mother.'

'I won't.'

She watched him go between the laurels towards the house. He was desperately unhappy. He would miss Harry Hughes far more than he would miss her if she was suddenly removed from him.

She clenched her hands harder still. If Harry had been sacked because of anything Uncle Edwin had done, she didn't care. She didn't care.

The rest of the story was sorted out by Whitsun. Some money had been found in Harry's locker which had belonged to an eleven-year-old. It was all hushed up, but

154

there was no question of him being articled to the cathedral solicitors any more. His father used his influence and secured him a position as lamp-boy at Longhope station. He went into digs and rarely came to Gloucester. And Albert seemed to withdraw from everyone, even March. He stuck the rest of that school year, but his spare time.was spent in the garden or the attics. And he wanted no company.

8

It was from then — Harry's expulsion — that March felt her life turn sour. Her exclusion from Albert's real presence was a continuing sore that did not heal, even when they both left school that summer and started with Will in the workroom. She chose to find the work boring, though had she known a year ago that she would spend her entire day with Albert she would have been overjoyed. Now she resurrected the old idea of being a personal secretary and used her tiny salary to pay for lessons in writing Mr. Pitman's shorthand.

Her plans for going to Bath were also balked when Aunt Lizzie's continued ill-health was diagnosed as consumption, and she was hurried off to a sanatorium by a frantic Uncle Edwin.

April told May that she thought March was 'simmering'. Neither girl tried to talk more intimately about it. March's temper outbursts were experiences to be avoided at all costs. They knew that after an eruption March would be serene and happy, but still they had no wish to precipitate the eruption. So March continued to 'simmer' and to become resentful; and as bitter as a girl of fourteen can become.

For Albert, this was a time of sanctuary. He was unexpectedly dexterous at transforming written measurements into a French-chalk outline on material and cutting a superbly fitting garment. Rarely were alterations needed. By using identically patterned woollen worsteds for three suits, he saved enough cloth to make

March a winter costume of impeccable line and smartness. She trimmed the collar with fur and borrowed a hat of Florence's that tipped over her eyes. When the tedium of button-holing became unbearable, she would go to the bandy room and parade in front of the big glass in her new clothes, pretending to be a 'secretary'. It became her solace and the height of her ambition.

That winter was marred too by ill-health for April and Teddy. Normally robust, the two of them were plagued by sore throats, each time diagnosed by a terrified Florence as diphtheria. The children, transplanted from the hot-house atmosphere of Midland Road School to Chichester Street Elementary, picked up every germ that was around. They hated the change. They whined and were intractable, and their quarrelling, reaching the ears of March in the workroom, did not endear her family to her.

On Teddy's birthday and Christmas Day, they were confined to bed, only saved from complete misery by visits from Bridget and Tolly. They played Happy Families on a large tray, then Bridget invented a mother-and-father game wherein she and Teddy sat in one bed, while April was a sick child in another, and Tolly a general dogsbody. Bridget and Teddy kept falling out of bed and April kept crying. Tolly was relieved when his father called to take him home.

In January it was decided that the children should have their tonsils removed. It was a mild winter with no frost to kill the germs and the School Inspector had shamed them three times already with enquiries regarding their non-attendance.

Gladys Luker said, 'I know someone 'oo 'ad it done. Spat blood for a fortnight they did. Couldn't eat nothin'. Couldn't speak 'cept for a squeak now and then.'

Teddy said sturdily, 'Don't believe that.'

April enquired, 'Who was it Glad?'

'A girl,' Gladys said unspecifically. "Er said it was agony. Absolute agony.'

The phrase 'absolute agony' confirmed it for April. She quavered, 'I don't want it done.' Her voice rose. 'Mother! I don't want my tonsils out —' She stood up from the stairs where the three of them were sitting and ran down the passage towards the kitchen. 'Mother . . . Mother . . . I don't want —'

Teddy said, 'I reckon Bridget would faint if I spat blood. I'd like that.'

'What? Seeing her faint?' Gladys asked jealously.

'No, stupid. Spitting blood. I'd wait till dinner was all out on the table then I'd say excuse me and I'd —'

'You won't be able to talk. The girl what I'm tellin' you about, 'er couldn't talk. Just gave a squeak now and then.'

'All right then, stupid. I'd —'

Florence arrived post haste. 'What are you saying Gladys? I wish you wouldn't frighten April. I can assure you Teddy, there is nothing to having your tonsils out.'

'Have you had yours out?' Teddy asked directly.

'No, but . . .' Florence could not help smiling at the trap he had set for her. She put her arms around his delightful stockiness. 'Darling boy, do you think if there was the slightest risk I would permit you —'

Of course Teddy knew she would not. But April, snivelling in the background, knew that adults did things against their wishes sometimes.

'Listen.' Florence gathered them both to her. 'You be good about this and you can have a present. Nothing to do with Christmas or birthdays. An extra present.'

'What?' Teddy pounced.

'Anything. Anything you like. Within reason.'

Teddy looked at April and took a breath. 'A scooter?' he asked.

'Yes. All right.' Florence did some quick reckoning.

The Risings were still rising. 'Yes. I think I can promise you a scooter.'

Teddy smiled beatifically. 'We'll be good.'

April whispered, 'It won't hurt, Mamma?'

'We'll be *good*, April,' Teddy said sternly.

April bit her lip. It was all right for Teddy. He had gone on having accidents in spite of the lesson he had learned on Mr. Goodrich's tree. He simply was never frightened.

She went to Barton Street with her father, and while he had coffee with Mrs. Daker, she stood shyly at the counter staring across it at David. He stared back quizzically, his head on one side.

'Well my Sweet Primrose?'

She looked uncomprehending.

'April brings the primrose sweet —'

She finished triumphantly, 'Scatters daisies at our feet!'

He smiled. 'That's better. You forgot to be shy. Now — what can I do for you?'

She had to disentangle her tongue from her back teeth, then clear her throat. 'Teddy and me . . . Teddy and I . . . have to have our tonsils out. Next week. We have to go to the infirmary and have our tonsils out.'

He looked at her for a long moment with his black eyes blank, then his mouth turned up slightly as if he'd thought of something pleasant. He came around the counter and lifted her on to it.

'You're scared,' he said, with just a touch of scorn.

She flushed. 'I'm not —'

'You're scared like you were when I chased you up the stairs and into the bathroom.'

'I wasn't scared. And afterwards . . . I wasn't scared. I enjoyed it!'

He flung back his head and laughed and she saw the way his Adam's apple bobbed in his throat like a marble in the neck of a ginger-ale bottle.

He said, 'Things that are frightening are also

159

exciting, April. Remember how you faced up to being scared and called me a wicked name? What was it?'

She shook her head.

'All right then, don't say it again. But you must use it inside your head about the tonsils. Do you understand?'

She looked at him. After a while she nodded very slightly.

He said briskly, 'Good. It shouldn't be hard. Look it in the eye. You'll have gas — a face mask I expect. You breathe very deeply and then you sleep. That is all.'

She thought about it doubtfully. Then she came to the important part. 'Afterwards . . . after the bathroom . . . you danced with me. That was what made it so exciting.'

He seemed to consider, though he knew already what he was going to say, she could tell from the smile which still pulled up the long thin mouth.

'You won't feel like dancing. But I'll visit you. Every day I'll call on you if your mamma will permit it.'

April let out a great sigh. 'She will permit it. Oh David. . . .'

He tucked some of the mass of dark gold hair beneath her bonnet and his smile became wide and open.

'Oh April . . . Primrose Sweet.' He lifted her to the floor again and prepared to join the others in the parlour. 'Remember, you can only be brave if you are frightened first.'

April knew this was true because her father had reported similar strange paradoxes from old Mr. Daker's repertoire. And old Mr. Daker was next to a disciple.

They made a detour via Eastgate Street on their way to the infirmary. Marshall's Toys wasn't open at that hour in the morning — they had to present themselves at Outpatients by nine o'clock — but the scooter was still displayed in the window after nearly a year.

'It must be dear if no-one can afford to buy it,' April said apprehensively, looking at her mother, clinging desperately to the thought of dark David who brought ecstasy with him.

'Stupid!' scoffed Teddy. 'They've sold dozens! They send to the factory for more each time they sell one.' He glanced up at Florence. 'Girls are silly sometimes Mamma, aren't they?'

'What would you do without April?' Florence reminded him gently.

Teddy frowned with concentration, then admitted generously, 'I couldn't go to school without April. And nothing is so much fun if she isn't there.' He looked around his mother's skirt at his pale sister. 'I love you,' he said frankly. 'And March and May.' He glanced at the gleaming red scooter. 'And Bridget,' he added.

'What about Albert and Papa?' prompted Florence, urging the children inexorably away from the window and towards the Cross.

'Of course.' He looked surprised that she could ask. 'And you. You more than me,' he concluded matter-of-factly.

Florence swallowed. Her own love did not blind her to the fact that Teddy was innately selfish; his charm lay in the fact that he knew it. So she had to believe him now. She closed her eyes, momentarily dazzled by the grey January morning. The years since Teddy's birth had been filled with such joy and peace that she thanked God for them every day. She thanked him now and added a fervent prayer that the forthcoming operation would not hurt her son. Quickly — hardly an afterthought — she included April in the prayer. The she opened her eyes and looked down at April, bonnet brim tipped towards the pavement.

She said, 'We'll play snakes and ladders this afternoon April, shall we?'

The bonnet brim came up. 'That would be nice Mamma.' April tried to smile. 'I am expecting David to call too.'

Florence squeezed the small hand. 'Gentleman callers already,' she teased.

'Oh David belongs to May,' April said seriously. 'But she won't mind. May never minds sharing anything.'

Florence thanked God again. May, her favourite until Teddy's birth, was not only beautiful, but since her visit to Bath many years ago, was strong too. And with the disposition of an angel as well as the looks. Sometimes Florence wondered whether she was too fortunate. A devoted husband and five lovely children, a beautiful, spacious home and enough money to help others. She turned into Southgate Street, prompting the children to say their good mornings to the old newspaper-seller already ensconced there. From her cramped and sunless childhood had sprung this flowering. And all because of Will. Dear Will.

April was never to forget the ordeal of having her tonsils out. The lights, the indignity of the gag in her mouth, the gas — she never understood why it was called laughing gas — that threatened to suffocate her forever, enclosed as she was in a mask too big for her. But most of all it was the lights, which burned into her as electric light was to do for the rest of her life, and silhouetted the gargantuan figures who bore down upon her and consisted only of eyes . . . eyes . . . eyes . . . then her mother, gently patting her cheeks and saying, 'It's all over and done with, little April. Come back to the big wide world . . . it's all over and done with.' And then the racking sobs came that hurt her throat and made her spit blood just as Gladys had prophesied.

A nurse delivered Teddy into Florence's arms; he was already coming round. She supported the two of them, April one side, Teddy the other. When Teddy lifted a groggy head and whispered hoarsely, 'Can we go and get the scooter now Mamma?' she wept and laughed at the same time. April never forgot that either.

Fred Luker came for them in his Austin. The nurse

gave April a fresh gauze pad and told Teddy not to keep talking. There were other instructions too, about food and drink. Lots of water. April knew she would never swallow again. Fred carried her out to his car where it said 'Ambulances only' and tucked her into the back seat, clucking all the while. April found it a most comforting sound. When Teddy started to speak, Fred stopped clucking long enough to say, 'Tha's enough young 'un. You 'eard what that there nurse told you.'

At last they were back home. April had never been so pleased to see it before and the sight of Will provoked more tears. Albert, who hated 'waterworks' as much as ever, spent an unusually long day in the workroom from where it was almost impossible to hear the distress of his sister. Teddy looked at the group around April's bed, his father holding her while she retched, his mother stroking her sweat-dark hair, his other sisters running back and forth with basins; he had found the lights and the masked men very interesting, and his throat was no sorer now than it had been when he had tonsillitis. If April thought to have a lion's share of the scooter by making so much fuss, she must have another think. Grinning to himself, Teddy curled up in his bed and slept.

David came in the evening. He was not allowed to see April who was sleeping at last, so he sat with March and May in the parlour and talked about the new National Health Insurance Act which Mr. Lloyd George was presenting to Parliament. March was too proud to ask for enlightenment, but May questioned him closely and thought it sounded very fair .

'Not for me. Nor for your father,' David said in his young-cynical voice. 'We're our own employers, so the ninepence for fourpence nonsense won't help us much, will it?'

'No ... but *we* can help ourselves,' said May. 'I expect Mr. Lloyd George is thinking of all the people who are in the *power* of their overseers and such like.'

'Or thinking of himself and his own political future.' David said quickly before May's sweetness could bring him to his knees. Her fairness shone like a sun in the gas-lit parlour and made March look plain and prim by contrast. He wished March would go away and wondered whether Florence had commanded her to stay as a chaperone. His heart quickened at the thought; did they take him that seriously? He had loved May for nearly a year and she must guess that his call on April was merely a ploy to see her. Yet she was so young and so innocent . . . innocent as the day she was born. How this could be when her close friend was the Luker girl, he did not know, yet so it was.

March said suddenly, 'Could Father — and you — stick the whole ninepenny stamp on your card? That would be fair, wouldn't it?'

David was at a loss, but would not admit it. He looked at March's clear, light-brown eyes and thoroughly disliked her.

'I can't see anyone agreeing to sticking stamps on a card,' he scoffed. 'The British John Bull is a sight too intelligent for that, I'll be bound!'

'Probably,' said March, losing interest. She and Albert still found David Daker insufferable; it was one of the few topics they could discuss fluently. The way May and Sibbie whispered and giggled about him made her absolutely sick. And April was as bad. She stood up. 'I'll fetch some more coal.' She took her time picking up the bucket, expecting David to be there before her. He made no move and she knew he wanted her gone. She walked stiffly into the hall where Rags met her, mewing to be let out into the frosty night. Deliberately she stumbled into him and sent him yowling ahead of her into the kitchen. 'You nearly sent me flying Rags!' she said loudly, in case Florence was within earshot. But no-one was downstairs, they were with April, or entertaining David Daker or sitting late in the workroom over something quite unnecessary. She opened the kitchen door

164

and watched Rags scutter through it. If only Aunt Lizzie would come home. If only she could get a job as a secretary. If only Uncle Edwin hadn't mentioned Harry Hughes' name to the bishop. If only . . . if only . . . if only Albert really loved her. As she loved him.

David said, 'May. I wish to ask you something. Privately.'

May said comfortably, 'Certainly David.' She smiled encouragingly. This was a potentially romantic situation and she must remember every detail to share with Sibbie at school tomorrow. The glowing fire, the gaslight on David's wiry hair — it was a pity it was so very bushy — his intense dark eyes.

Suddenly he dropped to one knee before her and put his hands on the arms of her chair so that she could not get up.

'May. Dearest, beautiful May. Will you marry me?'

May gasped and sat tight back as far as she could from the intense dark eyes which were now much too serious. She wanted to clutch at the arms of the chair and push herself further away, but that would mean touching his hands. There were dark hairs along the backs of his hands. He must be seventeen now. Seventeen.

He said, 'May, I didn't mean to frighten you. You must know I love you to distraction.'

She said squeakily, 'It's all right. I'm not frightened. But I think you had better sit up again. March will be back and will think it most odd to see you down there.'

'But May . . . I love you!'

'Oh David. Oh David.' She clasped her hands on her lap and gripped hard. 'Oh David . . . I'm only thirteen!'

He lowered his head and there was a sense of respite. 'I'm sorry dearest, I meant to wait. I really did. But I cannot think of anything else but you — all day and all night. Just give me a word — one word and I'll be patient. Say you'll think of marrying me.'

165

Without his eyes on her she could see it all as wonderfully romantic again. Nevetherless she still repeated helplessly, 'I'm only thirteen.'

He looked up and fixed his eyes on her. 'You'll be fourteen in three months, May. Will you give me an answer then? Juliet was fourteen.'

It was the right thing to say. Juliet. Romeo and Juliet. It was so romantic. She wanted desperately to get away and think about it, she also wanted to giggle.

'I don't know what to say. Please sit up David. I'm worried about your trousers and whether March will come in — and all sorts of things! I can't think about it properly.'

He coughed a sort of laugh. 'Oh May. Sweetness — yes, you are truly sweetness itself. I'll sit up if you will tell me you think of me just a little.'

'I think of you often David.'

'And you do not hate me?' he persisted.

'I would hardly visit the shop with Papa if I hated you.'

'Then you must love me a little.'

'I don't know! I talk of you and I think of you and I like you —'

'It is enough! There, I keep my promise.' He stood up, dragged a hassock to her chair and squatted by her, clasping one of her hands in both of his. 'Just go on thinking of me. All the time. Believe that I am thinking of you. We will see each other as often as we can and when you are sixteen — oh God, two whole years — we will be married.'

May was alarmed. 'Oh David. I'm not sure. Really.'

He laughed, his dark face radiant. 'You will be sure by then my darling.' He pressed her hand to his cheek and she felt the heat of his skin. 'Oh May. I did not mean to speak so soon. Surely not many girls become engaged when they are thirteen —'

'David, I have not become engaged!'

166

'Just between us May,' he pleaded. 'A secret. It will be fun.'

May bit her lip. That was true.

He stood up, knowing when to leave.

'Remember when you go to bed tonight my love, David is thinking of you. Every hour of every day he is thinking of you.'

It was so innocuous, no harm in it at all. May put her hands to her face, glad that he had gone, yet regretful too. She went to the mirror and looked at herself. Her hair was wild and her face unbecomingly red. She stared, then began to giggle. She could hardly wait to see Sibbie tomorrow morning.

By the end of the week Teddy was scampering along the landing in his bare feet, playing through the banisters with Rags and even slipping into the freezing bandy room to pick out a tune on the piano's black notes. April stayed where she was, improving daily but unwilling to leave the security of her bed. She wondered too whether David would stop his daily visits once she was up. He came promptly at seven each evening and sat with her until Florence brought up bread and milk at half-past. Then he pretended to eat a spoonful himself and fed her in between. The agony of swallowing was nothing when he was there. Once, when she was particularly fretful and refused to drink water, he seized her wrist and twisted the skin. 'How much of this can you stand, little April?' She bore it gaspingly for several seconds, then he held the glass to her lips. 'Quickly. Drink now. It won't hurt any more.' And with her wrist still burning and smarting, it hardly did. She told her father about it and he laughed his surprise and recounted once again his early experiences with old Mr. Daker. April understood it all. You paid first for happiness. She was happier than she had been for ages because David came to see her every day. And she had paid for it by having her tonsils out.

167

Bridget and Tolly came as usual to play with the invalids. Bridget had a nurse's uniform and donned it with great importance.

'I'm going to look after you,' she announced. 'Tolly, you get into April's bed and I'll take your temperature.' She extracted an enamelled tin thermometer and shook it busily. 'Hurry up Tolly. April, make room for him and lie down. You're at Death's Door.'

'I'll be the doctor,' Tolly said quickly, not liking the look of April's rumpled bed. 'Then I can play snakes and ladders with April and take her mind off her troubles.'

Bridget looked at him scornfully as she jabbed the thermometer into Teddy's mouth. 'Miss Midwinter sent her best wishes to you both and Miss Alicia asked if she might call with some hot-house grapes. I said yes.'

'Oh yes,' mumbled Teddy happily. He removed the thermometer. 'Hot-house grapes and a scooter.' He looked slyly at Bridget.

Momentarily confused she stared at him. 'Scooter? Oh the scooter. I'm doing my best Teddy dear, you must be patient.'

'No need.' He passed the thermometer across beds to April. 'No need at all is there April?'

'Mmm?'

'No need to be patient about the scooter,' he reminded her significantly. Then giving up all pretence at finesse, he blurted, 'We've got it thank you Bridget Williams. And no thanks to you!' he added contradictorily.

'How do you mean, you've got it?'

'We got it for having our tonsils out bravely!' he informed her triumphantly. 'Our own mother and father bought it for us and it is to be delivered next week when we are 'llowed to go outside.'

Bridget stared for only another instant, then she heaved a gigantic sigh of relief. 'Thank goodness.' She smiled modestly. 'I thought it would take longer than this.' She marched over to April, removed the thermometer, examined it and shook it down vigorously. 'But you're right of course. No need for gratitude.'

Teddy spluttered annoyance and April and Tolly stared. Bridget held up her hands. 'It's my doing. Idiots. You didn't think it just *happened* did you?'

'How your doing?' Teddy jumped out of bed with frustration. 'How can it be your doing when you didn't even know about it?'

'I knew all right. But not when it would come, nor how it would happen.' Bridget sighed again. 'I *prayed* for it. Every morning and every night. I prayed to God to send Teddy Rising a scooter from Marshall's Toy shop. And He did.' She spoke quietly, reverently, casting her eyes to the ceiling. Teddy tugged furiously at his nightshirt.

'I told you. Our mother and father bought it!'

'They were instruments.' Bridget had a good repertory of words. It was one of the many things April missed about Midland Road, the session when they 'collected words'. Bridget put away the thermometer and produced a stethoscope. 'Yes. They were instruments of God. And *I* asked God to send you the scooter.' She fitted the earpieces in position and said thoughtfully, 'I must remember to say thank you in Sunday School.'

Teddy's nightshirt creaked threateningly as he tugged it down as if holding in his temper. 'You don't have to wait till Sunday to say thank you,' was all he could find to say.

'It's better then. God's always in church.' Bridget's smug matter-of-factness was too much for Teddy, he collapsed back on his bed groaning.

'Does it hurt Teddy dear?' Bridget was over him anxiously. 'Now just lie quiet — give me the thermometer April — oh, I've got it in my bag — I'll just wipe this fluff off —' Teddy groaned again because it stopped Bridget talking about God. She devoted all her attention to him, smoothing his forehead, then gently brushing his hair. It was delightful. He might marry her one day then he'd be looked after all the time. He opened his eyes and mumbled through the tin-tasting tube, 'Wanna gla water.'

'A glass of water my darling?' Bridget crooned above him. 'There's none in the jug. Eridget will get it for you.' Apparently she was nurse no longer. She ran off downstairs while Teddy chewed on the tin and April and Tolly climbed ladders and fell down steps and hardly realised time passed.

In the kitchen March said, 'What do you want? I'm supposed to be laying the tea and I certainly don't want you under my feet.'

Bridget was always wary of March. She said, 'I only want some water for poor Teddy. I'm looking after him in my nurse's uniform. D'you like it March? I've got a thermometer and a stethoscope and lots of bottles of pretend medicine and —'

'Get the water and go on upstairs then.' March tried to shoo the child away kindly but she longed with all her soul to shove her hard. Bridget's good background was her only excuse in March's opinion: apart from that she was impossible, encouraging Teddy in his rowdiness and making him think he was so wonderful. March banged down five plates and thought bitterly that it would be she who took a tray for three upstairs. No, a tray for four, Tolly Hall was there too! She began to cut very thin bread, having to spread Goodrich's yellow butter to hold it together.

She bit her lip angrily. Children were all spoiled now; she remembered when she and Albert and May had been little, how they had had to work. When April was born she had done all the washing for weeks until Aunt Lizzie had rescued her from drudgery. She thought of Aunt Lizzie and her anger melted into tears. If only she could be with her, how different it would all be. Then she frowned suddenly at a recent recollection, her thoughts

170

switching unexpectedly to Teddy and April. Was Bridget really putting a toy thermometer in their mouths?

Tolly and April were deep into their game, so as usual, all Bridget's attention was lavished on Teddy. She held him in the crook of her arm while he sipped at the water, then she kissed him and laid him gently back on the pillow. 'Now I have to listen to your chest.'

She fitted the stethoscope into her ears again and lifted his nightshirt. He woke up suddenly and pushed it down, but not before Bridget, only child, had seen what she had seen. Her eyes opened wide.

He said, 'You can get down my neck. Not up there, if you don't mind.' But he was grinning without embarrassment because he shared a bath with April and in any case had never had inhibitions since those early days when he had 'performed' almost anywhere and received nothing but praise.

Bridget's curiosity was thoroughly aroused. 'No, I can't. There isn't room. Besides, I have to examine you. All over.'

'Oh no you don't —'

'I *do*! I'm your nurse and you have to do exactly what I tell you. Besides,' she looked pious again. 'You shouldn't argue with me Teddy. Not after I arranged for you to have that scooter.'

He sighed exasperation but lay back resigned, eyes closed. 'Oh. . . . all right.'

His nightshirt came up and the stethoscope was cold on his chest. But not for long. 'I might have to hurt you a bit,' Bridget said briskly. 'You must try to be brave.'

'I am brave. Always.' But she did hurt. He dared not open his eyes to see what she was doing and was surprised April did not protest. But April and Tolly were deep in their card game and Bridget had her back to them.

And then the door opened.

Bridget had his nightshirt down and the bedclothes

up in an instant, but March had seen. She stopped for a moment, affronted and shocked beyond words. Teddy clasped the sheet to his chin and said defiantly, 'Bridget's a nurse. She's got a proper uniform look March, and here's her ther — thermom —'

March recovered herself and walked around the cringing Bridget to place the tray on the bamboo table between the beds. 'Thermometer,' she said smoothly. 'It's called a thermometer Teddy. Now, I've cut this bread and butter very thinly, so I want you two to have a slice each. And there's milk to drink. Bridget, perhaps you will see to things, dear.'

Bridget could hardly believe her ears. She busied herself at the tea tray, eyes down, and after a few moments of plumping April's pillows and looking over her shoulder at her hand of cards, March left them again. Bridget avoided Teddy's eyes as she passed the bread and butter, but Teddy himself seemed not to realise anything was unusual.

March was waiting in the hall when Bridget and Tolly came downstairs.

'You father is here Tolly,' she said, wrapping him in his coat and handing him his cap. 'In the kitchen talking to Albert.' She turned to Bridget. 'Your car isn't here yet Bridget, but you may as well put your coat on ready.' She watched, leaning against the newel, as Bridget struggled into her thick coat alone. The gas hissed and Tolly could be heard laughing in the kitchen. 'Sit on the hall chest to change your shoes,' she instructed in the same detached voice. The small girl obeyed, red-faced and silent. March waited until she was in bonnet and gloves, then she said, 'Bridget, you've been putting that awful tin thermometer in Teddy's and April's mouths, haven't you?'

Bridget looked up for a startled instant, then whispered, relieved, 'Yes March.'

'Do you realise it has probably poisoned them?'

Another startled pause then Bridget gasped, 'Oh no, they use them in hospital! I know!'

'In hospital they are made of glass and they are clean.'

'This one is clean March! Look — I wiped it on my hanky — look —' she began to tug open the little case containing her toys. March held up her hand.

'They have to be boiled, Bridget. To kill the germs.'

'Oh . . . oh March!'

'If Teddy or April should die, it will be your fault,' March continued implacably.

Bridget's eyes looked about to fall out. March went on, 'We will say nothing about that. Nor anything else that happened this afternoon, Bridget. Do you understand me?'

Bridget was a long time understanding, but at last she nodded, terrified.

'On one condition,' March paused. She had not had long to think this out and she did not like confiding in this child even if she did have her in the palm of her hand. But there was nothing else for it. 'I want a job Bridget. I want to be a secretary. Do you know what I mean?'

Bridget stared anew, another long time taking in the change of topic. March prompted impatiently, 'Well? Do you know what I mean by a secretary?'

Bridget nodded again. 'Like Miss Pym is Grandfather's secretary,' she whispered.

March was satisfied. 'Like Miss Pym,' she agreed. 'You are to persuade your father — or your grandfather — to give me a position as a secretary, Bridget. If you will do that we will say nothing about this afternoon.'

Bridget sobbed, but she understood now. These were the tactics used at school. Secrets were kept by a system of barter.

She said, 'Daddy and Grandfather have already got Miss Pym, March! What can I do? They won't listen to me. Not even Mamma is allowed to talk about the business! Oh March — I can't — I can't!'

'I think you can,' March said with more assurance than she actually felt. 'I think Miss Pym has too much work to do for the two of them. I think she would enjoy training me. And I am very efficient and come from a good family . . . you know all this Bridget. Surely you can remember it by yourself?'

Bridget was sobbing rhythmically now, but little hiccoughing sobs that did not interfere with her hearing. She nodded quickly as March paused. Then she said, 'And you promise you won't tell them about Teddy? I couldn't bear it if they knew about — about —'

March smiled. 'There's your father now, isn't it? I think I hear the bell. . . . Of course I won't mention the business of the —' she hesitated deliberately, looking down at Bridget with her transparent eyes. 'Of course I won't even breathe the word thermometer!' She opened the heavy front door and walked to the car. 'Ah Mr. Williams. Will you come in for a few minutes?' She knew he would not. The car throbbed obediently but was difficult to start and Mr. Williams did not have a flair with the handle like Fred. They exchanged pleasantries as Bridget climbed in beside her father. Edward Williams had always been glad of his daughter's friendship with the Risings, believing that the large family must be good for his only child. Besides, Miss Midwinter had assured him of their excellent background.

He said, 'Thank your mother once again for her hospitality Miss Rising, won't you?'

Bridget piped up quickly, 'Oh, it was March who got our tea and carried it up on a tray and looked after us Daddy. March is very official.'

Mr. Williams laughed. 'I think you mean efficient my darling. There's a nice compliment for you Miss Rising. And unsolicited too.'

March, pleased with Bridget's quick wit, sighed,

174

'I've just been confiding my ambitions to your daughter Mr. Williams. She has a sympathetic ear.'

Edward Williams suppressed a smile at this fifteen-year-old's quaint phrases. But he also approved them.

'I've never noticed it myself Miss Rising,' he teased.

Bridget protested and, amid the laughter, they drove away.

March bit her lip again and wondered. Still, even if it came to nothing at all, it had probably scared the girl out of her wits and she'd never touch Teddy again. Horrible little madam. And Teddy deserved a jolly good smacking for permitting her to do such a thing.

Dick thrust his way into the kitchen a week later and announced in his gruff mumble that he was 'off'. Will and Florence were clearing up after a picnic tea eaten half in the kitchen, half in the bedroom with the two invalids. Will was looking forward to his evening visit to his mother with her quota of sewing for the next day. Doubtless he would bump into Hettie somewhere along the way.

He said, 'Don't follow you, Dick old man. If you're off to the Lamb and Flag, that's not news. I'll join you myself later.' He guffawed, but Florence frowned, looking at Dick as he stood huge and uncomfortable by the gas stove.

'I'm off to London,' Dick said briefly. 'Where I went before. There's a living of sorts to be got there — no-one will 'ave me down 'ere with my record. I'll send money back when I can but I want you to keep an eye on Sylv.'

Will was surprised but not displeased. Florence was aghast.

'Dick — you cannot leave Sylvia now! You are all she's got.'

'She's got Daze. An' 'er ma. I can't give 'er nuthin'. Not now.'

Florence was horrified at the hardness of him and the finality of his decision.

'What does she say?'

'I must do what I please.'

Florence looked at Will in distress and could see she would get no help from him. Her mind was overworked with concern for Teddy and April, but she did her best. For ten abortive minutes she argued with the silent adamant Dick. When she gave up at last, standing before him drooping, he said, 'I dun't want her sent away. She en't daft nor nothin'.'

'Dick of course we won't —'

'An' I don't want 'er ma to keep pesterin' 'er to work. She dun't want to do nuthin' except sit. She'll heal 'erself soon enough.'

'She will. I know she will, Dick. But what if she is ill — how can we get in touch with you?'

He shrugged and said nothing. After a few more moments he held out his hand and Florence perforce took it. She remembered how she had seen him first, chained and in uniform. If she had been a different type of woman she might have wished that Sylvia had hever clapped eyes on him: he had brought very little happiness with him.

Will said, 'I'll walk down the street with you.'

Florence said, 'Oh *Dick* — goodbye.'

He barged awkwardly to the door. 'Look after Sylv,' he said again. And followed Will into the night.

Once in the street, he overtook Will and put his foot on the doorstep at thirty-three as if barring Will's way.

'We'll say goodbye 'ere I reckon Will. Dun't want Sylv upset nor nuthin'.' He did not give his hand to his brother-in-law. Will, hoping to see Hettie, murmured something. Dick said, 'I dun't want you seeing Hettie Luker while I be gone. 'Tisn't safe and will get back to Flo one o'these days.'

Will blustered. 'What the devil are you talking about man?'

'I saw you, dun't you recall? I sawed the two of you last year and I've kep' me eye open since. Without me 'ere, Mam's goin' to twig dam quick, then there'll be trouble. So dun't go seein' 'er no more.' There was no condemnation in the level voice.

Will said angrily, 'I don't know what business it is of yours —'.

'Sylv loves your Flo,' Dick explained simply. 'I 'ad to tell 'er about Hettie Luker so she can make sure no word gets out.' He paused while Will continued to splutter his outrage, then said, 'Dun't excite yourself Will. Sylv en't goin' to say nuthin' to no-one in case it gets back to Flo. But 'er'll 'ave a word with you mind, if there's any more of it!'

And with these admonitory words — from Dick Turpin of all people — he opened the door of Will's old home, went in and closed it behind him. Will had a glimpse of splintering boards in the hall and a smell of mice, then Chichester Street was his again.

He stood there and swore quietly into the damp February air. It was bad enough Dick knowing, but Sylv! He wouldn't be able to look at her again, he wouldn't be able to face her. His own sister.

Then a deeper sadness took hold of him. He had lost Hettie. He'd have to lose her, he couldn't risk keeping her. And part of him loved Hettie.

Sibbie said, 'I couldn't come round last night. Our mam was that upset! I don't know what's got into her. She sits and cries and rocks herself all the time . . . it's awful May.'

'Perhaps you should have the doctor,' May suggested. 'He's coming round to see Teddy again today. Should I run back and ask Mother to send him to you afterwards?'

'Better not. She'd skin me for running up a bill. Fred says he'll put a drop of brandy in her stout tonight and see if that'll buck her up.' She tucked her hand in her

177

friend's arm. 'Tell me what David said last night. Did he get down on his knees again?'

May giggled. It was a typical February morning and Florence had lent the girls her grey umbrella. May lowered it over their heads, giving them a spurious privacy, and felt with her free hand in her pocket. 'He went down on his knees the moment Mamma took April up to bed,' she said. 'And the next minute, he gave me . . . this!' She opened her gloved hand and there, gleaming, was a ring with a single garnet in a claw setting.

Sibbie stopped in her tracks and drew in a hissing breath. 'May! Is it real? Is it an engagement ring?'

'He didn't say — mind the brolly spoke in your eye Sib — he just asked me to keep it. Then he put it on my finger for size and kissed it! He kissed the ring and my finger! He sealed it there — isn't it the most romantic thing you have ever heard in the whole of your life?'

Sibbie was a-twitter, jumping up and down and jogging the umbrella so that the rain poured down her neck. 'You're engaged May! You're engaged, and you're only thirteen! Oh May!' She threw her arms around her friend's neck and hugged her ecstatically.

At last they reached the school playground, late as usual. Miss Pettinger was counting the heads in each line and they joined their class just in time.

Sibbie hissed, 'Oh May . . . I do love you. We still share everything, don't we?'

'Of course,' hissed back May, one eye on Miss Pettinger. 'I've got blackcurrant jam — from our own bushes. What have you got?'

'Dripping. As usual. But we share everything, don't we May?'

'Of course,' May said again and remembered David and his complete devotion. It was quite worrying in a way. A responsibility. She was glad she had Sibbie to confide in.

It was Doctor Green's fourth visit in four days. He used a

tablespoon to look down Teddy's throat, then he felt all around his neck and took his temperature and pulse. On the landing he frowned and sucked in his lips consideringly.

Florence gripped her hands. 'Is it diphtheria Doctor?' she asked.

'I don't think so Mrs. Rising. If it was diphtheria there would be signs in April. I've also visited Kitty Hall and her little Bartholomew is very healthy. He's been here frequently I understand.'

'Yes.' Florence tried to smile. 'If only it's not diphtheria —'

'It's a very severe infection, Mrs. Rising. He has a nasty throat and a high temperature. I am wondering whether the fever hospital —'

'Oh no! Please Doctor! Surely we can look after him at home?'

'It is not easy. You will need a sheet at the door, soaked in disinfectant. Separate dishes and cutlery — everything sterilised.'

'We can manage Doctor. Teddy must not go away.'

'Very well. Yes. If you're sure. I'll be back this afternoon with some medicine. Meanwhile, if you can get him to drink some milk it will help to sustain him.'

'Yes. Yes of course.' Florence left March to see the doctor out and went back to Teddy. She was anxious, but not frantic by any means. Teddy had survived so much and he had recovered from his operation better than April had done. Now he grinned at her in quite his old way and whispered, 'Has the scooter come Mamma?'

'Yes my darling boy. We've put it in the stables, but you may try it up and down the passage as soon as you get well.'

He murmured, 'Let April have it.'

Florence smiled as she began to sponge his forehead. 'It's for both of you dearest. But April won't want to try it until you are well.'

He frowned and said quite fiercely, 'That's silly. Make

179

her have a go now. Right now.'

He became so fretful about it that Florence went downstairs and asked Albert to fetch her a cabbage, and while he was at it to bring back the new scooter from the stables. Only when Teddy could hear April dabbing her foot frantically up and down the hall, did he smile and close his eyes. Then the sheet was hung at his door and he and Florence were together until his death a week later.

On the day of his funeral it rained unceasingly for twenty-four hours and that evening's *Citizen* was full of news of the floods, not only at the Causeway and Sandhurst, but girdling the city itself as the many streams entering the Severn rose and burst their banks. The black umbrellas clustered around Teddy's grave like an outcrop of mushrooms and the handful of earth thrown on the tiny white coffin was a mud-pat in three seconds flat. Will and Albert supported Florence somehow and her two eldest girls stood close to her, while her sister-in-law was behind her.

Somehow a message had been got to the Rising uncles, and they clustered around their mother. Other members of the family from cottages and in service around Newent who had never seen Teddy, lurked unsheltered by the grim avenue of poplars and bared their heads to the cruel rain as the vicar's voice intoned dust to dust and ashes to ashes.

April, at home with Gran, let out a high wail just at this moment and held out her arms as if she could keep Teddy back from wherever he was going. But no-one had been able to hold Teddy in life, let alone in death. His motivation had always been curiosity unbridled by fear or apprehension. His last words had been 'Don't cry Mamma. I'm not going to cry.' And Florence, true to her character as well as her promise, had not wept again. They all wished she would. Her dark, blank eyes reminded them horribly of Aunty Sylv; her helpless idle hands more so. Three times since his death she had

180

fainted without warning, and Doctor Green asked
March to be sure to give her a slice of raw chopped liver
every day with her other food. She refused it steadfastly.
She had eaten it before to stay alive for Teddy.

The floods receded slowly. In Barnwood the Williams
were cut off from their work and school, but their newly-
acquired telephone brought them the news of the Risings' loss. They told Bridget as gently as possible and she
took it without blinking or speaking. That night, as soon
as it was dark, she left the house and walked as far as
the Pitch where the water lay dark and deep, guarding
Northgate Street like a moat. Carefully she waded into it
until she was up to her neck, shivering, weeping and hysterical. Then shrieking, 'Teddy! Teddy!' she threw herself forward and for five terrible minutes of chaos was
borne up by her clothes, during which time the boat
which ferried people across the floods heard her
screams and rescued her unharmed.

Two weeks later when she was taken to school again,
she threw herself in front of a tram and would have been
killed if her father had not scooped her frantically to him
and hurled them both to the ground.

Again she was hysterical and her father took her to his
office in King's Lane and held her to him while she
sobbed herself quiet. 'My darling girl . . .' his worry and
grief made him sob too. 'I know you are terribly sad at
losing your little friend, but you must learn to bear these
griefs. Teddy is safe in heaven.' They had already told
her this a dozen times, but it seemed not to help her at all.
He changed his tactics. 'Listen Bridget. Is there anything
— anything at all — your mother and I can do to make it
better? Would you like April to come and stay with you
when you are well enough? Would you like to go away
somewhere — with her of course . . . anything, darling.'

Bridget held onto him tightly and her weeping gradually abated.

She whispered frantically, 'I want March to be . . . I
want to help March somehow. She wants to be a secre-

tary — I told you Daddy —'

'My dearest girl —'

'I know you laughed, but listen — please listen Daddy. If March could be your secretary I should feel I'd done something to help them all. It's the only thing — the only thing — oh Daddy, Daddy —'

He kissed the top of her head and rocked her until the next paroxysm of grief abated.

Then he said, 'I'll see what I can do. Yes, yes. I promise you, Bridie. All right dearest, don't cry, all right. . . .'

They clustered round Florence protectively, making sure she saw none of the many callers. But Harry Hughes was different. Harry brought the careless happiness of schooldays with him. February had given way to March and the wind howled around the house and bent the trees double.

He paid his respects and presented Florence with a tiny nosegay of snowdrops picked around the railway line at Longhope. They seemed to give her some pleasure.

'And I've got a new job. In the signal box at Churchdown.' He grinned at Albert. 'Still menial, but I can take signalling exams and try for a box of my own one day.'

Albert hit him between the shoulder blades, more animated than he'd been for months. 'That's splendid old man. D'you want lodgings? We can offer you any of the attic rooms I reckon. Can't we Mother?'

Florence smiled blindly and Harry said, 'I'm fixed up at Churchdown thanks old chap. But when my turns work out right, I could come in and we could go to old Filbert's choir practices. What d'you say?'

Albert glanced at March, expecting her to share his happiness.

'That will be marvellous. Won't it March? Won't it just?'

March found an excuse to leave the parlour and discovered the afternoon post lying on the hall floor. There was one for her. Typewritten.

She opened it without much interest. It was a letter requesting her to attend for an interview at Charles Williams and Son, Auctioneers of King's Street, on the third of the month. Tomorrow. Her birthday.

She looked at the window where the coloured glass glowed in spite of the windy sunless day. Harry was back. And she was going to be a secretary. She felt sick and cold.

She moved slowly to the stairs and sat on the polished wood, moving her sightless gaze to the row of felt slippers.

Then she lowered her head and wept.

9

The war came slowly to Gloucester. April thought it
would entail hiding in the apple trees and shooting at
Germans over the wall as they charged down Chichester Street in their funny policemen's hats. But as the
months dragged by and not even one Zeppelin hove in
sight over the cathedral spires, she felt let down. The
seven years without Teddy had been the Slough of
Despond, and like the Pilgrim, she thought anything,
even disaster, would be a better state.

The *Citizen* printed Mr. Asquith's speech in full, and
Will read it aloud to the whole family, sending over to
thirty-three for the other Risings and assembling them
solemnly in the kitchen as if they were already
besieged.

' "If I am asked what we are fighting for . . ." ' Will
had had to resort to glasses the previous year and he
paused and looked over them at the gathering of
women and children; Albert stood behind him reading
silently over his shoulder. ' ". . . vindicate the prin-
ciple that small nationalities —" '

'What does vindicate mean Daddy?' April interrupted.

Daisy corrected her scornfully, '*Vinegar* silly. He
said vinegar.'

Florence corrected in her quiet voice, 'No, it is vindicate dear. It means . . . er . . . what does it mean Will?'

Will hesitated and March said, 'It means justify.
Make good. Let's listen, *please*!'

' ". . . . that small nationalities are not to be crushed in defiance of international good faith by the arbitrary will of a strong and overmastering great Power." '
Will breathed deeply and removed his glasses. Albert took the paper and continued to read silently. Will said, 'In other words, we're not going to let little Belgium be ground underfoot by those Germans and their Kaiser.'

Gran looked bewildered. 'Belgium? What's they to us? That's what I wanna know. Never 'ardly 'eard of Belgium.'

'It explains it here Gran.' Albert went to her chair and squatted by her while he told her about the Treaty of London signed right back in 1839. She tutted exasperation at the foolishness of it all and rested her liver-marked hand on her favourite grandchild's shoulder. March and May exchanged glances. May had completed her apprenticeship at Helen's Hair Salon in Saint Aldate Street, and March had been at Williams' for six years. Both wondered what difference the war would make to their lives.

Florence voiced all their questions. 'What will it mean? To us, Will? What will it mean to us?'

Will took her hand and rubbed it comfortingly, but it was Gran who answered the question.

'Nuthin' at all,' she said scornfully. 'Not nuthin' at all. The wars out in Africa didn't alter nuthin' for us, and neither will this one.'

And it seemed she was right. Germany walked over Belgium and trenches were dug on the Western Front and it seemed like stalemate. Nobody was terribly interested in the Russian advance on the Eastern front, so nobody was very surprised when, on April's thirteenth birthday, news came through that they had been driven far back into their own country again. The horrors of Gallipoli and Mesopotamia were all so far away. A hospital was opened in Great Western Road: a series of wooden huts in which were practised the first ghastly attempts at skin grafting and piecing together broken faces. Food was short, but then it had never been plentiful. A munitions factory was opened in Brockworth which was a few miles past Bridget's house in Barnwood. A light railway ran to it from the station for transporting shells; Bridget told the Risings that the noise reminded her of California subway which she enjoyed. Mr. Edward arrived at the office in King's Street groaning because he had not been able to sleep.

Social life was more exciting: when a dance was in aid of Army welfare, Florence could hardly insist on a chaperone for her girls. It would be impugning the characters of those poor soldiers and they had surely suffered enough. So March, May and Sibbie soon were used to going out alone and being asked to dance by young men who had not been introduced. Albert refused to accompany them.

Otherwise Gloucester became a little more shabby and definitely less genteel. People with money were apt to take it to Cheltenham when it came to spending. The Promenade there was full of expensive, good quality shops, and customers were still treated with deference and not mere civility.

Ready-made clothes were Will's anathema. Denton's on the Cross supplied ready-made shirt-blouses and gym-slips for the girls at the high school. The Co-op could sell half a dozen navy-blue melton cloth winter coats in less time than it took him to measure one up. He undertook alterations for both shops, but alterations were well known to be slave labour. He paid Albert a wage; Florence, Sylv and his mother worked for their board and keep, he had no money to pay them. Of course once the war was over all the young men who had lived in uniform for so long would want suits. Meanwhile the Risings kept their head above water; March paid half the rent and May gave her mother five shillings a week towards the food. They were certainly not 'rising' any more.

Things were no better in the Barton and early in 1915 David surprised everyone by joining up. Mrs. Daker sold haberdashery, eked a precarious living, and blamed May for it.

Will had time on his hands and he was bored. He accepted that nothing would ever be the same without Teddy, but his spirit still craved the simple happiness which was its birthright. He rented some shooting on Robinswood Hill and he and Albert tried for a rabbit occasionally. He insisted on Florence taking a walk with him Sunday evenings after church, and he still loved the way she clung to his arm as they strolled through the park. It made him feel strong and protective. But then, when they got home, there was supper and May chattering about the wounded soldiers who had gathered at the back of the church behind the pillars where their poor faces could not be seen; and Florence would go to her room. And he to his.

He could not avoid Hettie Luker. She sat at her door in the summer evenings as she always had, calling across to Lottie or his own mother. When he took off his cap and stopped to speak to her, she had a way of watching his mouth and smiling that almost set him on fire. But though at first she had tried to persuade him to meet her in the stables at the Mews Lane entrance, he had always said 'Better not'. He could feel Sylv watching him and it was as if he had to spend the rest of his life proving to her that Dick had lied and there was nothing at all between himself and Hettie. Hettie appeared to hold no grudge. Her smile was always there for him. He could have gone mad with jealousy when Alf began boasting about his prowess again in the Lamb and Flag.

'Forty-five y'know Will. It's a good age to make a woman pregnant, you gotta admit. B'God, it en't for want of trying, I'll tell you that!'

Will could imagine and wished he could not.

He said, 'Seen the *Citizen*, Alf? Those poor devils are still on the beaches in Turkey. Thank God they sent the Colonials in there.'

'Ah. No-one in their right minds 'ud want to be out in that lot, eh? Some silly sod sent our Fred a white feather in the post yesty. He din't like it at all. I says to 'im I says, you stop at 'ome and keep the job going m'lad. Else we'll all be in the bloody wuk-'ouse!' Alf laughed and slapped his thigh. 'Our Fred in't too pleased about new babby. Not that much pleases 'im these days. 'E was all right when 'e could dash around in that blasted car of 'is, but since we went back to dray work, 'is face is like a yard o' pump water.'

'Things aren't the same,' Will said. 'Nothing's the same any more.'

Alf laughed again. He had something to laugh at after all. 'Old age, that's what got into you Will. Now drink up and get back to that pretty little woman of yours an' see what you can do!'

'Flo isn't the same either . . .' Will knew he'd drunk too much because tears gathered in his throat. 'She hasn't been the same since Teddy went.'

Alf recognised his mood and slipped easily into it. 'You're right there Will. 'E was a bright little whippersnapper. Everyone did think the world o' that kid o' yours.' He clapped Will's shoulder. 'Give 'er another one, man! Blimey, if I can do, so can you. Same age as my old Het, in't she?'

Will did not bother to answer him. He walked home unsteadily, thinking of Hettie's infidelity and the loss of Teddy.

'Still got Albert,' he muttered as he bolted the garden door behind him. 'Still got our Albert. And little April.'

In January Mr. Asquith decided that Lord Kitchener's volunteers were not sufficient to continue with the war, and the word conscription was printed in the *Citizen*. Fred Luker did not wait for his papers to arrive.

When March came out of the office in King's Street at six o'clock one bitterly cold February night, he was waiting for her beneath a gas lamp. She tried to brush past him as she had brushed past him so often before, but he would have none of it.

He fell into step beside her, his rough clothes contrasting oddly with her immaculately tailored suit. She was still thin, and shapeless, but her carriage was like her mother's and she looked a lady.

'I want a word with you March. If you please,' he said curtly, no longer slurring his words, every consonant sharp.

March said, 'I'm tired. I've been at work since half-past eight this morning.'

'I haven't.'

She refused to ask why not. She had not seen Fred Luker alone since that acrimonious meeting when she was fourteen. When they had been in each other's company she had realised he was making a great effort to 'better' himself. The old type of cab driver had disappeared; the new ones were more like chauffeurs in decent uniforms. But when the Lukers had sold off the Austin because of petrol shortage he had seemed to revert to type again.

He said irritably, 'I've signed on. Joined up. I'm going to be a gunner. Artillery.'

She stopped in her tracks. Her feet were so cold she couldn't feel them, and the tip of her nose could be like Lottie's for all she knew, but she forgot all that in sheer surprise.

'Why?'

He shrugged, suddenly embarrassed. 'They'd have taken me soon anyway. Besides ... I can't stick Chichester Street any longer.'

It was galling that so often Fred Luker's feelings mirrored her own.

She said, 'You fool. You've built up that business and now it'll go. Look at Daker's.'

189

He smiled, pleased she was showing interest. 'I thought about that. Pa will keep it going. Somehow. Just enough for me to have something to start on when I get back. And I'll be getting to know a lot more about mechanics.' His eyes gleamed at her in the lamplight. 'Don't you see March? I'll come out with a damned sight more than when I go in.' He took a deep breath. 'I'm going to buy a charrybang when I get out. When this lot's over. You see.'

'If you come out.' The war might not have affected them yet, but the casualty lists in the paper were evidence that they affected others.

'Christamighty March! I'll come out! You know the Lukers — they come out of anything!'

She looked at him for an instant, then turned up her collar and breathed into it to warm her nose. They rounded the cattle market past the Saracen's Head. He cleared his throat.

'It's like this March. I want to know where I stand with you. Before I go.'

She quickened her pace and straightened her back to ramrod stiffness. He hurried to keep up with her.

'Look here March — you might as well talk to me because I'm not going to let you go till you do!' Determination made him breathe heavily. 'I'm going off to the Front dammit all! You could at least give me a civil answer!'

She crossed the road ahead of him, her boots making the wooden blocks of the road squelch slightly. He stamped after her.

'You still think you're the high and mighty Risings, don't you?' A train rattled over the bridge, sending gobs of steam to enshroud them; the stink of sulphur was in their nostrils. March used the concealment to rub her nose frantically on her sleeve. Just like Lottie Jenner, she thought furiously, blaming Fred for that too.

'You're not rising any more!' he yelled as they

190

emerged into Northgate Street and turned by the pillar box. 'More like sinking I'd say! Yes, a damned sight more like sinking!'

'How *dare* you speak to me like that, Fred Luker,' she whirled on him furiously. 'How dare you raise your voice —'

'It was the bloody train making such a rattle,' he said sulkily.

'And swear! Who do you think you *are*?'

'Never mind all that, March. You didn't bother about keeping me in my place when you wanted me to teach you to drive, did you?' She drew in a breath and he went on hastily, 'All right, all right. We were kids then. And you wanted a favour of me. And you were right sweet to me. And you knew I loved you. Don't shake your head like that March, you knew it, kid or no kid. And I haven't changed — in that way. I still love you.'

She said quickly but in a low voice, 'Well, I don't love you. I'm sorry Freddy. I've tried to show you these last few years without being . . . hurtful. I can't help my feelings.'

Suddenly he caught her arm and held her back; she tried to shake him off and could not.

He said grimly, 'You'll never love anyone except your Albert — I've known that for a long time March!' He held her harder still as she struggled furiously, her face screwed up against even hearing him. 'But I think, up to a point, you *can* help your feelings, March! Yes, I'd say you can help them very well indeed!'

She kicked at him with her boots, only just holding herself from screaming because there might be people in the darkness. He shoved her roughly against the Goodrichs' wall and pinned her there with the weight of his body. The closeness of him was overwhelming and she knew she was near hysteria.

He said, 'Dammit, you'll listen to me if it's the last thing you do!' He grabbed her arms as her hands went for his face. 'You'd help your feelings all right, my girl, if I had a bit of cash, wouldn't you? That's why you never really broke with me — not proper you didn't. In case I struck it rich with the taxi. Wasn't that it March? Eh? Eh?'

He spoke right into her face whichever way she turned it. She gasped a sob. 'Get away — get *away* —'

'Why? Is there just a bit of feeling there you can't help, March? Marcie?' He pushed his mouth against hers before she could turn it again. He laughed breathlessly. 'There is — Christamighty, there is! You felt something then, all those years back, when you gave me your little-girl kisses!'

With a gigantic convulsion she pushed him off and began to stumble up the road. He ran with her, holding her arm to support her but not attempting to stop her again. They came to a gas lamp and she turned her face away in case he should see the tears and the running nose.

He said, 'March, just listen. I want you to marry me. One day I'll be rich, I promise you that. Then . . . when I'm rich . . . will you marry me?'

She tried to go faster but she had a stitch and her breath was like a dog's. She slowed enough to pant, 'I hate you! You shouldn't have said . . . what you did. It's only natural for a sister to love her brother! I hate you —'

He interrupted impatiently, 'I don't care about Albert. What goes on with you two — that's up to you. You can't marry him, that's for sure. And I'm the only person in the world who will understand about him. Christ, by the time I come home on leave he'll be gone too —'

He stopped as she halted and leaned over with a groan. She had spent sleepless nights already, praying fervently that Albert would never be called on to fight. She closed her eyes.

Fred released her arm at last and drew away. After a while she began to walk up the street and then he followed at a distance. She held her side, telling herself she had a stitch. She still hated him because just when she needed his support most he let her go on alone. Somehow she got indoors and left her coat and beret on the newel post, desperate to join Albert in the kitchen. And when she opened the door from the dark passage on to light and warmth, there he was laughing with Father over an awkward customer.

She looked at them all, seeing them anew. Mother was pouring tea for April and May, Aunt Sylv, still Mother's shadow, was buttering toast and cutting it into trian- gles, Daze was chasing a tea-leaf floating in her cup. March found her eyes were burning from the sudden change of temperature.

They often made her feel isolated and different, but tonight they made her feel lonely. If only it weren't so long until her week's summer holiday with Aunt Lizzie. If only Mr. Williams would give her two weeks' annual holiday instead of just one. If only Fred Luker hadn't said that about Albert. If only she had been content to stay in the workroom with Father so that it did not seem as though she had actually profited by Teddy's death. If only . . . if only. . . .

Florence said, 'Come by the fire March dear, you look perished. How good it is to have you home. Now we are all together.' Her look warmed March's very soul, and her words included Teddy; even Aunt Sylv's husband and dead baby. As March sipped the tea which Florence handed to her, she knew that in one way Fred had been wrong: the Risings would never sink. Florence would hold them up.

News of the surrender at Kut arrived two weeks before Albert left for France. 'It's up to you now son!' Will said heartily, clapping him on the shoulder. 'Can't get anywhere against the Turks, so you'll have to see what you can do with the Huns!'

Albert grinned dutifully. Florence said, 'At least

193

you're fighting Christians. Those barbarians out there make me shudder!'

Albert did not have much opinion of Christians after the King's School, but he hugged his mother reassuringly and said over her head, 'We might get in another shot at the rabbits before I go, eh Dad?'

'Good practice!'

They all combined to make Albert's departure seem no more than a holiday venture. Florence had the look of a frightened horse at times and was refusing food again. March also picked hopelessly at her meals.

Gloucester boasted two hills besides the Pitch: Robinswood on the south-west edge of the city, Churchdown on the north-east. Compared with the surrounding Cotswolds and the far Malverns, they were mere tumps, but they were full of coppices and dells, and after five minutes' clambering, Will and Albert felt themselves as deep in the country as they had felt on their Kempley trips. The weather had been wet since April's fourteenth birthday, but now a watery sun lit up every drop of water and made it a pearl. The rabbits would soon come out and begin to feed. The two men, both wearing breeches with stout socks pulled over them, squatted comfortably among some bushes, guns over their knees. The silence was companionable, broken at last by Will with a deep sigh of regret.

'You're the best tailor in the city Albert,' he said suddenly. 'You've got a knack for cutting. Dammit, that costume you made March eight years ago still looks as good now as new.'

Albert shrugged, too apprehensive at the immediate future to share his father's feelings of frustration. 'I was fairly good at arithmetic. It's just arithmetic.'

'And something more. Don't know what. Flair they call it.' He sighed again. 'Damned waste. That's all I can say.'

194

'Not just the war, Dad. Business wasn't too good anyway.'

'And that's the fault of the war too, son. Don't you forget it!' A third sigh elicited no response from Albert. Will said, 'I'm getting stiff. Where are the little blighters?'

Albert grinned, relieved. 'Let's move up. That dell's a bit shady, maybe they'll be out further up. In the sun.'

They stood up and began climbing. Will panted. 'One thing. You're going at the best time of year. Summer ahead. They say the mud and cold are worse than the German bullets.'

Albert laughed. 'Hope so Dad. We've had plenty of mud and cold in our lives and they haven't done us much harm, have they?'

They both laughed. Anyone could put up with mud and cold after all. Then Will said, 'Mind you. I don't blame Harry for keeping out of it. Wish tailors came under the reserved occupation thing, same as railway signalmen.'

'Same here,' Albert agreed, but without passion. He was going and that was that.

'Don't blame anyone for keeping out of it,' Will gasped, stumbling over a molehill. 'It's not our war. Damned French . . . all their doing. And the Russians of course. Nothing but trouble where the Russians are. Look at the Crimea.'

'What about Belgium though Dad?' Albert paused, seeing a movement ahead. He brought his rifle slowly up.

'Fat lot of good we've done the Belgians,' said Will, halting too and following the direction of Albert's barrel with his eyes. 'They're done for. Good and proper. Been better for them if we'd let the Kaiser take 'em over in the first place.'

Albert's gun fired and threw him back a pace. They both stared. Will said, 'You've got him son! You got him! There's some meat for the pot!' He lifted his head

and pointed his beard to the sky as he laughed triumphantly. 'My God. The Germans had better watch out
when you get over there, hadn't they? Eh? E,Albert?'

Albert shouldered his gun and put an arm on his
father's arm as they trudged up to collect their kill. It
couldn't be too bad out there after all. He could shoot a
gun and he could put up with mud and cold. It wouldn't
be too bad.

March suffered badly after Albert's departure, but still
she suffered silently. She was too grieved for an out-
burst of temper, though this was what her reined spirit
required. Her small spites towards Rags, Daze, Gladys
Luker were not enough to give catharsis. She knew she
was on the way to becoming an embittered old maid.

Two days after Albert had gone, Harry called, obviously at his behest. They made much of him, April
spearing bread on the toasting fork and almost burning
herself at the range in her eagerness to make his tea,
Will coming in from the workroom to discuss the contents of the *Citizen* with him. March watched it cyni-
cally. She had had yet one more day of dull boredom at
the office. Miss Pym had no intention of permitting her
to become more than a dogsbody, and with Bridget's
father awaiting his commission there was hardly any
work for March to do.

Harry ate his toast and told them they mustn't worry
about Albert because he could look after himself better
than most. Then he pulled out his fat turnip watch and
declared he'd have to run for the train.

'Would you walk round to the station with me,
March?' he asked. 'It's a pleasant evening and I'd be
glad of your company.'

March had no wish to accompany Harry Hughes anywhere, but Will, doubtless primed by Albert, joined his
encouragement to Harry's. Sulkily she fetched her
short coat from the hall and they went down the path in
single file. It was bad enough with Harry fidgeting about

behind her between the laurels, but much worse when he skipped to the outside once on the pavement. March almost longed for Fred Luker's unthinking ill manners; in an odd way they bred ease between them.

She said crossly, 'I thought you were in a hurry. We'd better step it out hadn't we?'

'Train isn't until seven-twenty,' he replied, insisting on taking her unwilling arm.

'I thought you said you'd have to run for it,' she reminded him ungraciously. 'If I'd realised we had plenty of time I'd have waited for April. The walk would have done her good.'

'Actually, I thought it would be a good thing if we were on our own, March.' He snuggled her elbow into his jacket with horrible intimacy. 'We can talk about Albert and —'

'I don't wish to talk about Albert, thank you Harry!' March jerked herself free. 'And if you wouldn't mind I would prefer to walk separately. I am afraid I am not used to the smell of the grease you use on the signal levers.'

Harry flushed at the intentional insult. 'I — I washed and changed before I came, March. I apologise if —'

'It's not your fault of course.' She considered making a joke about Albert's army uniform and its particular smell, but Harry was not thick-skinned and would realise she was furious that he was here and Albert was not.

He stumbled, half in the gutter and half out, in an effort to preserve a little space between them. 'It — it's just that — I thought with Albert away, we might do something together, March. Summer's coming and there are some pretty walks around Churchdown. You could come out on the train and —'

'We try to spend as much time as possible with Mother. I'm sorry Harry.'

He said quickly, almost jealously, 'You find time to go to the hospital dances.'

It was too much for her and she replied coolly, 'Yes. Of

course you could come too. Only it's for men in uniform.'

He flushed darkly and was silent as they took the high pavement beneath the railway bridge; then as they turned into George Street, he mumbled, 'Albert would like to think we still see something of each other. That's all.'

She thought of Albert in his rough, ill-cut khaki with the flat cap making a triangle of his pale, ascetic face. He was taller than any of them now, with May's slenderness and April's curly red-gold hair. He had kissed her cheek before he left and told her that she was not only his cleverest sister — he was proud of her position as secretary to Bridget's father and she had never told him how menial it was in reality — but the most elegant too.

She said quietly, 'You know you are always welcome at home, Harry. Surely you saw that this afternoon.'

Mollified, he nodded vigorously. 'I feel as much at ease with your family as my own, March. More so.' He stared at the outline of the station buildings against the cold April sky, needing an excuse for his damp eyes. 'He said. . .Albert said. . . he would miss me most of all,' he told her gruffly.

March felt pain like a physical wound in her chest and bile rose in her throat. She mustn't lose her temper. Not here in the street with people passing and that man in the bathchair. . . .

She said tightly, 'I must go. Goodbye.'

She waited for no answer and almost ran back to Northgate Street. Harry stood and watched her with his jaw hanging, she saw him as she turned the corner. She did not wave. How she hated him; how she hated Albert. Everyone. The war was not just in France, it was here in her very soul. In her work which she had schemed for and wanted above everything . . . except the price she paid for it. And in her feeling for Harry, who had recovered after the disgrace of his expulsion and was consequently in a job that kept him out of the army.

A voice spoke behind her, making her jump. 'Penny for 'em March Rising! Or are they worth more than that?'

It was Sibbie Luker, still May's best friend and therefore over-familiar with all the family. She had come straight from the pickle factory in Worcester Street where she worked from seven in the morning until seven at night. The handkerchief which bound her hair away from the dangers of the machinery was in her hand and her abundant mouse-brown tresses were loose. She looked what she was — common.

March said shortly, 'I've been to see Harry Hughes on to the train.'

Sibbie darted speculative sideways glances at her, then suddenly said, 'Poor old Harry. I'll go and have a word with him too.' She suddenly changed her voice and mimicked the captain who drilled the young recruits in the barrack square at Bearland. 'Carry on March!' She giggled. 'Not that you'd know how I reckon!' Then she turned and ran back, calling Harry's name loudly. March hurried on, determined not to walk home with Sibbie Luker. Yes, they were the people she hated most. The Lukers.

Harry stopped as he heard his name shrieked down the length of George Street. Other people halted too but Sibbie Luker didn't care about that. He waited for her to come up, her brown hair — almost March's colour — flying about her face, and the smell of vinegar about her surely drowning any trace of signal grease that might still hang about him.

He said, 'What's up? Something wrong with March?'

She shook her head and hung on to his arm while she panted her breath back.

'Shan't see much of you now, shall I?' she gasped. 'Thought I'd say — good luck!'

He had to smile. After all she was half Rising, practically living there with May. And she was pretty and lively and warm.

199

He said, 'You're the only one to say that. Everyone gave Albert all their luck.'

'As bad for you as for him, I reckon.' She sucked in a huge breath and relaxed, smiling back at him. Her lips were bright red from the continual nibbling she always gave them. She jerked her head sideways. 'Come on, else you'll miss your train. I'll come on to the platform and give you a wave.'

'That'd be nice.'

He offered her his arm and she dimpled at him as she took it.

'Don't mind the smell then?' she asked with charming frankness.

He sniffed, closing his eyes in simulated delight. 'Heavenly,' he murmured. They both laughed.

He hung through the window of the train and admired the swell of her breasts and the blue of her eyes. She kept smiling and showing her teeth, then, as the guard blew his whistle and waved his green flag, she grabbed the door handle, pulled it open and jumped into the carriage.

'What are you doing?' he said, startled.

'Coming with you!' A porter chased the train and slammed the door disapprovingly. She bit on her lip, grinning like a mischievous child. 'Never bin on a train, and it's a nice evening and —'

He was appalled; still the conventional law-abiding Harry. 'You haven't got a ticket! And what about your people — they'll be expecting you home!'

She gave him a shove and he sat down hard. 'Don't be a kill-joy Harry Hughes! My folks expect me when they see me! And surely you can buy me a ticket the other end?' She sat by him and hugged his arm. 'I couldn't bear to let you go alone Harry. You looked so . . . alone!' She laughed at this. 'Enjoy things when you can Harry. Christamighty, we might be dead tomorrow!'

And with another impulsive move she reached up, dragged down his head and put her open mouth to his.

200

Shocked, he pulled back, but then, staring mesmerised at her open face — not so much frank now as downright brazen — he was caught by her mood. Albert was gone and March made any future calls to Chichester House an uncomfortable prospect. And Sibbie was here. He put his arm around her waist and squeezed until she shrieked for mercy. After that it was easy.

David was wounded.

Mrs. Daker had the news from the War Office and closed the shop immediately so that she could rock and keen in the back parlour while interested neighbours took it in turns to offer consolation. Tolly Hall, calling for thread for his mother who now took in sewing, brought the news to Chichester House, and an unwilling May went down that same evening to pat Mrs. Daker's shoulder and assure her it might very easily be worse.

She had a letter from David a week later and read extracts to the family as soon as she got home from work. With her golden curls tipped well over her forehead she was a walking advertisement for Helen's Hair Fashions, and her beautiful skin was strangely unlined by the expression of deep sympathy she so often wore. At least ten of the disfigured soldiers at the Great Western Hospital were madly in love with her and she was something of an expert in dealing with them.

'It's shrapnel. In the right thigh it seems. He's a little vague. . . .'

Florence said, 'He does not wish to pain you, dearest.'

April, never one for the proprieties, said in agony, 'It must hurt there.' She touched her own groin through the thick folds of her petticoats. 'Poor David. Will he be able to walk?'

'He's using crutches at the moment darling.' May smiled bracingly at April. 'It's good news really. He'll be invalided out of the army now.'

April's face changed expression. 'I hadn't thought of that. Oh May, you'll be able to get married now.'

For an instant May looked startled, then she said comfortably, 'He'll need time to recuperate, April dear. We'll have to see.'

Will lifted Rags off the chair by the empty range and put him gently on to the floor; Rags was an old man now. 'I'll be glad to see David Daker back. We helped each other out before, perhaps we can do it again. Business couldn't be much worse. Still, David can do most of his work sitting down. If necessary.' Will himself sat down and put his feet in the fender, although the June sunshine shone through the open kitchen door, bringing with it all the scents of the garden which Albert would have loved so much.

March said with suppressed violence, 'Trust David Daker to fall on his feet. Just a year out there and now he'll be safe home, probably with a pension, and everyone telling him how marvellous he is!'

Florence said reprovingly, 'March dear. Poor David is wounded.'

March replied inconsequentially, 'Yes. But Harry Hughes isn't!'

April's face was still radiant. She asked, 'How soon will he be home, May? We could have him here and nurse him, couldn't we Mother?'

Florence gave her gentle, sad smile but it was May who said quickly, 'Of course we couldn't April. Whatever would Mrs. Daker say? Anyway, he says here it will be two or three months before he's allowed out of hospital.'

Sibbie arrived then, hatless as usual, smiling even as she chewed her underlip.

'Good evening Mrs. Rising . . . and Mr. Rising.' Her smile widened as she looked at Will. It always did. It worried him no longer, but it seemed to imply a special intimacy between them. She stayed by the door, looking towards May and March now. 'I called to say I won't be able to manage the Saturday hospital dance.'

May's reaction was immediate. 'Oh, Sib. It won't be

so much fun without you. Why can't you come?'

'Some people — friends of the family — have invited me out to tea. At Churchdown.' Sibbie looked around, but the Risings were basically incurious and accepted this unlikely statement.

March said crossly, 'I would hardly call the hospital dances fun, May.' And April said, 'David can go to them when he gets back, can't he May? Will I be able to come too?'

Sibbie was staring at May. 'You've heard from David? Oh — oh May. Is he coming home?'

May stood up and handed the letter to Sibbie. 'I'll walk down the garden with you while you read it.' The two girls drifted out, Sibbie opening the stiff paper avidly.

March said, 'Strange, isn't it, how May is always otherwise engaged when it's time to wash up.'

April smiled beatifically. 'I'll do it by myself tonight March. I'm making up a new poem and I can say it out loud.' Will laughed fondly and April's smile turned fully on him. 'Well, I'll say it to Rags then Daddy!'

He looked over his spectacles. 'I love you, little April,' he said out of the blue.

April was now the tallest girl in Chichester Street and nobody there allowed her to forget it. She dimpled, thoroughly pleased. 'I'm nearly as tall as you,' she reminded him.

He shook his head. 'You'll always be little April to me.'

Albert's letters were peculiarly unsatisfying. He wasn't allowed to say much. When news came through of the attacks along the Somme, the family could make more sense of the letters they had received earlier. But the details Florence wanted to hear — what kind of food he had and how he slept — were missing. He commented on the lack of trees, flowers, birds. 'The shelling makes everything a desert,' he wrote. They simply could not imagine that. The *Citizen* quoted Ludendorff as saying the German troops were absolutely exhausted. Mr. Lloyd George took over from Mr. Asquith and there was a wave of optimism. The boys playing in the gutters of the Barton sang, 'Bugger orf Ludendorff'. But then little Rumania was defeated and nothing seemed changed.

A week before March's annual holiday in Bath, a telegram arrived from Uncle Edwin to say that Aunt Lizzie had collapsed and had been admitted to a sanatorium near Chippenham. Mr. Edward Williams — Bridget's father — had by this time obtained his commission and March asked old Mr. Williams if she could leave immediately to be with her aunt.

'If my son were not away, I have no doubt you would persuade him to grant you compassionate leave, Miss Rising.' The alderman had never entirely believed Edward's flimsy reasons for employing this young girl. 'I am a harder nut to crack.'

March swallowed and went back to her cast-iron three-bank typewriter, determined not to beg. She had never really cared for the way Bridget's father obviously indulged her either; it was a constant reminder that her position as his secretary had not been gained on merit alone. But now she wished with all her heart he was here. The alderman was right, he would have let her go.

They had news of Aunt Lizzie's death on the Friday evening before March was to travel to Bath. She would not believe it, even when Florence looked out the clothes they had worn to Teddy's funeral. Aunt Lizzie could not have left this life without a last intimate chat, a last smile, a last promise that next year she would be fit enough to ride in a motor car and that March should drive it.

The beauty of Bath, displayed as it had been that first time from the railway station, tore at her heart. Summer was heavy in the old Roman town; the tiny cafés had put tables out on the pavements in a continental way; punts were on the river. There was a terrible poignancy to such gaiety.

Uncle Edwin met them, looking old and frail in his black. He was bent as if literally a broken man. He escorted them into the sitting-room and stood watching them while Rose brought in tea.

'It seems only yesterday ...' he gazed at April standing erect by her mother's chair. 'Yet you were in a cradle and your sisters just little girls.'

May took his arm and led him to his old chair by the window.

'We sat here, d'you remember Uncle Edwin? You and Albert played dominoes and I fell asleep.'

And March remembered how she had sat with Aunt Lizzie and been the special pampered child for the first time. And how jealous Albert had been. It was over. Over for always.

The coffin was open on the table in the dining-room, and after tea they all filed respectfully past it. It was yet another blow to March. She had expected a welling grief that in itself would be an assuagement. She imagined being escorted to her room prostrate, weeping; May staying with her and April being sent up with a light supper. But it did not happen. The waxen figure among the satin ruffles was a shell, just as Mother had always said. The life had gone — the soul — the person: Aunt Lizzie.

Tense to the point of shaking, she lay in bed that night deliberately remembering, in an effort to find the release of tears. A few sentimental drops coursed down her cheeks but that was all. Next door she could hear April weeping and being comforted by May. April, who had hardly known Aunt Lizzie! Angrily she turned in bed, then much later heard her mother talking quietly to May. They were sharing a room and her father was in the bed she herself had had when she had been ill all those years ago.

When at last the house creaked confidentially to itself, she got up and wrapped herself in a shawl and went downstairs as quietly as she could. She had no idea what she wanted to do, but her steps took her into the dining-room again. She felt no fear, not even awe as she stood just inside the door, looking at the outline of the coffin in the dim light of a bead of gas above the mantelpiece. If anything, her mood was one of reproach. She wanted Aunt Lizzie to be there so that she could say to her 'You promised so much, and now you've gone without fulfilling anything—' but before she could approach the table and look again, Uncle Edwin's voice spoke from a chair in the corner.

'I knew you'd come,' he said. 'I've been waiting.'

He stood up slowly and painfully and walked into the aura of light. He was still dressed and March guessed he would not change now until after the funeral tomorrow. His prominent eyes looked blank and staring.

'You're Lizzie. You're Lizzie all over again, my dear. I always said that, didn't I? I told you that when you were a little girl.'

She nodded but could find no words to reply.

He looked into the coffin. 'She couldn't have any more children. She lost them — every one, you know, my child. Every one. When you came that winter of 1902 it was as if you were her child. She saw it and so did I.' He held out an arm and March came slowly towards him and looked down at the mask of his wife. Nothing stirred inside her.

He whispered, 'While you are alive March, she cannot be dead. Remember that. Do not grieve. It is my comfort and it must be yours too.'

He put his flaccid arm on her shoulder. It was heavy.

'You can have anything that was hers, my dear. Anything. You know that, do you not?'

She took her eyes from the figure in the coffin and made herself look at him. His stare was still blank yet he seemed to be waiting for her comprehension, so she nodded again.

He went on in the same sibilant hoarse voice. 'I told you once you can turn to me at any time. For anything. I want you to turn to me, March. Do you understand?'

Again she nodded. He seemed to be giving the words a significance they did not have. She wondered whether she ought to ask for something special. Was there a brooch or necklace that had been a favourite of Aunt Lizzie's?

He repeated insistently, 'Will you? Will you promise to turn to me? Will you?'

She forced a voice from her throat. 'Of course Uncle. Of course.'

'On her soul, March. On my Lizzie's soul.'

He slid the heavy arm from her shoulder and found her hand and drew it over the coffin. She was frightened at last. But then quite suddenly, he placed her hand on the edge of the oak, went to the gas jet and turned it higher. He smiled almost normally.

'Thank you March. Tomorrow, we shall sustain each other. And when the time is right you will come to me. Won't you?'

She removed her hand and clutched her shawl tightly around her shoulders.

'I will Uncle. Of course.'

'I knew you would. I knew you'd come tonight. God bless you March.' He straightened his bent back with an effort. 'Now, off to bed with you. We don't want you catching another cold.'

He followed her into the hall and closed the dining-room door with a click. When she was halfway up the stairs, he said quietly into the darkness, 'Remember, everything that was hers will be yours one day, my dear. Everything.'

She did not wonder what he meant. Obviously Aunt Lizzie had spoken to him on the subject and he had written his will accordingly. She dropped the shawl on to the floor and got into bed, drawing the clothes tightly around her. He was an old man and did not look strong. Would the house and everything belong to her eventually? They could all live in Bath then. And Albert would be with them again.

She fell asleep quickly and with a smile on her face.

10

After the formality of receiving their Bibles from Miss
Pettinger, the leavers that year congregated as usual
behind the coke heap. Gladys was sure of a job with
Sibbie in the pickle factory, but many local girls were
now employed in a munitions factory at Brockworth
and Gladys yearned to join them.

'Go on April, let's 'ave a go,' she urged, pushing the
ubiquitous Daisy back to her own side of the playground. 'They picks you up in a lorry every morning
and brings you back at night. What d'you think?'

'I think my dad won't let me,' April said gloomily. She
knew Will was planning to apprentice her as a dress-
maker and the prospect did not attract her very much;
on the other hand it certainly did not repel her like the
idea of the munitions factory. Gunpowder choking your
lungs and your skin turning yellow. . . . But officially
she had to seem eager to make shells.

' 'E will if you goes on at 'im long enough,' Gladys
said with truth. April could usually get her own way
with her father.

Daisy once again scrambled up the sliding coke pile
and lifted her red face over the top.

'Get off!' snapped Gladys. 'When you're fourteen
you can come this side. Till then —'

'Miss Pettinger sent me!' gasped Daze furiously. 'So
now then Gladys Luker!' She wiped a filthy hand on her
pinafore. 'Miss Pettinger wants our April in her room.
Right away! An' if 'er says what a long time I bin with

the message, I'm a-goin' to tell 'er you pushed me down the pile — an' you're not allowed 'ere anyways!'

Gladys made a sound of disgust and raised enquiring brows at April, who shrugged with a *sang froid* she certainly did not feel and moved off briskly while trying to look unhurried.

Miss Pettinger had a visitor with her. At first April did not recognise the tall thin figure standing by the window, dressed in the black bombazine that had been almost a uniform of respectable ladies ten years before. Then she came forward and put a pair of pince-nez on her nose. It was Miss Midwinter.

April had not seen her old teacher since she left the little private school with Teddy seven years before, but immediately she was back in that special aura. Miss Midwinter was wearing her pince-nez, therefore the pupil should stand. April was already standing, so she bobbed a small curtsey. Her amazement was complete when Miss Midwinter actually held out a gloved hand and shook April's limp one.

'My dear child. I've been hearing all about you from Miss Pettinger. You have fulfilled your early promise.' Miss Midwinter actually smiled as she made this pronouncement. She picked up April's familiar red school report and tapped it on Miss Pettinger's desk. 'An excellent record my dear. I am proud to have started you along the Road to Knowledge.'

This was too much for practical Miss Pettinger. She shuffled some papers to show she had work to do.

'Miss Midwinter has come here with a proposal to put to you, April,' she said matter-of-factly. 'Perhaps you would both like to sit down.'

April waited until Miss Midwinter billowed down on one of the hard school chairs, then fetched another for herself. Miss Pettinger's hands fidgeted among her papers. They were red and knuckly and it crossed April's mind that they accomplished very varied work besides instructing. They inflicted punishment that

209

was extremely painful even when just, they stoked the coke stove and mopped up various messes. And on occasions — few and far between — they soothed. There were many calls on them, so it was not altogether surprising when Miss Pettinger again took the field.

'Miss Midwinter has a place in her school for a pupil teacher, April. Your name occurred to her and —'

'I have *always* had you in mind, April,' Miss Midwinter amended austerely. 'Your conduct pleased me a great deal when you were with me. You are a member of an old and respected family —'

'And you are leaving school at fourteen,' Miss Pettinger took over blandly, 'which of course most of Miss Midwinter's pupils do not.' She smiled frostily. 'I daresay most of your girls continue their education at the girls' high school, Miss Midwinter?'

In the pause April said innocently, 'Bridget goes there. Bridget Williams — you remember, Miss Midwinter?'

Miss Midwinter regained her aplomb. 'And your dear sister works for Alderman Williams. As his personal secretary I understand.'

It was obvious Miss Midwinter had already spoken to the Williams. April lowered her eyes. Bridget by the sound of it. According to Bridget the Risings were still the next in line to the Royal Family.

Miss Midwinter swept on grandly, 'You will want to discuss it with your parents, my dear. And then perhaps you will all come to see me together.' She rose and gathered her bag and a lacy scarf while April skipped to the door and held it open. She swept out. 'On Tuesday,' she commanded finally.

Before then Miss Pettinger called at Chichester House and put the matter in very plain terms. 'Miss Midwinter will be getting a helper —' she refused to use the term pupil teacher '— at a very low cost.' She looked straightly at Florence, then at Will as an after-thought. 'On the other hand, April will get excellent training and if she is still of a mind to teach in two or three years, I will give her the necessary experience to make her an uncertificated teacher.' She sighed. 'Who knows, by then there may be some way she can obtain a certificate.'

Will was exultant, this was a badly needed fillip for his pride.

'I knew I was right to send the two babies to that little school,' he said to Florence as soon as Miss Pettinger left. 'My goodness Flo, it'll be something to have a teacher for a daughter, eh? And our March private secretary to the mayor. May probably owning her own business before long. And Albert fighting for King and country.' His eyes grew moist. 'Something to be proud of, eh?'

Florence smiled at him, thinking how selfish she was to wish for the old days at number thirty-three, with the flaking ceilings and Aunt Lizzie's lace curtains. She nodded. Then looked at April questioningly.

April said, 'If I can be a teacher one day and make you proud of me —'

Florence said quickly, 'We shall always be proud of you, April. Whatever you choose to do.'

Will said, 'That's settled then. Perhaps things are looking up. At long last.'

David came home. And April was the first to see him.

Not the least of her reasons for inclining towards the work at Midland Road was that it would mean she would pass the Barton shop twice each day. Before David's arrival she called regularly on her father's behalf, and Mrs. Daker, who disliked her the least of all the Risings, was able to tell her the exact date and time that David would arrive. She got to the shop at four-thirty on that date, her hair, put up for the authority of her position, falling out from beneath her old sailor hat, one of May's

211

dresses straining across her shoulders.

David was sitting huddled by a small fire in the back parlour and did not stand up. His face, turned momentarily towards her in greeting, was more guarded than ever, the eyes burning in the waxy paleness.

'Little April Rising, by all that's good and true!' He managed a grin. 'I thought it might be your sister when I heard the shop bell.'

April was as usual suddenly shy in his presence. 'May doesn't leave the salon until gone six. Seven some nights. She — she'll be so pleased — so happy . . . oh David, how are you?'

He said lightly, 'I think I might have a slight chill. Nothing to speak of. Sit down Primrose. Sit down.'

She was delighted by the name and obediently pulled up a chair.

'It's not cold David. I haven't even got a jacket. You must be ill.' She leaned forward, her concern deeper than May's ready sympathy. 'What about your leg?'

'I walk with a stick. Hoppity kick.' He grinned again. 'Teddy would have enjoyed that little rhyme. Yes?'

'Oh David. I can't bear it. You were so strong.'

He said roughly, 'I'm one of the lucky ones, Sweet Primrose, and don't you forget it. I'm home. I'm alive. I can walk fairly well. See. Hear. One day I'll feel warm again.' He forced himself back from the fire and looked at her properly. She breathed fast and tried to smile. He nodded as if satisfied. 'Yes. You're just as beautiful as ever, though you look as if you might be falling apart slightly this afternoon.' He took her hand quickly at her look of dismay and held it between his. The chill of him was instantly communicated. 'Is it because you're pleased to see me, little April? Could it be that?'

She was completely breathless. 'You know it is, David. Oh David. I've prayed and prayed that you would be safe.'

'And I am.' Again the light mocking tone. 'And now enough of me, Primrose. Tell me about you. May wrote

212

that you were a skivvy teacher at that awful hole in Midland Road.'

She gasped a laugh. 'I suppose that is it exactly! Did
May really say that?'

'Of course not. She made it sound good — as May
always does. She says that you'll end up as headmistress.' He released her and stretched for the fire
again. Impulsively she got up and lifted the smoking coal
with the poker to produce a little blaze. He grinned
wryly, 'Ah . . . April. I would have had to wait for ever
for news from you.'

She said steadily, 'I wrote to you. Every week.'

He glanced sideways, surprised. 'I got two letters.
Poems. No more.'

'I tore them up after I'd written them. Didn't you like
the poems?'

For answer he fumbled for his wallet and produced
two familiar pieces of paper. He watched her as she
blushed deeply, then replaced them and pulled out a
wad of pink notepaper.

'May's letters,' he said briefly.

The blush receded; she was well pleased to be
included with May. Then he pulled out a single sheet.
'Sibbie Luker.' His smile was back. 'Was there ever
such a lucky man? Letters from three beautiful girls.'
He opened Sibbie's letter and glanced at it. 'Do you go
with them to the dances at the hospital, little Primrose?'

'Not yet. Mother says I am too young to go without a
chaperone. And Harry cannot take us because he is not
in uniform.' She ducked her head. 'You could take us
David.'

'But shall not. May is very popular I assume.'

'The soldiers often call. There is one called Marcel.
They are terribly wounded, David. May would not —
would not —'

'No. I understand.' He looked at Sibbie's letter
intently. 'How will she feel about me walking with a
stick — hoppity kick?'

Distress brought her to her knees by his chair. 'How can you ask that? She loves you, David!'

He looked into the eager young face, blue eyes full of pain. Then he leaned over and kissed the wide forehead.

'Of course. Of course little April. It's so simple, isn't it?' He looked and saw her close her eyes as her mouth worked uncontrollably; he sat up straight, tipping his head and sniffing exaggeratedly, 'Oh, you smell wonderful, young lady! D'you know that? Robin's starch and Puritan soap and a touch of lavender bag and the merest hint of camphor about the hat!'

He kept his head back with a fixed ecstatic expression while she laughed vexedly and stood up.

'I'll tell May you're here. But you must come round, David. Please come like you used to. Not tonight because I can see you're still so tired and cold, but tomorrow. Will you come tomorrow to tea and supper?'

He returned to the fire. 'Very well. I'll come tomorrow.'

'I'll call for you after school. Oh David — welcome — welcome home!'

She went through the shop in a happy whirlwind, even blowing a kiss to Mrs. Daker as that lady went through a tray of ribbons with a customer. As she ran up Barton Street she kept her face lifted to the autumn sun.

'Thank God,' she said inside her head. 'If you'll just send Albert and Fred back home, we — we'll —' she could think of no offering enormous enough to bargain with. 'We'll be so grateful,' she finished lamely. Then she was in Eastgate Street and there was Marshall's toy shop. After all, God had Teddy. He could not want more.

David waited until seven, when surely April would

214

have told May and she would be round to see him, then he
stood up with difficulty and got into his jacket. Mrs.
Daker was horrified.

'You're just going out when I am cooking supper?'

'It seems I have to, dear Mamma. I am engaged to be
married if you recall.'

'So?'

He shrugged. 'If she will not come to see me, I must go to
her,' he said briefly as he limped through the tiny
kitchen.

It was hard going; further than he remembered. The
sun slanted down Chichester Street: the Luker woman
and Mrs. Turpin were still in their doorways and Lottie
Jenner making for the Lamb and Flag with great
determination. Either they had forgotten him or thought
him of no account; none of them acknowledged his
passing. It occurred to him that they were used to
wounded men limping their ways towards the Rising
house.

He went to the kitchen door, led there by sounds of
chatter, and was welcomed vociferously again by April,
with real pleasure by Will and Florence, but with some
restraint by March and May and — he saw later when
the excitement died down — by Sibbie Luker.

May was all apologies.

'April said you would come tomorrow evening, dear.
We're going to a dance at the hospital — Mr. Luker is
taking us in the trap. We really can't let them down.
I'm so very sorry David. Oh dear. . . .' She looked at
him with genuine distress, then brightened. 'But of
course, you're in your uniform! How lucky — you can
come with us!'

'And I'm wounded too. How fortunate.'

There was an uncomfortable pause, then March said,
'Do we have to go, May? This is the first time we've seen
David for ages.'

'Darling, I know you don't enjoy going.' May kissed
her sister's cheek. 'But they look forward so much to

215

seeing us. Think of Albert.'

David smiled at March. 'Yes. Do not feel you are putting me about, March. I promised my mother I would be home for supper.'

May looked relieved. 'Oh, that is all right then I suppose. And it's marvellous to *see* you David dear!'

He stayed long enough to watch them drive off. Sibbie could have been mistaken for a Rising now, so long had she associated with them and modelled herself on them. Her hair was still mouse-brown, but her pale blue eyes fringed with very dark lashes were striking, and her mouth, which she constantly pouted or nibbled, was full and more luscious than the sensitive Rising mouth. She smiled prettily at David and said she was sorry he couldn't come with them, and he smiled back and said if he'd known she was going he would have made different arrangements. Everyone laughed and Sibbie made a *moue* and bit her bottom lip.

David watched them down the road; like three white gardenias in a flower pot they looked. He made his farewells to Will and Florence. April walked with him down the garden to Mews Lane because he could not face Mrs. Luker and Mrs. Turpin again. They hardly spoke. She wished she had told him about the dance. He looked very cold and his face twisted as he leaned on his stick.

She said quickly, 'I'll call for you tomorrow after school. Half-past four.' And turned and ran indoors in case he thought she noticed his pain.

He stumbled into Mews Lane, and there, leaning against the wall of the stables, was Sibbie Luker. She smiled, showing white teeth.

'I said I felt sick. Pa dropped me off home and I came through the back. I thought you wouldn't want to walk down Chichester Street again.'

'Very perspicacious of you Sibbie.'

She said, 'D'you get my letter?'

216

'Yes.'

'I wasn't boasting. There's others now. Harry Hughes for one. I know exactly what I'm doing David.'

'I'll bet you do.'

She smiled again then turned and opened the stable door and led the way inside. David limped after her. In the corner lay April's red scooter and over one of the beams hung a rope from which Teddy had swung. Sibbie took David's free hand and drew him into the complete blackness of a stall where remnants of old straw still lay.

David was not gentle and he laughed when she cried out.

'Come down into the pit with me Sibbie Luker,' he murmured, crushing her hard on the brick floor beneath the straw. 'Come on. It's what you've always wanted, isn't it?'

And Sibbie remembered the nail in her back and told herself that David's anger was better than his disinterest.

The year drew to a close. There was the silent grief of Teddy's birthday and a quieter Christmas than usual without Albert or the prospect of a visit from Aunt Lizzie. Uncle Edwin, pressingly invited by Florence, declined to leave Bath but suggested that this summer it might be possible for March to visit him 'as promised'. Florence was puzzled by this but did not go into it. In many ways March had seemed more settled and contented since the funeral and Florence supposed that Edwin had 'promised' some of Lizzie's things — maybe even a small cash gift. Things like that mattered to March.

The engagement between May and David continued much as it had before the war. May had decided they had best wait until David could get the business on its feet again. There was small hope of that and in any case he appeared to have very little interest in the business.

217

Mrs. Daker still sold her buttons and thimbles, and when April called in with ointment, strawberries, books of poems, even buttercups gathered from the railway bank, David was nearly always sitting before the fire drinking scalding tea.

He was unfailingly pleased to see her however, and encouraged her to talk. It was to him she spoke of the books she read, the poems she wrote, the children she taught. She confided in him almost completely. Not quite. He was still May's.

May herself was in a dither. When Marcel Beauvais from Ostend proposed to her beneath the frost-encrusted apple tree, she thought it was the most romantic thing in the world. But then, she could remind him gently that she was already engaged to be married. She would be twenty-one in the spring, and the only thing she was sure of was that she did not want to be married to any one man. Yet she wanted to be married. It was crazy. She told Sibbie how she felt and Sibbie had difficulty in checking her laughter.

'My dear darling May . . .' she hung on to May's arm, gasping. 'I know *exactly* what you mean!'

It was one comfort.

Then at the end of January, Albert came home on leave.

He did not have David Daker's facility for putting on a face. It was obvious to his family that his experiences in the trenches had been more — much more — than uncomfortable. His ability to find happiness in a flower or a simple joke had gone for ever. When Will rallied him heartily, 'You showed 'em then lad, eh? You showed the Hun!' Albert crouched over his knees and studied the oilcloth as if his life depended on it. He showed a little pleasure however when Harry called and even asked him to stay the night.

'Now hang on old man,' Harry held up his hand. 'I start late turn tomorrow afternoon. We can't all swan around like you, you know.'

March watched angrily as Albert grinned without resentment.

'Well, you don't have to get back tonight at any rate. We could walk down to the river. Have a pint at the Saracen's Head.'

Harry raised his brows at this suggestion and said, 'Nice barmaid there, eh old man?'

March said sharply, 'You can't possibly go out tonight Albert. It's going to snow!'

'What difference does that make?' Albert smiled. 'Remember how we used to have snow fights, Harry? Remember Evensong that time when we hid snowballs in our cassocks and shoved 'em down —'

Harry looked uncomfortable; the days at the King's School had been expunged from his list of memories. Unlike Albert. All he could do was remember. Every sentence began 'Do you remember —' as if they had been the happiest days of his life.

Harry stayed and they walked as far as Sandhurst in the pitch darkness, talking foolishly like overgrown schoolboys. The next morning Harry produced a bottle of rum and they lay on their beds still drinking and talking. Harry, unused to liquor, was soon giggling.

'And what are the mam'selles like, Albert? Eh? What are the bits of French skirt like? Compared with here?'

The rum had an unwelcome effect on Albert, driving him back to places he had no wish for. He shook his head fiercely.

'Don't know what you mean, old man. When you're off duty there are prostitutes. Don't know about them.'

'Oh come on Albert! You must know! If I can manage it in Churchdown surely you can manage something in la belle France!'

Albert leaned on one elbow. 'How do you mean?'

Harry, bursting with importance and the longing to boast, said smugly, 'I've got a girl.' He pumped out a laugh. 'I've *had* a girl. I've got a girl. And I can have her again any time I want.'

There was a long silence while Albert assimilated this. Then he frowned. 'I thought you and March were friends. Can't have anything like that going on when you and March —'

Harry flumped back on to the bed. 'Oh she wouldn't have anything to do with me, old man. I tried. Don't think I didn't try. But March never thought much of me you know. I meant to tell you before — right at the beginning ... anyway I'm all right now. Quite all right. Thanks very much.'

There was another long silence, then Albert said painfully, 'Who is it? Anyone I might know?'

Harry was convulsed again. 'I should think so. I should think you might know her any time you so wish!' He rolled over and looked across the intervening space at his friend. 'It's Sibbie Luker, old man! Marvellous she is — an absolute corker! If you like I'll put in a word.' He leered drunkenly. 'I'm not possessive Albert. Not where you're concerned, old man. Always been pals, always will be.'

Albert shifted on to his back and stared at the ceiling with his blue eyes.

'No thanks, old man. Thanks all the same.'

'Any time. Any time, old man.'

'Thanks. . . . Time you were going, old man.'

Harry sat up, hiccoughing loudly. 'You're right. As ever. Walk to the station with me, old man?'

Albert said dreamily, 'Not now, old man. I'm tired. G'night.'

Harry chuckled again as he staggered to the wash-stand and splashed his face and combed his hair. By the time he left the room, Albert was asleep. And they talked about licentious soldiery!

Alderman Williams was at a Council meeting and Miss Pym had a cold. At three o'clock March pushed her remaining work into a drawer and left the office. The snow still held off but the low yellow-grey sky kept people off the streets and she was home in ten minutes flat. The house appeared to be empty. Florence had left a stew in the slow oven on the left of the range and was doubtless sitting with Aunty Sylv. Will might be anywhere looking for work. And she had doubtless passed Albert as he went for another aimless walk. She sobbed with frustration, then paused as a sound came from above.

Albert sat on the edge of his bed cleaning his revolver. There was no sign of Harry but the stench of rum was everywhere. March thinned her lips disapprovingly.

'Honestly. . .Albert. I don't know why you're so keen on that wretched Harry Hughes. If Mother could smell this room, what d'you think she'd say?'

He looked at her blankly, then tipped some oil on to his rag and began on the barrel of the gun. He did not use his whole hand as March did when she cleaned the top stair rods, twisting the slim brass through the Brasso as quickly as possible; he used one finger swathed in the cloth and very slowly and gently rubbed it along the length of the barrel.

She said, 'Are you all right?'

He nodded.

'I left work early. Thought I might see you walking back from the station with Harry.'

'No. I didn't go. I was tired.'

'Have you slept?' she asked in a kinder tone.

'Yes. I think so. I was lying down.'

'Would you like some fresh air? We could walk down to Fearis' and buy some muffins for tea.'

'All right.' He rubbed on however. 'March. Do I smell?'

'What of? No, of course you don't.'

'It smells out there all the time. I thought I could still smell it.'

'You've had about fifty baths anyway. It's that rotten drink I suppose Harry bought.'

She sat on the other bed and watched him. He stopped

rubbing and held the gun up, examining it carefully.

'I haven't shot anyone yet, March. Honestly,' he said.

'Well, point it the other way. I don't want to be your first victim.'

'It's not loaded. I've got cartridges though.' He looked thoughtful. 'I could kill myself if I wanted to. Some of the chaps shoot themselves in the foot. So that they're sent home.'

She got up and went to the closet.

'Come on. Here's your tunic and cap. Put the gun on the wash-stand, you can finish it later. Take the brolly. It might snow.'

She got him dressed and down the stairs. He leaned heavily on his father's big black umbrella as they negotiated the path between the laurels. When they were in the street she took his arm, thankful the weather kept Hettie Luker and Aunt Sylv indoors.

He did not speak and his weight grew heavy on her arm. They turned into Northgate Street and trailed behind a small party of men from the hospital walking into town. There were two wheel-chairs pushed by nurses, three or four men on crutches with the white of bandages showing beneath their caps. March held Albert back. She could imagine what their faces would be like.

The road dropped away beneath them and the high pavement with its rickety iron railings was close to the metal girders of the railway bridge above. March made a small cooee to get an echo and provoke a response from Albert, but he looked straight ahead, apparently not even hearing her. There came the unmistakable snort of an approaching train. The bridge trembled and the usual reverberations were everywhere; smoke and steam descended to cut off the light. They were in a murky tunnel of noise.

Suddenly Albert screamed. She could not hear him but his gaping mouth and distended nostrils and eyes told her what was happening. Clutching the umbrella he turned frantically, ran along the railings until he came to a gap and jumped the four or five feet down into the road. Horrified, March followed him from above, calling fruitlessly into the bellow of sound, hanging over the railings with outstretched hand.

Albert ignored her, not seeing her; he flung himself full length along the tram lines and brought the umbrella to his shoulders. Sighting along it towards the group of soldiers, he began to make explosive noises between his teeth. At first these were inaudible, then as the train receded into the distance, they could be heard plainly. 'Putch! Putch! Putch-ch-ch!'

He scrabbled to his feet and ran crouching until he was beneath the soldiers and wheelchairs. He pointed the umbrella. 'Got you!' he screamed. 'Got the bloody lot of you — filthy, bloody swine — buggers —'

March reached him. She lifted her skirt and scrambled anyhow over the railings, landing by his side with a spine-jarring thump. She encircled him with her arms and held him to her with all the fierce strength of her thin frame. He struggled for an instant, then as suddenly as it had begun so it ended. He turned into her neck and began to weep.

One of the nurses joined her and helped the two of them back on to the pavement.

'It's shell shock. You know, do you?' she asked in a low voice. 'He should see a doctor.'

'I'll see to it. I'll see to it. Thank you — thank you very much. I'm so sorry if it has upset anyone —'

'Please. We understand. May we help you home?'

March moved her head so that she could see past Albert's cap.

'No. I can manage. We can manage. Come Albert. Come my dear.'

She led him down Mews Lane. Someone had hooked the umbrella over her arm and it was a frightful struggle

223

to straighten her hat and go on down the rough passage, with Albert's stumbling feet threatening to trip her every inch of the way.

'Come on. Come on dearest,' she whispered, thrusting at the garden door with her foot and easing him down the path. She prayed her parents would still be out and the back door open. Her prayers were answered. She sat Albert by the range and made hot tea and held it to his shaking lips. Then she filled bottles and urged him upstairs.

Once in bed he seemed to recover a little.

'I'm all right now March. All right now. If only I could sleep. I can't sleep you know. Not properly.'

'You'll sleep my darling boy. Close your eyes.'

'Don't leave me March.'

'I won't leave you.'

'As soon as I sleep, you'll go. I know you will.'

She threw her coat on to the other bed and unhooked her skirt. In her petticoat she climbed in beside him and took his head on her shoulder as she'd done when they were children.

'I'm not going to leave you, Albert. Go to sleep.'

He smiled and lifted his mouth for her kiss.

'March. I love you. I'd forgotten.'

'I know my darling. I know. Go to sleep.'

And she held him to her and stroked his ginger hair and smiled through her tears. He was hers. She would get him out of the Army if it meant shooting him in the foot. And he would be hers always.

But she reckoned without Albert. The next day she did not go back to the office, too scornful of her job even to send an excuse. She told Albert that he was not going back to France, that she would engineer it somehow. He shook his head quite gently.

'March, I shall go back. It's all right now. I'm clear and up straight again. I know now why I'm doing it. Remember what I said all those years ago March? You

224

said you'd die for me and I said —'

'I remember. We were children.'

'It's all right March, I know that. But I've got to have things clear — clear and simple. And that's all it is, isn't it? That I'd die for you.'

'I want you here Albert. Alive and here.'

He was silent, looking down at the oilcloth again in a way that frightened her. Then he said, 'Please March. Let me go.'

She whispered, 'I — I don't understand, Albert.'

He shook his head helplessly. 'I don't understand either. But perhaps if I stay now, I won't be the sort of person you can love.' He waited while she protested, then went on, 'You think it could not be so. At this moment that is what you honestly think. But later. . .' he looked up suddenly. 'March. You despise Harry, don't you?'

She swallowed, not wanting to answer in case she forfeited his precious exclusive love.

He smiled. 'If I stay my dear, I might become like Harry one day.'

She drew away and looked into his face. For an instant she saw him as others must see him, the everyday anonymity of him, the pale ginger hair, mild blue eyes, thin high cheek bones. If he stayed he would always look like that. Perhaps.

She kissed him quietly. 'All I ask is . . . come back Albert. Please.'

He held her again. But he did not reply.

It was strange how the family took this burgeoning love so calmly. Of course March knew it had always been there and the others must have seen it too. Now they closed ranks to give March and Albert the precious time they needed. March did not go back to the office and neither Will nor Flo pressed her to do so. Harry was dealt with in the front parlour by May or April, and after two calls he stayed away. The threatened snow arrived and closed them off from the rest of the world. They cleared a

225

path to the winter cabbage patch with much laughter and returned to make cocoa for Florence and Will and talk of other times.

March was transported into a world of delight that she had never guessed could exist for her. She knew that in the midst of his terror she was somehow making Albert happy, and this increased her own happiness to a point where she could only just support it. All this love just created more. Florence spoke freely of Teddy. They sang around the piano in the bandy room and remembered Aunt Lizzie calling them all 'beautiful'. Gran came over and held the hand of her favourite.

Quite suddenly it was over. Early one morning they congregated in the kitchen for the last time. Albert kissed them all, even his father.

Will said, 'After. . . . It'll be better, son. We'll start again. A brass plate — "Rising and Son". What d'you think of that?'

'We'll make our own designs Dad,' Albert agreed. They hit each other on the shoulder.

Florence smiled. 'You're a mutual admiration society,' she said.

They were always pleased when Florence teased them. Albert said, 'We're a mutual admiration society Mother!'

March was the only one to accompany him to the station. She held his arm high because he had to shoulder his kitbag, and they went down Mews Lane to avoid seeing people.

'We're like an old married couple,' Albert said, smiling at her without embarrassment.

'Yes,' said March, thinking only that she mustn't cry. It was one of the qualities Albert appreciated in her; she did not weep tears of sadness, only of temper. She must make it easy for him to leave.

No-one they knew was on the platform, and amid the many parting couples they were completely anonymous. The train arrived from Cheltenham and Albert found a compartment and stowed his bag in the netted rack above his seat, then let down the window and hung through it. March tugged off her gloves and put her fingers in his.

They did not speak until the train began to move, then he said above the hissing steam, 'Thank you March. Thank you.'

She opened her eyes wide, willing the tears to sub- side. An iron-tyred trolley passed by, shaking the plat- form. She was running alongside the moving carriage; Albert's fingers had loosened but hers still gripped.

He leaned out at a dangerous angle and their mouths touched jerkily.

'Let me go March!' he shouted. 'Now!'

She forced her hand open and stood still. He went from her in a cloud of steam, snatching off his cap and waving it as if he were going the short distance to Newent or somewhere similar.

Carefully she counted the dark blue and white Mazawatee tea advertisements on the sooted brick walls of the station. There were thirty-seven.

April smiled at Mrs. Daker as she went through the shop, and received a blown kiss in return above the head of a customer. In the back parlour, David was reading the *Citizen*: casualties for the month of January.

'You look better today,' April said, ignoring his reading matter. 'And your mother looks very happy too. She blew me a kiss!'

'She calls you a little bit of spring in winter,' David said mockingly.

April was used to these moods by now. She said briskly, 'And you call me Miss Primrose. Very nice.' She sat down opposite him and produced a drawing from her bag. 'I wanted you to see this protrait of my employer.' It was a ghastly caricature drawn by one of the younger children, recognisable only because of the enormous pince-nez.

David smiled obediently. 'How many more like this?'

'Seven. I had seven of the naughty ones this afternoon. So I asked them for pictures of people they disliked. Four of them did Miss Midwinter. Three the Kaiser.'

His smile widened a little. 'You'll get the sack of course. You know that.'

She opened her bag wider so that he could see the other pictures. 'I've absconded with the evidence,' she assured him. 'My word against theirs.' At last his smile became a grin and she relaxed. 'You really are better, David.'

'I've got some new medicine.' He reached for it from the mantelpiece. A brandy bottle. She tightened her mouth, but before she could speak, he said, 'How is May?'

'Well. A little depressed since Albert left. You will be with us on Sunday as usual again, so you will see for yourself.'

He let that go, merely taking a mouthful of brandy direct from the bottle.

'And March?' he asked afterwards.

April frowned. 'Like a tightly coiled spring.' She stood up as if she could not bear to watch him with the bottle. 'March cannot . . . cannot . . . *receive* our help. She shuts herself off from what we could give her. Mother — you know Mother, David — she pours love out to her and it could be a soothing balm. But March won't — cannot take it.'

He looked at her straight back and carefully put the bottle on the floor out of sight. 'You are very perceptive, April.'

She thought he was still mocking her and she said angrily, 'If that is what I am — then I cannot help it! And it hurts, David!'

'It's the difference between you and May.' He spoke

almost to himself and then laughed abruptly. 'Don't ever be a nurse Miss Primrose — you're much too subjective.'

There was a short silence while she considered asking him what he meant, then did not. She came and sat down again, registered that the bottle had disappeared, and said, 'David. You still won't talk about the war. I know that. But how is it . . . how will it be . . . for Albert?'

His eyes were without expression. 'Ask Fred Luker when he comes home on leave.'

She smiled slightly. 'I can't do that. Fred is good with cars and you and Albert are good with cloth.' She stood up again and got ready to go. 'You see, Mr. Luker came in for a word with Albert and he said —' she lengthened her face and used Alf Luker's voice exactly, 'Fred do make 'is bloody gun talk! Bloody talk!' She tried to grin down at him. 'And of course that makes sense. Because a gun is a machine like a motor car. But cloth. . .' she stopped on a question.

David shook his head. 'There's more to it than that, little April. Much more. Albert. . .Albert will be all right.'

She said passionately, 'I don't believe you! And I'm not little any more! I'm almost as tall as you, David Daker!'

And she was gone, pushing clumsily through Mrs. Daker's little kitchen into the back alley and slamming the door behind her.

March knew that old Charles Williams was angry with her for taking leave of absence during that last week in January, yet she refused to tell him that her brother had been home on leave. Even so, when written notice that her employment would cease in mid-February was placed on her desk by a triumphant Miss Pym, the shock of disgrace made her physically ill. She emerged from the tiny lavatory on the half-landing, still white and shaking, and asked to see Mr. Williams. Miss Pym informed her that the alderman was at the Guildhall, but would grant her an interview the next day. March threw down the letter.

'You can be my messenger then. I won't be here. That was all I wished to tell him.'

Miss Pym drew in her chin. 'You realise you will forfeit one week's salary by such a foolish action?'

'A week's salary? Is that all?'

March walked down the stairs with a sense of release. She had wanted the post urgently enough to blackmail a small girl ten years ago, and because of that it had always been dust and ashes in her mouth. She was well rid of it.

But although her family uttered no word of reproach, she knew their feelings. To be 'given notice' was not to be given references, and it was unlikely March would obtain another position of equivalent importance. She told herself she was happy back in the workroom sewing the occasional button-hole and tidying up after her father, but then Sibbie arrived one evening in March, half-excited, half-subdued, and announced that 'every cloud had a silver lining'. After some fidgeting and embarrassment she explained that dear little Bridget Williams had put in a good word for her and she had a job in King's Street at guess where — Williams and Son!

Politeness could not hide the general astonishment; only March kept an expressionless face. Sibbie explained that she was sick to death of the pickle factory and Gladys said munitions were no better, so she'd been trying to get an office job for some time. And she was so sorry that March's bad luck had turned to good for her, but she simply could not let such a chance slip through her fingers.

It was May who said, 'Of course you couldn't, Sib. March would have recommended you herself if she'd any idea that you wanted a job like that.'

Later, even Florence expressed surprise at the appointment.

March said bitterly, 'You know how she got the job, don't you?'

May said defensively, 'She's a hard worker March —'

'She certainly is!' March made for the door. 'But she can't type or do shorthand or add up a column of figures!'

April looked at May. 'What did March mean?'

'Nothing darling. Gossip. Sibbie is sometimes a little over-friendly with the soldiers. . .you know.'

Florence nodded. 'Single girls cannot be too careful, May. I've always said this.'

Surprisingly, Will spoke up. 'Sibbie Luker — all the Lukers — are good generous people. Very generous.'

The very next week news of the Passchendaele assault began to come through. The dreaded name Ypres was mentioned again, and after the gas attacks two years before everyone knew that no good could come of it. The casualty lists lengthened and were published weekly instead of monthly.

Albert's named appeared in April, two days after the War Office telegram arrived. Albert Edward Rising. It described him as a beloved son but it did not say that he left a sister as good as a widow. It made no mention of his simple straightforward love for Rags the cat, the daffodils at Newent, an organ note soaring into the fan-vaulted ceiling of Gloucester cathedral. To most people he was as anonymous in death as in life.

Yet as a postscript, perhaps as an offering, Harry Hughes enlisted that same day, was sent out to France and was never heard of again.

11

March could shed no tears. It was as if the discipline she had laid on herself at Albert's leave-taking stayed like a curse to desiccate and wither. Grief took her as it had taken Florence and Sylvia; she could do nothing. For hours she sat in the workroom staring at the needle in her hand. Obediently she would lay the kitchen table and take her place with the others, but unless prompted she forgot to eat. Nobody was over-anxious on her behalf; they were all paralysed by Albert's senseless death, and though they knew March's grief was more intense, they felt the least they could do was to allow her to suffer it quietly and in privacy.

Helplessly, drearily they went about the business of celebrating April's and May's birthdays. For April, Florence boiled eggs and sat the cosies on them as she had always done on special occasions, but no-one made any comment. When it was May's turn she gave her a pair of stockings almost surreptitiously, as if it were an act to be ashamed of. May held her mother's thin face to hers for longer than usual.

'We shall be happy again,' Florence murmured steadily. 'Don't be cast down, my dearest.'

May whispered, 'So long as we have you. . . .'

Grief came differently for the other Risings. Gran, bent and nearly double now, recalled the old days lugubriously.

'Plenty o' men about then there were,' she said, remembering the kitchen table at Kempley surrounded by Jack and Wallie, Will and Albert. 'Now look at us. All women save Will. 'E got the 'ole kit and caboodle of us on 'is shoulders I reckon. All my other boys scattered to the winds. My ole man dead and buried. And now two gran'sons...ah-eh...ah-eh...' she lifted her head piteously to Florence. 'I allus said we'd be proud of 'im. I allus said it. And Christamighty we can be proud of 'im right enough. Can't we? 'Tis all we got. Our bloody pride.'

'Be quiet our Mother,' Will said sharply.

But Flo took the almost bald head in her hands for a moment.

'They've gone to a better place Gran. We know that.'

'Ah...ah, my beauty.'

Will, looking at them, felt the terrible weight of them all for the first time in his life. His mother, Sylv and little Daisy. Florence, May, March and April. And only April and May working.

March knew that what she was experiencing was a form of madness. She was in a wasteland amid such desolation and isolation that the existence of her own dwindling body seemed an offence. A displacement of air that was unnecessary. The obvious solution occurred to her at intervals during the endless days and nights. But even desperation took an effort. Aunt Sylv probably had an ancient supply of laudanum and she could beg a little over a period of time until she had sufficient. There was the railway line; but that meant leaving the house which she never did now. There was the gas stove, but someone else was always within range of its lethal hiss. She knew that one day fairly soon, she would make the effort. She could not even look forward to it because looking forward needed energy.

On June 22nd Fred Luker came home on ten days' leave. There had been other leaves which he had spent in France; no-one in Chichester Street had seen him since he joined up eighteen months previously. There was a grand get-together at the Lamb and Flag — the singing could be heard from the front bedroom at Chichester House — and the next day he presented himself, neatly uniformed, to offer Florence his condolences. He saw no sign of March and sent her his regards.

He then spent three days in the Forest of Dean talking to the small mine-owners there with whom he and his father had dealt before the war. He was more self-assured now and saw that the old business of hawking coal around on the dray wasted precious man-hours. He suggested that in the future peace, the surface coal-mines might join in a co-operative to supply large concerns like the schools, the Gas and Coke companies, the engineering firms sprouting along the Bristol Road.

Cautiously the Forest miners told him they would need something in writing from such large concerns. Fred spent another three days in Gloucester sounding things out from that side. Nobody could see the end of the war, and no-one was interested in discussing peace until it came. And then they would want something binding in writing from the miners. It looked like a deadlock, but Fred knew it wasn't. He spoke the same language as the miners and could talk them round the next time; and if not, they were a gullible lot. Pragmatism and dishonesty were often the same thing.

The day before his leave was up he called again at Chichester House. This time March was in the kitchen with her parents. He was shocked at the sight of her; not just her thinness but her bowed shoulders and blank face. On her part March felt a definite sense of shock penetrating the depth of her madness when she glanced up briefly and took in the familiar yet foreign figure before her. Fred seemed taller than when he bent over his precious Austin. His shoulders were very wide and his neck thick and strong. He reminded her of the caricatures of John Bull that abounded in the press: pugnacious, thickset, completely determined.

He took a chair opposite Will and watched them almost clinically. They were like figures in a dream.

He said deliberately, 'I wondered if you had any news of Harry Hughes?'

March became still. Fred's voice was the same, rough to the point of harshness, yet with a note of authority that was new. His attack was the same too. Perhaps even more direct. Brutal.

Will shook his head. 'He's been gone about six weeks. It was a sudden decision. When he heard. . .when he heard. . . .'

Fred said, 'When he heard about Albert's death. Yes.' He glanced at March. 'You knew he was friendly with Sibbie? He told her he wanted to be wherever Albert was. He told her that Albert was the best friend he'd ever had or would ever have.' He cleared his throat. 'I wanted to tell you that. It might help.'

Florence also glanced at March, then murmured, 'We see so little of Sibbie now and had no idea she saw anything of poor Harry. Probably then, she is worried by the lack of news?'

March stared at the floor. Sibbie and Harry, Sibbie and old Charles Williams. She didn't care about it any more. It didn't matter.

Fred nodded. 'Yes. She was so worried she went out to Longford and called on his father. But he had heard nothing either.'

Florence poured the obligatory tea and answered questions about April and May. No-one mentioned March's name; Fred did not speak directly to her and her parents broke through her silence only with a smile. But when it was time for him to leave, Fred tucked his cap under his left arm and held his right hand towards her.

'I'll go the back way Mrs. Rising. Thank you for the tea. March, will you walk through the garden with me?'

March looked up without full comprehension and he repeated slowly, 'Come on March. You won't need a jacket, the sun is so warm.'

She shook her head dumbly. He picked up her limp hand.

'Yes. I want to talk to you.' He looked at Florence. 'You can spare March for half an hour, Mrs. Rising?'

Florence smiled encouragement. It would do March good to get outside. 'Of course Fred. March dear, a little air will be good for you.' She took March's elbow and urged her up. March walked like an automaton by Fred's side. 'Give our regards to Mrs. Luker —' Florence opened the door and the heartless sunshine poured in.

Will said, 'Yes. Our regards to your mother, Fred.'

Fred did not reply.

The garden was burgeoning; the currants and gooseberries behind the nets sent a heady smell across the rough grass. Albert's fruit bushes. They would be called Albert's fruit bushes always. March staggered a litle, leaning more heavily on Fred. The rough khaki beneath her fingers was terrifyingly familiar. She felt a mounting pressure in her throat.

'You're quiet Marcie.' Fred's voice was gentle as he used her special name. 'Won't you say anything to me?'

Fred had been to the same places as Albert had been. Fred knew what it was like; knew that some men shot themselves in the feet in order to be sent home. March turned her head so that he could not see her face. She had done that before. When her nose had been running.

He said quietly, 'Please speak to me Marcie. Tell me that I should be dead. That it should be Albert here with you. Say anything you like.'

Of course. Fred knew about her feelings for Albert. Fred knew about her bitter anger. Fred knew . . . everything.

They came to the miniature apple orchard where the tiny apples were already dropping into the grass beneath. Fred stopped beneath the biggest tree.

'Albert would be pleased with this crop I reckon. He loved the garden didn't he?'

March tucked her chin on to her chest and bore heavily on the rough khaki arm. She wondered whether she might fall down.

Fred went on. 'Not as much as he loved you though Marcie, eh? Our Sib told me about his last leave.'

She choked and cringed lower.

He said, suddenly brusque, 'Stand up straight March! 'Tisn't like you to cower and grovel, it isn't in your nature. You had what you wanted from life. You had someone's complete . . . *self*! If Albert had lived you'd have lost him again — oh yes you would. To Harry. Or someone like Harry.' He opened the gate into the lane, pulled her through and shut it with a bang. 'You know that, March. And even if you'd kept him it would have been like having a tame dog about the place! That's not for you.'

She turned, her hand raised to strike him and he caught it in his.

'Be angry in a minute March, but listen first! You've got him — don't you see? You've got him now, for always! No-one can take him away from you! Can't you understand that's why *I'm* so bloody angry?'

She stared at him, eyes wide, then shudderingly, she let the spring in her relax. He watched her carefully. Her shallow breathing became deeper and quicker by the second.

He said, 'Come on. In here if you're going to cry.'

He pushed at the old stable door with his shoulder and drew her into the musty gloom. She looked wildly around her. There was April's old scooter and a rope hanging from a beam. Her breathing was fast, too fast and convulsive. Fred. Fred was here. In khaki. Understanding everything.

She gasped a scream as she collapsed, and he caught her and held her tightly as if he expected grief to disintegrate her slight body. Indeed the sobs that racked her might easily have done physical damage without his supporting hand on her rib cage, his shoulder for her jerking head. For five long minutes the gale blew itself past crisis point, leaving her as weak as a kitten. Now his hold was different; he cradled her, rubbing his thumb along her spine, wiping his cheek to hers to clear the tears. It seemed natural that after a period of this soothing, he should begin to kiss her. First her eyes and then her ear lobe, back to her eyes and down her long thin nose and then her trembling, shaking mouth.

She did not protest. The uncontrollable passion of her grief spent, something else flickered into life; a physical feeling that was not unlike the beginnings of temper. She let it take its course. Soon there would be a time when she had to make a decision: to stop or go on. For now it did not matter. The warm mouth came back to hers, and this time she was conscious of it. Her own lips moved beneath it, tremulously but with a definite response. At once, the soothing hands slid up her back and held her head to steady it, and the kissing went on. She permitted it deliberately; the moment for decision was still not upon her, and meanwhile the warm hands and mouth did not intrude into her grief but were a kind of homage to it.

Fred waited for the sudden tension in her spine. It did not come. He leaned away from her at last and looked into her face. It looked back at him, the mouth open on a sob, the eyes swollen and half-closed.

He said, 'I'll make it all right for you Marcie. Just trust me.'

She made a sound of protest as he laid her in the straw, but that was because it was cold and she wanted his warmth back with her. She welcomed him when he lowered himself on to her, not even realising that the moment of decision had come and gone. There was no room in the world for anything except him; he was no longer Fred Luker who had given her driving lessons. He was a nameless someone who knew everything and did not condemn. His complete acceptance of herself was the balm she needed, and once she accepted that, his expertise awakened every suppressed instinct within her. She gave herself to that first experience of sex as she had given herself to her tempers as a child; with an abandon that was exhausting, exhilarating and brought complete peace.

She lay still again while Fred cradled her.

'My darling. My beautiful darling.' He was near tears because she made no effort to rearrange her clothes. He ran his hand along the slim length of her leg. 'I've always loved you Marcie. Always. But I never knew how much.'

She looked up at him. 'Tell me. How much? How much do you love me?'

'Oh Christamighty Marcie. More than anything. Anyone.'

'More than Sibbie?'

He laughed hoarsely. 'More than any o' that lot. You're part of me now Marcie. I can't tell you how much I love you. You're my life.'

She sat up slowly and began to button her blouse. As his hand still stroked her she trembled with remembered joy.

'I'm glad you don't love me better than life. You must live. You must live. If I am your life then you must live. Do you hear me?'

He said steadily, 'I hear you Marcie. I'll come back. I promise you. And if you'll trust me, I'll make everything all right for you again. That's a promise too.'

She stood up eventually and let him pick the straw from her hair and clothes. Then she left him quickly, frightened that this sense of peace would go if she stayed too long and realised what she had done.

She slept the whole night through and her dreams of Albert were no longer nightmares that stayed with her when she woke. Now, he seemed faceless, almost formless. He was with her as a warmth and comfort. It was as if she was absorbing the essence of him. Wasn't that what Fred had said? That she had him for ever now?

She did not go to the station to see Fred off. It was a Saturday and Hettie, Alf, Sibbie and Gladys made a retinue which grew as it progressed. Lottie came 'for the fun of it' and Daze tagged after Gladys to hear about the goings-on at the munitions factory. There were plenty of noisy tears and good luck wishes, but no-one seriously thought Fred was in any real danger. The Lukers could survive anything, even old Ludendorff and the Kaiser. Sibbie swung her mother's arm on the way home and Hettie remembered how happy she had been with Will Rising. And how he had ditched her the minute his sister got wind of the affair.

Sibbie grinned sideways, pumping her mother's arm painfully.

'Ah . . . I was just thinking something, our Mam. Us Lukers. We're a fine lot aren't we? Not quite good enough to be loved, but good enough for plenty else, eh?'

Hettie sniffed back her tears and looked reproving. 'Now our Sib. You can't 'ave it all ways my girl and you've chose —'

'Oh ah. I can Ma. I can have it as many ways as I choose — you wait and see.' She laughed. 'Just you remember, we're better than a lot of folks round here. D'you know that? Better than most.'

Suddenly Hettie was infected with her daughter's resilience and laughed through her streaming eyes.

'Not just better girlie. We're the best!'

They swung into Chichester Street still laughing. Indefatigable.

Will was drunk and he knew it. He was often drunk these nights, and everyone understood and did their best for him. But tonight nobody's best was good enough. He wanted Hettie. Or Florence. He wanted Albert or Teddy. Or old Mr. Daker. Even Harry Hughes would have done.

240

Lottie was not in the Lamb and Flag, and Alf Luker was helping with a moonlight flit. Will drew in great lungfuls of the September evening air and reeled against Goodrich's wall, then followed the bricks down to thirty-three.

'Ma?' He hammered on the door, then squatted on the boot-scraper. 'Ma, come and let me in! Give me some bread and cheese and onion so's the girls — ladies — can't smell my breath! Come on Ma, come on —' the door opened and he fell in. His mother supported him with difficulty.

'No, Will. No food tonight. There en't none 'ere.'

'Cruel. Cruel, Mother. Where's our Sylv? Oh, with Flo as per usual, I'll be bound.'

'Yes. She's keeping Flo comp'ny. Like she do most nights when you're at the public.' Gran looked down the hall. 'Now come on our Will, stand up. That's it. Off you go and 'ave a bit o'walk. Walk it off afore you goes in. Nice night like this — do you good. Come on now —'

'I wanted a bit o' company Ma. Talk. About Teddy and Albert and poor ole Pa.'

'Not tonight Will. Dessay that young Daker 'ud be glad of a chat though. Why dun't you go and keep 'im company. Our May en't too keen, is she?'

'What d'you mean? They're engaged aren't they?'

'Engaged! Look over those glasses son. Our May dun't want to marry the lad.'

He had bundled himself down the steps by this time and stood on the path, surveying her hazily.

'Bin understood for years Ma. Years. Fixed up when she was fourteen or something.'

'More's the pity.'

'Like me and Florrie they are. Same as us.'

'Is that what you want for May then our Will? Same as what you got with Florrie?' Old Mrs. Rising's eyes, faded and rheumy, fixed him for an instant then flickered away. 'You get on down the Barton for an hour, our Will. Talk to that young Daker.'

There seemed nothing else to do. Stinking of whisky, he avoided the Cross and went down past the Army hospital which now sprawled over land owned by the railway company, and approached Barton Street along the embankment. Soldiers and girls were everywhere, looking at the full moon and at each other. A portable gramophone blared, 'Pack up your troubles in your old kitbag and smile...smile...smile....' Will wept maudlin tears and thought how he would take poor wounded David Daker over to the Waggoner and buy him a whisky and talk about his old man who had stood on his head. And maybe about Albert. Oh, and May. Cheer the lad up.

He went down the side way and tapped on the kitchen door. Nothing happened so he went in. The place was deserted. Kitchen and parlour were neat and tidy for the night. Will stood in the middle of the shop looking around indecisively, wondering whether he should write a note. The next instant his spine jarred with shock as a sneering laugh came from behind the workroom door. He was still facing towards it, eyes wide, when it was followed by a scream; a female scream. Then another laugh, triumphant yet cynical. He lifted the counter flap and shoved at the door in sudden panic; when it gave he hung on to the knob and went with it, almost falling into the small, dark room. And then he had to continue to hang on grimly, bent nearly double to absorb the physical shock of what he saw.

There was David Daker, white-faced, eyes like chips of coal, shirt sleeves rolled to the elbow, crouched above the cutting table as if bringing his peculiar concentration to bear on one of his paper patterns. But the pattern was Sibbie Luker. Her milky body lay spread-eagled before him in complete abandon, the red marks of his fingers still blotching the perfect skin. Her arms were upflung in surrender and her head hung from the edge of the table so that Will saw her face in reverse, contorted and horrific.

242

She recognised him before he recognised her. She screamed again, her scream enunciating the words, 'Oh no!' Then she jack-knifed her naked body and began to cry piteously. For a long second they stayed like that: Will staring incredulously; David leaning with assumed nonchalance against the edge of the table, Sibbie huddled upon it, naked and weeping.

Then Will said, 'Get your clothes on Sibbie. You're coming with me.' He went into the room and presented the girl with his back. 'And as for you —' he addressed David scornfully. 'Your liaison with my family is at an end. If ever you try to speak to any of us again — and that includes Miss Luker — I will report you to the police immediately.'

David said insolently, 'For what? Making the most of the local whore?'

Will felt quite sober. He breathed deeply twice.

'For perverted practices, more like. You dirty swine — you —'

David said coldly. 'Be quiet man. You don't know what you're talking about. You don't know anything, do you? How old are you — forty-five, fifty? All that time — all those years — and you haven't learned a thing!'

Will hardly heard him. 'To think — to think I wanted you to marry May!'

'Not really.' David's smile was chilling. 'You thought you did. You thought you did the Dakers a good turn — helping us out when my father died — permitting me to fall in love with your daughter. But you never really forgot we were Jews did you?'

Sibbie said, 'I'm ready Mr. Rising.'

Will turned. She was so like Hettie, a hurt and damaged Hettie. He tried to sound gallant as he crooked his arm.

'Come on then. We don't want to stay longer than we have to.'

She took his arm timidly and he escorted her through the shop, parlour and kitchen. He knew it was the last time he would see the place where he had first started tailoring. David made no attempt to follow. They walked the length of the Barton and Eastgate Street without speaking, but in the quiet of the Catholic churchyard she began to weep again and collapsed on to a flat tombstone, pulling him to a stop. He had to remind himself that she was a woman of twenty-four; she looked such a child sitting there knuckling her eyes.

He said sternly, 'Now, now Sibbie. All over and done with. Try to forget it. Turn over a new leaf. Let this be a lesson to you.'

She said in a small voice, 'You — you know about me, Mr. Rising?'

'Know about you?'

'What he said. David Daker. You already knew what I — that I —'

He said briskly, 'I know you've been a silly girl Sibbie. Letting attention go to your head and —'

She burst out weeping again. 'You'll never respect me now! I can't bear it! That you of all people — the one person in the world I look up to — care about —' She threw herself from side to side and Will stood awkwardly by her and held her steady against his right leg.

He said sensibly, 'Of course I respect you Sibbie — I'm probably the one person who can understand you, my child. For one thing I've always been a second father to you — isn't that so?'

'May and me have shared everything. Always. And when you were good to Ma I used to pretend you *were* my father.'

He sucked in a quick breath. 'Yes. Well. Then you know I can understand you — your warmth. And sympathy. Because ... because of —'

'Because I'm like Mam?'

He swallowed his next breath and tried to continue smoothly. 'You hardly deserved to come up against

244

someone like Daker. He's returned from the war with a crazy streak in him. Maybe it will caution you Sibbie — as it has certainly cautioned me.'

'Is it really the end of him and May?' Sibbie asked without distress. 'I think it's best. He's a funny one Mr. Rising. Real funny.'

He tried not to think what she meant and knew he would think of it often. The white flesh, so familiar yet so young and taut; the red finger-marks . . . everywhere.

He said quickly, 'We must both forget him, Sibbie. He won't trouble us any more, he's got some shame.' Thank God May had escaped that. He felt sick at the thought of May on the cutting table. Yet he had seen Sibbie Luker there and had not felt sick exactly.

She said pathetically, 'I loved him 'cos of May, see. I know it sounds wrong, but that's why I let him do it. Because of May.'

Will remembered she had met the young swine under his roof in the first place. 'I understand, Sibbie. I told you, I understand. Now come along like a good girl and let's get you home.'

It was almost dark. She stood up and took his arm again and leaned on him as they went down Mews Lane.

She whispered, 'There's only been him and the alderman. You do believe that?'

'The alderman?' Will was shocked again, not unpleasurably. 'D'you mean old Charles Williams? He must be seventy if he's a day!'

Sibbie said simply, 'I like older men. They're kinder.' She swallowed. 'I thought you knew about him.'

'No. I. . .March insinuated. I wouldn't listen.'

Again she wept. 'Oh God. What must you think —'

They were outside her gate. He held her up.

'Why? Why did you do it, Sibbie?'

'I don't know. They gave me presents. I don't love them. Only one man I've ever loved. And I've lost him now.'

She was crying so much, so wholeheartedly, he had to

put his head down to hear her. Suddenly she seized his cap and held it hard as she kissed him.

'There!' she choked. 'I know I've lost you so I might as well take what I can anyhow!' She clung to him like a leech. 'Oh Will — I've always loved you — I wouldn't lie to you — ever since I was a little girl.'

Hettie had used that phrase, he recalled. 'I wouldn't lie to you. . . .' He put his arms around her waist and let her kiss him again.

He knew he was drunk. Very drunk indeed. The night sky reeled around him. He tasted her tongue and felt her sharp teeth and melting body. Then, tantalisingly, she pulled away from him and was gone, and the slap of the wooden door against its jamb made him sway. He stood there, waiting for the world to settle. Then a voice spoke from the complete blackness ahead of him.

'Still at it then Will?'

Will literally left the ground, turning a half-circle in the air to face the speaker.

'Who the hell is it?'

Some of the blackness gathered itself together and materialised beneath the moon. It was Dick. Sylv's ne'er-do-well husband who had disappeared ten years ago and had been presumed gone for ever by everyone except Sylv herself.

He said prosaically, 'Me. Bad penny.' He stood before Will drooping slightly from the shoulder, shabby, ill-kempt and . . . in khaki. 'I were just leaving. Said me goodbyes and were off.'

Will waited for his thumping heart to settle and his thoughts to turn over again properly. This — this — soldier — had been in talking to Flo and Sylv.

Will said roughly, 'Didn't even think to say hello to me — is that it? Christamighty, is that a uniform or what?'

Dick shrugged. 'Petty offenders were given the chance to join up. I joined up. Now I'm on the run.'

Will's fuddled mind searched back. 'You were over with our mam, weren't you? An hour or so back? She

246

wanted to get rid of me so she could fetch Sylv without me knowing.'

'I bring trouble,' Dick reminded him. 'I'm a deserter, Will.'

Will refused to be shocked; he returned to his gripe. 'Christamighty. Sometimes I think none of you want me in this bloody family at all.' The whisky made him believe what he said; he was head of the Risings and should have been consulted about Dick.

Dick said, 'They calls it 'arbouring. The military police know about Sylv 'cos I put 'er name down as me nex' o' kin. Once they've searched thirty-three they'll be over —'

'You're my sister's husband,' Will stated, full of righteous indignation. 'If I can't help. . . . Sylv was good to Flo when Teddy died. Did you hear about Teddy? And Albert? We got to stick together Dick.'

Dick shuffled. 'Thought you'd call me a coward.'

'We've heard enough. Nobody says much but we've heard. Albert. Fred Luker. David Daker.' He remembered this evening and stopped.

Dick misunderstood his benevolence. 'You dun't 'ave to worry about me saying nuthin' Will. I wun't say a word about that little girl —'

Will exploded. 'D'you think I'm offering you a bed because I think you'd tell tales? God, Dick, I haven't done a thing! Drunk too much but nothing else! Not since you left! Ten bloody years innit? Can you say the same?'

Dick shuffled again. 'Dun't want no bed Will. Mebbe the stables.'

Will was galvanised into decision-making. 'Right. The stables it shall be. Though you're welcome to the best bed in the house if you want it. No-one can say I've turned my back on my own.' The thought of giving Dick sanctuary uplifted him. He remembered another time when he had given Dick's wife similar sanctuary; his ennui finally disappeared. He sprinted through the garden, leaving Dick skulking in the back lane, and burst in on a gloomy gathering in the kitchen. Sylvia and Florrie were sitting stoically as usual while his mother waved her apron like a banner, prophesying doom for them all. April patted her uncomfortably, March stood by Florence's chair with an expression of withdrawn disgust, and May, practical as usual, brewed tea.

Will said, 'Quick. Jump to it. We want a mattress and bedding down in the stable for Sylv and her husband. Stop that crying Mother and take some tea down to Dick. Sylvia —' but Sylvia, her stolid courage melting with gratitude, was weeping at last.

Will enjoyed the furore which he created. He stood in the middle of the kitchen, legs slightly apart, and gave out his orders like a general. The women, thankful to have something to do, scurried at his bidding. He was making things happen tonight in a way he hadn't done for years. Sibbie. Now Dick. April picked up a pillow and ran ahead of him, echoing his feelings with the uncanny knack she had when she said, 'It's quite an adventure really isn't it?'

No-one mentioned the fact that they were breaking the law. It was the autumn of 1917 and everyone was revolted by the war.

The next morning was Sunday and they all slept late, including Sylv and Dick in their makeshift bed in the stables. The constables found them there, took the bedding as evidence of collusion, and led Dick back to the familiarity of prison. Will, descending hastily in his nightshirt, was apprised of the situation by a policeman in a ready-made Co-op suit. 'It won't come to much Mr. Rising,' he said reassuringly. 'You'll get a chalking-off in court of course. That sort of thing. You'll live it down.'

'My business won't,' Will retorted bitterly.

He could blame nothing on Sylv, or even Dick. It

had been his own doing. It had been the drink. Sometimes he wondered whether the whole episode with Sibbie had been the drink too.

He told them about David's banishment that afternoon. April took a Sunday School class occasionally and she sat with her gloved hands clasping her prayer book very tightly as her father informed them that David Daker was not fit to consort with respectable people any more. May took the news submissively, as if she might already suspect as much. March was completely indifferent, Florence surprised and horrified.

April said clearly, 'Why? What's he done?'

'That I am not at liberty to tell you,' Will said ponderously. 'But I must make it quite clear it is not some small peccadillo. It puts him beyond the pale.'

April said conversationally to her mother, 'Perhaps he harboured a deserter. That would make him a traitor to King and country, wouldn't it?'

'April —' Florence warned.

Will flushed darkly. 'I wish I could think that young Daker cared enough for any other human being to give them succour. But he sees people as — as — carrion —'

April burst out, 'How can you say that Father? How can you? David was injured caring for people! He gave his leg just as Albert gave his life!'

Will was deeply angry with his younger daughter as he had never been before. 'Don't mention Albert's name in the same breath as his!' he thundered. 'And kindly take my word for this whole sordid business child!'

'I am not a child! Everyone thinks I am, but I am not!'

Florence said, 'April. Dearest.'

April looked at May. 'You won't listen to this will you May? You know yourself that David is the sweetest kindest man in the whole world!'

May put her arm around the shaking shoulders.

'You have always idolised him dearest. Like another brother. But I know what Papa means. I sometimes had the feeling . . .' she searched for words, looking into

249

April's tortured blue eyes. 'I sometimes felt that as far as David was concerned, I was an — an object. A valuable, precious object, but nevertheless . . . now listen darling, please! He treated me that way. He used to take me off the shelf, polish me and put me back —'

'I hate you all!' April said hysterically. 'You've always been awful to David — you've none of you understood him! He'd die for any of you — willingly. And he'd die before he'd admit it! You can't see anything — you're so blind and stupid and —'

'Be silent!' It was Florence's voice, level as ever, yet it halted April in mid-flow. Everyone was staring at her incredulously, even March, who years ago had been only too wont to burst out in just as uncontrolled a manner.

Florence pitched her voice lower still. 'Whatever you think April — however you feel — you have to take your father's word about this business. You know he is never unfair or unjust and that he is not a bigoted man. Now go away for half an hour — into the garden if you like. Think about what has been said. And then come back and tell us your thoughts, sensibly and without rancour.'

It was the longest speech Florence had made since Albert's death. April kept her lips together and breathed quickly through her nose, but she took the advice. And she thought about the prayer they had just said in Sunday School 'for the brave men who, with their courage and true valour, defend us from the evil foe. . . .' April pivoted on her low strap shoes and stared at the lush greenery around her. Who exactly were the foe? Where were they? At the beginning of the war she had been a child and everything had been neat. She should have known better. She should have known when Teddy had been taken away, that nothing — ever — was neat.

On Monday night Will went to the Lamb and Flag as usual and immediately knew that something was different. Lottie held his arm even after he had bought her a gin, and told him repeatedly he was an honest man if no-one else in the world could say the same. Alf guffawed at all his jokes and said that any time he wanted to drop in for a chinwag, there was always someone there, even if it was only Het or Sib. Mr. Goodrich, fetching a jug of stout for his old mother, pumped his hand as if they hadn't met for years.

Only after Lottie stumbled from the snug for an unexpected lying-in, did Will see that she had been sitting on that night's copy of the *Cheltenham Echo*. He glanced at it idly while Alf went for more beer. There was the usual news, American soldiers landing in France, French soldiers throwing down their rifles, Russian soldiers fighting each other, the poor bloody British managing as best they could with the new tanks supposed to be supporting them; and someone called General Allenby doing something in Palestine. Will wondered what Palestine had to do with the war.

His gaze went idly on through the lesser headlines and suddenly he sat up and glanced over the partition to where Alf was telling a pair of soldiers about Fred and his talking machine gun. For the moment no-one realised that Will Rising was alone in the snug reading a newspaper. He glanced down again. 'Gloucester tailor turns traitor,' it said. The words had to be consciously focused. He could barely discern the text and he adjusted his spectacles frantically rather than lift the paper under the light. 'On the night of September tenth, a deserter from the ranks of the Somerset Light Infantry was apprehended on the premises of. . . .'

Will wet his lips and sat on the paper himself. He was sweating. If it hadn't been for the headlines he might have imagined the article was strictly factual — the word 'harbour' did not appear. But that stark and catchy line slanted the whole report. Made it 'newsworthy'. The sweat dried cold and he felt sick. It was so easy to remember those few words, 'Gloucester tailor turns traitor.' Nobody who knew him would take them seriously, but his present business depended on people who did not know him that well. All his old customers bought ready-made clothes; he needed the nouveau riche with 'county' aspirations. And they would remember that he had been labelled traitor.

Alf's voice said above him, 'I'm just off Will. . . . You all right me old mate? You look a bit green.'

Will made a face at his glass. Had Alf brought in the *Echo*? Or had it been Lottie? Or even Sid Goodrich who never gossiped yet had obviously known about it.

Will stumbled into the street by the light of an enormous circular harvest moon. He wanted to go somewhere and cry because the whole world was against him: even his little April.

A hand gripped his arm and held him from falling into the gutter.

'Come on my handsome. Just here. Lean on the wall and take some good deep breaths.'

It was Sibbie Luker's hand and Sibbie Luker's voice and smell and — and essence. He obeyed her, sobbing openly. She continued to hold him.

She whispered, 'Sat'y I cried on you. Now you cry on me Will. Go on, cry it all out.' He tried to tell her about the paper and she put a finger on his lips. 'I know. Pa told me. One bloody thing after another.' She did not remove the finger, it moved back and forth across his lips. 'It makes what I got to say worse. But I have to say it Will. Otherwise you might write me off for good an' all. And I wouldn't want that.'

'I'd never write you off Sib. I told you, you're like another daughter to me —' he stopped speaking because her finger was now inside his mouth.

She laughed. 'I don't think so Will. You're not like a father to me anyway. Not now.'

His weeping stopped but he was still breathless. She was pressed against him and her hand came away from his mouth and explored his face slowly. It was a sensual experience new to Will. His liaison with Hettie had been boisterous and innocent by comparison. He was almost frightened. But certainly not miserable any longer.

252

She went on softly. 'Listen Will. Yesterday old Charles Williams offered to buy me one of them little bungalows down by the canal. My own place, Will. The deeds 'ud be in my name.'

It took a minute to sink in and then Will removed some of his weight from her and took a sharp breath.

She flattened her palm on his cheek and held on to him. 'I knew you'd be shocked. In a minute you'll walk away from me — you're bound to. I'm a kept woman now and you've been trained to keep away from kept women. But later on Will, just think. My own place. I can sell it for a couple of hundred probably. Or keep it. As soon as the old man's dead, I'm free.'

He jerked his head away from her hand and tried to take a step. He staggered and fetched up against the rough bricks of Goodrich's wall. She laughed again.

'Yes, I know. It'll take some getting used to. Probably even poor old Ma will disown me. But I don't care Will. You'll get used to the idea — all of you — and you'll come to me because I'll be the only one among the lot of you with a bit of money and my own place.' He took another shambling step and another. There were two yards between them. Her whisper reached him even when he'd trebled that distance.

'Don't forget last Saturday night, will you my love? How you saw me bruised and naked and at the mercy of all men — yes, even you. Because one day you'll wonder just who is master and who is slave. I promise you that Will Rising. I promise you that!'

That night he dreamed vividly. Sibbie was indeed naked and covered in red marks. He was rubbing salve into them. Very gently.

12

A letter arrived from Uncle Edwin asking Florence
to 'spare' March for a visit. He knew that April
would be back at school and May as busy as ever,
but from her last letter he gathered that March was
still at home, and if this was so, perhaps Florence
and she would like to come and have a week or two
in Bath. Florence's name was apparently an after-
thought.

March said, 'Not yet Mamma. I feel so unwell all
the time.'

Florence was anxious. 'I thought you seemed so
much better since Fred Luker came home on leave.'

March flashed, 'What do you mean?'

'Nothing in particular March. I was grateful to
Fred for talking to you and helping you to accept
Albert's loss.'

'I'll never get over Albert's death,' March said
fiercely.

'I did not say you would get over it dear.'

'My being unwell has nothing to do with Fred!'
March swallowed a mouthful of bile determinedly.
'I'm run down, that's all.'

'Quite. That is why this invitation has come at a
fortuitous time. Now listen to me dear. You were
Lizzie's favourite niece and I am sure Edwin has in
mind that one day you will inherit some of her
things.'

March stood up. 'I must go Mother,' she gasped.

Alarmed, Florence half-rose also but March waved her down and made for the back privy. Ten minutes later she returned, insisting it was the margarine.

'Horrid stuff. I'll never get used to it,' she shuddered. Flo was still anxious. 'Some arrowroot,' she said. 'You must take arrowroot and lie down.'

So the subject of visiting Uncle Edwin was shelved.

Florence's anxiety was not only for March. The other two girls were looking 'pale and peaky' as she informed them often. April, starting her second year at Midland Road, had no more illusions as to her real position in the school. In case she had been nurturing secret ambitions, Miss Midwinter informed her that when she and her sister retired, the school would be sold as a going concern. 'In fact child, when the right buyer comes along, we shall not hesitate. Our retirement depends upon it as you will realise.' She did not assure April that the new owners would be persuaded to keep her on as 'pupil teacher'.

April longed to call in at the Barton and talk it over with David, but had eventually succumbed to Florence's pleas and promised not to try to see him. Nevertheless she still hoped she might encounter him accidentally. She was always re-buttoning her shoe outside Daker's, or standing to watch a train thunder over the level crossing.

May was frankly lonely. Her engagement to David had served as protection only for a long time now, yet without it she felt bound to turn down other male friendship. For one thing she discovered that she could not even imagine the kind of man she wanted to marry. She had loved so many: Teddy, Albert, David and all her many suitors among the wounded soldiers. But none of them exclusively.

She was not a stupid girl and this discovery horrified her. She asked April whether she was shallow and her sister's passionate reassurance to the contrary did not entirely convince her. Her chief morale-booster —

255

Sibbie — was no longer around. Disgraced for ever by her own action. May had wept when the news was brought to Chichester House by Lottie Jenner. March said scornfully, 'You're well rid of Sibbie Luker. She was nothing but a sycophant.' May had looked up the word. Had Sibbie really sucked up to her for her own gains? But what exactly had she gained? Except a spurious friendship with Bridget Williams which she must have used in some way to ingratiate herself with old Mr. Williams. May said later with defiance, 'Sycophant or no sycophant, I miss her most terribly.'

Florence arranged a holiday for the three girls with Aunt Sylv and Daisy.

'There's poor Sylvia with her husband in prison. March still grieving for Albert. And though April and May have taken everything in their stride I can see they are both below par.' She looked at Will. 'You too my dear. Would it be possible for you to have a few days away?'

'Of course not,' Will said irritably. 'And I don't see how Sylvia can do it either. Nor March. Neither of them have done much work for me over the last two months so neither of them have been paid!' Florence's surprise did not escape him, though he did not look at her. 'And as for April and May, they are our breadwinners. Do you think they can throw up their jobs just for a week's change?'

Florence said quietly, 'No, I don't think that, Will. But I think if I spoke to Miss Midwinter, she might let April —'

'The girl has just had four weeks' holiday Flo!' Will let his ennui erupt into impatience.

'I could try.' Florence refused to be ruffled, which annoyed Will more than ever. 'And if not, then May and March could go. May has had no annual holiday from the salon this year.'

'Good God woman! I just told you that March has no money for any holiday! Nor Sylv —'

256

Florence's voice dropped a tone. 'I have a little put by, Will. The fare to Weymouth is eight and fourpence and they could get rooms for ten shillings. Sylvia is a careful housekeeper. I think she could feed them for another pound. That is under five pounds all told. For the five of them.'

Will stared. 'And you have saved five pounds?'

'Yes.'

He tried to laugh. 'I'll have to cut down on your housekeeping.'

She flushed slightly. Will's donations were minimal. She said, 'Mrs. Hall gave me a little work my dear. Now I no longer help you, the afternoons are long and I was glad —'

'Kitty Hall? Gave you work?'

Florence's flush deepened. 'Blankets to darn. Very easy.'

There was a pause, then Will said, 'Prison blankets. My God. My wife darning prison blankets.'

Florence pleaded, 'It did not last long Will. And I've had in mind for some time . . . since we lost dear Albert . . . that the girls would need a holiday.'

Will went to his chair, lifted out Rags and dropped him to the floor. It was typical of Flo that she wanted a holiday for everyone save herself. At one time that would have made him weep with love.

He settled himself heavily. 'Please yourself my dear. You earned the money and managed to save it. Spend it how you wish.'

He tried to feel benevolent. There were men — Alf Luker only just down the road — who would have 'borrowed' that money for whisky. After all it was his by right. Everything of Florrie's was his by right. But he had always been a fair and just man. Always.

Miss Midwinter was a match for Florence. Smilingly she treated the suggestion of a further week off from school as merely ludicrous.

257

'The maternal instinct Mrs. Rising . . . I am always dealing with it as you might imagine. But of course April is a woman now and must take on a woman's responsibilities.' She led the way through the tiny yard that was the playground. 'We are quite pleased with her, you will be glad to hear. Quite pleased.' She glanced through a window where April could be heard chanting 'Mrs. D. Mrs. I. Mrs. F.F.I. Mrs. C. Mrs. U. Mrs. L.T.Y.' 'Yes. Quite pleased.'

April kissed her mother warmly that night and laughed with genuine amusement.

'Thank you for trying, Mamma. Miss Midwinter admits that your maternal feelings are natural and a credit to you, but might be a little confining for me!' Even March raised a smile. April went on mischievously. 'If you could hear what she thinks of the maternal feelings of some of her parents you would be thankful that she knows you are a Rhys-Davies!' Florence was bewildered. 'Oh Mamma,' April reminded her with mock severity. 'Have you not realised that a Rhys-Davies is simply incapable of having anything but fine feelings?'

Florence tutted ruefully but was thankful that May's salon had agreed to her week off when she wanted it.

'And dear Sylvia has agreed to go on the understanding that she looks after you — you are not to do a thing, she says!'

In fact they all embarked on the Weymouth week for Florence's sake more than their own; only Daze was as excited as they all should have been at the prospect of a holiday by the sea. Miss Pettinger had secured her a position as mother's help to Mrs. Woodward at the chemist's, but the baby was not due until November and Daze was bored.

Weymouth was as they had imagined from Florence's description. She had gone there with Grandma Rhys-Davies as a small girl and had been enchanted by the watering-place strung along the deep

258

bay with its bathing machines and clock and its pierrot
show. The pierrots had given way to a concert party
known as the Happy Hey Days. Aunt Sylv promised
that if their money allowed they would go to the show.
Daze jumped up and down with excitement. May,
smiling at her, went straight to the tiny box office and
booked seats for that very night.

'My treat,' she told them, pressing Daisy's hand
warningly in case March should feel affronted. But
March stood apart as usual, drooping a little in the
warm September sun and looking definitely 'pale and
peaky'.

Sylvia nodded acceptance. She had thought May
should have paid for her own railway ticket at least.
Flo had always been soft with her.

'We'll 'ave a 'igh tea then,' she said. 'Kippers and
some o' the cherry cake Gran put in my case.' Daze was
permitted to jump unrestrained. 'But this wun't 'appen
every night my girl! Tomorrow when it gets dark, we
can 'ave a game o' cards.'

They strolled along the prom, Daze and Aunt Sylv
trailing some way behind March and May. May was
fascinated by the fashions. She squeezed March's
arm, aghast as a girl not much younger than they were
themselves passed by wearing a dress without sleeves.

'That simply is not decent,' May murmured. 'I
wonder whether Mother would let us make something
similar for next summer? So short and simple.'

March murmured without interest, 'Grecian.'

'Greasy?'

'Modelled on Greek costumes,' March explained
impatiently. 'All right if you've got nice arms.'

May giggled. 'Imagine Lottie Jenner. Or Aunt Sylv.'

March said, 'May. I think I must go back to our
rooms. The sun is so hot.'

May was immediately all concern, fetched the key
from Aunt Sylv and escorted her sister back to their
furnished rooms above a banana warehouse. March

lay on one of the beds, her forehead damp and her hands slightly shaking.

'Darling, you're ill. Oh March, you poor darling. What can I do?'

'Go away,' whispered March ungratefully. 'Oh. And fetch me a pail.'

May arrived with an enamel slop-pail which March used as soon as she was alone. She lay back exhausted and thanked God that the others were going out tonight. She could take her mother's ardent advice and rest.

Even without March — perhaps because of that — the evening was an unqualified success. The Happy Hey Days were a bunch of bright young things with little talent but a lot of enthusiasm, carried almost entirely by someone called Monty Gould. May, constantly referring to the programme, saw that the comedian who walked jauntily onto the platform wearing one of the new trilby hats, twirling a cane and saying, 'I was walking down the street the other day when . . .' was called Monty Gould. The young man who leaned against the piano and sang to the pianist to 'Come into the garden Maud,' was also called Monty Gould. The male half of the Dancing Duo was the same.

Monty Gould had the audience on his side from the very beginning. He made them laugh, he made them cry, he had them jigging and breathless with his tap dancing. When he came to the edge of the stage and asked them to join in a song for 'our boys in France' they cleared their throats and smiled mistily.

Even so the beginning of the chorus was ragged, and May's clear soprano rang true above his pleasing tenor.

'Keep the Home Fires burning . . . while our hearts are yearning. . . .'

He turned immediately in her direction, not pausing but letting a smile lighten his dark, handsome face as he sang more strongly to offer her encouragement. A few determined singers accompanied them but after a faltering hesitation May responded to Monty Gould's encouragement and soared away as she so often did in the bandy room. 'Till the boys come home.'

When the song was over there was a moment's hush, then clapping broke out almost frantically, and amid its roar Monty Gould ran to the side of the stage, took the steps in one bound and found his way to May. He took her hand and urged her to her feet. The wavering spotlight played on them and the applause continued for the beautiful blonde girl who looked like an angel. May dimpled exquisitely, just as she had in the Corn Exchange after singing 'I'm a dainty dancing fairy' and then the young man turned towards her and lowered his head to her hand in a way that the Belgian soldiers had never dared do because of their poor faces.

May looked down at the smooth dark head, so unlike David's wiry mop, felt the dry hand on hers, so unlike David's nervously clammy fingers, then looked into the brown eyes as they lifted to hers. She felt a small thrill begin in her throat and tremble down her spine. His eyes were clear brown like Florence's and March's . . . and Teddy's. Yes, Teddy's, because they were filled with laughter. She stared into them with parted lips, and helplessly her own smile widened and the next instant they were laughing joyously. As if they shared a joke; or the war had ended; or they had come into a joint fortune.

The audience might have thought the whole thing was rigged, except that Aunt Sylv stood up and detached the young man in no uncertain manner, sending him back to the stage and sitting the young lady down with two unmistakable gestures. Laughter broke out everywhere. Undeterred, Monty Gould parodied the walk of the browbeaten clown of the moving pictures, Charlie Chaplin. He spoke a word to the pianist, turned and, completely transformed, sang

261

to May, 'We have come to the end of a perfect day, to
the end of a journey home. . . .' May, breathless, told
herself it meant nothing, but did not believe herself.

Aunt Sylv was furious.

'If your mamma could have seen that little exhibi-
tion,' she muttered as they left the theatre, meeting
familiar smiles from complete strangers, 'I just don't
know what she would have said!'

May squeezed her aunt's ample arm. 'Dear Aunt
Sylv. She wouldn't have objected too much, I think. Not
when she saw . . . him.'

They emerged into the September night. The moon
hung over the shallow water of Weymouth Bay,
providing a pathway straight to France and the
unbelievable horrors over there.

'And why might that be?' Aunt Sylv asked with unaccustomed sarcasm.

May sighed at the moonlight.

'Because he was like Teddy. And everything Teddy
did, Mamma understood.' She squeezed again with
affection. 'And darling Aunt Sylv, I know you understand too. Of all people, you understand.'

Aunt Sylv stopped looking around for Daze and
joined her niece in staring at the moon. 'A-a-ah,' she
sighed.

Daze appeared, dragging Mr. Gould behind her. May
and Aunt Sylv hung on to each other.

'He was looking for you, our May!' Daze said,
grinning from ear to ear, her sailor hat falling off her
head, her hair ribbon sliding away. 'I saw him and told
him I was your cousin and he asked me to — to —'

Mr. Gould was not so dynamic outside the brightly lit
confines of the small theatre. Now there was something
else about him; something small boy and appealing.

'I wanted to thank you.' He did not let go Daze's hand
and the pair of them looked more than ever like something from a silent film. 'The show tonight — there's
never been one like it. And it was your doing.'

May swallowed. 'Not at all Mr. . . . .Gould. I shouldn't have pushed myself forward like that.'

'You were natural. That was what they liked. In all that tawdriness, you were natural.' He smiled nervously at Aunt Sylv. 'You have the advantage of me, ladies. My name being in the programme.'

Aunt Sylv was silently cautious as always, but Daze shouted, 'This is me mam. That's May Rising. Me cousin.'

May expanded quickly, 'Mrs. Turpin . . . we're pleased to meet you, Mr. Gould.' She pulled Daisy to her. 'We have to go now dear.' Mr. Gould looked vulnerable without Daisy's sticky hand in his. May swallowed her natural sympathy. 'Thank you Mr. Gould. Good night.'

He recovered himself. 'But not goodbye surely? Mrs. Turpin — are you here for the week?'

Aunt Sylv made a noise like a cross sow. Daisy, hugging May's hand now, said, 'The 'ole week. Innit lovely?'

'Yes. Yes.' He spoke simply. 'We change our repertoire on Wednesday. May I offer you some seats? It would give me great encouragement to know I have well-wishers in the audience.'

Daisy said,'What about March?' She ignored May's shushing sounds. 'March is May's sister and is proper poorly tonight. But by Wednesday she might be better.'

'Four seats,' Mr. Gould promised beseechingly.

Surprisingly it was Aunt Sylv who said brusquely, 'I don't see why not. Give March a bit of a treat wouldn't it?' She began to draw the two girls away.

May said more graciously, 'Thank you Mr. Gould.' And then when his beautiful Teddy-smile dawned, she added, 'I shall look forward to it.'

March was not enchanted by the news of her unexpected treat on Wednesday; drained yet still queasy, she could think of no prospect that could possibly enchant her. While May and Daisy cleared away their supper and laid the breakfast for the next morning, Aunty Sylv visited her niece in the tiny bedroom which she was sharing with May.

' 'Tisn't very roomy our March,' Sylvia said, tidying around as she knew Florence would have done had she been here. 'But 'twill do for a week I reckon, eh?'

March said weakly, 'There are a lot of rustling noises underneath. I hope snakes don't come in with the bananas.'

Aunt Sylv crouched down, adjusted the chamber-pot to where the sagging bed springs gave it more clearance, and listened.

'Shouldn't 'ardly think so. Monkey mebbe. I'll ask the men tomorrow.' She sat back on her heels. 'Lovely smell they makes mind, don't they?'

March tried to close her nose against the sickly-sweet banana smell. She remembered Albert telling her his trick for not smelling Gran's boiling sheep's heads, and weak tears rose to her eyes.

Aunt Sylv said abruptly, 'Who's the father, our March? Come on, you can tell me. I bin through all this remember. Just tell me an' I'll make sure 'e gives you a ring and makes it all legal and proper.'

March was completely shocked. So shocked she forgot her weakness and sat bolt upright on the hard flock mattress to stare at Aunt Sylv as if she'd announced the end of the world. Which, as far as March was concerned, she had.

Aunt Sylv levered herself up on to the other bed with difficulty and held her big shoulders close to her chest.

'Come on my girl. I know babby-symptoms when I sees them. Lucky for you I'm the only one 'oo does.'

March's face changed slowly and subtly from blank amazement to realisation and then to horror. She made no attempt to cover up.

'Oh no . . . oh no . . .' she whispered.

Aunt Sylv said matter-of-factly, 'Funny 'ow things work out. Now, if Sibbie Luker was still friendly with your May, she would a known a month ago and it would a been all round Chichester Street and 'alfway to Bristol by now.'

March breathed, 'I can't believe it — I can't!'

'You know 'ow babbies come our March? Flo 'as *told* you 'asn't she?'

'No. May. May knows, Sibbie told her years ago. Oh God. I thought it had to be dozens of times.'

Aunt Sylv was genuinely surprised. 'Why? Christamighty, I thought you girls was supposed to be so quick and bright an' all. Think about it a bit our March. Once is enough.'

March never doubted her aunt's diagnosis. Now it was given she saw that there was no other answer.

'Din't you miss?' the incredulous voice went on. 'Din't you put two and two together when you missed?'

March suddenly collapsed over her crooked knees. 'I never keep account of — of that. And when I realised how late ... I thought it was because I was ill.' She began to weep noisily. 'Since Albert died I haven't always ... it hasn't always ...'

Aunt Sylv stood up and patted the thin back quickly.

'Now, now, girlie. Cry quiet if you must. We don't want May or Daze in asking questions. There, there.'

Aunt Sylv was no expert with comfort, but March was rarely receptive to it either. She suffered the thumps and choked back her sobs somehow. For a few minutes more she hugged her knees, her forehead pressed close to them. Her aunt stayed awkwardly above her, waiting.

Then March drew a breath and spoke quickly. 'He made me. I wasn't well — it was all so terrible after Albert was killed. It didn't seem to matter. Nothing seemed to matter.'

Aunt Sylv was on familiar ground again. She nodded. 'It's a bit o' comfort. An' you thinks to yourself, it can't do no-one no 'arm.'

It hadn't been quite like that but March moved her

265

head in agreement. The turbulent copulation with Fred in the stable had been a comfort, yes. But it had been a triumph too. And an erotic delight which — especially now — she dared not admit.

There was another pause. From the other side of the door they heard May and Daze go into a duet. 'We have come to the end of a purr — fect day. . . .' March said desperately, 'What am I going to do?'

Aunt Sylv repeated, 'Tell me 'oo it was. I'll go and see them —'

'I can't! I can't!'

The rough voice humoured the panic-stricken one.

'Was it Harry Hughes? He's the only one I can think of and if it was 'im we're sunk 'cos I reckon 'e's dead and gone with Albert. If it were one o' they soldiers from the 'ospital then —'

'Oh my God! Of course it wasn't Harry!' March raised a ravaged face for an instant then buried it again. 'It was Fred Luker.'

Aunt Sylv could not hide her surprise.

'Fred Luker? You? Oh I know he always trailed after you when you were a kid. But I didn't think you gave two straws for 'im!'

'I don't — I don't — I told you —'

'Yes. Yes, you told me.' Aunt Sylv registered that the singing next door had stopped. 'That's almost as bad as Harry Hughes, but not quite. End o' June 'e were 'ome weren't 'e? 'Tis just past two months. Lottie Jenner might be able to do something. There might be time.'

'What d'you mean?'

'Get rid of it. Lottie's done a few in 'er time.'

March sat up and shook her head. 'Not Lottie Jenner. No. Not that.' How could she explain that they had always looked down on Lottie.

Aunt Sylv said, 'Well, you can write to Fred. He'd get leave and be 'ome in three or four weeks I daresay.'

March found herself in a curious state of mind. It was the only thing to do. Write to Fred and tell him he had to marry her. It was degrading and everything she hated. Yet . . . she did not entirely hate the idea. If she had a choice it would be different of course. But she had no choice. Fred had no choice. They must be married as soon as possible. Just for an instant she let herself remember Fred's hand moving along the inside of her thigh. She shivered.

'I'll write,' she said in a low voice. 'I'll write tomorrow.'

Aunt Sylv stared down at the red-brown head. 'Are you sure child? Can you really marry one of the Lukers and make a go of it?'

March lifted her shoulders, shrugging off the large hand.

'I've got no choice, have I?' she asked.

Aunt Sylv had had no choice either. The father of her three children had already been married to someone else. She sighed deeply.

'No. Not really March. You ain't got no choice.'

As it happened March did not have to wait until Wednesday to meet Mr. Gould. The next afternoon, as they lay in canvas chairs on the fine golden sand, he stopped before them and tipped his straw boater charmingly.

'This is a lucky meeting!' he said, his eyes on May. 'I thought as the afternoon was so bright, I would take the air.'

Aunt Sylv gave a dry, cynical cough. March, who was composing a rough draft of her letter in pencil, looked up unwelcomingly. Daze, who might have oiled the situation as she had the previous evening, was nowhere in sight. May did her best. Mr. Gould touched March's unresponsive hand and looked baffled.

May smiled. 'Have you time to fetch a chair and sit with us, Mr. Gould? We should be glad of your company.'

'It would be the greatest pleasure, Miss Rising.'

He almost sprinted along the beach to the stack of chairs. May said happily, 'What a charming coincidence. We were rather dull by ourselves, weren't we?'

Aunt Sylv lengthened her mouth in a kind of smile. March said, 'I was not dull, May. I was writing home.'

'Darling March. But do take the trouble to talk to Mr. Gould. I want you to tell me if he reminds you of . . . someone.'

March put away her notepad and pencil ungraciously, but hardly needed to open her mouth. Aunt Sylv limited herself as always to monosyllables. Mr. Gould and May were quite capable of sustaining a conversation throughout the long golden September afternoon; and did so. Many facts emerged. He was twenty-eight to her twenty-two. He had a 'weak chest' so was unable to serve his country, but as the Happy Hey Days had performed in all the barrack halls in England he liked to think that in his small way —

'You probably do more for the spirit of our cause than many a serving soldier!' May said enthusiastically.

'Thank you Miss Rising. Thank you.' His colour deepened gratefully. 'We played Bournemouth last week and at the end of our last performance I was handed a white feather.'

'Oh my goodness,' May said, hands to face.

'It was a frightful experience. And on stage too.'

'I wish I'd been there,' May declared passionately. 'I would have stood up and announced to the whole auditorium that in spite of being medically unfit to serve in the field, you were doing more than your bit to keep our fighting spirit high!' Her cheeks flushed, like his, and her blue eyes flashed. She looked magnificent.

He sighed. 'Ah Miss Rising. . . . Actually Miss Maud Davenport, who does several numbers with me, did go to the front of the stage and say something of the sort.'

May paused, ravaged suddenly with an unaccustomed emotion which she hardly recognised as jealousy. 'I am so glad,' she said at last.

He saw at once that he had erred. So he then told her that the 'company' was his only family. Both his parents had died when he was small, and he had been brought up by grandparents in North London who had sent him to a small private school where 'drama' had been prominent on the curriculum.

'My younger sister went to a private school also,' May breathed, delighted to find another link between them. 'She teaches there now. Our brother went with her.' She lowered her voice. 'He died when he was six.'

'How frightful! Yet . . . you *knew* him. And you have sisters too. I have no-one.'

Daze returned and pestered to be taken to the Punch and Judy show. Mr. Gould and May strolled along the sand with her and stood on the outskirts of the crowd, smiling at Judy's squawks but hardly hearing them. May told him about Albert and how terribly March missed him, and that was why she was out of sorts. She told him about Florence saving up so that they could have this week away. She even mentioned the decline in Will's business. He said, 'I envy you your family, Miss May.'

She noticed the change in address and dimpled. 'I would like to share them. They would be most happy to welcome you if you are ever in Gloucester, Mr. Gould. The house is always full of callers.'

'It would indeed be a pleasure.' He smiled absently at the vociferous applause all around them for Punch's antics, then added abruptly, 'And is there a special caller, Miss May? I cannot believe you are not engaged to some lucky man.'

May, too, smiled over the heads of the crowd towards the striped box with its tiny stage.

'Well . . . I am not. And there is no special caller.' She turned to him and her polite smile disappeared. 'There was someone. Yes. As a matter of fact he was a childhood sweetheart. We were expected — everyone expected . . . I had a ring. But the connection was meaningless and when my father forebade it earlier this summer, I will confess I was relieved.' She added in a low voice, 'I have told no-one else how I feel. They realise that I am not heartbroken. But I have told no-one that I am . . . relieved.'

He looked at her with a gaze that was now steadfast.

'I am honoured that you have told me,' he said. The crowd began to break up and he changed again from serious to mischievous. 'Let's run from your cousin! Wave to her — yes, she's seen! Now come on!'

At once the moment was transformed into fun. Daisy ran screaming after them and Mr. Gould pulled May behind the bathing-machines, then expertly beneath the promenade where the paddle boats were stacked. They emerged the other side, doubled back gasping with laughter, and slowed to a respectable walk as they came within sight of March and Aunt Sylv.

March made another effort. 'Did Daisy enjoy the show? Where is she?'

Mr. Gould spoke up to cover May's threatened giggles. 'She enjoyed it a great deal from the sound of her applause. She was with us a moment ago.' He glanced around innocently as Daisy came panting up, hurling accusations. 'Ah, there you are child!' he boomed in music-hall tones. 'Rescued at last from the Perils of Punch!'

March and Aunt Sylv exchanged glances as the other three were finally convulsed by their own laughter.

By Wednesday afternoon March's letter was in the post and she felt a great deal better. Strangely, when she thought of her future it was with a small thrill of something like excitement. Perhaps it was because she suddenly had a future. Or perhaps May's twitterings were infectious. Even March could see that May had never felt like this before. Aunt Sylv said straight out, 'The girl's head over heels in love.' And May herself did not deny it. She could think of nothing and no-one but Monty

270

Gould. She wanted to touch that sleek dark hair and look into those light brown eyes again . . . drown in them. . . it was the most romantic thing that had ever happened to her. Yet she had known of its possibility. That was why she had waited . . . yes, she saw quite clearly that it was all ordained.

They returned from the beach after another accidental meeting with Mr. Gould, to find the afternoon post waiting for them on the dark stairs that led up to their rooms. Florence's handwriting was recognised immediately. The envelope was addressed to Aunt Sylv, and while the kettle boiled for tea she slit it open and passed it to March to read aloud to them all.

March did not get very far. Reading on while May commented, 'Darling Mamma, the notepaper even smells of her!' she stopped suddenly and drew in a shuddering breath. May said, 'What is it March dear?' But March could not reply. May took the paper from her numb fingers and read it for herself. Tragically she looked up at Aunt Sylv. 'It's Fred Luker. He's listed as missing believed killed. Poor Mrs. Luker is taken ill and Sibbie is back home looking after them all.'

Daisy said perfunctorily, 'Poor old Fred. Still, he might be all right I suppose.' She glanced at her mother. 'Will we be allowed to speak to Sibbie our Mam? If she's there all the time it will be difficult not to.'

Aunt Sylv said tersely, 'We'll see. Now go and make the tea our Daze — two spoonfuls 'll be enough mind. And May, take this sixpence and pop down to that shop that sells off buns at closing time.'

May was surprised. 'We've got bread and butter.' She saw Aunt Sylv's expression and nodded. 'I won't be long.' She went through the kitchen. 'Don't go in for a bit, Daze dear. This sort of thing makes March remember Albert all over again. She's very upset.'

She was so upset that there was no question of her going to the show. The news seemed to bring on one of her queasy turns again. Aunt Sylv put her to bed with

271

the tea when it was made and said she would trust May and Daisy to behave themselves for the evening and she would be outside the theatre at nine o'clock sharp to meet them. May was so thankful that March's sudden relapse did not bar her from seeing Mr. Gould that she spared very little thought to Fred Luker's predicament or the effect it had had on her sister. The slightest thing upset poor March these days and at one time she and Fred had been quite friendly.

May and Daisy sat in the front row holding hands, prepared to enjoy every second of the evening. Which they did. Monty Gould concluded the show with a song generally sung by a saucy soubrette in music hall who would cast her eye to her partner or even up to the boxes. Monty Gould sang it seriously to everyone there, even the harassed usher. 'I love you dearly, dearly and I hope that you love me. . . .' Only then did May discover that she and Daisy were still hanging on to each other for dear life. She looked round and grinned sheepishly, wishing that it were April sitting there sharing these precious moments. Then she saw tears in Daisy's eyes. She smiled, and the fourteen-year-old smiled back then sawed at her nose with the back of her hand. 'In't 'e lovely our May?' she whispered. 'In't 'e the loveliest man you've ever seen?' And May hugged the thin shoulders suddenly.

Aunt Sylv did not waste time with idle regrets or even grief.

'Pretty kettle of fish this is,' she remarked, going into the small bedroom as May and Daze had left. 'But to be honest my girl, I couldn't see much hope of happiness for you with Fred Luker.'

March, lying frozen in the bed, staring at the ceiling, said cruelly, 'You should know about that. You never had much out of your marriage, did you?'

Aunt Sylv looked at her sharply, surprised by this show of spirit. 'Don't you be too sure of that March

272

Rising, neither. Dick an' me, we were 'appy enough when we was allowed to be. We was two of a kind. You and Fred Luker — chalk and cheese.'

March turned her head and stared at the window instead. 'Doesn't matter now. We won't get the chance to find out.'

Aunt Sylv folded her arms. 'It'll 'ave to be Lottie Jenner, that's all. She won't talk. I'll see 'er an' —'

'Not yet.'

Aunt Sylv said warningly, 'Once you're much over three months you can't do nothing March. And Flo mustn't know — it 'ud kill 'er —'

'All right, all right. I'm talking about a day or two. Not a month, not even a week. Just two days after this week.'

Aunt Sylv was unaccountably nervous. 'What you thinking about girl? You can't do nothing yourself mind. An' if you start jumping about . . . it gen'lly strengthens you whatever they do say.'

March said, 'It doesn't look as if I've got the energy to do much jumping about, does it?'

'Then what? I don't want nothing 'appening March. Flo trusted me with you two girls.'

March turned her head into the pillow and her voice was muffled.

'There's someone who might help me. My uncle in Bath. On the way home I'll call on him. It'll be all right Aunt Sylv. Letty and Rose are in the house, even Mother couldn't object to me spending a night there. After all, I was Aunt Lizzie's favourite niece.' She sobbed, suddenly remembering Aunt Lizzie. And Albert. And Fred Luker.

Aunt Sylv said doubtfully, 'I don't know what that old man can do, I'm sure.'

March said fiercely, 'He's got money. And money can buy anything!'

Aunt Sylv did not argue with that.

*   *   *

273

The following afternoon Monty Gould proposed marriage to May and was accepted instantly. They discussed arrangements in a sort of trance. They were both over twenty-one, but he would come to Gloucester and ask her father's permission formally. Everything was going to be absolutely straightforward. Everything was going to be absolutely wonderful.

Aunt Sylv said crossly she wished she had never come to Weymouth in the first place and what Flo was going to say she couldn't guess. Daisy hugged her and told her that she was as pleased as Punch about the whole thing really. She smiled unwillingly.

When May was asleep that night March punched her pillow and stared dry-eyed at her own abdomen. 'I hate you Fred Luker,' she whispered with absolute conviction. 'You promised . . . you promised. . . .' And then she almost physically shut him out of her thoughts and lay down, hands over the place where 'it' must be. She did not have time to think about Fred now. Somehow she had to persuade a great deal of money out of Uncle Edwin. Enough for her to go away on a long holiday by herself. The difficulties were enormous. And not only in Bath either. Mother would protest in amazement at the idea of her daughter traipsing around the country on her own.

March tightened her mouth. She was twenty-four. She was a woman.

A sudden wave of nausea made her hold her breath and when it had passed she was cold and shivering. Oh God . . . she was a woman.

13

Will and Florence found it difficult to understand just what had happened at Weymouth. Sylvia, suddenly cowardly, had gone straight in to number thirty-three, and May, in a state of euphoria, seemed hardly to notice she had arrived home without her sister.

'Mamma — April — Father — it has been the most wonderful week of my life. I have to tell you — I know you will say it is too sudden — but that is the way it was, so I must tell the truth.'

Florence said, 'Darling girl. It is wonderful to see you. Leave the suitcase there, April, and let us have tea. Is March having hers with Granny?'

May settled herself at the table with an expression of bliss.

'Boiled eggs! And no-one's birthday! Oh Mamma, it's as if you knew there was something special to celebrate! Sit by me April — how beautiful you are darling, your hair is so much curlier than mine and when it's loose like that . . . March is in Bath, Mamma.'

'In Bath? On her own?'

'She was anxious about Uncle Edwin and said she had been selfish to have a week at the seaside when she should have been comforting him. But that's not what I want to tell you. I have the most wonderful news —' she decapitated her egg as if she expected a rabbit to leap from it, then smiled as if it had. 'I have met the man I am going to marry. In Weymouth. He is beautiful — he reminded me of Teddy when first we met. But there is also something of Papa about him. His name is Montague Gould. Monty for short. Isn't that sweet Mamma? Monty. It sounds so right don't you think? May and Monty. Oh my dears, I am so happy!' And as if to prove it beyond doubt two tears collected and rolled on to her cheeks.

April was the first to respond. She gave a sort of squeak and flung her arms around May, sweeping both their eggs out of the cups and setting them rolling across the tablecloth oozing yolk. Florence sat very still, staring down at a leaf floating in her tea. Will finished stirring his and replaced the spoon with a clatter, leaning back in his chair and saying, 'Well! Whatever next? Goes away for a few days by the sea and comes back going to get married! To a perfect stranger!'

May was not put out. Laughing in spite of her tears, looking through April's spread hair, she said, 'Perfect is the right word Daddy. Perfect for me.' She turned her blue eyes on her mother. 'Oh Mamma, I do love him so. He's made everything so — so *right* for me!'

Florence looked up and smiled slightly. 'Wasn't anything right before?' she asked gently. 'You have been our ray of sunshine, May. I did not know things were not . . . right.'

'How could they be, Mamma? All that has happened —' she reached out beyond April's shoulder and caught her mother's hand stretched towards her. 'But now . . . there's a meaning to all that. I know now why I was put on the earth. It's so difficult to explain.'

April said passionately, 'I know what you mean May.'

'I think we do too. Don't we Will?' Florence turned her gentle face down the table. Will shrugged almost irritably, but May knew she had all the support that was necessary. She began on a description of Monty's charms.

Will said gruffly, 'Why isn't the fellow in uniform? Not one of these conchies is he?'

'Of course not Daddy! He has a weak chest and was

not fit enough for the army. But my goodness, he does more for the country than many a soldier, yes, I can say that in all truth Mamma! If you could see him perform —'

'Perform? What is he? Some circus fellow?'

'Daddy, please don't be horrid. Monty is — is —' she knew that he was a music hall artiste, but could guess the reaction that would provoke. 'He is an actor,' she said with dignity.

Only April was delighted with this information. Florence looked worried, Will did not like it. He was suddenly insanely jealous. His sons had been taken from him and now he was to lose his daughter.

'I cannot allow a daughter of mine to run off with an actor fellow,' he said pompously.

May, still holding her mother's hand, responded to the gentle pressure and simply laughed. 'Daddy. Just let me tell you about him. The way he held the audience in the palm of his hand, yet is so alone. No family. I want him to belong to ours. I want you all to feel —' she swallowed and gripped her mother's fingers tightly. 'I want you to feel that Monty is another son.' She sobbed. 'Oh my dears, there is room here for a son, surely? Papa darling, he is completely different from David. So willing to love and be loved! To be with Monty is like being in the sunshine.' She turned to Florence impulsively, hardly realising that April had withdrawn herself. 'Mamma, d'you remember how it was with Teddy? That feeling of happiness — of something exciting about to happen — of everything being amusing and — and fun?' She saw that Florence remembered only too well. 'That is how it is with Monty!'

Florence tried to maintain her smile. 'I think you are in love, my darling girl.'

There was little more to be said. Will asked unanswerable questions about the young man's income and Florence wondered worriedly how May would manage to make a home in theatrical digs, but they could see that May was determined. The questions were shelved until Monty's arrival next weekend; speculation — the enjoyable kind — was embarked on.

April, ready to dislike the young man because he was different from David, was forced to kiss her sister's peach-like cheek. She said sturdily, 'I hope he knows how lucky he is!'

May held her sister to her. 'We are both so lucky,' she said quietly. 'We thought how easy it would have been to miss each other. If the company had not got that week's booking at Weymouth. If Mother had not persuaded March and me to take a week's holiday. It is terrifying to think by what a narrow margin we found each other.'

Will remembered thinking how lucky it was that smallpox had driven Flo out to Kempley. But now the memory was a tinny echo and meant little. In some ways it put him against the match. He looked from one to another of his family; it was at moments like that he felt most alone.

'And as for March . . .' he growled. 'I've got an order for a suit so I hope she won't hang about in Bath too long.'

March continued to rehearse what she would say to Uncle Edwin as she walked past the abbey and began the long climb up the terraces of Bath. Aunt Sylv had given her sufficient money for a cab and checked that she could use her railway ticket the next day, but March did not know what might happen at this interview; she kept the florin where it was, inside her glove, in case she needed to buy food or a bed for the night. She swallowed on a dry mouth: Uncle Edwin had always said she was like Aunt Lizzie; would he now believe that she was also consumptive — a fact to be kept from her family — and needed six months' rest? She swallowed again. At least she wasn't going to be sick. When the saliva ran, that was the time to find the water closet.

She pulled the doorbell with a hand that trembled slightly. She had left a Gladstone bag at the station with a few of her things rifled from the big case she shared with May, and she suddenly felt ridiculous standing there in a linen coat and skirt she had made herself, as if she had called for a casual hour instead of on a desperate mission. But when Letty opened the door and immediately exclaimed her delight, her nervousness disappeared and she was able to lie calmly.

'Letty, is my uncle at home? I took a cab in between trains hoping to have an hour or so with him.'

'Oh Miss March — Miss March! He'll be that glad to see you! Oh this is a lovely surprise I'll be bound! Come in, come in. We haven't seen anything so pleasing since — since —' she lowered her eyes. 'Since you know when.'

March patted her shoulder. She had been the only one of the Rising children to treat Letty and Rose as servants and not equals, and strangely enough they loved her for it.

'Never mind, Letty. I'm here now. Where is my uncle?'

'In the dining-room, Miss. He spends a lot of time there these days.' Letty dropped her voice sepulchrally. 'Where 'er coffin was.'

March nodded as if it was the most natural thing in the world, though her heart sank when she remembered how oddly Uncle Edwin had behaved in that room before the funeral. Letty did not announce her, seeming almost reluctant to approach the door, and March paused before knocking and looked back.

'Letty, is there a fire in the sitting-room? No? Then ask Rose to light one, will you? And we'll have tea in there like the old days.'

Letty paused, one foot on the basement steps. She and Rose both suffered from rheumatism and were not used to coal-carrying any more. But March had a look of the mistress about her, and it was nice to feel there was a hand on the helm again just for an afternoon. Letty smiled and creaked downward.

Uncle Edwin was sitting with his back to the door, staring across the gleaming expanse of the dining-table to the window beyond. The room, which had seemed so bright when Aunt Lizzie presided over meals, was in reality all heavy mahogany and stifling velvet. March could smell the dust. She said timidly, 'Uncle . . . it is me. March. Come to see you as I promised.'

He turned slowly like a mechanical figure on a stand. His face had sunk cadaverously, his hair was sparse and iron grey, and his eyes, colourless and dull, stared at her expressionlessly for a long moment without surprise. Then he held out a hand.

'I've been waiting for you. Sit down.'

She took his hand, looking around for a chair. They were tucked neatly beneath the table, but when she moved to go to one, he kept her by him, looking up at her. She stood next to him uncomfortably.

He whispered, 'It's time. We've waited a full year. That is enough surely?'

'I should have come sooner Uncle. But you heard we lost. . . .' Her voice trailed away.

He said, 'Your mother wrote to me. You know grief now, my dear.'

She nodded. He drew her closer and put the back of her hand to his cheek. She could feel the roughness of stubble.

He said, 'We will comfort each other, March.'

'If only that could be so, Uncle.'

'Of course it can be so, dearest. Do you not remember our words of last year? That is why you have come. It will take time. It will not be easy. There is a difference in our ages and I am no longer strong. But it has always been there, March . . . between us . . . the understanding.'

Her lips were as dry as parchment. 'Yes Uncle,' she whispered, hardly knowing what he meant, yet remembering the presents and the kisses and the sense of power.

He droned on. 'Before Lizzie left me, I knew that you were meant to take her place. And then she commanded it.'

'Commanded —?'

'On her last day. She said you were to have everything that was hers. Everything. I did not understand her at first. I thought — her clothes, jewellery. She came to me empty-handed, March, the Rhys-Davies never had a penny.'

'So I understand Uncle.'

'But then I knew. When we stood here together, March, I knew. And I saw that you knew too.' He rubbed her hand harder and she tried not to flinch away. 'Lizzie intended you to inherit me, March. That was her last wish.' As he spoke he seemed to be gaining energy from somewhere. His beard rasped on her hand agonisingly and his voice was stronger. March was paralysed with horror. Tears of pain started to her eyes and she swallowed and swallowed again, desperately.

He said, 'I sit here often March, thinking back. And I see that when you arrived that first time, as a child, she recognised something in you that was a facsimile. She began training you then, my dear, to take her place. Talking to you. Telling you about her background. About me —'

'She never spoke of your affairs, Uncle.'

'She was never disloyal, I know that. But she spoke of the way to . . .' he chuckled softly, '. . .to *manage* me. Did she not? Gentle persuasion — did she not tell you to use gentle persuasion?'

The highlighted memory, once so precious and secret between her and Aunt Lizzie, now made her gasp with horror.

'I see she did.' He removed her hand at last and looked down at it. 'My dear, I have made you bleed!' They both stared down at the prominent metacarpals, the middle one traced by a line of bloody graze. Then Uncle Edwin put his mouth to it and sucked. The pain leapt up her arm

281

and she gave a little cry. 'My dear, I am sorry . . . sorry . . .' he kissed frantically with puckered lips and then touched her hand with extended tongue. 'Is that better?'

She longed to pull away and run from the house, back to the security of Florence.

She whispered, 'Much better Uncle. Much better.'

He saw her tears and tried to stand up to take her in his arms. Somehow she moved naturally towards the door and said shakily, 'I've asked Letty to light a fire in the front room. Shall we go in and have tea now?'

She did not wait for his reply but went into the front room. It was warm there, in any case, after the sun of the day. She spread her hands to the blaze of the newly-lit fire and when Uncle Edwin came in she was drawing up one of the many small tables to accommodate the tray which Letty had just brought in. She smiled up at him. 'This is nice,' she said. 'See, Letty has fetched us some muffins. Like old times.'

She must be careful. Very careful. Until she knew exactly what he intended she must give away nothing.

In the event Monty Gould arrived at Chichester House before March, clutching roses for Florence and some precious tobacco for Will and a book of Keats' poems for April. It was a very good beginning.

May's tales of her family had been based on a lifetime's memories and had ill-prepared Monty for the stark reality of the small, plump man wearing glasses, surrounded by three thin women. April had a cold and was less vivid than usual, and Florence, far from being the dark elegant creature May had described, was an old lady. Chichester House itself was too large and draughty and though October was still a week away, Monty was glad to congregate with the others around the kitchen range. Everything was shabby and depressing. Only May shone like a candle through it all. The sooner he married her and got her away from this, the better.

As for the Risings, they saw an extremely good-looking, well-dressed young man. Inclined to flamboyance at first, he soon discarded that manner like a change of costume, and became simple and straightforward. In his wide-eyed frankness, Florence did indeed see Teddy. In his comradeliness, Will glimpsed Albert. When he nodded over the newspaper April sensed her father.

Will said bluffly, 'Have to take you along to my shoot my boy. Robinswood Hill. Nice bit of country and we might get a rabbit for the pot.' He had not gone to Robinswood since his trips with Albert.

'I say. Thanks a lot sir. I'd enjoy that.'

They brought home a rabbit each and Will was in good spirits.

'We've settled it all May. Your young man seems set on a Christmas wedding, so the sooner you see about the banns the better.'

Florence was secretly horrified, May overjoyed.

'Oh Daddy — I knew you'd love him. I knew it!' She hugged her father's arm, sensing that his enthusiasm would diminish if she hugged Monty.

Florence said quietly, 'So soon? I had not thought to lose you so soon.'

It was Monty, with his unerring instinct for saying the right thing, who picked up her hand. 'Please do not talk of losing May, Mrs. Rising. This will always be her home and she will often be in it.'

Will nodded. 'Young Monty has persuaded me that there is a lot to be said for racketing around the country, Flo. They can often racket this way!'

May smiled encouragingly at her mother. 'Listen. I'm going to go up and light the candles on the piano and we'll have a sing-song in the bandy room. I want you to hear Monty sing.'

April said, 'The candles are nearly gone. Shall I light the gas?'

May shook her head. 'No. Just the candles. I'll bring some more.'

When they gathered ten minutes later, April understood May's insistence on doing without gas. The candles flickered on her golden hair as she accompanied Monty, and they made his brown eyes luminous. He sang alone at first, his light tenor sounding like Albert's in the closeness of the room. Then they sang in duet; all the old favourites. 'We have come to the end of a perfect day.' 'Keep the Home Fires burning.' 'Come into the garden Maud.' April watched her mother and wanted to weep.

Monty left on Monday morning from the Midland station. He was playing in Blackpool that evening; it was a long engagement and he promised to find digs for two. They had already advanced the date of their wedding to November.

May leaned up to the carriage window and kissed him chastely and he murmured, 'Thank you for everything darling. They're just as you said — a wonderful family — a beautiful home —'

May smiled. 'They adored you darling. And when you shot that rabbit —'

'I was a gamekeeper in a play once.' He grinned at her horrified expression. 'Nothing else to it darling.'

May wept a little as she walked on afterwards to Helen's. It made her look pale and interesting and Helen, as well as some of the more privileged clientele, thought it was terribly romantic. She hoped it would snow on her wedding day. She began composing a letter to Monty telling him this and describing the snowflakes as 'confetti from heaven'. Perhaps he might write a song of that name.

At five-thirty on Tuesday a telegram arrived from

March. It said 'Married today. New Inn 7 pm. Love March and Edwin.'

Florence read it twice before taking it through to Will in the workroom. He was reading the paper but bundled it hastily behind the sewing machine as she entered. The enormity of March's message did not get through.

'What does she mean?' He looked accusingly over his spectacles as if Florence was keeping something from him. 'Married? Is she married? Who has she married?'

Florence felt a sensation creeping up her spine and knew it to be a species of fear.

'Look at the signature.'

He looked and his frown deepened. 'We knew she was with Edwin of course. But has he had the audacity to agree to her marrying someone? I've never liked his manner where March is concerned, but if he thinks he can step into my shoes —'

'He wouldn't . . . he wouldn't . . .'

'I'm not so sure. And what does this mean? New Inn. Do they mean our New Inn? If she has got married, then she's ashamed of him. Won't bring him here. New Inn indeed?'

Florence said without hope, 'It might be Edwin who has remarried.' She looked through the window. 'Here is April. Perhaps she can help.'

But April could not and neither could May when she arrived. The telegram was taken over to number thirty-three and read to Aunt Sylv and Gran Rising. The former said sharply, 'What does Flo make of it?'

April shook her head. 'Nothing. We don't know what to make of it.'

Aunt Sylv looked as if she might say something significant, but all that she actually managed was, 'Looks as if March might put in an appearance about seven o'clock. You'll know then I s'ppose.'

'Yes,' April said. There seemed little doubt that March had married someone in fact. And May was marrying her actor. April felt a twinge of something like fear.

*   *   *

By seven, they were all assembled in the kitchen. The minutes ticked by and no-one came. May dismissed it as a joke. Florence said, 'If nothing happens, you must go to Bath tomorrow Will, and bring her back. I don't like her staying there now that Aunt Lizzie has gone.'

And then just before eight, the door bell jangled in the hall. April flew to the door and in the dim light saw that March stood there alone.

'Oh thank goodness!' She drew her sister inside gratefully. 'We wondered what to expect. We're all here waiting for you — come on.'

March did not hang back. She saved her exclamations until she reached the kitchen door by which time they sounded theatrical.

'Why are you here? Didn't you get my wire? The New Inn at seven o'clock — I wrote it quite clearly and the clerk read it back to me. We've been waiting for you. Edwin has ordered the most sumptuous dinner —' She ran out of breath and took another quickly before anyone could speak. 'At half-past seven he let me take the car and come to fetch you! Yes my very own car — what d'you think of that? It's a Wolseley. Grey with a darling tonneau. April you'll love it! You must come and stay with us and I'll teach you to drive.'

It was Gran who stopped the flow. Her voice came out in a squawk which rivalled her own cockerel back at Kempley.

'You've married your uncle? Is that what you're saying girl? You've married that old man?'

March, her tirade silenced, swallowed two or three times and ran her tongue around her lips. Then she drew herself up.

'Edwin and I have always been close. Yes, close. He

286

is shy and retiring otherwise he would have come and asked properly Papa. He — he needs a companion —' she shook her head at Flo's exclamation of horror. 'I am fond of him. Truly. And the best way seemed to be —'

Will said wildly, 'It's against the law! A niece cannot marry her uncle!'

'There is no blood relationship Papa. We have been married in the Baptist church today. Quite legally —'

'In Bath?'

'We did not think you would wish it to be here.' March slipped off a glove and displayed her ring. Her hand was yellowy white and a scar ran down its length. 'Please don't be angry. Come back with me and eat a meal. Please. I cannot bear it if you turn against me — I cannot bear it!'

There was another silence. They stared at her ring. Then May said, 'Oh March. Oh darling. What have you done?'

March looked at her desperately. 'The only thing I could do! The only possible thing! I have nothing — I *am* nothing! Uncle Edwin has always loved me!' She took a step towards her mother and saw the distaste in the brown eyes. Her hand clenched, the bones standing out skeletally. She said in a choking voice, 'Very well. If you will not celebrate with me — or wish me well — I'll have to manage on my own.'

Aunt Sylv said, 'March — wait a bit — sit down and talk to your ma and pa. Tell them —'

'No!' said March harshly. 'No Aunt Sylv! If they can't accept my marriage, I don't wish to talk to them again!'

Gran spoke in her hard old voice. 'Leave 'er be Sylv. She's made 'er bed. Now let 'er lie on it.'

March laughed wildly. 'It's — a very comfortable bed thank you Grandmother! More comfortable than any bed I shall find with you!'

And she turned and left Chichester House.

*   *   *

October came in wet and windy, the Indian summer giving up almost overnight to winter. It became obvious that the much-vaunted capture of little Passchendaele had cost too much; April heard a rumour from Gladys Luker — who had it from Sibbie, who had it from old Charles Williams — that the German casualty list was far lower than the British. If killing men was what the war was about, then Passchendaele, Messine, Ypres, counted for little. April felt a sinking frustration and guessed that David had felt the same all along. If only she could talk to him . . . he would understand that the events in her family — the high romance of May's sudden match and the sordid pragmatism of March's — were like shadows of the war. David understood things like that.

April missed March more than she had thought possible. When Albert had come home and given himself so whole-heartedly to his family again through March, her sister's happiness had been a revelation to April. She had been permitted to love March as she had very occasionally loved her when they were children. They had talked of very ordinary things: school affairs and the possibility of buying a second-hand car after the war. When the news of Albert's death had driven March into the waste lands, April had always hoped that she might be the one March would turn to. She was home each evening long before May, and tried to do the things May did so well. She cut her sister's bread for her, stirred her tea, fetched a cushion. That guardianship was not only taken from her suddenly, it was proved to have been useless; March had evidently not even noticed April's special care and love.

April felt she might be taking over March's role of frustrated emptiness; looking ahead to May's departure, it seemed almost inevitable. It was impossible to take May's place, with her ranks of followers. April was still too young in Florence's opinion for the dances at the hospital, and in any case May's ready sympathy was not hers. She could have given her life to one of May's pathetic young men, but a kiss and a loving glance were quite beyond her.

She threw herself into the work at Midland Road and felt guilty because she enjoyed it. Gladys put her feelings in a nutshell when she asked one Sunday afternoon as they walked home from the church: 'Don't you feel left out o' things April?'

She did. She felt that the great events of the world were passing over her head.

Gladys went on scornfully, 'There were a whole lot of us weren't there? Daze, you, me, Bridget Williams — stuck-up donkey — and Tolly Hall. An' your Teddy of course. An' I'm the only one out o the lot of you that's doing any bloody thing about the war effort!'

It was true. Bridget was at the high school and Tolly had actually won a bursary to the Crypt School. Daisy was now ensconced at the chemist's and was allowed to serve in the shop when they were busy. She talked high and mightily about getting shop work later on when the baby was old enough to be left.

Gladys turned the knife in the wound. 'I bet ole Teddy would 'a lied about his age and been in the trenches by now!'

April said feebly, 'Don't be silly Glad. Teddy wouldn't be fifteen till Christmas Eve.' But she wouldn't have put anything past Teddy.

As if to reinforce her feelings of inadequacy, Kitty Hall arrived that very evening with a pile of blankets for Florence to darn. Tearfully she confided that Tolly wished to join a group of volunteer schoolboys forming an ambulance corps. The boys had already raised enough money to buy an ambulance and were talking to the Red Cross about the scheme. Kitty's husband, Barty, was inclined to think the whole thing would make a man out of little Tolly and refused to interfere. Kitty had all Florence's sympathy but the only comfort she could offer — and perhaps the best — was a murmured, 'They won't consider it my dear. Boys of fifteen — it would be ridiculous.'

April wasn't so sure. She met Bridget a few days later and found her enthusiastic about Tolly's scheme. Bridget had gradually transferred much of her hero-worship from the image of murdered Teddy to Tolly Hall, who had shared so much of Teddy's short life, and she tried hard to inject quiet Tolly with a little of Teddy's adventurous spirit.

So it was that when April saw the advertisement in the *Citizen* she was ripe for some sort of rebellion. It said, 'Give your hair to the war effort!' And underneath in smaller print it offered to send one whole pound to the Red Cross for every length of hair donated. The address given was in Alvin Street, a narrow ancient thoroughfare of slums running between Worcester Street and the cathedral. April sauntered that way when she came out of school. The number given was enamelled on a peeling doorway next to a second-hand furniture shop. She intended merely to enquire for further details, but as soon as she opened the door on to a bare, noisome hallway, she was lost. A squat Italian woman appeared from beneath the stairs which rose out of the hall; her eyes ran over April's respectable figure and took in the mass of hair beneath the knitted beret. She said, 'Y-e-es?'

April said nervously, 'There was a piece in the paper. About — er — giving one's — er — hair for the Red Cross.'

The woman's face cracked into a congratulatory beam and she seized April's hands and made a sort of obeisance over them as she overwhelmed her with praise. April could not get a word in. She was led down some basement steps and into what had been a coal cellar. Two or three chairs stood around a tall mirror. A man was having a shave, wrapped in a sheet. April backed away.

'I did not realise — a gentleman's barber shop —'

'We wish to show our patriotism my child — just as you!' She dusted a chair and ushered April into it. 'But how to do it? All we have is our skill with the scissors. Then we must use this skill, yes? Just as you have just your hair perhaps? Now the cover-up —' April was swathed in the sheet whipped from the other customer. 'The hat over here . . . the hair pins. A-a-ah. Papa! Look at this beautiful hair. Two pieces would you say? Three?' She pushed her face before April's. 'How does that seem to you child? Three pounds for the Red Cross. And you will hardly notice it. The hair is so thick and curly it will twirl around your face so and so —' She did things with a greasy comb and April, staring appalled into the long mirror, saw that her hair did indeed twist and twirl becomingly over her ears and forehead. Rather Byronesque.

She swallowed. 'Three pounds.' It was a great deal of money.

'So. We will begin.'

The barber left his customer and came over. Wordlessly he clubbed April's hair close to the neck and handed three large tresses to his wife who immediately went to a table, bound the cut ends and dripped wax on to them from a candle. It took no longer than five minutes. April would have put her hands to her face in horror had they been free. As it was, she clenched them fiercely beneath the enveloping sheet and tried not to cry. The man, still without a word, went back to his customer, and the woman, holding the three swatches of hair up in delight, came back to April. She saw her distress and cooed congratulations while she laid the tresses carefully out of April's sight and picked up scissors.

'Now, my angel of mercy . . . we make you very pretty.'

With small flips of comb and scissors, she began. The hair was taken up the nape of the neck at the back and into a feathery fringe in front. April, swallowing and feeling sick, watched a transformation in the mirror. It took longer than that first frightful severance. Fifteen — twenty minutes. The woman was carried away by her own artistry.

'Now my child. You shampoo tonight. And as the hair dries, you comb it this way. Up. Always up. You understand?' April nodded dumbly and allowed herself to be uncovered and led back up the stairs. She stood in the street outside the chipped door feeling vulnerable . . . cold . . . bald! She couldn't go home, she couldn't face them. May would be appalled and sympathetic. Florence would be horrified. And Will . . . April and her father had not been very close since the David débâcle, but he would still be hurt about her hair.

She scurried from Worcester Street into the Northgate like a criminal. Then suddenly turned past the cattle market and began to run in earnest; towards the Barton. She did not ask herself why; she just ran. It had been a grey, rain-filled day and was almost dusk; a light shone from Daker's window, illuminating the boxes of cottons and silks. She held her side and breathed deeply. Then opened the door and went in.

The bell pinged and the thick smell of cloth enfolded her reassuringly, just as it did in Will's workroom. David was behind the counter, measuring ribbon on the brass rule set into the wood. His customer blocked April from his view. She turned her back and fingered a roll of silk, praying Mrs. Daker would not come to serve her.

Luck held. The customer said, 'That was barely the two yards, you know.' And David murmured something and obviously added another inch because there came a satisfied grunt and the customer continued, 'I measured carefully but there are the turnings and so on.'

'Quite.'

April had not heard David's voice for nearly three months and the monosyllable started her heart beating violently. She had an impulse to lean her head down on to the silk and restrained herself with an effort.

He had to pass her to open the door for the customer, but his back was towards her back and he gave no indication of recognition. Behind the counter again there was a short silence. She waited for him to ask whether he could help her and rehearsed how she would turn and whip off her beret in one movement and say brightly, 'What do you think?'

Then he spoke very quietly. 'What are you doing here April?'

She felt her strength disappear through the soles of her feet and the tips of her fingers. Her carefully rehearsed greeting went to the winds. She only half-turned. 'How did you know?' she asked weakly.

He shrugged impatiently. 'How could I not know. Idiot.'

He looked the same. Gaunt. Still haunted.

He said unemotionally, 'Christ. Why are you here? Surely your father told you never to speak to me again?'

She whispered, 'David. I'm so sorry. So sorry.'

'Did he tell you why?'

She shook her head and he laughed shortly. 'Of course not. So why are you here?'

She said painfully, 'I was glad. Glad. When Daddy refused to let May continue with the engagement. I was glad. I'm sorry David.'

'You'd better go.' He did not move. His hands on the polished wood were clenched. 'Go on.'

She went slowly towards him. 'I've always loved you. Ever since — ever since March's birthday party. I wouldn't have hurt you for anything David, but — but — if you are hurt, I could help you.'

He stared for a long moment, his eyes wide and burning black. Then he held out one clenched fist as if he could stop her advance.

'You don't know what you're talking about, little girl. Christ, you're as bad as your father aren't you? Tarred with the same stupid, ignorant brush! Love. Sympathy. Consolation. You and your family make me sick. Sick!'

He did indeed look as if he might throw up then and there.

She stopped, breathing quickly. 'David, don't send me away. I *can* help you. You know I can help you, whatever it is that is gnawing —'

He gave a sort of growl of sheer rage and slammed his fist on to the counter. 'Be quiet! Every word you say makes it worse — can't you see that? Christ, I thought you were the one who had a little — a little —'

'Perception. You said I was perceptive.'

'Don't remind me of my own words for God's sake. You could dredge up enough absurdities to get me committed — just as your father would like to get me committed.'

She was horrified. 'Daddy? No — no, he wouldn't even —'

'Just go away, April Rising. Go away and keep away like Daddy told you! Go and tell the casualties at the hospital how brave they are — how wonderful. They might believe you although you don't know what you're talking about. You're fifteen April! For God's sake, you're fifteen — and you come in here —'

She was weeping, not covering her face which contorted pitifully as the tears rolled down it. He groaned.

She whispered, 'I can't help being fifteen. Not knowing . . . anything. I *do* know I love you! And I do know that you don't love me! That is enough . . . that is enough.' Suddenly she remembered something and reached up to pull off her beret. 'I tried to help. I tried to do something . . . *something*. They're going to pay three pounds to the Red Cross for my hair.'

There was a thick silence in the shop. Somewhere to the rear Mrs. Daker rattled a saucepan against the gas stove. David stared.

Then he said, 'Where did you go?'

'A barber's shop. In Alvin Street.'

'You know they won't give a penny to the Red Cross?'

'I did think about that. But I'm sure they will. She —

she was an Italian and they're very patriotic. And anyway . . . that was what I intended.'

'So that makes it good? Your intentions were good so that makes the whole thing dinky-doo? Does it?' His voice was savage and she began to cry again.

'David, I know it sounds silly. But you *must* understand. I'm — I'm *trying* —'

'Did it occur to you that *if* they give three pounds to the Red Cross they are doubtless getting ten more out of the deal? Do you honestly still believe that people do something for nothing?' He dropped his forehead suddenly on to his raised fists. 'I thought you were intelligent. That's what I meant by perceptive, I expect. Intelligent. And you're stupid. You're stupider than May and I wouldn't have believed anyone in the world could be stupider than May!'

She sobbed, standing helpless and vulnerable with her hands by her side, one of them clutching the beret. He did not dare look up and see her; the short curly hair around the face that was heart-shaped instead of oval, the drowned violet eyes . . . he willed her to go. To leave him in peace.

But not April. She said at last, 'What should I have done then? Kept my hair?'

He breathed twice then said, 'Gone to the Red Cross yourself. Offered the — the stuff — direct. If they're not actually selling it they probably know the best market. Oh God, I don't know. Go home April.'

She blurted, 'Tolly Hall is younger than me and he's going to join a medical unit and —'

'Go *home* April!'

'I'm nearly sixteen, David. And people can get married at sixteen.'

'If you don't get out I'll just leave you here.' He began to turn towards the door into the little back parlour.

She said desperately, 'All right I'll go. But . . . but I'll do something David. I'll make you proud of me — I'll do something!'

She dashed the back of her hand across her face and blundered out of the shop. She stood a moment, collecting herself. Luckily the street was almost empty and she rammed on her beret and gloves and hunched her shoulders protectively around her naked ear lobes. But from the depths of her misery rose a new determination. She *was* going to do something positive about her life and David would be proud of her. Purposefully she made for the Black Dog Inn where the bus dropped Gladys every evening.

It was another week before April could present her family with a *fait accompli*. They had been appalled and admiring about her hair and it had been May's consoling kisses that had hurt most of all. She could not tell them then of her intentions in case they eroded them with their understanding caution. As May had shampooed with her own special Cuticura soap, first assuring her how pretty her new curls looked, then exclaiming when they were wet, 'Oh my dearest girl, there's nothing here — absolutely nothing *here!*' April had decided to keep it all to herself until she had actually arranged it. And that was what she did.

Eight days later she addressed them as they gathered at the supper table.

'I've left Miss Midwinter darlings. Today actually. And on Monday I start on the bench next to Gladys. At the munitions factory. Filling shells.' She laughed artificially. 'I had to do something about . . . it.'

Nobody argued. May had bought some satin slippers that very day from a girl who worked at Slade's Shoes in the Promenade at Cheltenham and found it hard to think of anything else. Florence extended a hand, smiling a small, inverted, dismayed smile, and April knelt before her and let her denuded head be patted lovingly.

Will said heavily, 'March lost her position. May's giving hers up. Now you. All three girls.'

May protested vigorously. 'Papa, how can you say

that? Poor March was most unfairly treated — that was made obvious when Sibbie Luker was taken on by that awful old man! And as for me —'

Will shook his head. 'I know. I know. Excuses — reasons — for every one of you! But see it from my point of view for once. My business has run itself into the ground. I'd give anything for the chances you girls have had. And don't blame Sibbie for seizing the opportunity March made available to her.'

Florence was moved to protest. 'Will my dear! May was criticising Sibbie for more than that, as you well know! There now —' she dropped a kiss on April's head. 'Let there be no more talk . . . defeatist talk don't they call it? We must be . . . forward looking. May is going to be married to a dear boy who will look after her and make her life interesting. And April is going to help to win the war. What more could we ask, Will?'

Will was in no mood to be optimistic. He said, 'I could wish for my sons. And for my other daughter who has sold herself more blatantly than Sibbie Luker could ever do —'

'Will! Please!' Florence was ashen-faced, the hand on April's curls suddenly clenched.

Will was not prostrate with apology as he would have been at one time. He thumped himself heavily on to his chair and looked at the table without joy. 'Blackcurrant jam again,' he grumbled. 'I thought we might have dripping toast today. Something seasonal.'

May tried to bring the atmosphere back to normal. 'Blackcurrants are very good for you Papa,' she said briskly, taking over the teapot while Florence controlled herself and April scrambled into her place. 'And we shall need to have plenty of it for April this winter. The girls at the factory turn quite yellow, some of them. It's something to do with breathing the T.N.T.'

April began to eat silently. Her news had not had the effect she had feared. But the sudden eruption of resentment from her father had been like a bursting

297

boil. She glanced at him from beneath her new fringe. She knew he thought of her as his special child; she knew he thought that she had let him down. Was there no way that you could please one person without displeasing another?

Muddled and angry, April munched obediently through her blackcurrant jam sandwich. She didn't care if she turned bright yellow. She would be proud to do so. May simply did not understand .

14

March told Edwin of her pregnancy in the middle of November. His delighted astonishment knew no bounds.

She was sitting in Aunt Lizzie's chair next to the fire in the sitting-room; it was her favourite place in the whole house. He held out his hands to draw her to her feet and when she declined to move, he knelt on the hearth-rug and put his head in her lap in an attitude of worship that was balm to her soul. She rested her own head on the antimacassar and laid reluctant fingers on his hair; encouraged, he slid his hands into the small of her back and pressed his cheek to her stomach. She allowed him to stay there while she counted twenty fairly slowly, then said gently through his murmurings, 'Edwin dear. Do you think it is quite safe to put pressure on baby?' And he immediately staggered to his feet, fetched her a footstool, drew a chair to her side and patted her shoulder. She saw that his face was wet with tears.

He said, 'Are you certain about this dear heart? Tell me everything. When did you know?'

'Oh Edwin . . . it would be indelicate to speak of it.' She turned her head towards the fire. His breath stank.

'But dearest,' he was remembering, calculating. 'If you haven't seen Doctor Maine, you cannot know. After all, I have been only once to your bed.'

She took a sharp breath to show him she did not approve of such frankness. She did not let herself remember that one night.

'Edwin. Dearest.'

'You must let the doctor examine you, March. You cannot know for certain.'

She sat forward and held her hands to the blaze. 'I knew that night, Edwin. That is why I have ... abstained ... ever since. I was thinking of your son, Edwin. There must be no risk.'

'March. Child. How could you have known such a thing.'

'I *knew*, I tell you!' She rounded on him angrily. 'A woman does know these things. And I have been proved right!'

He fell to his knees again and gathered her to him. 'I'm sorry my love. Sorry.' She let him kiss her, keeping still and unresisting as she had when a child. The kiss went on and on. Not until she tasted his foul tongue did she realise where it was leading and pushed him away.

'No Edwin!' she said sharply.

He was thoroughly roused. 'Why not sweetheart? Why not? It is perfectly safe — put your trust in me, March. I know about these things —'

'Is that why your first wife lost four children?' She spoke clearly and cuttingly, knowing she had to put an end to his advances once and for all. He stared up at her. 'Yes, did it occur to you that it might have been your fault? Four miscarriages?' She was all righteous indignation, believing in herself with complete self-delusion. 'My God. I've done my duty, haven't I? I'm bearing you a son Edwin! Isn't that enough for you?'

He was reduced to tears again, holding her hand and begging for forgiveness. Letty came in with the tea things and caught him still at it. She glanced at March, noting the high flush and the hand still protectively across the abdomen.

March said, 'Thank you Letty. Take the coal bucket with you please.' And as soon as the door closed, 'Would you pour the tea Edwin,' she asked. 'I am so tired today. I don't know why.'

'My darling ...' Edwin fussed around her and she

watched him with a half-smile.

'I hope you're not going to treat me like an invalid, Edwin,' she said. 'I'm perfectly healthy you know.'

And she was. When the sickness had gone she had recovered very quickly from the separation with her family which she thought at first would kill her. And she had a new defiance too which helped her enormously when Letty gave her those queer looks, or the neighbours cut her, or her life in Bath with an old man became so boring she wanted to scream. She would show them all.

When the baby was born her family would come round: Florence would be unable to resist the call of grandmotherhood. March might drive down to Gloucester in the Wolseley and take them all out for a spin. Yes, she'd show the Risings all right. And she'd show Fred Luker too, dead or alive. She'd show him that she could do better without him. He might be able to transport her to a plane where everything was wonderful, but she'd show him that even after that experience, she could manage — she could manage. . . .

Montague Gould married May Rising in the distinguished Saint Catherine's church at the top of Wotton Pitch. It was a proper wedding. Will borrowed twenty pounds from Sid Goodrich and hired the Cadena for the breakfast. Monty backed a lucky horse and used his winnings to buy real champagne, some of which he drank from May's slipper. The Citizen printed a long list of guests which still did not hide the absence of the bride's older sister. It provided a bit more gossip to add to the story of traitorous goings-on at Chichester House. May did not care. She was so happy she could hardly believe it. As she hugged April in the privacy of her bedroom before the ceremony, she tried for a moment to pretend that she missed March.

'March and Sibbie,' she sighed, adjusting her veil. 'I never thought I would get married without them being there, April.' Then she smiled at their mirrored faces. They both knew that March's unhappiness would have cast a shadow on the proceedings. May hugged April. 'You're here, that's the important thing. And after all —' she re-adjusted the veil. 'Sibbie shared everything a little too freely. Perhaps it is better she doesn't share Monty!'

They both laughed at such a ridiculous idea and went downstairs to join Florence and Will. The mood was one of hectic excitement. Will was enjoying himself; Monty had won him over completely. Florence could have wished for a quieter, more serious occasion, but she too trusted Monty by now. April, in her long straight muslin dress, came into her own for the first time. Her short curls, threaded with a blue ribbon, completed the picture of a Regency lady. She was confident in her own beauty and knew the contented self-assurance that May had always known. Monty's friends — members of the 'Company' — flocked around her admiringly. She remembered the scene in Daker's shop just three weeks previously, and knew that the trembling, vulnerable girl of that day had gone. Her love for David was rejected but she could still be proud of it. She tipped her head in a way Teddy had had — 'leadin with his chin' Will had called it — and smiled as she caught May's flowers. In spite of everything, she was a Rising and could rely on that if nothing else.

For May it was a whirl of excitement that matched the froth on her father's beer, the bubbles of the champagne. When she and Monty waved their goodbyes through the train window, she knew she had memories she would treasure for ever. But the future held more.

Monty kissed her and she snuggled into his arms without any of the reservations she'd felt with David. Monty never invaded her. His kiss was companionable as well as sensual. She sighed ecstatically and together they watched the telegraph poles whizz past the window of their compartment hypnotically enchanted.

It was only momentarily annoying when the compartment door slid open and two soldiers clumped in to join them. They glanced coldly at Monty and he thumped his chest and coughed. May intuitively took her cue. 'Is it bad again dearest?' She took the snowy handkerchief from his breast pocket and made a to-do about shaking it out. 'Lean your head back and hold this to your mouth.'

The soldiers exchanged glances. One of them leaned forward. 'It's this fog, lady. Shouldn't be out in it.'

May's smile was gentle and resigned. 'I'm afraid we have no choice — er — Corporal. My husband is on urgent war work.'

Monty held her hand and squeezed it.

When they were at last in the privacy of their bedroom in Blackpool he thanked her and she tried to explain.

'You are brother to me as well as husband. You are everything. I want to be everything to you my darling.'

'You are, May. Oh you are.'

She remembered all the things Sibbie had told her about men and made even the unhooking of her stays into a ritual. Incredulous and delighted, Monty carried her to bed.

'You are my darling. Oh you are,' he murmured. They were a perfect match.

March's letter shocked May as much as it did Will and Florence. She showed it to Monty after the evening performance.

'I didn't think she really loved Uncle Edwin. Not in that way.' She looked at Monty, distressed. 'I assumed it was an ... an arrangement. For companionship. Or something of the kind.'

Monty shrugged. 'The arrangement was extended, presumably.'

May was appalled. 'You make it sound so mercenary. Like Sibyl. No Monty, it's not like that. March told me once that Uncle Edwin had promised to leave her everything when he died. She had no need to sleep with him for money!'

Monty, bored with the subject of March and her unlikely marriage, kissed his wife and made love to her in his usual satisfactory manner. Much later, however, she returned to the subject as she held him in her arms. 'Monty. . . .'

'Yes, my darling.'

'It would be nice to have a baby wouldn't it? Like March.'

He shook his head against her shoulder. 'Not a bit sweetie. You get fat and haggard and then you go through a lot of pain . . . I couldn't bear that.'

'It would be me bearing it Monty. And I wouldn't mind a bit if it meant having a baby at the end of it.'

'With a maid to do the napkins like March will have?' He kissed her. 'I want you with me dearest. Always. Just you and me.'

She laughed adoringly and kissed the top of his head. 'You're to be husband, brother, father and . . . baby. Is that it?'

'Yes please May.' He glinted his brown eyes up at her before fastening his mouth on her nipple. Still laughing, she rocked him against her. He would change his mind. Of course.

Will's reaction to March's news was red-faced and blunt.

'It's disgusting! She led us to believe she was going to be a companion to the man! They've been married less than three months —' he rounded on Florence. 'Christamighty woman! You do realise this will make us grandparents and cousins in one fell swoop, do you?'

Florence's emotions were far more complicated. She said hesitantly, 'At least it *is* a marriage. I thought

March might intend taking all and giving nothing.' She shook her head. 'I should go to her. I think her pride will not let her come home after what happened that night.'

'You won't get a welcome from Edwin if you go,' Will warned. 'He was always a queer devil. I remember him lurking about when I took the children there first. Hardly spoke a word.'

Florence frowned, finding it too difficult to comprehend. 'Lizzie could never keep a child you know.'

'I do know. And how he must be boasting now. An old man of over sixty.'

Florence made no reply and somehow her silence angered Will more than a reproof would have done. Or perhaps it was Edwin, fifteen years older than himself, enjoying married bliss while he — while he lived like a monk. And in more ways than one. They did not need to make any vows of poverty.

Determined to do something, to break through Florence's reserve somehow, he snapped suddenly, 'I can't run this place any more, Flo. We'll go back to thirty-three. Live with Mother.'

He hoped she would protest or at any rate appear dismayed. But she looked up at him and gave one of her rare smiles.

'Oh Will. How wise of you dearest. We should have done it before. But now, with May and March gone, it's ridiculous to stay here. And Sylvia will be delighted.'

Will went to the door, unable to stay in the room with her any more. Teddy . . . Albert . . . two of the girls . . . and now the house. And she didn't care.

He reverted to the subject of March savagely. 'She's nothing more than a whore!' His voice rose. 'Your daughter is nothing more than a whore!'

That would hurt her. He slammed the door between them and knew that would hurt.

April found no great satisfaction in working at the munitions factory at Brockworth. At first there was a sense of comradeship with the other girls which was sufficient to convince her she had done the right thing. Gladys, thrilled to have a special friend to work with, drew her into the clannish atmosphere of the shell shop on the first day. She was never introduced formally, but names attached themselves to faces beneath the head-scarves: Mavis . . . Clara . . . Ginnie. They were what Gladys called 'good sorts' and would forge your name for you in the book if you were late and give you a 'lend' of some of their special cream which bleached the yellow out of the skin. Then there was Connie who was a bit of a toff, and went for a walk well away from the shed during the dinner break so that she could smoke her little cigars. And Stella who smiled secretively as she confided what her ma got up to while her pa was away in France. Stella had bored a hole in the ceiling so she could get a bird's eye view of her ma's bed. It seemed very like the Lukers! There was a lot of jumping and laughing.

But this comradeship was not quite enough. April could not treat the whole thing as a bit of fun as Gladys did. She was not, after all, very proud of her bright orange fringe which proclaimed her as a war worker for all and sundry to see. When they missed the bus because Gladys overslept, the orange hair enabled them to get a lift on the light railway which ran direct from the station along the London Road and out to Brockworth. The engine-driver hauled them both into his cab, pinched their bottoms and called them names. April did not find it as amusing as Gladys obviously did.

The work itself was physically hard. Some of the girls could fill sixty shells in a day and sing as they did so. April, frightened to open her mouth in case she breathed down the poisonous T.N.T., could manage thirty shells if she worked non-stop. The stiff oilskins which they wore did not help movement. She was exhausted.

Connie watched her pick over her dinner one day just before Christmas. It was carrots floating in stewed lamb and called Lancashire Hotpot.

'Come on outside for a turn with me youngster,' she said brusquely, climbing over the bench and clumping off without waiting for April's yea or nay. April looked at Gladys, startled, then followed willy nilly. Connie trudged across the gravelled yard where the bus would collect them that evening, and on to the rough grass beyond. Then she felt inside her overall and produced her gold cigar case.

'Come on. Have one. Do you good.' She lit a short cheroot and passed it to April who puffed experimentally. 'You're wishing you'd never come, aren't you?'

April puffed and breathed in and choked. Connie thumped her back peremptorily.

'Sorry.' April's eyes poured tears. She tried to grin. 'How is this supposed to do me good?'

'Nerves.'

They trudged and April puffed and coughed occasionally. It was better out here under a grey sky full of snow than in the shed where they ate dinner. In one week's time it was Christmas and they would have two days off work. In six days it was Teddy's birthday. He would have been fifteen.

Connie said, 'Finished? Time to go in. Tell yourself that the more bloody shells you fill the sooner the war will end.'

April was shocked at the aristocratic way Connie said 'bloody'. She tried to match her sang froid. 'Vital war work. Yes.'

Connie shook her head. 'No. That sounds as though you approved of the war.' She ground her cigar under the heel of her rubber boot. 'That's what's getting you down, d'you see? Making these things which will kill more men.'

'Is it?' April hadn't thought that far; she was always too tired to think.

'I expect so. You taught little kids before, didn't you?' Connie grinned, her teeth very white in her yellow face. 'That was war work. You could teach them not to fight

307

wars. Good stuff. Now you've swapped to something else. Not good stuff. So just tell yourself that the next shell you fill might be the one to end the war. You'll be all right then.'

April dropped the rest of her cigar and stepped on it in imitation of Connie. She felt better. Whether it was the cigar or the philosophy, she did not know.

The move back to thirty-three went smoothly, and if Will had thought it a punishment for his two remaining womenfolk he had to revise that thought quickly. They and the three 'other Risings' found it a relief. A concentration of their forces as it were. As Gran said, 'There we was, a-rattlin' about over 'ere, and you a-rattlin' about over there. And 'ere we all are as snug as bugs in rugs. No more rattlin'!'

Florence held out against taking her old room, but when they followed Alf Luker over with the big bedstead, she discovered Gran had emptied it of all traces of her things and directed Alf there in spite of protests. April slept with her mother and Will went into the attic room immediately above them.

Florence said softly that first night, 'Well my dear child, here we are again. Where we started together, you and I. Except that you were in a drawer then.' April loved her mother talking like this and encouraged her to go on. Florence put her head back and looked at the ceiling. 'See the cracks? What do you think they look like?'

April studied them seriously. 'A map of Norway?'

It was wonderful to hear her mother's delighted laughter.

The old terraced house had gone downhill badly in the ten years since they left it. Neither Gran nor Aunt Sylv had much interest in housekeeping for its own sake, but now that Florence and April were installed they all found it worthwhile. With a will the four women set to work. Kitty Hall brought them some paint pots with prison paint still left in them. They thinned it assiduously and began on the hall. Will, giving up all pretence at working in his old front room, walked the streets rather than witness their concerted energy. He had half-hoped that his mother and sister might drag Flo down to their level, but he remembered now how Sylvia had raised herself when she'd stayed with Flo before. And it was happening again. By the time May visited them at Christmas the old house looked sprucer than it had in their day, and May was ecstatic in her appreciation.

'I wish Monty could see this!' she exclaimed. 'You've done wonders. We were so anxious when we heard you were coming back here.'

Will said defensively, 'Why didn't he come down for Christmas May? Thought he might be slumming it? Was that it?'

'There's a rehearsal for the Boxing Day performance.' May kissed her father placatingly on the top of his head. 'Actually I didn't ask him to come. I wanted you all to myself. Just for once.'

Nobody commented on this, though there might have been a connection in Aunt Sylv's next remark. 'Ah. Another new year next week. Nineteen eighteen — sounds kind of queer don't it? Mebbe it will be the last year of the war. Then they'll let my Dick out o' prison.'

Will stared down at his hands and noticed for the first time a liver mark across his knuckles. And he wasn't fifty yet. He'd never stand living in this place with Dick, that was certain.

May said, 'It's strange about love, isn't it? I didn't understand before and now I do. Dear Aunt Sylv.'

She made it sound as if she and Sylvia were in a special club. Yet all the women there knew what she meant. And so did Will.

The move back across the street brought one small ray of comfort to the only man of the family. Hettie Luker still called most evenings to drink her stout in the kitchen with Gran and Sylv. The old lure of warmth and comfort and laughter was gone for him, but occasionally she would mention Sibbie's name, forbidden though it was. He listened avidly and said nothing. In the face of his silence, Hettie eventually became defiant.

'She's got a nice little place down there,' she addressed Gran, but Will knew she was talking to him. 'It's made of wood and it's got a verandah overlooking the canal. You can watch the barges go up to the match works. There's sailing boats now too. One of her friends took her out in a skiff last summer. Lady's life.'

Gran said sourly, 'So I 'ear. Price is a bit 'igh for most of us I reckon.'

Hettie snapped, 'It's no more than what we've paid most of our married lives. You 'ad seven young uns. So did I. An' we ain't got no nice little 'ouses by the water.'

Sylvia said pacifically, 'She was always a generous girl was Sibbie. She used to share her sangwidges with our May and gev her a lovely bottle of bath salts one birthday. I'll always remember that.'

Hettie looked mollified but continued to attack. 'An' there's May going from pillar to post in those theatrical lodgings, not a stick nor stone to call her own —'

Sylvia said firmly, 'May's 'appy. And she knows she's making her husband happy.'

Hettie was silenced. Will stood up and went to the door; there was no more to be heard that night. He said suddenly, 'Daresay Sibbie makes a lot of people happy.'

They all stared after him. And Hettie smiled.

March woke to a prickling sensation in her groin. It was half-past three by Aunt Lizzie's little carriage clock. She switched off her torch and lay down again, knowing quite well what it was and not wanting to admit it even to herself. Doctor Maine had never examined her properly, and had used the information she had given him to forecast that the date of the baby's birth would be June the twelfth. It was now March the twenty-third. Babies born after only six months

310

carrying never lived, so March could not permit her baby to be born just yet. The prickling sensation swept from her left thigh across her swollen pelvis to her right groin. She savaged her lip and turned over. Edwin would never believe her. He'd know . . . he'd turn her out.

But there was nothing at all she could do about it. Fred Luker had impregnated her on June the twenty-third, and exactly nine months later she was going to give birth. The pains grew steadily stronger. She bore them until first light and then rang for Letty, but before the thump of Letty's bedsocked feet sounded in the attic above, she heard Edwin move next door. With a gasp she arched her back and hit the wall behind the bed with her fist. He arrived immediately, hunched with anxiety, his old-fashioned nightcap pulled down to his ears.

'What is it my love? A bad night?'

He came close to the bed and saw March's twisted body and waxen face. 'My God. Something's gone wrong!' His panic was contagious. 'It's Lizzie all over again — oh God, oh God! What have I done to be punished like this?'

Letty bundled through the door and took in the situation at a glance. 'I'll go for the doctor,' she volunteered, pulling curling papers out of her hair as she spoke. 'Get Rose up, will you sir? She'll make tea for madam. And yourself.'

March was alone again. She had never imagined pain like this; she would not be able to stand it for long. It was supposed to go away occasionally, she was certain of that. This was incessant. Every few minutes it flared to a crescendo, but it never went away. It was half-past six now and this had started at half-past three. Three hours.

The doctor came and shook his head at her. 'Much too soon,' he grumbled as he examined her. 'Hardly dilated. Nothing much. I'll send a nurse. Relax for a while. You might not be in labour yet. It's too soon.'

Tea arrived, but March had no spare time to drink. Letty tried to hold her head and put the rim of the cup to her lips, but before the hot liquid reached her she screamed and twisted, spilling the tea over the sheet in her effort to get away from the pain. She was vaguely conscious of the arrival of the nurse, but time had no meaning any more. There was only one meaning. She was being punished for her wrong-doing. It was amazingly clear to her now, that everything that had happened in the past year had been a punishment. Losing Albert had been a punishment for betraying Harry . . . just as losing Teddy had been a punishment for blackmailing Bridget. And losing Fred had been a punishment for that ecstasy in the stable. And this — this was a punishment for deceiving her uncle, and, in a way, her dear Aunt Lizzie.

She fought it until she was too exhausted to fight any more, then she jerked and whimpered and called for her mother. Florence became a symbol of purity and goodness that might beat the evil in herself.

'Mother!' she cried, opening her eyes and seeing only the nurse's washed-out grey ones above her. 'Mamma . . . I want my mamma!'

'Not long now dearie,' said the nurse reassuringly. 'You're doing nicely. Very nicely.' She went to the windows and pulled the curtains across the late afternoon dusk. A small coherent part of March's mind did a sum: it must be fourteen hours since this began. She whispered, 'I can't go on. Why don't I die?'

The nurse actually laughed. 'My goodness, we're not going to die dearie! What a thing to say!' She bustled back to the bed and did something unspeakable between March's crooked knees. 'Time to start work, I think. Yes, I think we can get down to it now.'

March's son was born at six o'clock the next morning and weighed just under seven pounds. Edwin, on his knees in the dining-room, did not question anything. Lizzie had heard his prayers and had permitted him to keep this child. The nurse made no comment and Doctor Maine assumed that Edwin must have known all along. When he came to the bedroom and knelt again to weep on the back of March's hand, she knew breathlessly that she had got away with it. Pain had been sufficient punishment and in the circumstances, although the memory was still too near, it had been worth it. They both looked down into the cot where the tiny boy child slept, his groping hands pinioned within the bindings. His scraggly hair was inclined to be ginger and March had noticed that his eyes were pale blue.

She said, 'I'd like to call him Albert Frederick.'

Edwin would have agreed to anything and he had always known of her devotion to her older brother.

He whispered reverently, 'Little Albert.'

Suddenly March understood how her mother had felt about Teddy. It came to her like an epiphany, startling and clear. She reached down and put the flat of her hand gently on the baby's head. There was an instant connection; he became part of her as he had not been when he was actually inside her body. She leaned down and stared at him. He was ginger like Albert . . . he could be Albert again.

She said, 'Leave me now Edwin, I must feed him.'

'I'll stay dearest. Don't worry about me.'

She lifted the baby and held him to her shoulder as she said calmly, 'No. Leave me Edwin dear. I would prefer it.'

She waited until he stumbled to his feet and retreated. Then she began to undo the bindings around her breast.

It was perhaps because of her intense joy in little Albert, that March began to feel homesick. She and Edwin were now officially Baptists so there was no christening which might have tempted Will and

Florence to bury the hatchet. March's note on the reverse side of the formal card announcing the birth did not elicit more than a stilted letter from Florence saying that they were thankful for March's safe delivery. It was obviously written against Will's wishes. Unexpectedly it was followed by a letter from April sending her love and hugs for her darling nephew.

March begged Edwin to permit her to invite April to stay.

'I realise you cannot countenance my mother and father yet,' she said in a conciliatory voice, although she had refused to discuss their attitude with Edwin at all since the awful night when she had returned to the New Inn alone. 'But April is so sweet. And she would love to see Albert.'

Edwin said pompously, 'I doubt very much whether she would be allowed to accept any invitation I might offer, March. But in any case sweetheart, I do not wish her to be leaning over my son, infecting him with the explosive material which must cling to her.'

'Edwin! She is the cleanest, most fussy —'

'I think not, March. My son is too precious to risk anything.'

That was another thing. Edwin never referred to Albert as their son, always his. It forced March to remember that in fact he did not belong to Edwin at all — a fact which her initial self-deception now made almost impossible to believe, even secretly. More and more she inclined to the more acceptable idea that the baby was a reincarnation of the dead Albert. It made her more homesick. It made Edwin more repulsive.

The summer dragged on. Startlingly, in spite of the Allies making no noticeable headway, it became apparent that the Germans could not maintain their enormous front. Rumour had it that Ludendorff was making some attempt at peace negotiations. In Gloucester, April began to see an end to her work and it was like a promise of light in darkness. In London at the Variety in Deptford, May saw peace as a personal salvation also. In the relaxed atmosphere of a country not at war, Monty's lack of uniform would not be held against him and he would get engagements that were suited to his talents. She might rent a little house in Gloucester near her mother and become pregnant. To be home again and with a baby would be heaven.

And in Bath, March knew that the peace would provide her with an excuse to go home. Not even Edwin would begrudge her that.

15

Saint Catherine's was for weddings, ancient Saint
John's for thanksgivings. On that afternoon of
November the eleventh, it was crowded with the
irreligious hordes from the streets around the Northgate for a special service of praise. Many had not even
read the notice outside, but had crept in to kneel in the
dark interior to weep for one reason or another. Hettie
Luker was there with four of her children, praying
superstitiously with crossed fingers for Fred and her
other boys. It would be like Fate that would, to keep her
hoping for the last fourteen months then pole-axe them
all right at the end. The soldiers from the Great
Western Hospital were packed into the front; they had
been notified of the service and had turned out in what
uniform their torsoes could support. The smell of disinfectant combated the woodworm and dry rot odour of
the church itself. They sat dumbly, their twisted faces
turned to the altar candles perhaps envying the ones
who had 'given their all'. Their nurses provided
splashes of red and white colour that remained in
April's memory for many Armistice days to come.
White flesh and red blood.

April and Florence sat near the back, alone at first,
then joined by Aunt Sylv and Daze. As the service progressed, not understood by most of the congregation,
yet soothing in its very ancientness, April put her head
on her hands and wept difficult, repressed tears that
made an agony of her throat and hurt her head behind

316

her eyes and felt as if they were wrung from her innards through her mother's old wooden mangle. She wept for them all, May and March as much as Teddy and Albert. But mostly she wept for Florence, who did not lower her head but knelt upright and stared at the starry candles until her pupils were mere pinpoints in her beautiful ravaged face. To April she represented all the losses of the war, and more. She seemed suffering itself.

Afterwards, subdued and silent, they trailed back home. Gladys left her mother and walked with April and Daze; Florence and Sylvia linked arms. From London Road a solitary figure hurried ahead of the Saint Catherine congregation: it was Bridget. 'I had to be with you,' she said apologetically to Florence. 'Mother says I can stay if you don't mind.' Florence laid her gloved hand briefly on the smart velvet bonnet. 'We're glad to have you,' she said.

Gran and Will were in the kitchen of number thirty-three, a pot of tea and piles of toast waiting. Will was half-ashamed of opting out of church, half-defiant. Church was not for him, yet he needed something, some outlet for relief or regret or whatever it was that welled in him. It was he who suggested that they visit the Cross as darkness fell.

'There'll be singing. And they're burning dummies.'

'Pagan rites,' murmured Bridget, her eyes kindling in spite of herself. She was half-sorry the war was over before she could accompany Tolly Hall to France in his brand new ambulance, wearing a nurse's outfit not unlike the one she'd had as a child.

Florence said, 'I think I would prefer to be quiet, Will dear. Take the girls why don't you?'

April was surprised to find she wanted to go. She said, 'Will you be all right Mother?'

'Leave 'er be,' Gran said, shooing them all into the passage. She closed the door on the hubbub of finding coats, hats and gloves. 'We got our mem'ries to sort out. Eh Flo? An' that's about all we got I reckon. Mem'ries.'

Florence gave her gentle smile. 'It's all anyone has, Gran,' she said.

The Cross was jammed with people and Will had to burrow a passage through them for the girls to see anything. Keeping close to the wall of the Bank, they wormed along until they were almost beneath the effigies that were supposed to represent Hindenburg and the Kaiser. From Westgate Street people were still pulling logs and whole trees to heap on the pyre. The fire brigade stood ready to water the walls of Dentons, and the roar of voices singing 'Pack up your troubles' rose to a squeak now and then as railway detonators went off, factory hooters wailed and through it all the church bells clanged incessantly.

The noise literally scattered the wits; tears accompanied crazy laughter, strangers embraced. April found herself clasped to the bosom of an enormous woman smelling of rancid fat. She hugged her in return and was passed back to a man in overalls who was yodelling. The others had disappeared, engulfed in the maelstrom of bodies; it was the forfeit to be paid, the loss of individual identity to the whole. At first April paid it gladly, lifting her voice with the others, weeping and laughing and embracing indiscriminately as the pile of wood was fired and the flames licked around the dangling effigies.

The mass hysteria was so complete as to be physical; she felt that without everyone else around her holding her together, she would literally disintegrate and run into the gutters of the Cross like rainwater. Soldiers, lightermen from the canal stinking of beer, gypsies from the Westgate waste land, housewives and boys and girls older and younger than she was herself, swung her round, shouted at her, grinned and sobbed. The firemen played a spray of water around the fire so that rainbows flickered across the old stonework of the buildings and raucous screams arose here and there as people were wetted. April caught a glimpse of Gladys riding high on someone's shoulders, then Daisy swung past. Of Will or Bridget there was no more sign. It was licensed madness . . . chaos.

Suddenly April was in a pocket of emptiness; still, panting, deserted. She felt her own heart beating with a heavy metronome menace as she looked into the cloudy, moonless sky. There was a pressure in the air, as if the city huddled around the firelit scene, containing it as it had contained other madnesses. The leaping flames and crazy faces linked Centurion, Conqueror and Cavalier. And now the Kaiser. In a sudden panic she pushed through towards Eastgate Street. Hands pulled at her clothes like briars, but now she fought them off as if she were trapped in a nightmare. Long ago she had lost her hat and her short curls stood on end. She clutched at them with both hands and opened her mouth to scream. And a voice said, 'It's all right April. I've got you.'

It was David Daker.

She held him with her hands and flung her strong young body against his, determined he should not leave her. They reeled backwards and he gasped as his leg took their combined weights.

'April . . . it's all right! What the hell — Christ what the hell are you doing here? Does your mother know where you are?'

'Yes. Yes of course. Oh David . . . I was frightened. And there you were. Like you always were. Oh I love you!' She tipped back her head and bellowed into the uproar. 'I love you! I love you!'

'For Christ's sake!' He backed again and came to a wall where he leaned. In the lurid light his face was chalky. 'You're mad. Let me go —'

'No!' She tightened her hold convulsively. 'You must let me hold you — I don't care if I'm hurting you. You must suffer for me —' she was hysterical. And nearly as tall as he was. She pulled at his neck and kissed him. He became very still, the typical Daker stillness.

'Why were you frightened?' he shouted at last. 'Did someone . . . did something happen?'

She shook her head violently. 'It was the night. No moon. Like witchcraft.'

He nodded, understanding. 'It might have been a night like this when they burned Bishop Hooper,' he said.

'Oh David . . .' she looked at him through tears. 'I do love you. Why don't you love me?'

'Because I mustn't.' He edged back behind a buttress of Saint Nicholas' church and she, clinging to him, went as well. 'You — you're at the Brockworth factory,' he panted. 'Tolly Hall told me.'

'Yes. A year I've been there. David —'

He went on roughly. 'Straight after you came to the shop that time. After you'd given your hair. You little idiot. Sometimes I could kill you —'

Hope was resurrected. 'I don't care about that, David. What did you mean, you *mustn't* love me?'

'It's my good deed. My one good deed.'

She did not understand him and the cacophony was too great for discussion. She said, 'I wish we could stay here for ever like this.' Her tears were beginning again, the mangle turning. There was a concerted shriek as the ships' sirens down on the canal blasted off in unison. David suddenly bawled 'Blast it! Blast and damn it! I mustn't love you — I mustn't!'

Rockets shot into the air and in their light she saw his dark face descending on hers. He kissed her. Not as she had kissed him with puckered lips and a little smacking noise, but slowly, with penetration as if he would enter her body then and there. She was startled at first, her eyes opening wide, trying to see into his. Then as the kiss went on and his hands moved gently and persuasively to her waist, she relaxed against him tremblingly.

And then it was over. He removed her limp arms from his neck and pushed her gently back against the buttress. And left. He did not ask how she would get home, he did not say goodbye. There was a long moment when she felt his pain as an agony in her chest, then he was gone.

She stood where she was, bumped by people, wetted by the firemen's water, her face burning and her body a pulsating cluster of nerve-ends. She did not know what she wanted, only that whatever it was was all-consuming. After a while she began to walk towards her home, and as her passion cooled enough to permit her to think of David without trembling, she knew that she had won him. Somehow. He might try to persuade her otherwise. Because of May. Because of his dark moods. It didn't matter what he said. He knew and she knew.

She reached number thirty-three in a dream of tremulous delight, almost frightened by the strength of her own happiness. And there, where he had crawled, was the body of Rags who was the same age as April herself. She leaned over him, her hands pressed to her mouth to keep back the vomit. He must have ventured too far from his quiet backwater; his rear end was squashed and exuded unmentionable bloody entrails. She ran for her mother and they wrapped the poor body in an old sheet and laid it in the wash-house.

Then they wept together, holding each other as they rarely did. It seemed a final farewell to the war. To death itself. A last sacrifice to the gods. They had a right . . . they had earned the right now . . . to happiness.

Will watched the three dummies burning amidst the rainbow spray of water and felt none of the catharsis of everyone around him. Christamighty, what had it all been for? The ashes floated down and were knocked to the road and stamped on like so many

321

of his hopes. For the umpteenth time he paraded the list of his losses through his mind: old Daker, Teddy, Albert, Harry, his own father. As an aftermath there was the sourness that now existed in the remnants of his family life. May and March gone, little April turned against him. And Flo ... Flo. Tailor turned traitor. Tailor turned traitor. What was he supposed to *do* ... how was he supposed to *live*? All he wanted was a little happiness. He was starved, shrivelled for want of it.

He turned to go home, and there, waiting for him, as naturally as if it were a daily occurrence, was Sibbie Luker.

She grinned widely, not trying to speak through the din, not advancing, jostled on all sides, separated from him by linked arms yet unmistakably waiting for him to look round and see her. He felt his face stretch wide and a frisson run through him from top to toe, before someone shoved him on the shoulder and sent him sideways between two shrieking women holding their skirts to their thighs and attempting the can-can. He thought he had lost her in the crowd and then she was lifted high and her face was turned to his again, still smiling, but asking for nothing.

He watched her for a long moment before the hands that held her slid beneath her armpits. She was more beautiful than he remembered, with Hettie's wildness minus her unkemptness. Her mass of hair was loose around her shoulders just as it used to be when she came straight from the pickle factory; but her skin was whiter than April's, her lips as juicy red as always, her eyes violet in the flaring firelight. She was as vivid as the flames and rainbows, and like the flames and rainbows she belonged to everyone.

He caught up with her far down Southgate Street, nearly at the infirmary gates. She had her back to the wall of a house, her arms spread-eagled, the one hand clasping a window ledge as if she was frightened of being swept away. People still milled around, but

322

thinly, and he knew her attitude was a challenge to him. He could pass her by, or he could take her as she was. There could be no apologies, no alteration to her way of life.

He stood before her, panting yet not exhausted. Slowly he put his hands on the wall, either side of her head, and lowered his body to hers. It was like coming home.

She whispered against his ear, 'Are you sure? You must be sure.'

He couldn't find words to reply but he did not move, and after a while she put her mouth to his and he kissed her with a deliberation that was a commitment in itself. She let him finish then tipped her head and began to caress him with her parted lips. Not with Hettie — certainly not with Flo — had he known such an innocently erotic embrace. He slid his hands over her thick flannel coat, letting her take all his weight so that she groaned softly.

'Christamighty Sib! You've got no drawers!' he discovered. They were the first words he had spoken to her and she tried to laugh against the pressure of him. And suddenly he was infected with laughter too. The happiness that he had craved came to him — realised because this girl that he lusted for was as careless and carefree and amoral as her mother before her. He saw the evil phrase 'kept woman' in a new light. Sibbie had been kept . . . for him. To compensate for Hettie, who had compensated for Flo.

He put his arms around her waist and held her to him in a huge bear hug, his beard pointing to the moonless sky as he laughed. And at last she took her arms from the wall and clasped him too, and her laugh became triumphant. She knew she could have summoned him to her almost any time during the past year, but this had been worth waiting for. He had come to her. She laughed with him until they were both fighting for breath. Then she gasped, 'Now Will Rising. D'you want to come and have some supper with me in my little house by the canal? Or d'you want to go straight back home to your family?'

He did not have to answer. They swung down Southgate Street together and over the level crossing into Bristol Road. And David Daker, roaming the streets like a caged animal, saw them and watched them until they were out of sight, with his black eyes narrowed.

And then he too went home, thinking of April. For the first time he permitted himself the luxury of thinking of April exclusively. Surely Will Rising and Sibbie Luker being together meant that he was entitled to think of April without sullying her sweet eagerness. He told himself sternly that two wrongs could not make a right; the fact that April's father had succumbed to Sibyl Luker's importunings did not whitewash what he himself had done. Yet somehow it made his . . . what had Will called it? — perversion . . . possibly forgivable.

And he knew that April would forgive him. That had been the trouble from the beginning. April would always understand and forgive. She needed protection from herself.

But now. Was it different now?

She had responded to his kiss. He sweated when he remembered it. At first she had been frightened; then she had trusted him; then she had responded. She was as unlike May as it was possible for a sister to be. She was completely unconscious of self, where May was conscious of little else. May had married an actor; perhaps together they would enact out the rest of their lives. It seemed suitable. But April . . . April was different.

He walked past the Pump rooms and followed the railway line to Barton Street. His head ached and his heart thumped and he did know what he could do. Then, after all his soul-searching, he remembered how she had come to see him last year, against her father's wishes. To show him her hair. Unbidden, a small smile appeared on his frozen face. It came to him with complete certainty that the matter was out of his hands now. April must know that he wanted her, and that would be enough. Of course he could go away . . . run away. But he knew he would not do that. His roots were in Gloucester just as hers were. Besides . . . he was much too curious to leave now.

As he unlocked the shop door and let himself in, he began to chuckle. He was ten years older than she was, but she had lived with older people for so long that it did not matter. It would be interesting to see what she would do next. Interesting. Exciting.

His mother, upstairs, sat bolt upright in bed and listened. She had not thought the Armistice would make any difference to David at all, yet here he was laughing his head off as if he'd won the war all by himself!

May and Monty spent Armistice night in Piccadilly Circus with thousands of others, and by the time they dragged themselves back to their digs in Kilburn, Monty was as drunk as a lord and May not much better. He would have slept immediately, but she, remembering her dream of peace, kissed him incessantly until he was sufficiently awake to want her.

'We mustn't . . . we mustn't . . .' he grumbled as she moved seductively against him. 'I'm not prepared Mamie . . . don't do that.'

But she went on doing it. 'It'll be all right baby. There. Mamma's baby. There then.'

He giggled helplessly into her neck. 'Have your wicked way woman! I am powerless against you,' he declaimed in a slurred voice.

'Quite powerless.'

She smiled ecstatically into the darkness of the small cramped room. A baby conceived on Armistice night. If it was a girl she would call her Hope. If a boy . . . if a boy . . . Victor. It was all happening just as she had planned.

March, unwilling to wean Albert, was tied to the house that night, and Edwin, dutiful as ever, stayed with her. They watched through the sitting-room window as fireworks lit the sky and Letty and Rose came up the area steps and waved to them before scurrying into the darkness. March held Albert to the glass though he was half-asleep.

'I can tell him later that he saw the Armistice celebrations,' she replied to Edwin's protestations. 'It won't hurt him. He can have his ten o'clock feed a little early to make up for being disturbed.'

'You should wean the child, March,' Edwin said austerely, refusing to move from his chair when she began to unbutton her blouse, though he knew she liked to be on her own during feed-time. 'He is eight months old now and quite strong enough to manage a cup.'

March did not protest too vehemently. She still hoped that Edwin might let her go home for a few days soon. 'I enjoy feeding him, Edwin dear. It is my duty.' She closed her eyes as the first pain shot through her breast. Then it was all right. Even when, towards the end of the feed, Albert closed his new teeth on her nipple she only laughed.

Edwin said, 'You have other duties March. To me. Those you neglect.' He got up and pulled the curtains across the windows though she was behind a screen. He turned up the gas. Her breast ballooned through the opening of her blouse. He sat down by her.

She said in a low voice, 'Edwin. You know how I feel. We have been blessed with Albert. I think — I think that is enough.'

'Well, I do not.' He stretched in his chair, desire making him more than usually pompous. 'You are a young woman, March, and it would seem I am still potent. I could have more sons. I want more sons.'

She held Albert very close. He had never been as direct as this before. She dropped her voice to a whisper. 'We will see dearest.' When she went into her

326

own room, Edwin was standing by her bed, disgustingly naked.

'No Edwin,' she said faintly. 'I cannot. I am still feeding —'

'Tomorrow you will finish. Rose shall take over with watered cow's milk. Come March. Come my darling. Let Edwin take care of you again.'

She had to hold herself against fighting him. Her tears seemed to inflame him and her unwillingness was put down to modesty. It seemed to take a very long time before it was over and he lay panting beside her. She leapt out of bed and donned her nightgown with trembling hands. When she slid in again very gently, he was asleep, still naked and stinking. She lay on the very edge of the bed, her sobs dry now and terrified. At midnight Rose and Letty returned and went breathily upstairs and she heard Rose crooning gently to the baby. Then the long hours of night went on. There was nothing she could do. Illness would mean he would be with her all the time . . . she couldn't bear that. She looked into the future and it was like a long dark tunnel.

Men came home sporadically all through November and December and still there was no news of Fred. Nor Uncle Dick. Nor Gran Rising's sons. Neither Sylvia nor Gran pined however. They were realists to the core and both knew that though they loved their menfolk they were often better off without them. It was different for Hettie. Fred could pull the business together. Fred would sort out his father and his brothers . . . make sure Gladys didn't follow in her sister's footsteps . . . take the strap to Henry when he stole. Hettie needed Fred badly.

He arrived in time for Christmas, eighteen months since he had been home last. He held court at the Lamb and Flag and though he recounted the barest outlines of his life in a labour camp in Silesia, it was all around the street the next day that he had lived behind German lines as a Polish peasant, outwitting the Hun right, left and centre. He presented himself at number thirty-three and was accosted by April, all agog.

He smiled grimly. 'Well. I reckon I did outwit them in a way April. I stayed alive. Not many did that.'

She said, 'We're so proud of you Fred. You and David. You won the war for us.'

He shrugged. 'Dunno about that. Listen kid. March — tell me about March.'

April, sentient in her love for David, hardly knew where to begin. They were in the passage of number thirty-three; no longer was there the delightful privacy of all the rooms in Chichester House. She glanced towards the kitchen.

'She was lonely after Albert died. Then you. We all thought you were dead. So . . . so —'

'So she ups and marries her uncle.'

'Fred, try to understand. They're happy.'

'Have you seen them April? Ma tells me none of you have seen March since she was married.'

'It's difficult to explain Fred. Father was so hurt you see. But we know she is all right. She writes to me quite often. About Albert Frederick. He sounds perfectly beautiful.'

'Albert Frederick?' Fred frowned, looking more like John Bull than ever.

April said, 'The baby. Named for Albert. And for you I suppose Fred. I hadn't thought of that before.'

Fred said slowly, 'My God. She had a baby. That was something Ma didn't mention.'

April felt suddenly uncomfortable. 'Perhaps she didn't know. We don't talk about it a great deal actually.' She bit her lip. 'Actually Fred we haven't seen him. I wanted to visit but apparently Edwin did not think it a good idea because I was working at the munitions and —'

'Albert Frederick.' Fred looked past April into the dim recesses of the passage. 'Albert Frederick. Yes.

That . . . that's nice for March.'

April felt on surer ground. 'Very nice,' she agreed enthusiastically. 'March is going to have him photographed for his first birthday.'

'When is that?'

'March the twenty-fourth. I'll bring a copy over for you to see, Fred, shall I?'

He grinned, his teeth as white as his mother's in the dim passage. 'I can't wait till March kid. I'm getting a new car tomorrow. I'll pop down and see them all. Sort something out.' He reached behind him and pulled open the front door. 'Perhaps she'd like to come back with me. Spend Christmas with her family. Like old times, eh?'

He went into the street and April hung on to the door, looking at him doubtfully.

'I don't think she'll do that Fred. She would hate to come back to this house again.'

His grin was indefatigable.

'We'll see. Wouldn't hurt to get one of the attics ready though.'

April went back inside, still puzzled. But then she too grinned, leaning against the newly painted wall, closing her eyes, turning her face to the ceiling in sheer gratitude. Fred home. And David . . . David in love with her. Her father came down the stairs.

'Hello my little April.' He took his hat from the stand and struggled into his overcoat. 'Are you saying your prayers again?'

'Yes Daddy. Yes, I am.' She felt guilty as she belatedly helped him with his coat. She could always get her own way with Will; everyone believed that. But she would need prayers to help her with this. She said, 'Daddy, even if I do things that might hurt you, I still love you. You know that, don't you?'

He turned and planted a kiss on her nose. She was the same height as himself and more like him than any of his children.

He said, 'I hope so, kitten. And . . . and if I do things . . .

sometimes . . . that don't seem right to you . . . well, the same applies.'

She laughed. How could he ever do anything that wasn't quite right? She held the door for him. 'Where are you going just at tea time?'

'See a man about a dog.'

It was one of Monty's silly comic phrases. Will had adopted many of them lately. 'I was walking down the street the other day. . . .' 'That's no lady, that's my wife.' Flo would tighten her mouth and look reproving, but she knew it showed his fondness for May's husband. For them all. Since the move to number thirty-three, Will was like his old self.

16

Fred drove his new car with care, hardly noticing the bare countryside of winter, certainly not taking any pleasure from it. The car, a bull-nosed Morris, had belonged to one of the archdeacons in the cathedral close and had been laid up for two years because of the petrol shortage. Fred had worked on it for two days before he went to the fuel dump at Churchdown and bartered for black-market petrol. He had no wish at all to be stranded on his way to Bath. He knew exactly what he had to do and had planned the day with the precision of a battle offensive. The element of surprise was everything. He dared not give March time to think, to plan, to scheme towards a compromise. The two days he had spent on the car had been risky; April might have written to her sister to tell her of his return. But Fred had always felt a relationship between machines and the Risings. He had made his first real contact with March through the Delage. If his present car broke down now, so would his hope of gaining March.

He felt his way through the gears, getting to know the machine through his senses just as he knew the woman. At Almondsbury he stopped to let the engine cool. He took two of the cans from the back seat and topped up the petrol tank. Then he went into the George Hotel and booked a room for that night. He sat on the running board of the Morris and let his thoughts take a different direction while he smoked a cigarette and consciously rested. He thought of the miners down in the Forest of Dean and how he would organise them.

There had been coal fields in Silesia and a man who came to the labour camp to negotiate with the Germans about their fuel. One of the Germans had worked in London before the war and described the man as a 'fly one'. Fred had put in a question now and then and built up a fairly accurate picture of the man. He was what Fritz called an 'entrepreneur'. He sold his fuel at very much more than he paid the miners. Yet they could not manage without him. Fred studied the end of his cigarette. Warmth and food. They were basic human necessities which had to be supplied whatever was happening in the world. And war made them desperate necessities. He narrowed his eyes against the thin spiral of smoke. Warmth and food had to be transported. And these entrepreneur-blokes were go-betweens.

It was all so logical that it pleased mechanically-minded Fred with its sheer balance; he saw it as the sources of need and supply being perhaps a few degrees apart, and himself a pendulum swinging between them. At the same time this logical sequence of events conveyed no calm and tranquillity to him; there was an urgency to the business that brought him to his feet. If he could see his opportunity, so could others. This business with March must be settled quickly for more than one reason; he must get down to the Forest. In both cases — March and the miners — there was no time for diplomacy. Frontal attacks were called for.

He found the address without difficulty and drew up behind a grey Wolseley. Letty answered his ring immediately. Behind her, Edwin was settling a magnificent fur coat on to March's shoulders and was himself dressed to go out. There was a short, uncertain pause, they all stared for a startled instant, then March put a hand to her mouth just as Letty said, 'Was there something sir?'

Fred said nothing; when he spoke it must be only to attack. March said faintly, 'Fred. Freddy. My God. Is it really you?'

Edwin frowned. 'Do you know this man, March?'

Fred noted the word man. Not gentleman. March swallowed visibly.

'Edwin. . . of course. It's Fred Luker. You remember our neighbours in Chichester Street — the Lukers?' She looked again at Fred. 'I cannot believe this. You were presumed dead.' Her voice took on a note of accusation.

Edwin said pompously, 'Mr. Luker. Yes, the name is familiar. Well, as you see. young man, we are just about to take a drive. However, we can postpone it for a —'

March said suddenly, 'Fred, why have you come? Are they all right at home? Mamma —'

Fred stepped inside, took the edge of the door from a surprised Letty, and shut it behind him.

'Your family are very well March. Very well indeed. Happy.' He saw a door on his left and went swiftly to it. 'Shall we go in here?'

Edwin tucked his chin into his collar disapprovingly. March dithered for a moment then hastily followed Fred into the sitting-room. The fire, banked for their return, smoked blackly behind the guard. Fred glanced around him, taking in the carpet, curtains, upholstery; the sheer comfort of the place brought a grim smile to his face. March hadn't changed. He watched her closely. She went behind a chair near to the fire, her chair perhaps, a spoon-backed velvet thing. She held on to it for dear life and met his gaze with something like fear in her own.

'Why have you come Fred? What has happened?'

She expected an emergency; anything else would have been heralded by a letter. Well, this was an emergency.

He waited until Edwin closed the door then said flatly, 'Plenty has been happening by what I hear. But. . .for now, I've come to take you home. Where you belong.'

March's eyes widened and she looked frozen where she was. Edwin gulped in a huge breath. 'Look here my man — you are talking to my wife. If you have something to say, we will listen. But make no mistake, she belongs here. This is her home.'

Fred said in the same unemotional voice, 'No. She has stayed here with her baby to spare others. Her home is with the father of her child.' Nobody spoke. Shock stretched Edwin's old face almost free of wrinkles. Fred gestured at March. 'Go and pack. Get the baby. Come back here.'

March made a small whimpering sound but did not move. Edwin stood in front of the door as if barring it, his breathing very audible, blood now pumping up his neck. He spoke at last, explosively, saliva slurring his words. 'Get out you. . . . That's all I'll say to you, neighbour or no neighbour! Missing in action or not! Just get out before I call the police!'

Fred looked coolly at him. 'Listen. It's not your fault. I could lie and tell you her mother is ill and she's needed at home. But this has got to be final. There's no time for lies. The baby is mine. Mine and March's. I was home on leave in June 1917. Work it out for yourself.'

March whimpered again and slumped over the back of the chair. Edwin, dribbling chin thrust forward, stared for a long time at the hard, pugnacious face before him, then turned slowly towards her.

'Is this true? My God . . . is this true March?'

The question was answered by her silence, her bowed head, the hunched shoulders beneath the fur coat.

Fred repeated quietly, 'Fetch the boy, March. Pack your things.'

There was a pause; the two men continued to look at March. At last she lifted her head slowly, met Edwin's intense gaze and flinched visibly.

'This is my home!' She spoke tremulously to him. 'Aunty Lizzie wanted me to have everything. Edwin you know what she said — she —'

'You. . . .' Edwin spoke on an indrawn breath of disgust. 'You . . . *bitch!*' He breathed out and spittle frothed his colourless lips. 'There was never any love — there was never *anything!*'

'It was mine!' she protested, her voice rising with self-justification as she realised she had said the wrong thing, taken the wrong attitude. March could not backtrack, it was not in her nature. 'You told me yourself it was mine! And, my God, I've paid for it! Deny that if you can!'

'So . . . a whore as well as a bitch!'

He looked as if he would fall over where he stood. Fred said quickly for the third time, 'March, do as I say. Go and pack.'

Edwin rounded on him with a snarl like a cornered animal. 'She shall not take anything! Take *her* with you for God's sake! And your bastard child! But she came here with nothing and that is how she will leave!'

That took the spirit out of March. She clung frantically to the chair as if she would never be parted from it.

Fred's voice was hard as he used words he had used before. 'Stand up straight March! You are mine and what I have is yours. We have a son too. Fetch him and let us go.'

Edwin swung round again and watched as she straightened slowly and began to make for the door like an invalid. Perhaps he hoped she would plead with him, but as her hand went out for the door knob, acknowledging defeat he said pettishly, 'Don't think you can take that coat my girl! Paid for with my money is that coat!'

She stood still and let the coat slide from her shoulders to the floor, then she left the room. The two men faced each other across the fireplace.

Fred nodded his head at the chair. 'Sit down. It's hit you hard. D'you want a drink? Whisky?'

Edwin said, 'If I were a younger man I would kill you. I

335

should kill you. My wife . . . my son. You don't know what you're doing. That is your only excuse.'

Fred gave a wintry smile. 'I know exactly what I'm doing. I've always known I wanted March Rising and I've got her. Now sit down and let me ring for that woman to bring a drink.'

'No! Letty — Rose . . . they mustn't know.'

Fred shrugged. 'Suits me. She's coming back to Gloucester for a visit then — that should satisfy them.' He glanced at the floor. 'In that case you'd better let her take the coat, hadn't you? If she walks out in the stuff she came in, they're going to wonder.'

Edwin sat down abruptly. 'She can have the coat. Nothing else.' He looked up. 'I can't believe this. She's above you. You're common.'

Fred snorted half a laugh. 'Yes. You're right. But I know March like I know my car. And I can manage her. Just like I manage my car.'

Edwin made a sound of disgust and put his head in his hands.

After a while March came through the door again, carrying Albert over one shoulder and wearing the linen suit, very tight across the chest now. Fred looked hard at the baby, noted the blue eyes and gingery hair and smiled again. Then he leaned down, picked up the fur coat and draped it over March's shoulders. 'It's very kind of you to spare your wife for a visit to her family,' he said, directing his voice at the open door.

He guided her into the hall, picked up the Gladstone bag she indicated at the bottom of the stairs and opened the front door. She waited at the top of the steps as if not trusting herself to descend them safely; he put a hand under her arm and they went down together to the waiting Morris. She did not glance at the Wolseley in front. She handed Albert to Fred and slid into the front seat of the small car as if it were a limousine. Fred held his son, smelled the baby smell

336

of him, looked over his copper-gold head at the slim ankle on the running board, and smiled again.

He couldn't stop smiling, even when March began to cry as they drove through Bath.

'What have you done Fred Luker! My God, I've got nothing! No blankets for Albert. No clothes. Nothing!'

If she expected Fred to tell her that she had him, she was disappointed. He guffawed loudly above the sound of the engine.

'You've got the coat girl! Reckon that'll fetch two or three hundred! Just what we need to start the business!'

She felt as if he'd turned a cold-water hose on her.

'Business?'

'Our business girl. We're going to make money, remember?'

'So it was the coat you wanted, not me?' The old familiar temper stirred in her like a resurrection. 'You're hateful Fred Rising! You come back to life — turn up — claim Albert and me as if we're left luggage! And all you can think of is how much money you'll make from Edwin's fur coat!'

'No. Oh no. That's not all I can think of, March. I've booked a room at the George in Almondsbury. I'm thinking a lot about that. I hope you slept well last night because you're not going to do much sleeping at the George.'

'How dare you speak to me like that!'

'As if you were a whore?' He looked at her sideways. 'I knew that a long time ago March. I've bought kisses from you. I've bought your favours, often. But I didn't buy you that day in your stable, did I March?'

She sobbed, 'You're hateful Fred Rising! Hateful!'

'Because I know all about you?' He stopped smiling and said seriously, 'You're a fool March. The only person in the world who really knows you and still loves you — what more could you want?'

Her sobs died away. 'Do you really love me Fred?'

'Yes,' he said flatly.

'How much?' she asked as she had asked before.

'Enough to make a fortune for you. To buy you clothes and a car and make you the most important woman in Gloucester. I was going to do it on my own, but he cropped up.' He jerked his head at Albert. 'So we do it together now March. The first thing we did together was get that coat. I'll show you the next thing when we get to the George.'

She sat haughtily silent for two minutes. Then she pulled down Albert's bonnet and ran her mouth sensuously over his head.

'You showed me that before,' she said with a curious mixture of repressiveness and provocation.

'That was just a beginning, March.'

That night Albert cried lustily for Letty's attentions and for the first time in his short life was ignored.

'Let him get on with it,' Fred advised. 'His racket covers ours.' He put his warm hand on the inside of her thigh and felt her instant response. Albert screamed in the corner and the bed creaked ominously. March surrendered to Fred with the same fierce abandon with which she had surrendered to her tempers. Her physical loathing for Edwin, her cerebral devotion for Albert, her maternal obsession for baby Albert all went into the long sexual intensity of that night. Fred might know, he might love her in spite of everything, but that did not mean he could understand or forgive. There was a fierce aggression in his love-making that matched her own. It seemed right that it should be orchestrated by the furious yells of their son. It seemed right that when at last the baby fell into an exhausted sleep, they should also feel quieter, more tender.

He said, 'Marcie. Tell me you love me. You've never said it.'

'You know I do. How could I . . . you know I do.'

'Say it.' He held her against his neck and stroked her long brown hair. She closed her eyes and tears filled her lids.

338

'I love you Freddie. Don't leave me again. You won't will you?'

'Marcie. . .Marcie. I'll never be far away. That, I promise.'

'But. . . . What shall we do Freddie? If we live together — the disgrace! I don't think I could bear it. And Albert —'

'We can't live together girl. I'm not going to make you that kind of important woman. Not like our Sib.' He felt her flinch and held her more tightly, 'We're going to play Edwin's game for a bit. It won't hurt us. You're going to have a long stay with your ma. Tell her what you like. Tell her he's got something catching and you've taken Albert away for his safety — she'll understand that. And he won't start no divorce, you could see that. So we'll have two or three years' grace.'

'Two or three years? Fred, you just told me you'd never leave me —'

'I said I wouldn't be far away. And I won't be. I'll be over the road. I'll be coming over each day to see if you'll give me a hand with my new business. Typing, suchlike. Your ma will be pleased to think you've got an interest. She'll be pleased when I take you and the baby out for a drive on a Sunday afternoon.'

She was silent, secure in his arms, feeling a faint relief that perhaps she hadn't burnt quite all her boats. She turned her head and tasted his neck. There were bristles even on his throat.

'Have you got a typewriter then Freddie?'

His laugh vibrated in her mouth. 'Not yet. It's one of the things the coat will buy. You can choose it.'

'Oh Fred. It's such a lovely coat too.'

'Good job. It's got to buy you a complete wardrobe. You can't turn up at your ma's without a change of clothes. And for the babby too.'

'Don't call him babby please Fred.'

'Albert Frederick then.' He put his hand under her chin. 'Thank you for that Marcie. When April told me that, I knew I had to come for you.'

'Oh Freddie. Shall we go to sleep now?'

'In a minute, Marcie. In a minute.'

The next morning while she fed Albert, he told her the bare outline of his thirteen months in Silesia, but more of his plans to sell coal. At first she was horrified.

'Coal? You're going back to coal-hauling? I thought you wanted to get a char-a-banc. Or another taxi?'

'The boys can do that side. I've got bigger fish to fry. And you can help me, March. Edward Williams is back from the war. I want you to call on him.'

She was aghast. 'I was dismissed from the office!'

'Not by him. He's got cause to dislike the change made by his father.' He grinned sideways at March. 'You know the alderman has paid for Sibbie's bungalow down by the canal?'

'I don't want to talk about that please, Freddie.'

'All right by me. But you've got influence there Marcie. I want you to use it.' He came behind her and ran his fingers down the length of her spine. She said nothing and he reached around and removed her nipple from Albert's mouth.

'Fred — really —'

They tussled and Albert roared.

'Fred —!'

'Say you'll go and see Edward Williams.'

'All *right*!' Order was restored. 'That was despicable Fred! No, don't laugh, I mean it. It was blackmail.'

'I shall be using it often Marcie. On everyone. It's how business is done. And it seemed to work on you.'

'I don't know whether you're serious or not.' But Marcie smiled too. Because it suddenly struck her that if Fred was going to take on all that desperate manipulation that life seemed to call for, the guilt would at last be taken away from her shoulders. She sighed. 'I hope it's all going to work out as you say Freddie.'

He put his arms around them both. 'Of course it is Marcie! Of course it is!' She had never seen him like this before: jubilant. Another thought occurred to her; the war had taken, but it had given too. Fred had gone away sullen, discontented; an underdog. He had come back confident and assured and very much master of his fate.

She said, surprised, 'Freddie, I really do love you. You . . . you've given me back something. Myself.'

His smile died and he drew back, encircling her still, but leaving her free to lift Albert and turn him into her other breast.

He said quietly, 'You couldn't have said anything nicer to me Marcie. If I don't do anything else in life, that would be enough. To give you back yourself.'

She glanced up from the sucking baby, slightly alarmed. 'But you will do something else in life, won't you Freddie? You meant what you said about the business?'

He laughed again, falling against the bed and rolling about helplessly. She was reminded that in spite of his self-assurance he was still a Luker: lots of noise, lots of laughter, thumping bed-springs.

He said, 'Oh Marcie. . . my Marcie. You'll never change. We'll make such a pair. Such a pair my girl. No-one will beat us!'

It was surprising how well the family took her unannounced arrival. She had known her mother and April would succumb immediately to Albert's charms, but she had wondered about Will. However, after the straight look he could barely restrain his pleasure in his first grandchild. There were a few sarcasms: 'How did you persuade Edwin to let you loose?' and 'I thought you would arrive in your own car and try to impress us.' But they were said with a smile, and he held Albert as he had always held his own babies, with casual expertise. On Christmas Day he did not have to see a man about a dog, and he surveyed them all with obvious pleasure. 'We're beginning to look something like a family again. Eh April? Eh little April?'

341

May did not come home for Christmas, but in mid-January a letter arrived from her addressed exclusively to Florence. Florence read it with a little smile. May too was expecting a child. She hugged the news to herself for the rest of the day. How pleased darling Will would be, especially if it was another boy. Will was made for family life, for children and their endless routines and demands.

It was a Monday morning and as she carried the smalls across the yard to the wash-house it started to snow, the gritty flakes showing up against the dark grey of the gasometer. Both Granny and Sylvia were out 'doing the rough' at their various houses and she had the place to herself, just as it had been in the old days.

She dippered some hot water from the copper into the sink and began to squeeze Will's combinations, combs very gently. What enormous satisfaction there was in the small things of life, and how everything turned full circle if you could only wait patiently for long enough. March had called her son Albert. Would May call hers Teddy? Flo smiled gently at the thought. How incredible it was, this life. How incredible and how indestructible.

April tidied up her classroom at the Midland Road School with meticulous care. Miss Alicia was suffering from a 'touch of the bronchials' and she had taken over her room and her work. She knew that immediately she left, Miss Midwinter would make a tour of inspection and if so much as a piece of cotton obtruded itself from the tiny work baskets, there would be a stern reprimand. 'A neat classroom is the sign of a good teacher' was one of her many maxims. But April could not summon a hint of impatience for the whole frustrating experience that was Midland Road School; she was too happy to mind what happened in her day-to-day existence.

In any case her teaching days would soon be over. There would be no pupillage at Chichester Street Elementary now; certainly no training college when she was eighteen. She must marry David when she was seventeen and work with him in the shop. In her crazy exultation on Armistice Day it had not occurred to her that David Daker could actually need her. But during her secret and tentative visits to the shop since, she had realised that she could make David laugh even when his leg was hurting him most; and when he was laughing she could encourage him to handle cloth again and begin to sketch designs.

At the beginning of December he had spent a whole afternoon in his cutting room and two weeks later had produced a loose velvet jacket for her with what he called 'raglan sleeves' and a stand-up collar that framed her short curls to perfection. While he had worked, she had minded the shop and was heartily congratulated by Mrs. Daker herself on taking the princely sum of thirty-five shillings in three hours. It amounted to a clear profit of five shillings. In a nine-hour day there were three lots of five shillings. Fifteen shillings a day, six days a week. It was a fortune!

In the New Year when it was too cold for snow, old Doctor Green died of the Gloucester disease, bronchial pneumonia. Kitty Hall, one-time maid and wet nurse for the doctor, came to April tearfully and asked whether young Mr. Daker could make her a loose jacket and matching skirt in black velvet to cover her very ample proportions. For the funeral. No expense to be spared for her dear Doctor Green.

For decency's sake, April held the tape measure while David measured her, then made tea and held Kitty's hand as she offered stumbling solace.

'You're born to this job April,' sighed Kitty at last, standing up to leave. 'You can put Daker's back on the map, like it was in the old days when your father did his apprenticeship here.' She patted her nose and looked at April over her workmanlike handkerchief. 'But your ma's going to get to hear of it dearie. I won't breathe a word. But someone will.'

April swallowed her own forebodings on this score. 'I think Mamma would understand,' she said. But neither of them really meant Florence.

Kitty sighed again. 'Wish my Tolly was home. Not only for my own sake dearie, but for yours. I've always said to him that now Teddy has gone, he must keep an eye on you. You and him got on well when you were kiddies didn't you? But what with him going to the Crypt and that Bridget Williams going to high school — well, they seem to be thrown together. She's even talking of joining him in France you know!' Kitty's mouth thinned disapprovingly. 'I told her he'll be home before she's halfway across the Channel! He calls it mopping-up operations, I call it dogsbodying. Those Frenchies are using him and the other boys to skivvy for them in their military hospitals!'

April ushered her to the door and let her smile linger as she closed it, like the Cheshire Cat's. David, hiding behind the cutting-room door, said, 'You're indispensable, April Rising! What should I have done with her if you hadn't been here? Does she ever stop talking?'

'A coat and skirt!' said April gleefully. 'That's seven guineas at least David! Seven *guineas*!' She sobered suddenly. 'Doctor Green's always been good to us. Isn't it strange — and wonderful — that even now . . .' she faltered to a stop and David put the palm of his hand against her cheek, which was all he dared to do with his mother in the kitchen and customers liable to come in at any moment.   •

So April tidied up her classroom carefully but with great speed, because David was waiting for her and she could stay there only an hour in case Florence grew suspicious. She slid into her old indestructible melton coat because the green velvet jacket was another of her many secrets, pulled her knitted beret down to meet the collar, and went out through the tradesmen's door into the snow and early darkness.

The subway reminded her of Teddy and Bridget and

344

March and she was glad again that March was home with baby Albert and appeared to be so content. April was realising her old dream of replacing May as March's nearest sister, and it was with joy — and surprise — that she saw her ministrations being accepted with warm appreciation.

Only this morning March had taken her early morning teacup from April's eager hands with tears in her eyes. 'Darling . . . if you knew. It's so good to be home!' She drank her tea and looked at the smears on the side of the cup with a smile. 'Dear April. You didn't wash this cup in soda water did you? Didn't Mother ever tell you that china washed that way would never hold tea smears?' She laughed at April's downcast face and put the cup down to hug her. 'I'd rather have tea made by you than any other kind, whatever the cup!'

April skirted the park to the Spa Pump rooms so that she could see the beginning of the new memorial to the fallen soldiers of the war. Albert's name would be there of course. And poor Harry Hughes'. But not David's and not Fred's. Her bargaining with God had done some good.

Someone else was staring at the enormous marble slabs piled in readiness. It was Connie. Connie, who smoked cheroots and made the last shell to be fired in the war. April watched her as she stood there, obviously 'County' in her tweeds and brogues, a small felt hat pulled firmly over her hair, hiding it as effectively as the head-scarf had done in the factory. Then she reached into her sleeve and produced a handkerchief and dabbed quickly at her face. She was crying. Carefully, swallowing her own tears, April retreated and turned down Arthur Street. Who would have thought it? Connie had lost someone in the war. How amazing that Stella had not found that out; Stella who had cut a hole in the ceiling so that she could watch her mother being unfaithful to her father.

Luckily there was no-one in the shop, because nothing

could have stopped her going straight to the counter and saying to David, 'I love you. I love you so much David.'

David looked at her, still not believing after two months that it was happening and he was permitting it to happen: the constant secret visits, the interest in the business, the sudden outbursts — as now — of her strangely adult, passionate love.

He said in his objective way, 'Why don't I remind you you're only sixteen and don't know the meaning of the word love?'

'Because you've given up all that protesting. Because you knew all along that I fell in love with you at March's fourteenth birthday party. Why wouldn't you allow yourself to see it, David?'

He shrugged. 'Perhaps I did. Perhaps I encouraged it. To feed my ego. I wouldn't face up to the fact that the one sister found me faintly repulsive, but I suppose I knew that too. So —'

'You are not to talk like that David!' April's colour flamed, not for her own pride, but for his.

She broke the rule that he had made by his example, and came close to him, putting her arms around his waist and holding him forcibly to her.

'David, listen. I think you and May were in love with an idea. May's idea was wrong from the very beginning, but yours . . . yours was killed in the war.' She regarded him straightly from twelve inches away. 'That's why you turned to Sibbie.' He jerked physically and would have torn away from her but she had been prepared and held grimly to him. 'Don't — don't hurt yourself my darling. Did you think I didn't guess? Did you think I didn't know how it was? To lose an idea — to go from the highest to the lowest? Ah David . . . David . . . that was when my love changed, from adoration to understanding.'

He was still now, very still within her arms. She loosened her hold and he stayed where he was, his eyes burning into hers. She whispered, 'On my way here I

346

saw Connie. She worked at the munitions factory. She was hard . . . tough as nails. But now — ten minutes ago — she was by the new war memorial, and she was crying. Perhaps I should be there crying too . . . we lost Teddy and Albert after all. But — but — I'm happy David. It's selfish, maybe it's wrong. But I can't help myself. I'm happy.'

She cupped his head in her hands and he did not resist her. Very slowly she brought their mouths together. She kissed him as he had kissed her two months ago on Armistice Day. Deliberately she built passion between them, making her body soft against his hardness, exploring his mouth with her tongue. His hands came to her shoulder blades tentatively at first, then harder until it was as if he tried to mould her body to his own. And then, when she thought she must cry out with wanting him, a peculiar sound came from upstairs. A hoarse, croaking sound that made them pause, then draw apart and look at each other, she wildly, he with a hint of his ironic smile.

He said softly, 'It's all right. It's my mother. Singing.'

April listened, identified it, nodded and then smiled into David's eyes, so brilliantly that he blinked.

'Isn't that beautiful? I've never heard her sing before. She is always weighted with unhappiness. Oh David . . . isn't that beautiful?'

He did not take his eyes off her. 'Yes,' he said.

'Everything is.' Her face contracted with sudden conscience. 'Except for Connie. Except for . . . so many.'

'There is always beauty my darling.' He massaged her shoulder blades in a friendly way as he let her go. 'Oh April. I do love you so.'

She was radiant again. 'That's the first time you've really told me that David. That's the first time you've treated me like a woman and not a child.'

He smiled. 'You're seventeen in eleven weeks, April.'

'Yes. Seventeen. We could get married then if Pa would give his consent.'

David drew her to him again and kissed her. 'He will.'

347

'You know he will not. You are treating me like a child again.'

'No. This is one promise I can make to you my Primrose Sweet. If you still wish to marry me when you are seventeen, I will see your father and he will agree to it.'

'I — I almost believe you David! I feel you could do anything!'

'When I am with you I too feel I could do anything.' He laughed. 'But that one thing, I certainly can do.' Another kiss and then he said solemnly, 'April. Will you marry me? Please?'

Her reaction was that of a schoolgirl. And as her weight bowled him against the counter so that he winced with the pain in his leg, he recalled the day of his father's death when he had thought there would be no more happiness for him. He had not known then that as his father had departed this world, so April Rising had entered it, bringing with her an ample supply of the daisies of happiness. And he had dared to be embittered.

'Primrose. Sweet Primrose,' he murmured.

THE END

3VSNY000004802

F
SAL   Sallis, Susan

        A scattering of
        daisies